DICK SCHMIDT'S
CAREER

"Thoroughly developed characters drive this well-conceived financial tale. At the same time, nail-biting scenes abound."

—KIRKUS REVIEWS

"Dick Schmidt's latest novel, *Career,* is a thrilling page turner with non-stop action, engaging characters, and an attention to detail and locales that really bring the story to life. Caught up in the adventure, I could not put the book down. An engrossing, delightful read from start to finish."

—DOLORES SUKHDEO,
President and CEO, South Florida PBS

"*Career* gives readers an exciting glimpse into the fast-paced, high-risk world of finance, from a carefully researched 'insider's' perspective. The author also offers a fresh insights on the age-old familial issues that accompany cross-cultural romances. An exciting and suspenseful adventure, I highly recommend this book to readers of all genres."

—JEFFREY L. RODENGEN,
Best-selling author, Historian, Chairman and CEO
of Write Stuff Enterprises

CAREER
A NOVEL

DICK SCHMIDT

LANDSLIDE
PUBLISHING

Landslide Publishing, Inc.
201 Plaza Real, Suite 140
Boca Raton, Florida 33432

ISBN-13:
Softcover: 978-0-9975010-5-6
Hardcover: 978-0-9975010-6-3

Copyedited by
Carol Killman Rosenberg • www.carolkillmanrosenberg.com

Cover and interior design by
Gary A. Rosenberg • www.thebookcouple.com

Printed in the United States of America

To Barbara,
my true north

PROLOGUE

In 2007 and several years prior, the United States began laying the groundwork for an economic collapse when well-intentioned incentives designed to encourage individual home ownership led to a free-for-all in the housing market. Stimulated by low initial interest rates and a lack of attention paid to the qualification of purchasers of real estate, buyers were attracted to residential investment like bums to a free steak sandwich. The unintended consequences included extreme upward pressure on demand, which the nation's developers were only too happy to accommodate.

The resulting "bubble" sent shock waves throughout the global economy when the underlying mortgage obligations, which had since been bundled and sold to unwary investors, began to present with symptoms of instability. In fewer than 100 hours, the venerable investment bank Bear Stearns went from a highly valued member of the investment community to a pariah when they were taken over by J.P. Morgan in March 2008. The extent of the underlying problem did not become fully apparent until the following September when Lehman Brothers was allowed to go bankrupt, no one willing to step up to the plate to bail them out.

The financial effect of the eventual failure of the real estate market was compounded by the vast number of investment vehicles that were created for funding the ever-burgeoning mortgages.

1

Many of these and their derivatives, such as collateral debt obligations, credit default swaps, and the like were so complex that the investing public was unable to determine or evaluate what was being purchased, except in the most general of terms. So, when the house of cards tumbled, the ripple effect was massive. The recession that resulted absorbed entire insurance markets, industries, and banking institutions, requiring the largest ever government bailout in recorded history.

Robbie Wells

CHAPTER ONE

As the September sun cast longer shadows across the south docks of Bahia Mar in Fort Lauderdale, Robbie Wells peered casually over the wicker shelving jutting from behind Corky's patio bar. He fit the stereotypical image of a boat bum: long, unkempt hair, faded cargo pants, and a worn-out T-shirt split a few inches at the neck as though to give him more freedom. The scruffy figure was trying not to look too interested in the comings and goings of the watercraft in the adjacent marina; however, Robbie was in fact very interested in the departure of *Roy's Toy,* the 130-foot Westport that was bow thrusting its way off the T-head of F dock.

He watched as it slipped smoothly into the Intracoastal, heading south toward the Dania Cut-Off Canal for a scheduled haul out at Derecktor Shipyards. More particularly, Robbie was focused on the thirty-one-foot Cape Horn, the mega yacht's tender that was left tied to the floating dock where it was kept at the ready for a tow when the big boat departed on a cruise.

Robbie was somewhat familiar with the scheduled comings and goings of *Roy's Toy,* because he had struck up a friendship of sorts with the owner, as he had with many yacht owners in the Bahamas. During the summers prior to 2008, Robbie had developed a form of native celebrity that attracted tourists who cruised around Marsh Harbour and the neighboring Out Islands of the Bahamas.

In fact, Robbie was a rather complicated person, one who did not relate to structure or authority, which was rather odd in that he had completed three successful tours in the Navy as a sonar specialist on an Ohio-class submarine. In that time, he had impressed his superiors with his ability to understand the complexities of underwater detection and avoidance in a high-intensity world of nuclear cat and mouse in the silent depths below the polar ice caps.

Since his separation from active duty, Robbie gravitated to a more vagabond lifestyle sailing the waters of the Caribbean. He'd met some rather edgy characters along the way and delivered drugs between the States and the Bahamas to supplement his cash needs from time to time. He fell into his current lifestyle quite by accident, when he met David Nemeth, the lead singer of the rock group Ascension while they were on tour in Miami. David was looking for a source of cocaine, and Robbie was in a position to help him out. Their business relationship developed quickly into a bond of trust and friendship when they discovered their mutual love of the sea and sailing.

Robbie watched as the Westport disappeared around the bend in the Intracoastal heading south toward the 17th Street Bridge. Satisfied that it was committed to its planned trip to the yard, he put a five on the bar top, grabbed his duffle off the stool next to him, and padded off barefoot on the connector to the floating F dock. He walked purposefully, so as to look like he had every right to be there. When he reached the end, he threw his bag nonchalantly on one of the console seats and climbed aboard the dark-blue hulled Cape Horn. He opened the overhead storage compartment, feeling around for the keys he knew he would find there. He wasn't really stealing the boat, just borrowing it for a few hours for his current mission. If everything went as planned, he would be back before the evening was over, and the crew aboard *Roy's Toy* would not even know it had gone missing.

His fingers touched the spongy flotation fob on the key chain, and he snaked the ignition key, float plug, and kill switch out of the overhead, and hooked everything up. He was already familiar with the boat, having fished on it with the owner, Roy Connors, many times in the Exumas. He lowered the twin Yamaha 300s to the full down position and pushed the start buttons for each. They came to life immediately, purring softly, the four stroke engines barely audible. There was little wind, so he untied the half hitches in the bow and stern lines, saving the spring lines for last, tossed the bitter ends aboard, and jumped back on. In reverse, Robbie levered off of the rubber bumper on the floating dock and backed quietly away from the marina, moving slowly into the Intracoastal in the same direction the Westport had taken a half hour before.

Robbie kept a keen eye out for other boats, or for anyone who might have taken an interest in his departure. He bumped the throttles a touch, keeping them below a thousand rpm. The last thing he wanted to do was pull up in sight of the Westport crew where he could be spotted through binoculars. He followed the bends in the Intracoastal past the Lauderdale Yacht Club where it straightened out. It was late afternoon, and there was little traffic on the waterway, so he stayed to the middle and moved around the boat, bringing in the dock lines, coiling them, and hitching them neatly over the rocket launchers behind the console seats.

As he bent over, he noticed the large cooler under the seats and pulled it out to look inside. *Lucky me!* he thought upon seeing six bottles of Kalik Bahamian beer sloshing around in the container partially filled with half-melted ice. He pulled one out for himself and opened it, levering off the top from the top of another, and took a long pull of the cold brew. He held the cold bottle to the side of his neck to cool himself a little. *This day is shaping up pretty well for me,* he thought. *A nice ride on the ocean, make a quick ten thousand for my effort, and enjoy a few brewskis in the process. Not bad!*

7

He thought about that for a moment, but then it occurred to him, as it had previously, that it just didn't make sense. He spoke the scenario aloud to help him reason through it:

"I meet this guy in Marsh Harbour. He has a nice family. He's obviously very wealthy, because he has a new fifty-five-foot Fleming motor yacht that he keeps in the Bahamas all summer, and an airplane that he flies back and forth with. He explains to me that he has to disappear for a while, and he doesn't want anyone looking for him, so he concocts this story that he is going to fake his own death by ditching his plane in the Gulf Stream after declaring an emergency, but he needs a ride back to Fort Lauderdale or Miami. For providing this service, he is willing to pay me ten thousand dollars if I do it and keep my mouth shut."

Robbie kept mulling it over in his mind, and he could only come to one conclusion: This was worth *a lot* more than ten thousand dollars. He'd come to this realization more than once and so had made some preparation. Smiling, he patted the top of his duffle, then pushing on the top of it, felt the hardness of the 9mm Smith & Wesson inside.

The Cape Horn passed 15th Street Fisheries on the right and Pier 66 on the left, and Robbie admired the big boats that lined the face docks as he worked his way under the 17th Street Causeway and followed the markers east between the jetties toward the ocean. A gentle breeze was blowing out of the southeast, and the Cape Horn took the light chop on top of the gentle rollers with a kindly motion. The flare of the bow, coupled with the deep-vee forefoot of the hull, made for a dry ride as Robbie moved the throttles up smoothly to a cruising speed of four thousand rpm. At this pace, he estimated he would be on station at the coordinates he had been given in a little more than three hours, leaving him the better part of an hour of leeway for adjustments he might need or additional time to put an alternative plan in place.

With several hours of monotony to kill, he took long pulls on his Kalik and thought about the path that had led him here. The last two years had been lucrative for Robbie. He had some success bringing a couple loads of grass into the Bahamas, using the ruse of occasional boat deliveries to cover what he was doing. He had developed a reliable reputation as one who could deliver small and medium-sized sailboats to the islands for families who did not have time or patience to deal with the long passages required to get to the good cruising grounds of the Abacos or the Exumas. Using Robbie's services, they would arrive by local airline to find their sailboats cleaned and provisioned, ready to go. Word got around, and Robbie received opportunities to bring in all sorts of contraband in vessels that were unsuspicious looking to local authorities. He knew where to clear customs to avoid scrutiny and where to offload his illegal substances to avoid detection.

He'd hit the jackpot when he met David Nemeth in Miami after a concert. One of his "business" partners had made the introduction, knowing that Robbie could fix him up from recent inventory he had been asked to deliver. Robbie received a dual benefit in that he made a new friend of influence and was able to offload some inventory at retail, not something he was accustomed to. As their bond grew stronger, Robbie spent more time in South Florida where David kept his pride and joy, an Alden-built, shallow-draft centerboard schooner ideally suited for Florida and the Bahamas. It was fifty-eight feet on deck with a generous bowsprit, but it could be sailed by two people who knew what they were doing, or even single-handedly by someone who knew how to plan ahead. Robbie and David had spent weeks aboard, jamming on their guitars and sailing the waters of the Lower Keys and the Bahamas. Robbie was euphoric with the arrangement until David got arrested with a suitcase full of drugs, the felony further compounded by the weapon David had on him when he was arrested.

Since it was not the first of many scrapes with the law, which wasn't unusual in the rock-and-roll community, the judge in Texas gave the musician some serious prison time, the better part of two years. To Robbie's amazement, David asked him to look after his boat, live on it, do whatever he wanted, just keep it up somehow and ready for David when he got out. Robbie willingly agreed and promptly set sail for Marsh Harbour in the Abacos on the *Mayan* where he knew the people were friendly and always enjoyed having a free spirit around with a lot of stories to share with them. Particularly in the summer, the harbor at the Conch Inn, the local social mecca, was filled with summer sailors looking for a good time in the sun. That was where he'd met Adam Schaeffer.

Adam Schaeffer had spent the last two summers in the Marsh Harbour area with his family—wife, Marjorie, and preteen daughters, Mary and Karen. They spent most of their time in the marina at the Conch Inn for the amenities and social life, making short cruises from time to time to the Out Islands in the area. Most afternoons concluded around the unusual pool at the resort, which had a deep end in the middle. It set up perfectly for impromptu "Wallyball" games, named after the original owner Wally Smith, which was basically volleyball played in the pool. The deep water at the net made it difficult for the front row to spike the ball. The games were always well attended, accompanied by gallons of rum punches, and served to set the social activities for the community for the next day. Most of the participants were cruisers in the area. Robbie was a notable standout with his long hair and disheveled appearance, but nonetheless accepted as a social director when he was in residence. He was recognizable, among other characteristics, by the fact that at four o'clock every afternoon he blew a loud note on a conch shell wearing an old volleyball cut out to look like a helmet, summoning the partiers to the afternoon's Wallyball game.

On many evenings, groups sat around the pool, and Robbie

played his guitar enthusiastically. Many of the songs he had composed himself and really weren't half bad, if truth be told. Sometimes the groups got more intimate and moved to one of the boats docked at the marina or anchored in the harbor. Young girls found Robbie's rakish handsomeness irresistible. He seldom went home alone, if he was so inclined. Everyone found his stories entertaining, if not all quite believable. However, in fact most were true. Robbie was indeed rather complicated. Who wouldn't warm up to a lovable vagabond who sailed the exotic waters of the Caribbean on his own schooner, living off the fish he caught from the sea? He was truly a character out of a Joseph Conrad novel.

It was here, two years earlier, that Adam Schaeffer and Robbie had become acquainted. Adam's girls were fascinated by the old schooner and asked Robbie if he would take them for a ride sometime. That led to an invitation for the family to sail around Lubbers Quarters to Tahiti Beach, where at low tide the family could picnic on the sand dune and wade in the current as it ebbed and flowed with the tide changes. Robbie made a great day of it for all of them, taking them snorkeling on one of the few inside reefs on the bank where Marjorie, Schaeffer's wife, felt comfortable, not being a water person herself. Over the summer they repeated the activity, once leaving Adam behind because he had to work at his office in Florida, planning to fly in for the weekend.

By prior arrangement Adam agreed to bring the *Marge Inn,* their fifty-five-foot Fleming cruiser, down to Little Harbor to meet them for the night. He arrived just as the sun was going down and the no-see-ums began their kamikaze attacks. Robbie helped him set his anchor a few feet off and pull the boats together so that they could raft for the evening. Everyone took relief from the bugs in the air-conditioning aboard the motor yacht, while Marjorie cooked up the grouper filets Robbie had speared that afternoon.

As they feasted, Robbie asked, "Adam, I always meant to ask you about the name of your boat. I get it that it has to do with Marjorie, but what's the connection?"

The girls giggled, and shouted in unison, "Daddy's in the brokerage business. Get it? MARGE INN. Brokers deal in margin accounts and the boat's our hotel, or inn."

Everybody had a good laugh.

Robbie could be subtly sensitive when he wanted to be. When the girls got tired as the evening wore on, Marjorie led them to their cabins. The three adults sat on the fly bridge and watched the stars, vibrantly bright in the islands where there was no dirty air or ambient light to dull their luster. Robbie sensed that a mood was developing, so he quietly slipped below and to the *Mayan*. There he untied the spring lines that attached the two boats, and they drifted apart on the tension caused by the spacing of the anchor placement, giving the family some privacy as the boats swung independently in the shifting currents and gentle evening breezes. He didn't hear the subsequent hushed arguing voices over the muffled drone of the Fleming's generator as he settled into his quarter berth behind the chart table on the *Mayan*.

The next day, after an adventure-filled afternoon on the reefs just offshore where Robbie showed the girls how to spear lobster, then tail and clean them, Adam pulled Robbie aside and made arrangements to speak to him about a private matter after they got back to the marina at the Conch Inn. Robbie sensed the seriousness of the request and understood that he was not to mention anything to anyone. Although his curiosity was aroused, he put it out of his mind for the time being.

Adam and Marjorie decided it was time to head out to make sure they would have enough tide to get over the sandbar that blocked the entrance to the Conch Inn Marina, not a problem for Robbie, who anchored farther out in the harbor. The girls, Mary and Karen, whined that they would rather sail with Robbie, so with little reservation, the adult Schaeffers pulled anchor and cruised slowly northward, picking their way around the shallow water at Lubbers Quarters, trying to keep the overhead sun from getting in front of them, which would prevent them from reading the water clearly.

Robbie knew the area like the deck of the *Mayan* and chose to sail off the wind outside the barrier islands on a broad reach where the schooner could use her full waterline to maximize her speed. The girls sat on the weather rail, squealing with delight as the occasional wave splashed up high enough to douse them, as Robbie took his time setting each sail with the proper trim while the autopilot kept a steady course past Elbow Cay to the entrance of South Man-O-War Channel. The channel had no real markers to identify it, but Robbie knew exactly the bearing from Matt Lowe's Cay to jibe the big schooner and turn in for Marsh Harbour proper. Karen and Mary took turns steering the turn for the jibe, as this was beyond the ability of the autopilot. Robbie gave careful instructions regarding the timing, as he had to manhandle over a thousand square feet of sail for the jibe by himself. Fortunately, the winds were light.

Robbie secured the *Mayan* to the mooring he had customized for himself in the harbor late in the afternoon, too late for the Wallyball activities. He could see the *Marge Inn* tied up in her usual slip at the marina, so he loaded the smiling, somewhat sunburned girls into his Zodiac and motored them into the dinghy dock, returning them safely home to appreciative parents. The girls were amped up from their day of adventure and couldn't wait to share it with their friends on the dock at the marina, kids of other families cruising the local waters. Schaeffer made eye contact with Robbie and nodded toward the Conch Out Bar up by the pool. He told Marjorie he was going up for a beer and make a call to the office, that he would be back in about a half hour. She set about finding something for the family to eat for dinner.

Settled in a corner table where they would not be overheard, Schaeffer clinked bottle necks with Robbie, and they took long pulls on their Kaliks. "Robbie, I can't thank you enough for the weekend. You really made that special for my family, and the girls are on cloud nine. They're talking to their friends like they just completed a transatlantic!"

Robbie felt he was being manipulated, that Schaeffer didn't seem sincere, but he answered anyway. "My pleasure, Adam. You know I'm the unofficial chamber of commerce designee for the Bahamas, so it's kind of my job." He smiled. "Maybe you will be in a position to do something for me sometime."

"Actually, that's why I wanted to talk to you, but it has to be in the strictest of confidence. There will be some money in it for you, but if you decide not to do it, I have to know what I am going to ask you will stay just between us. Lives may depend on it," Adam added for effect.

"Come on, Adam. We've spent two summers together, right? You have to have some idea that I don't support this lifestyle off of a trust fund. You've seen some of the characters I do business with, and yet you've never heard a word from me about what I'm involved in. I think I have a track record that warrants some confidence. Tell me what's on your mind."

So, for the next twenty minutes, Adam Schaeffer outlined his plan to fake his own death for reasons he did not explain. When he was finished, he asked Robbie if he had any questions.

"Dozens, but they're obviously none of my business. I've had you figured all wrong, and you appear to want to step into another life of some sort."

"Something like that."

"So, let me see if I have this straight. At some unspecified time in the future, within the next couple of months, you plan to ditch your one-eighty-two in the ocean on a flight back here to Marsh Harbour, after declaring an emergency of some sort. You are willing to pay me ten thousand dollars in cash to find a suitable boat to meet you at the site and bring you back to Fort Lauderdale, no questions asked. That's all I have to do is pick you up and keep my mouth shut?"

"That's it," Adam said simply. "Can you arrange for a boat?"

"I don't think that would be a problem. I just need a little advance warning to make arrangements. Be a little more specific about your timing."

Adam thought for a minute. He didn't want to give away any strategic advantage, but he figured if Robbie were going to make alternative plans, timing wouldn't be much of a factor. He was also counting on the probability that this was a lot of money for someone like Robbie, who most likely wouldn't want to screw it up. "It's mid-July now. I still have some loose ends to clean up, so probably in about a month or so. I can give you a week's notice, and the exact coordinates of where I plan to ditch. I won't put the plane in the water unless I see your boat there, obviously. It will be near dusk, which will inhibit attempts for a search. We'll be long gone before the Coast Guard will be able to organize a search by air, and it will be dark before they can get a boat in the area. Small aircraft like these usually sink within minutes, so no one should be looking for me for very long. So, are you in?"

"I think I can handle my end of things," Robbie answered thoughtfully. "I don't want to appear too connected to you, so I suggest we not spend a lot of time together between now and when this happens. I'll give you a cell number you can contact to verify the time and location I will need. In the meantime, I think I will pull up stakes here in a few days and head for the Exumas. I can get a flight out of Nassau when the time comes to make arrangements for a boat to pick you up. You okay with that?"

What kind of schmuck does this to his family, especially a nice family like this? Robbie wondered, but he didn't dwell on it. Trying to make sense out of the emotional side of things didn't work well in Robbie's world, where many of the people he did business with were borderline psychotic anyway.

"Sounds like a plan," Adam said resolutely.

The two shook hands and left the bar separately, hoping their meeting would go unnoticed. Robbie motored his little blow-up boat back to the *Mayan* to smoke a joint and play his guitar, while he thought about how he would find a boat in Florida for his mission.

In the morning, he picked up a wharf rat to help him for the twenty-hour close reach down to Nassau. The twenty-something reminded Robbie a little of himself as a kid, eighteen years earlier, and it gave him someone to talk to during the voyage. Provisioned from the Golden Harvest, they took the easy way, motoring out South Man-O-War Channel, the way Robbie had come in the previous day, and clearing the reefs on the sound side of Elbow Cay, they set sail in a freshening breeze, making way almost due south across an east wind. By late in the afternoon the following day, Robbie had cleared the Paradise Island jetty and made his way to the fuel dock at Yacht Haven.

CHAPTER TWO

Robbie wasted little time in Nassau, just long enough to drop his wharf rat at Señor Frogs where he could mingle with his peer group, top off his fuel, rinse the salt from his sea voyage off his boat at Yacht Haven, and refill his freshwater tanks. In a little over an hour, he was on his way out the east end of the harbor toward the Yellow Bank and southeast to the Exumas. He anchored for the night at the east end of the harbor, suffering the exposure of a light chop blowing across the bank as a favorable trade-off to trying to navigate the Yellow Bank and its numerous coral heads in the fading light or at night, preferring instead to pick his way in the morning glare southeast toward Highbourne Cay, the first stop in the Exuma chain.

The next day, after a six-hour journey, the *Mayan* dropped anchor in fifteen feet of water outside of the marina at Highbourne. Robbie took his mask and fins and motored the Zodiac to the sound side of the island where he slaughtered five good-sized grouper and returned to the marina to try to monetize his catch among the mega yachts tied up there. The first yacht that caught his eye was a beautiful Westport 130 tied up on the face dock. The raised name boards on the trideck announced it was *Roy's Toy*. He approached the swim platform where a pretty young woman in a skimpy bikini was hosing off some beach equipment. Assuming she was crew, Robbie asked if the chef was aboard and would he like some freshly caught grouper.

She looked down at the disheveled-looking soul in the rubber boat. "I don't know; I'll ask." Then she shouted up a level, "Dad, there's some guy here wants to know if we want to buy any of his fish!"

A tailored-looking man, thin and tall, stepped forward to the back of the aft deck dressed in a T-shirt and shorts. At first he looked a little annoyed, as if inconvenienced, until he noticed the bevy of prize grouper in the bottom of the Zodiac.

"Wow! Where did you get those?" he inquired. "Can't be from the reefs around here. We were out there all morning and didn't see much of anything."

Robbie put on his most accommodating smile. "I guess you just have to know where to look. I got them all on the first set of heads on the other side of the island."

The girl, an attractive blonde in her early twenties, Robbie guessed, suddenly took an interest when she realized that Dad placed a value on what he saw.

Frankly, her dad was always bragging about what a good spear fisherman he was, but she hadn't seen much evidence of it on this trip. The cook on the boat had bought most of the fish they had eaten from locals.

The gentleman walked down the curved transom stairs to the swim platform for a closer look. "Those are impressive, I must say." Turning to his daughter, he said, "Mish, go get Cookie and tell him to come back here, see if he wants to make fresh fish for dinner." Returning his attention to Robbie, he asked, "How much?"

"Twenty apiece."

"For all five; you've got to be kidding!"

"You can only have four. The Nassau is for me." Robbie nodded to the crowd that was gathering on the dock. "If you don't want 'em, I'm sure there are other takers around here."

About then the chef arrived with the girl. When he saw all the fish he whined, "You expect me to clean all of those?"

18

The girl started laughing.

The older man, obviously the boat owner, compromised with, "Tell you what, if you filet them for us, and agree to go out on the reefs tomorrow to show us where you find them, you have a deal. Better yet, I'll extend the deal for anything we bring back tomorrow; we've got guests coming in next week. What do you say?"

Robbie eyed the smile on the blonde's face, winked at her, and said okay.

"That's our tender parked behind us; we'll take that," the owner said pointing at the navy-blue Cape Horn tied off astern of the big boat. Robbie grabbed the fish by the stringer through their gills and climbed out of the Zodiac. The owner of *Roy's Toy* thrust out his hand to help with the fish, and Robbie grabbed it, introducing himself with a smile, "Hi, I'm Robbie Wells." It was an awkward moment, the dynamics clearly having shifted to Robbie's favor.

"Hi, I'm Roy Connors, and this is my daughter, Michelle; we call her Mishie, or Mish. My wife is aboard taking a nap, but she'll be on deck before long. I'm the owner of *Roy's Toy*," he added, now feeling somewhat embarrassed about the name.

Robbie reached back in the dinghy for his ditty bag and withdrew a sheathed fish-cleaning knife, which he slid in the waistband of his swimsuit, and he made his way down the dock to the public fish-cleaning stand where he went to work turning the unfortunate grouper into dinner filets.

———✦———

Over the next two weeks Robbie made use of his new connection, something he was good at. As the Connors party entertained guests aboard the big yacht, the free-spirited vagabond became a source of entertainment for owners, guests, and crew. Robbie shared his knowledge of the sea in exchange for hospitality, a little money, and romance, but most important, useful information. He took the family sailing on his impressive schooner and held their rapt attention as he regaled them with stories of its owner, David Nemeth, well known to Roy Connors. As it turned out, Connors had acquired his fortune representing theatrical Broadway performers and musicians, and whereas most of his clients were more upscale, he did count a number of the more edgy rock musicians among his stable. He was well aware of the circumstances that had befallen the South Florida rock legend.

Robbie spent a lot of time with the crew of *Roy's Toy* as well. From them he learned that the big yacht was scheduled for serious maintenance upon their return to Florida in three weeks' time. He made subtle inquiries about the disposition of the Cape Horn while the big boat was getting a fresh bottom job, and he was pleased to learn that it would stay behind in the slip at Bahia Mar, since it would only get in the way at the crowded yard, and the crew would have no need of it anyway. Robbie noted that the timing was about perfect for his requirements, assuming that Schaeffer stuck with his original schedule. Casual talk also revealed that keys were always kept in the overhead storage compartment, so that anyone authorized to use the boat would know where to find them whenever he had need of it.

How convenient—just like a key under the doormat! Robbie remarked to himself. For reassurance, he volunteered to clean the tender after snorkeling or fishing trips, always verifying what the mates had told him, that the keys were always left in the overhead. He was never disappointed. Robbie was confident he could rely on access to the Cape Horn, assuming the scheduled yard work coincided with Adam Schaeffer's plan to "kill" himself. He decided that continued association with the Connors family would serve no use, so Robbie weighed anchor and headed southeast toward Staniel Cay to hang out for a few days before charging up his burner phone and checking on the status of his plans with the investment banker. He knew he would require about five days of hard sailing to get back to Fort Lauderdale, and he needed some cushion to allow for contingencies, should any arise. That gave him about ten days to kill.

Now, two weeks later in the second week of September, the afternoon gulfstream greeted Robbie with a gentle breeze out of the southeast as he started to power up coming out of the channel in Port Everglades. There was little traffic, so he had the quarter-mile-wide harbor entrance to himself. The Cape Horn settled in nicely at thirty-eight hundred rpm, and the deep-vee hull and flair to the bow made for a dry ride. Sitting on the molded captain's chair, Robbie fired up the GPS and punched in the coordinates Schaeffer had given him for the rendezvous, just north of Great Isaac light, marking the edge of the Great Bahama Bank, south of Grand Bahama and about seventy-five nautical miles ahead. As the chop started to build just a little, he cut the power back to a smoother thirty-five hundred rpm. The GPS showed two hours, forty-five minutes to his waypoint. He looked at his watch, just coming up on four o'clock. *Perfect!* he thought. *I love it when a plan comes together.*

He felt pleased with himself, and he reached below the seat and fished another Kalik out of the cooler and opened it, again levering off the top from another bottle. He wondered what he was going to do when he got down to the last one; he didn't see an opener anywhere around. Robbie started thinking about a plan of how he was going to get more money out of Schaeffer once he was safely aboard. It was a fine line and dilemma he faced, how to keep from hurting his victim, wherein he couldn't get any more money out of him and how to keep him under control while he figured out where the money was to be found.

One thing was for sure: This guy wasn't walking out on a nice-looking family and a respectable job, ditching an expensive airplane, and losing a motor yacht and whatever other personal wealth, which was most likely considerable, to start a new life somewhere unless he had salted away a sizable fortune. Robbie figured it was best that he not get too greedy and just pick the low-hanging fruit. He reasoned it was a good bet that Schaeffer would have a lot more cash with him than the ten thousand he was going to pay for the transport, and that was a good place to start. *Probably has a young girlfriend too,* Robbie surmised.

He figured his best play would be to confront Schaeffer before he got situated aboard, while he was still vulnerable climbing out of the water. That would also eliminate the possibility that Schaeffer might have some kind of alternative plan cooked up. After all, Robbie would represent a risk to Schaeffer for the foreseeable future if he was successful in faking his death, and therefore would be an ongoing threat. Yeah, that was the better plan, make sure his fare didn't come aboard prepared to try something cute, hold him at gunpoint and find out what else Schaeffer had to put on the table, and shackle him to the seat in front of the console for the ride back, where he could keep an eye on him.

It did occur to Robbie to help Schaeffer consummate his plan to die, for real, but homicide was not really part of his makeup. Besides, if Schaeffer pulled off whatever he was trying to achieve, he would never be a threat to Robbie, lest he risk exposing himself. He figured he had done about as much planning as he could, given the variables that faced him in the next several hours, so he just settled back in his chair and enjoyed the ride. He looked behind him and saw that he was already out of sight of land, so he knew he was at least a third of the way to his destination, which the GPS confirmed.

When the sun moved lower on the horizon behind him, the color of the water became a deeper blue, as the glare had been eliminated. The drone of the motors and the smooth ride with an occasional roll in the Atlantic swells started to put Robbie to sleep. He debated having another beer but thought better of it. Another hour passed by, and the sky deepened in color noticeably as the sun neared the horizon. Almost in a trance, Robbie got a shot of adrenaline as the GPS started beeping that he was arriving at his destination, the way-point flashing red. He zoomed in the range on the chart plotter and slowed as he approached the exact spot where he was to expect the aircraft to ditch. He figured Schaeffer wouldn't hit it within a couple hundred yards, but the least he could do was be where he'd agreed. When he was right on the spot, he put the engines in neutral and hit the stop buttons. His world went silent, except for the slapping of small waves against the fiberglass hull.

Robbie scanned the horizon to the west and listened for the sound of a small single-engine plane. He heard the plane before he saw it, because it was coming from a different direction than he'd expected, spiraling down in tight circles from several thousand feet in the air.

Jorge Gonzalez

CHAPTER THREE

From the twenty-fourth floor of the Bank of America Tower, the cityscape of downtown Miami lay before the small group assembled in the managing partner's office of the regional accounting firm. The Miami River and the expanse of Biscayne Bay were overwhelmed by the shimmering blue of the Atlantic Ocean, which lay just to the east. It was early afternoon at the beginning of July, so the sun glimmered off the water twenty-three stories below, an invitation hard not to notice by any of those assembled.

Paul Dickenson, whose office it was, smiled across his desk at astonished Jorge Gonzalez, having just given him the best news of his young life. Walter Adams, the audit partner in charge of SEC-affiliated clients, stood, also smiling, to congratulate Jorge on his new promotion to audit partner with the firm, and the assignment of the firm's highest-profile client to his care and responsibility. Technically Jorge would not be the partner in charge because he did not meet the firm's internal ops specs set out in its membership in the SEC Division for Firms of the American Institute of Certified Public Accountants. He would bear all the responsibility for completing the engagement, which was already underway, by the end of August. He was already very familiar with the engagement, because he had been involved with this client since he'd graduated from Florida Atlantic University with a degree in accounting in 1995, thirteen years earlier.

This promotion was a capstone in Jorge's career, and he couldn't wait to get off work and tell his parents. They were going to be so, so proud. He understood it had been as much their journey as his. Arriving in America at the age of seven, a frightened little boy and his family joined hundreds of refugees as they were corralled by authorities in the streets of lower Key West to begin the bureaucratic process of immigration to the United States. After a long and confusing passage across the Straits of Florida, Jorge only understood from his parents that this was a good thing, but nonetheless, he was happy the sea voyage part of the ordeal was over.

His aquatic passage began at the end of April 1980, when Jorge and his brothers were rousted from their beds in their small migrant shack on the sugarcane plantations southwest of the giant city, Camagüey. His father worked the fields in season, moving northwest to the fruit plantations in the alternate growing cycles. His family was dirt poor and struggled to keep a roof over their heads and food on the table by following the migrant agricultural flow throughout central Cuba. The plantation owners had provided the necessities that kept the system going until the Castro regime took over. Without the profit motive to move goods through the system, the distribution of living requirements became unreliable, despite the new government's attempts to see that everyone's needs were met. Many field workers moved to the cities where they were closer to the sources of power and the food and housing that power attracted.

Of course, Jorge and his two brothers were unaware of this at the time. They only knew that the family struggled and were often hungry. Carlos, the oldest, and Valeriano were required to go to school, something the government put a lot of emphasis on, but much of the time they set off on their own during the day to see that their needs were met. This particular morning was different, as Adriana, Jorge's mother, quietly corralled the children, told them to be quiet, and rushed to stuff what little belongings the family had into straw bags.

Santiago, their father, led them out through the makeshift village to the train station where they arranged for passage on an open flatbed railroad car, which they shared with twenty other people, mostly families like themselves. Peasants were scattered in groups surrounded by their belongings, mostly stuffed in cotton bags. Some used them as cushions for comfort from the splintery wooden flatbed.

"*¿Papa, a donde vamos?*" Carlos cried as he was lifted onto the flatbed unceremoniously. None of the children had a clue.

"*Vamos a America,*" his father answered gruffly. "Just get on the train."

Adriana urged them along. Santiago helped Adriana aboard, and they made a space for themselves among the others, sitting and lying on their bundles of personal effects. The locomotive far ahead sounded its shrill whistle announcing its intention to leave the station, and amid clouds of smoke and steam, accompanied by regular beats of *chug, chug, chug,* the cars started to roll slowly away from the brightening sky in the east.

Valeriano, age ten, was two years younger than his older brother, Carlos, and he usually deferred to his elder brother in family matters, but his curiosity could not be kept in check. "Papa! Tell us what's going on. Why are we on this train?"

Carefully, Santiago did his best to explain that he had learned the government was allowing Cubans to leave the country and go to America if they could identify relatives living there. All they had to do was find someone willing to transport them from the harbor at Mariel, on the north coast near La Habana. Their mother had a brother who lived in Miami and could vouch for them.

This explanation only led to more questions and confusion, which Santiago ended with a stern command of "*¡Silencio!* We will talk about it later, you'll see."

All this was lost on poor little Jorge, who was most interested in watching the countryside roll past the unguarded sides of the platform car at breakneck speed. He had never even seen a train before, and he thought this was the most exciting thing he had ever done. Eventually he fell asleep in his mother's lap for most of the journey. After eight hours and several brief stops, the train rolled into La Habana late in the afternoon and disgorged its cars of future refugees in the center of the city.

It was the last day of April, and word of the Mariel boatlift had already spread throughout the capital. Anyone with some type of motorized transportation was taking advantage of the opportunity to make a little money outside of the government subsidy by accommodating citizens who wanted to get to the harbor at Mariel. While Santiago began negotiating a ride for his family, Adriana did her best to find some food for her boys, who had not eaten since six that morning. She traded one of her strong straw baskets for some bread sandwiches brought along by a family she had met on the train. She was able to save the lump of pork she had brought with her from Camagüey, which she felt if rationed, could last the family about three days. After that, she didn't know what they would do.

Later, Jorge would recall, their ride to Mariel looked like a scene out of *The Beverly Hillbillies,* a favorite show in reruns while he was struggling to learn a new language. Three families and their life's accumulations were stacked above a stake truck as it smoked, rattled, and squeaked its way across bumpy coast roads from La Habana to Mariel, about thirty-five miles west of the train station. He was not prepared for the mass confusion as he and his family were deposited at the entryway to the harbor of the small fishing village at Mariel. Hundreds were camped in tents and cooking over open fires, gathered in groups of two to twenty. As Jorge's family made a place for themselves among the wannabe refugees, Santiago went into the marina proper to find what kind of authority was in evidence and to make arrangements for his family's transport to America.

After an hour, Santiago returned, round-shouldered and dejected, to report the discouraging news. "From what I have been able to determine," he explained to Adriana, "it is not at all like we were told it would be, at home in Camagüey."

"What do you mean, Santi?"

"Most of these people here have made arrangements to leave the island by getting an exit visa from the Peruvian embassy in La Habana. The marina fills every day with boats that have come from Key West or as far away as Miami to pick up those who want to leave, but no one is allowed out without the proper paperwork. We may have to go back to La Habana, and then it may take weeks for the embassy to contact your brother and have him vouch for us in order for us to leave here. And, even then, we will have to find someone who will be willing to take us. The soldiers here say they are not responsible for what will happen to us when we get to America, but most of the people here say there is no problem once we get there. We will be treated as refugees."

Adriana started to weep softly, trying to hide her tears from the children. Carlos and Val were running around scoping out the area, and Jorge was too preoccupied with the goings-on around him to notice her sadness.

"What are we going to do, Santi? We can't go back. We would be in so much trouble."

Santiago looked down at Adriana's lovely tear-stained face, the drops running thin lines through the grime of the day's travel on her cheeks. His heart ached for the pain she was feeling and raced for the fear he felt for the monumental misjudgment he may have led his family into. Her green eyes looked up at him, pleading for him to show the strength he did when he made the decision to leave this wretched island. He knew he had to be strong for her. With great confidence, he held her chin in his palm and stroked her cheek with his thumb. Softly he said, *"Mi amor,* everything will be fine. You and the children stay here and try to find a family that will take you in for a few days, while I go back to La Habana and make arrangements for the papers we need to leave. I will be back by Monday, and we will be able to leave."

Adriana felt comforted and smiled, looking up at her husband. He seemed so calm and assured. She knew she could hold out the few days he needed to work things out. So, with Jorge in hand, and the help of his big brothers, Adriana stopped by each house near the harbor entrance inquiring if anyone could take her and her three children in for a few nights, so she would not have to sleep outside without any shelter. She was taken aback at the hostility she encountered by most of the people she met, who were not sympathetic to her desire to leave Cuba. Most were downright rude; some were not that nice. After an hour and a half, it began to get dark. She returned to the comfort and relative safety of the campfires of the other refugees at the entrance to the harbor and made a space for her family among the others. Some were willing to share food, and, in return, Adriana shared some of the pork she had brought along. She didn't know how long it would be safe to eat anyway. For the time being, it was valuable for bargaining.

The next morning Adriana and the boys ventured into the marina to see what the situation was all about. There were a dozen finger piers all filled with boats, mostly small fishing boats, and a few cabin cruisers. Along the seawall were dozens and dozens of other misfit boats of all types, most in ghastly condition, rafted to one another five and six deep. People were milling around everywhere, and soldiers were present, stopping boaters and asking questions. Every minute or so another small powerboat arrived around the corner of the jetty and circled the marina, looking for a place to park, finally settling on rafting next to a previous arrival. She and the boys sat on the edge of the dock and watched the chaos in amazement. It occurred to Adriana that there was no structure to who came and went. It seemed that anyone who could get aboard a boat would be free to leave. There was no one to stop them.

As they watched, two masts close together, one taller than the other, came in between the rock jetties. Adriana was surprised to see that they belonged to one boat, a relatively nice-looking sailboat, kind of tubby, not very sleek, but newer, not a wreck like most of the other boats. It looked to be about forty-feet long, more like a sailing yacht. At the helm was a tall and muscular young man steering from the middle, accompanied by a beautiful young girl ready at the bow with dock lines in her hands. They both had long blond hair, his maybe a trifle longer than hers, and they were smiling and laughing at each other as they circled the marina looking for a place to tie up. One of the soldiers waved at them to approach the official dock by the government building, the one with the Cuban flags flying from atop a flagpole, where the only dock space available in the marina was located. *Not where you want to tie up, I'm thinking,* Adriana said to herself. *There's a reason nobody is docked there, and there sure are a lot of soldiers!*

Sure enough, as soon as the boat was secure, the large young man was brought inside, held roughly by one of the bearded soldiers, while the girl was left sitting under guard in the cockpit. After about forty-five minutes, the young man was led away by the authorities, and Adriana did not see him come back for the rest of the day. Around midafternoon she left the boys to look after each other and guard their meager possessions, while she tried again to find someone who would take them in for a few days. This time she had better luck, and a family in town made room for them in their back porch in exchange for some cleaning and gardening.

Each day the boys spent part of the day at the marina watching the goings-on, while Adriana worked for the family who had taken them in. On Sunday they reported back to their mother that the big blond sailor had been brought back, but it seemed he was not allowed to leave the marina, as the boat was still there.

On Monday Santiago arrived at the marina around noon, and seeing no sign of Adriana around the entrance where he had left her three days before, he ventured past the gate toward the docks where he found his boys playing around the piers with some other kids, while Jorge looked on. When they saw him, they stopped running around and rushed to him with big hugs and much excitement. Jorge stepped between his father's legs and held on, as though he needed protection from something, a fearful look in his eyes.

"*¡Papa!* I think we have found a way to America!" Carlos exclaimed, pointing to the family making camp in the grass alongside the face dock on the west side of the marina. An elderly couple sat wearily among their belongings napping, while their adult children minded the grandchildren, who had been playing hide-and-seek with Carlos and Valeriano.

"This is the Iglesias family, and they speak some American." Santiago looked at his son with some interest as the boy continued, "They say they have been talking to the girl on the sailboat over there by the government office"—he pointed across the harbor to the new-looking sailboat with two masts—"and she told them that she and her boyfriend are in some kind of trouble; they are not supposed to be here, and they are getting kicked out. They are leaving tonight, and we can go with them. It is a big boat."

Santiago thought about this for a moment, considering the bad news he had to report from his trip to the Peruvian embassy in La Habana. "Carlos, go find your mother and bring her back here while I talk to this Iglesias family about their plans."

The boy ran off to find his mother at the house where he had been sleeping on the porch. Santiago sat with the Iglesias family and asked about what Carlos had told him. They first asked him if he had any money, and when they found out they didn't, the young parents went back to reading their local newsprint, so Santiago focused on the grandparents, who seemed more obliging. They shared what they knew.

Santiago could smell the smoke of the cooking fires of the groups that were scattered around the area. Mariel Harbor was in a large bay, lined with long commercial docks along the east side, which were now filled with a growing number of small boats rafted to one another, waiting to find passengers to take back to Florida. The Marina itself was overcrowded with boats arriving and leaving in a constant flow of activity. It was boxed off in a square shape with docks inside. The scene was mildly chaotic.

He learned from his new friends that boats were coming and going all the time. Persons who had paperwork in order, usually exit visas obtained from the Peruvian embassy, were allowed to board boats heading north to Key West. Earlier in April, these departures were monitored by the soldiers who guarded the marina, but recently the sheer volume of refugees and the number of boats coming to pick them up made documentation difficult for the authorities, who were now willing to let people go just to get them out of the area, whose infrastructure was taxed beyond its limits. Fights were breaking out, and it was difficult for the military to maintain law and order.

Santiago explained that he had been unsuccessful in obtaining an exit visa for his family in La Habana, because he couldn't identify where to contact Adriana's relative in the United States, apparently a requisite, so he had returned empty-handed. In fact, he had learned this from others who had not been able to get inside the embassy, just as Santiago could not because of the crowds and the limited resources there to deal with them. Reluctantly, he had returned to Mariel and his family to work out an alternative plan.

Santiago begged the Iglesias family to let his family accompany them if they were able to make passage on the sailboat that was tied up in the marina. They met Adriana, who had just arrived from town, and saw the forlorn look on her beautiful face, and with the encouragement of the children who had bonded over the last few days with Carlos and Valeriano, they agreed to let the Gonzalez family join in.

Jorge's big brown eyes looking up at them had certainly helped sway them as well.

———— ᴍ ————

Jorge took the rest of the afternoon off from Arthur White & Company, Certified Public Accountants, his only employer since he had graduated from Florida Atlantic University in Boca Raton. He had taken his degree and 4.0 average to a regional firm instead of one of the big four, not because he wasn't sought after, he was, but because he wanted a faster path to the top with more hands-on experience. He envisioned one day starting a firm of his own, and he thought the training he would receive would have more transferability from a regional firm than a Coopers & Lybrand, where he would be a cog in a wheel, not a master of the machinery. So far, he was on track. Arthur White & Company handled publicly traded clients, same as the big firms, and it did a lot of intricate tax work, dancing in minefields of conflicting objectives where closely held businesses needed to report good incomes but did not want to pay tax on them. These were the challenges that made successes of locally owned CPA firms, not rooms of junior auditors verifying data from statistical samples generated by programs set up by mathematicians.

He couldn't wait to get to his parents' home in Little Havana to share his good news. His mother was going to be so proud, but not surprised. She and Jorge's father had sacrificed their whole lives to create a pathway for him to succeed, and he owed them everything. He was reminded again of the long overnight sailboat trip from the crowded harbor in Mariel with another family. Fortunately, the big storms that had blown through the Florida Straits a week earlier had given way to smooth water and a moonlit night, but little Jorge didn't know that at the time. Thirteen of them at the hands of a young couple, Durk, Jorge recalled his name, and his girlfriend had "borrowed" his father's forty-foot sailboat and sailed it from Tampa to be part of the great boatlift adventure in 1980. It didn't work out so well for Durk, however.

Young Durk thought he and his college sweetheart would be welcomed as saviors by the Cuban people when he got to Mariel, prepared to bring refugees back to America and freedom. Instead he was held captive for two days because he was not Cuban and his actions were considered suspicious. It didn't help that most of the boats arriving from the north were barely seaworthy, and his sailboat was quite new looking and didn't fit in with the rest of the flotilla. It reeked of capitalist extravagance. Just the same, his efforts were greatly appreciated by his guests. He was allowed to leave, and in the chaos of the activity, no one of importance noticed when he stopped by the rafted fishing boats along the eastern seawall and picked up the two families on the way out of the harbor.

The only boats following them were others full of refugees, and when the sun came up in the morning, they were greeted by a line of clean, white U.S. Coast Guard cutters, six abreast, in a formation four or five miles long, radioing requests to provide for any needed assistance to the menagerie of vessels making their way to Key West. They also issued instructions where arriving boats were to make their arrivals; as there were so many, they could not all fit at the customs dock. Only one of the Iglesias family could speak any English, and Durk and his girlfriend knew only a couple of words of Spanish, but the needs of the moment made communication possible for what was necessary.

After the family was vetted at the Truman Annex temporary processing center set up in the old Navy shipyard west of Whitehead Street, they were sent to a relocation center in Gadsden, Alabama, where the Gonzalez family was settled in subsidized housing with other families of limited resources who had found their way to the United States. Santiago found himself again in the fields working with the crops of the season, while Adriana was given a position in food service in the local school system. With the government assistance, their combined incomes gave them enough to get by, while the boys did their best to adapt to the ways of the American South in the school system. This was harder for Carlos and Valeriano, who were in seventh and fifth grades, where social patterns were already well formed.

Jorge had things a little better. His peers found him a curiosity and, as such, wanted to get to know more about him. They saw him struggle with a new language, but rather than make fun of him, they helped him. There was one boy in his class who had come from Central America and already spoke English. He was a great help to Jorge, but when he left for his own classes, Jorge felt very isolated, which made him all the more determined to learn the language of his new homeland. Jorge's brothers didn't fare so well. Picked on by their peers, Val and Carlos stuck together, forming a close bond, as they kept each other's backs. They got into fights often, defending their place in the school community, and the authorities of a conservative South didn't have a lot of sympathy for the darker-skinned new arrivals. The Gonzalez brothers, as they came to be known, were in trouble a lot, much to the consternation of their mother.

"Why can't you boys be more like Jorge?" she entreated, much to their dismay. "He is such a good boy, and he reflects well on the family. You boys make us look bad."

It might be assumed that the older brothers would come to resent this, but the opposite was the case. They adored their brother, and they had his back, too. One of the reasons Jorge had an easy time of it was that his classmates knew they would have to deal with the Gonzalez brothers if they made a misstep. Carlos and Valeriano were resigned to futures that had already been destined for them, but they were determined to see that Jorge would not share the same fate.

Life was very difficult for Adriana and Santiago, and the stress of long hours and worry for the older boys showed in their faces. Santiago began losing his hair in his early forties, and Adriana began turning gray, although the light beamed from her emerald eyes when she looked at her youngest son. In their first year in Gadsden, Jorge came home on Sunday from church, smiling happily. He had not yet learned English, but Adriana made him go to Sunday school at the local Catholic Church and attend Mass every week without fail.

"Mama, Mama!" he shouted as he came in the kitchen door. "They sang a song about home in church today."

"What was the song, Jorge?"

"I don't know all of it, but it was about Camagüey. Didn't we used to live there? They sang about it!"

Adriana was very confused, but she smiled at her little boy and said, "How nice, Jorge. Maybe they did it just for you."

A week later Adriana ran into the mother of Jorge's Honduran classmate and asked about the song they sang in church last Sunday. She understood when the woman explained the song was *Come Away, Come Away to Jesus,* sounding very similar to the young boy's ear as Camagüey.

Smiling, Jorge now thought about this, too, as he pulled in the driveway of the modest, brightly painted house in Hialeah. That story had become a family favorite.

He found his mother where she usually was, in the kitchen preparing a small meal to share with her husband in the evening, a tradition she could not give up, even though her boys had moved on with lives of their own. Jorge's brothers had not made much of their secondary education since the family had relocated to the Miami area after five years in Alabama. Carlos and Valeriano ran a gas station in the heart of Little Havana, servicing rundown cars of fellow refugees and supplying aftermarket accessories popular in the Latin American culture. Many of the transactions they sourced involved questionable provenance and were quite profitable; provided no questions were asked of them, no answers were proffered. The owner of the service station did not involve himself as long as he did not hear from authorities and his customers were satisfied.

When Adriana saw Jorge come through the kitchen screen door, she squealed in delight, *"¡Jorgi! ¡Que sorpresa!"* Then followed a look of concern on her face as she wiped her hands on her apron. "What are you doing here in the middle of the afternoon? Is something wrong?"

"No, Mama. Everything is fine. Better than fine. I came to bring you wonderful news. Is Papa here?"

Santiago worked in his cousin's restaurant in Calle Ocho, near Carlos and Valeriano, where he had taken a job after the family moved from Gadsden. Adriana waited tables part time in the busy season while Santiago cooked and managed things in his cousin's absence.

"What news is this?" Adriana's frown turned into a radiant beam, and her green eyes flashed.

Jorge felt his heart skip a beat that he had caused even a moment's anguish for his mother, who was as beautiful to him as ever. He could not see the graying of her hair or the lines the years of struggle and hard work had put in her face.

"I have been given a big promotion at my accounting firm. The partners have asked me to join them as a partner, so as of July first, I will be a part owner of the accounting firm and entitled to a percentage of its profits," he explained carefully. Adriana rushed to him and embraced him, coating the back of his dark suit with baking flour. "Wait, there's more. I have been put in charge of the firm's biggest and most important client," he exaggerated.

Adriana cried out softly, held him by the shoulders at arm's length, and looked up into his brown eyes. With great pride on her face, she said, "We must tell the whole family. Can you stay for dinner? I'll call your brothers; they'll want to know. Papa gets off at seven, and I'll add some pork and vegetables to what I'm making. We should tell our friends, too. We'll make it a celebration!"

"Not so fast, Mama. I still have some work to do. I just wanted to come by and give you the good news, but I can come for dinner, and it would be fun to see Carlos and Val. I haven't seen them for a while. But, please, just us for now. I don't want to jinx anything."

Adriana faked a false frown, but she was happy. "I just want the whole world to know what an important big shot my little boy, Jorge, is. I always knew you were going to make this family proud. Not that I'm not proud of your brothers, but they are always in trouble." She placed her hand on his cheek. "You never gave us any reason for concern; you have always been such a good boy." Adriana noticed the smudge of flour she left on his cheek, and shrieked, *"¡Dio!* Look what I've done." She turned Jorge around and started whisking the flour prints off of his suit with a wet kitchen cloth until it looked normal again. "There you go." She ushered him out the door. "Go back to your precious office and impress your new partners. We will all be here waiting for you to celebrate at seven thirty, or whenever your busy schedule makes it possible for you to fit us in."

Jorge smiled at her as he slipped out the back door. *Sometimes I don't know if my mother is Cuban or Jewish,* he kidded.

It took about twenty-five minutes for Jorge to drive his BMW 3 Series back to his office, where he sat at his desk and took stock of his situation. His new responsibility was Pension Strategy Partners, an investment banking firm that specialized in tactics to protect large actuarial portfolios such as pension funds from interest rate sensitivity in the marketplace. Their mission was to hold the line on portfolio values while maintaining laddered cash flows for anticipated employee retirements. This structural investment planning alleviated the strain on annual charges to corporate earnings arising from temporary fluctuations in interest rates. Jorge knew that the business model sounded complex, but it was really simple in his mind. When he tried to explain it to someone, he was usually greeted with a yawn.

As an auditor, his job was rather simple. To render the firm's opinion as to the fairness of the published financial statements and attendant regulatory filings, he needed to understand and document the accounting system and evaluate the systems of internal control the company had in place to safeguard its assets. The confirmation of the existence of the assets was relatively simple, as the majority of the actual pension fund money and investments were held by known major financial institutions, such as J.P. Morgan and other huge banks. He had only to confirm their custodianship of investments and catalogue the necessary cutoff dates for trades in process at the end of accounting periods. In this case, the fiscal year-end of Pension Strategy Partners was June 30. Most of the testing was done by mathematically proven statistical analysis, so the amount of physical records that had to be examined by hand was not so burdensome.

Yesterday, Jorge had been a manager on the engagement and had seen through all the year-end audit procedures, including validation of cutoffs. His time in July, which started tomorrow, would be spent finishing the review and testing of the system of internal control, and that process would be the same as last year. He would coordinate the remaining managers on the job to work the various cycles the audit process had been broken into, so that their efforts would produce results at the appropriate time. Some of his new responsibilities included reviewing changes in general ledger procedures, and for this he sought some assistance from the firm's senior audit partner, Walter Adams. Jorge concluded the day with a quick meeting of the senior audit staff to bring everyone up to speed with his new responsibilities and what would be expected of them going forward.

Later that evening, Jorge enjoyed a celebratory pork dinner with all the Cuban trimmings, *arroz congri, yuca con mojo,* and *tostones,* lovingly prepared by Adriana. Carlos and Valeriano couldn't resist attending the family dinner, if for no other reason than to have a chance to take a few cheap shots at their "big shot" businessman brother who wore a suit to work every day.

Jorge gave it all back in good measure. "Yeah, things are great, Carlos. How's the spinner hubcap business going?" he asked, making fun of the Cuban preoccupation with jazzed-up American cars, which made up a good part of the brothers' aftermarket parts business.

"Yeeeooow!" Carlos snapped his index and middle fingers over his head in a loud popping noise, ducking so as to avoid the low-flying zinger hurled in his direction. "You know, little brother, our business has very good margins when you don't have much cost basis in your inventory." He winked at Valeriano, who smiled back at him.

Adriana pretended not to understand the meaning, and Santiago looked the other way. Valeriano continued the questioning: "So, Jorge, who is this very important client you are in charge of?"

Jorge started to explain the business of Pension Strategy Partners, but he only got as far as the word "derivatives" when Valeriano interrupted him. "Whoa, slow down. Remember you're talking to your dumb-ass brothers who steal hubcaps for a living." Adriana crossed herself, frowning, and Valeriano said, "Bring it down to a level we can understand."

"Okay, I'll start at the beginning. You know I'm a CPA, right?"

"Yeah, stands for cleaning, pressing, and alterations," Carlos quipped.

Jorge ignored him, continuing, "So what we do, as a major firm, is not bookkeeping and tax returns, although we do a lot of tax-related work, but we examine the financial statements put out by bigger companies, ones that others rely on for their business purposes, like banks and stockholders. After a thorough sophisticated review, we opine, excuse me, give our opinion to you guys as to the fairness of the presentation of the statements, so the people who rely on them can do so with confidence. Does that make sense?"

"It does to me," said Valeriano. "Now I know why you don't do so much tax work. Who wants to report all their income fairly?"

The brothers laughed, their father just looked bewildered, and Adriana gazed adoringly at her big-shot son, who was obviously important to a lot of people.

"Then," Jorge continued, "our letter of fairness is published along with the financials for everyone to see."

The brothers nodded in understanding. They teased a lot, but they were happy for Jorge, and as proud as their mother at how far he had come from the cane fields of Camagüey. Not that they were dissatisfied with their lives, but just happy that a Gonzalez had broken the family cycle of poverty and made it to the professional world.

CHAPTER FOUR

Jorge spent the majority of his time during July and August in the offices of Pension Strategy Partners located on North Andrews Avenue in Fort Lauderdale just south of Cypress Creek Road. They had just two months to complete their work and put out their opinion on the June 30, 2008 fiscal year-end statements.

The building that housed the corporate offices was a trophy landmark, having been previously a branch location for a failed Florida bank. Its appearance was worthy of a venerable financial center with its coral stone walls and wrought-iron gates at the front courtyard. Two-story parking at the rear connected the garage with the first and second floors of the building, making access for occasional visitors—there were not many—and employees alike. The first contained lavish executive offices, trading desks, and a well-appointed lobby, and the second floor was given over to the extensive information technology and data-processing requirements. The impressive building served no operational purpose, about eight thousand feet for each floor, other than show how secure and confident it looked on Pension Strategy Partners' business brochures and website, inferring it was a solid place to do business.

Jorge and his staff spent most of their time during the audit fieldwork on the second floor where the center of the floor housed the elevator core, which was adjacent to a separate HVAC room. It was loaded with the additional air-conditioning equipment required by the heat-generating computers that were the heart of the business operations. Offices lined the perimeter of the second floor, and individual cubicles occupied the balance of the space. Access to the building was controlled by keypad at each of the three entrances to the building, the main one at the front, and one each at the rear to the parking garage.

Jorge headed for the glass-walled office on the southwest corner and tapped gently on the glass partitioning next to the identity plaque on the doorframe, which revealed that the office belonged to the Information Systems Director, Anita Berwitz. The raven-haired young woman looked up from her computer screen and smiled.

"Good morning, Jorge. What mind-numbing data do you want me to produce for you today?" Anita looked over the tops of her librarian-styled horn-rimmed glasses with an amused expression on her pretty face. Jorge warmed, as he always did, to her dimpled smile and gentle jab at the dreary work that was generally asked of her. He smiled back, comfortable enough to invite himself in to her office and sit in the chair opposite her desk.

As he slid into the modern, metal-framed chair he reflected on how gorgeous Anita looked if you got past the heavily framed glasses and somewhat dowdy clothes, which hid her rather curved female frame. She was not too tall, about five-feet-six, generally wore flat shoes, accentuating her curves and athletic behind, and her ample breasts spoke for themselves. In spite of all these notable features, what stood out was her drop-dead pretty face with full lips and dimples, which exaggerated her generous smile. Jorge took a moment to take all this in as he formulated what he was going to ask her. The two enjoyed a friendly, not quite flirty, interchange developed over the last several years during the summer when he was present for the annual audit. While they were in a professional setting, they each did their best to conceal the charge between them, but it was obvious to everyone else. He visited with her more now that he was senior on the job and had more interaction with management and operations heads at Pension Strategy Partners.

"Well," he began, "we're just wrapping up our fieldwork this week, so I wanted to stop by and tell you I won't be around much more this year. I do look forward to working with you next year, though I'll miss seeing you in the interim."

Jorge was not really comfortable dealing with women, unless it was in a purely business capacity on professional matters. Clearly, this association was outside of that comfort zone in his mind, and he really did feel he was going to miss working with this nice little Jewish girl, something else that was out of the ordinary for a parochial Catholic boy from a closely knit Cuban family. He felt clumsy around her, only confident when he was dealing in accounting matters, and he used the opportunities to explain his auditing process and theory to her.

Anita was inquisitive about understanding why she was asked to produce the information she did for him to meet his needs, and she was a willing listener on those occasions when he highlighted the underlying reasons to test and verify certain data the accounting department produced. He enjoyed telling her how overall it fit a puzzle for the auditors to satisfy themselves that the systems of internal control were safeguarding the company's assets, and why this understanding was of paramount importance before the auditors could render their opinion as to the fairness of the financial statements.

"You know, it doesn't have to be that long," Anita volunteered. "When do you actually finish up?" Anita hoped he would pick up on the suggestion, but Jorge was oblivious, a romantic relationship not really on his radar. He was too close to her to see the obvious.

"Well, the fieldwork is essentially done now; we just have to go back and compare our notes to the planning checklists we developed to make sure we have everything covered. Once the statements are finalized, and our management letter approved, we just need representation letters from the partners and key operations personnel, and the statements are released for filing. As you know, the PCAOB requires the audited statements be submitted within sixty days of year end, so for you that's August thirty-first. We're completely out of here by the end of this week and done for the year in about two weeks after that."

"Just to educate me, what's the PCA . . . alphabet you just referred to?"

"You mean the sixty days?"

"Yeah, those guys."

Jorge fumbled for a second with the acronym, finally sounding it out like a first-grader trying to mouth the alphabet. "P-C-A-O-B. Public Companies Audit Oversight Board. They are the first among many that require securities firms to file annual audited financial statements, and they want them in sixty days. Puts quite a crimp on us, 'cause that's a fast turnaround. Fortunately, your business is mostly monetized, so the audit verification is easy and quick."

Anita gave him a puzzled look. "Monetized?"

"Oh, that means that what you do is recorded in verifiable numbers in a short period of time, so our work is more objective, not say . . . like a hospital where results need to be measured in subjective outcomes as well as numerically, which makes the process much more complicated. For you, there's a transaction and the money is either there or it's not."

"Got it," she acknowledged. "So, did you find any fingers in the cookie jar?"

Jorge laughed. "You know, that's everybody's reaction, but that's not really what this is all about. Everyone thinks we're looking for fraud or theft, but we're really not. We will probably uncover it if there is, but our responsibility is to the overall fairness of the financial statements as a whole. So, if there is some minor theft, it may not be of concern to us unless it is of sufficient size to materially alter the statements taken in their entirety. We would probably be more interested in the effect that a theft would mean to the systems of internal control, and the exposure to other possible interference it might represent."

"You mean you don't care about the money I've stashed away from the petty-cash fund over the years?" Anita laughed, throwing her hands in the air.

"Not really." George looked serious, finally relaxing as he got her meaning.

"You need to chill a little," Anita said, noticing the delayed response to her attempt at a little humor. Returning to her previous prompt, she asked, "So, I shouldn't expect to see you until next year when you come back to start your fieldwork?" She hoped he would pick up on the earlier cue.

Jorge studied her inviting smile, and it suddenly dawned on him what she was after. He felt a little excitement well within him and ventured cautiously, "Unless you might want to meet for coffee sometime, if that's not inappropriate."

His reward came in the form of "That would be nice, and no, I don't think that's inappropriate."

Jorge was relieved and encouraged. She wrote a number on a Post-it. "This is my cell number, so you don't have to go through the switchboard." She held it out to him, and he stuck it on the outside of the working paper file he had brought with him as a prop.

"That's a date then. You can expect a call from me." He smiled and stood, looking down at her and feeling more confident and pleased with himself. He made an exit before he could say anything to screw things up, and headed for the small conference room on the other side of the floor where his staff had been allotted working space for the audit fieldwork. He spent about an hour finalizing the assembly of working papers and attention to checklists prepared by the senior and junior accountants, making a few notations and initialing what had to be documented. He used this opportunity to build coordination among his staff and make recommendations.

"I want you guys to think outside the box for a minute. Is there anything you have seen that you think may need a deeper look before I take this back to Miami and sign off on it?"

The five in the room looked over at him and pretended to be thinking of something to say that would sound intelligent. Audit staff were not often asked that type of question in earnest, and it was a chance to show off. A junior newbie fresh out of college leaned forward and raised his index finger.

"What is it, Chris?" Jorge acknowledged.

"Well, I'm sure you're on top of it. I'm obviously new to this engagement, but I did notice one thing," he said tentatively, not wanting to look stupid.

"What is it?"

"Well, I looked over the work papers from prior years to acquaint myself with the process here, and I couldn't help notice an increase in the activity in the omnibus accounts over the years."

One of the more seasoned seniors jumped in. "That's pretty normal. The omnibus accounts are just suspense accounts in each revenue sector that are set up to hold transactions in suspense until they can be posted to where they belong, so the accounting process doesn't get bogged down waiting for confirmations to come in, and the company can close out the accounting cycle."

Chris felt the need to defend himself. "I know that, we've proved them all out, and most balances are zeroed within a few weeks of the close of any interim accounting period. I'm just referring to the volume of activity." He looked pleadingly at Jorge for some acknowledgment that he wasn't a dummy for bringing it up.

Jorge wanted to reinforce the young accountant's initiative, so he responded, "Good point, Chris. Each of you was responsible for a revenue sector, and each has an omnibus account. I suggest each of you," he said, nodding to the other staff who had responsibility for revenue sectors that had similar omnibus accounts, "sample five or ten in your area, and follow them through, just to clean up the issue, now that it has been raised."

Jorge knew that the number of transactions selected should have been documented with a statistical sampling model, but in his experience, the number to be sampled always came out to between five and ten, so it wasn't worth the effort to run the computer model. It was a trick he had been shown years ago by Walter Adams, the senior audit partner at Arthur White & Company, and Jorge was confident that that was what he would have advised if he had been there. He noted the logic in the appropriate working paper file as a backup.

"I'm not surprised at the increase. The main business of this investment firm is to stabilize investment portfolios, and the number and types of hedges they use grows every year, so I would expect these suspense accounts to see more activity," he added.

Business concluded, Jorge told everyone he would meet them back in the Miami office later in the day to begin the monotonous job of pulling everything together, so the financial statements could be signed off. He was ahead of schedule, with almost three weeks before the filing deadline required by the PCAOB.

When Jorge got back to the office, he poked his head in Walter Adams's office to go over the decision he had made. After a brief description of the issue that had been raised by the staff earlier in the morning, Adams dismissed the matter as superfluous and told Jorge that he had done the right thing, the audit was already over budget, and that pursuing it further could only open up a can of worms that would end up amounting to nothing anyway.

"Okay, I'll just note our conversation in the file then," Jorge said.

"No, I wouldn't bother with that. You told me you already noted it in the working papers. That's good enough for our records."

The new young partner found this peculiar, since Adams had always been a stickler for documentation, but he trusted him and let the matter slide, a decision he would come to regret, as things turned out.

—⁓—

A little over a year before, in July 2007, the National Association of Securities Dealers, better known as the NASD, which provided oversight of firms that traded in public securities, had been reorganized into the Financial Industry Regulatory Authority, or simply FINRA. A nongovernmental, self-regulating, non-profit organization, FINRA was established to oversee and regulate the securities industry. With a burgeoning population of criminals taking advantage of the investing populous finding its epicenter in wealthy retirement communities, it was not surprising that two of its sixteen offices could be found in Boca Raton, Florida.

Following a very successful career in the brokerage business, Fergus Dennison decided to relocate to Boca Raton in preparation for his retirement and was promptly snatched up to head the local office of FINRA, where he now sat in his fifth-floor corner office near the Town Center Mall. He could just see the blue of the Atlantic Ocean between the condominiums lining the beach to the east. Fergus took a deep breath after reading the memo from the headquarters in Washington, DC, that had just been put on his desk, and exhaled softly through pursed lips. This semi-retirement job had not worked out the way he imagined when he first got to Florida. He was working ten or more hours a day, constantly commuting between Washington, Atlanta, and South Florida. He had never seen such financial carnage in his life, and it was getting worse by the month.

Since late summer, the markets had been weakening, resulting in failures throughout the securities industry caused by undercapitalized firms running out of liquidity. The investigations, mediation, and actual courtroom testimony were taking their toll on the aging businessman. Fergus's handicap had gone north of twenty, particularly frustrating in that he had imagined becoming a single-digit handicapper with the year-round golf afforded in what was supposed to be his near retirement years. Now his superiors wanted his office to expand surveillance of investment bankers in his area due to the looming failures on Wall Street, which now included some giant banking houses.

Bear Stearns had been acquired by JPMorgan Chase under duress earlier that spring, and rumors were circulating that Lehman Brothers was seriously undercapitalized. If those two could fail, it might well signal the end of the modern financial world as he knew it.

Fergus's boss in Washington, Howard McCall, wanted him to "get ahead of the curve," so to speak, whatever that meant . . . less time on the golf course that was for sure. He decided the easiest way to go about the job would be to canvas all of the investment banking firms under his jurisdiction and match critical items in their balance sheets against a template for general financial health that he would design based on criteria available from Washington. That way, if he missed something, it would not be his fault.

Dennison had only been in the quasi-public sector a year, and already he was thinking like a politician. He assembled the analysts in his office and set them about the task, while he organized the investigators into groups to look into more than twelve hundred investment banking firms in the state. About two dozen of those were boutique, smaller firms, which were the ones he had the most concern about. The bigger houses had to answer to much more scrutiny from the public, so he was less concerned about those.

Figuring it would take about a week to put his strategy together, Dennison booked some afternoon tee times. After the nerdy part of the comparative was completed, he would be required to make the actual personal visits to the firms that appeared to be the most vulnerable. Pleased with himself that he had managed to turn a problem into an opportunity for some free time, Dennison went out and shot a ninety-two from the white tees at the resort club he had joined.

After ten days of backroom work comparing second-quarter results from member firms, year-end from some fiscal year-end members, to his Washington, DC–approved template, only three firms looked like they merited closer inspection. One was in Orlando, and the other two were in South Florida. Dennison and his team decided to get the Orlando securities business out of the way first. So, in the first week of September, he and his team booked rooms in Orlando for an overnight and drove to the town that the Magic Kingdom put on the map.

The offices of the small firm were in the Citrus Tower on Orange Avenue, once the tallest building in the city, now just a solid address for businesses and law firms that wanted to show roots. A review of the management organization and highly leveraged customers revealed nothing particularly noteworthy, but the visit in itself brought attention to the owners that speculation on a weak foundation was not worth pursuing in this climate of market uncertainty.

The review of the bond house in Miami resulted in much the same conclusion. The principals were fast talkers who pedaled hard to value government bonds to banks in rural America, often marking up the prices egregiously. The sales personnel were typical of the business, wearing expensive suits and driving flashy cars. Much of their time was spent entertaining country bumpkin bankers, trying to impress them with their high-profile lifestyles to gain a personal relationship to the bond-buying decision makers. The business was pretty tacky, but there was not much exposure to the public, primarily due to the fact that investments were not inventoried for very long, as the sales desk did its best to flip them as quickly as possible.

Last on his list was Pension Strategy Partners, another boutique firm in Fort Lauderdale. This firm had garnered Dennison's attention for a lot of reasons. It was closely held, creating an environment for questionable decision-making, and it took speculative positions in the fringes of the derivative markets when it invested to hedge interest rate fluctuations for the large bond funds it managed.

Particularly notable were the pension funds that comprised the bulk of its customers. Pension Strategy Partners numbered a host of union-based employment organizations from the Northeast and Midwest, such as the International Brotherhoods of Teamsters, Electrical Workers, Longshore and Warehouse, and Dockworkers. Many of these blue-collar labor unions had histories of ties to organized crime, and government authorities suspected many still did, although the connections were far removed from the days of mobsters like Jimmy Hoffa. Still, there was a lot of money involved, the lines of distinction were blurry, and the environment of the member's workforce was a tough one. Management may have moved into the white-collar sector, but certainly it was not too far removed from its roots.

Dennison pondered his strategy as he left his office for Fort Lauderdale. He joined I-95 south around 10:30 in the morning on Monday, September 10. Traffic was light for a Monday, and he made it to PSP's offices on Andrews Avenue in less than a half hour for the impromptu meeting with the principals. He had only called them this morning to set it up, feeling that seeing their reactions to a request for a financial review without a lot of advance notice yielded better results than if they had a lot of time to prepare. After the initial in-person request for inquiry, he would send a team of office nerds to do the actual investigative work. When he got there, he was able to meet with two of the three principals. Adam Schaeffer, the person in charge of operations, was in the Bahamas, where he spent most of the summer weekends with his family, due to return around midday.

"To what do we owe this surprise visit from FINRA?" the taller of the two principals asked, his hand extended with a smile on his face.

Introductions were made all around as the small group retired to the fancy conference room on the ground floor, which housed the executive offices. Apparently, it was designed to impress, and it succeeded, with its caramel-colored woodwork and a view of the well-planted courtyard and its wrought-iron gate. It said this was where big decisions were made by people who knew what they were doing, just what it was designed to do.

When they were seated, Dennison began, "We usually begin an investigation with a personal visit, just to pave the way. This is really in the ordinary course of business, and we want you to know we are not on a witch hunt of any sort."

"Investigation? You said *investigation,*" the taller, seemingly more in-charge principal said, one eyebrow arched as if in disbelief. It was a question and a statement.

Dennison blanched and leaned forward, putting his palms on the conference table, trying to calm the situation. "That's exactly why I'm here; please don't be alarmed." The other two relaxed a little. He continued, "I don't need to tell you the markets are in disarray, particularly the interest-sensitive sectors, and FINRA wants to get ahead of the problems, so we are *investigating,* inquiring of, if you will, firms to be most likely affected by the circumstances. For example, it's no secret that Lehman Brothers may be in serious trouble because of speculative investments in mortgage-backed securities compounded by limited capital resources, to the point that bankruptcy may be in the picture."

"That will never happen!" the shorter principal chimed in. He seemed more excitable, dressed in more casual attire, a beige poplin suit with a blue, open-neck Oxford shirt. This contrasted with the taller man whose dress was Etonian, to say the least, in a dark-blue suit and regimental tie, heavy brogues on his feet. "The government will not let that happen. If Lehman can't find a partner, the Treasury will make someone take them over, just like Bear Stearns last March." As his nervous concern began to show, his right leg began pumping up and down under the conference table so enthusiastically that the tassels on his loafer began to make a tapping sound.

"Possibly," Dennison granted, "but the concern is still there. Nothing you have done has triggered this review." Dennison thought *review* sounded a little better. "It is routine." He brought out his copy of the PCAOB filing that had been made just a little over a week earlier and began to review the highlights with the two men. "Let's go over your overall situation from a thirty-thousand-foot level. We will have a small team of operations people in here this afternoon to review the mechanics of your data systems. We'll start with some general questions about your business model and how it is structured to make money, and then get into your capital resources . . . that all right with you?"

The two young entrepreneurs looked at each other, clearly seizing on the same thought. The taller one, named Stillson, took the lead. "We would suggest if you are going to get into any of the technical stuff, or specifics contained in the financials we have filed, that we have our independent CPA present. The firm is only about forty-five minutes away, and I'm sure the partner on the engagement can be available on short notice."

Dennison nodded agreement. "Why don't you call him, then. We will stick to general matters for the time being."

The remaining principal moved to the conference room door and gave instructions to his secretary to notify Arthur White & Company of the unannounced meeting and request that Gonzalez make the trip up to Fort Lauderdale to help. Returning to his seat he said, "The audit partner should be here in about an hour, and Adam Schaeffer, our operations chief, also a principal of the firm, should be here as well."

The three had a relatively relaxed, informal discussion about the firm, its goals and philosophy for stabilizing large bond portfolios, mostly pension funds, in a climate of erratic interest rates, and other background information. They also talked about how the three partners got together in the first place. Dennison took copious notes for his records. By the end of the meeting, they were on a first-name basis, Chris, Bradley, and Fergus, who told them he went by Ferg. Any concern among the office staff about the impromptu meeting was quelled as they observed the easygoing manner of the gathering.

Shortly before noon, the meeting increased by two as Jorge Gonzalez arrived from Miami about the same time as Adam Schaeffer made his appearance from the Bahamas. The discussion deepened in intensity as the group began talking about the operational details of the boutique investment firm. Sandwiches were brought in from a local deli, so that the principals of the firm could get as much of the review, as it was now known, out of the way. Three staff from the FINRA investigations office on Military Trail in Boca Raton arrived around two in the afternoon to begin the detailed work of going over the operations of Pension Strategy Partners. Schaeffer and Gonzalez moved with them to the second floor for this purpose, while Dennison concluded what was essentially the social part of the process, said his goodbyes, and drove the twenty minutes up I-95 to his office near Town Center to await the report from the operations team.

Schaeffer and Gonzalez introduced the FINRA techies to Anita Berwitz in the IT department where she could guide them through their checklists for the flow of accounting information through the data-processing systems.

Schaeffer was cooperative in all aspects of the investigation, but Anita and Jorge could not help noticing he seemed uneasy with the process, particularly as FINRA started getting into the area of journal adjustments to the interim financials, particularly the ones that were driven by authority, not automated in the accounting systems processes. At the end of the day, the FINRA team announced that they wanted to look at all the special journal entries in greater detail. Schaeffer seemed concerned about the time the investigation would take.

"How long do you think it will take you guys to finish up and file your report?" he asked nervously, looking at his watch as if the answer were contained in it somewhere.

The team leader replied blandly, "We will be here at least a couple more days. Our boss wants us to review all of the special journal entries at each month end, and each of your investment sectors has omnibus accounts for holding transactions in suspense, which are closed out after each accounting period. These will take individual review, then we have to write our report, so not before Friday at the earliest."

Schaeffer started to get a little agitated. "I don't get it. You've told us this review is routine, that nothing the firm has done has triggered it. We are not suspected of having any difficulties. Our 10-K and supporting schedules have been submitted to the Public Company Oversight Board. Our financials have a clean opinion from our independent auditors. Isn't this a complete duplication of work?" Turning to Jorge he added, "Arthur White & Company already did this in the course of the audit, right? So, hasn't this ground already been covered? Help me out here."

Gonzalez thought for a moment, not wanting to mislead anybody, although he, too, was getting a little annoyed at the intrusion. "Well, on a macro scale that's right, Adam. But our opinion is based on the statements taken as a whole, and the stuff these guys are looking at probably doesn't even meet a materiality threshold for an audit, so we may very well not have looked at each adjustment individually. Their concerns and objectives are not necessarily consistent with ours. Just let them finish and do their jobs, so we can get this behind us."

Anita, who had been following the conversation among the gentlemen, was pleased with herself, as she remembered Jorge talking to her about the very subject of materiality just three weeks earlier when she had jokingly brought up the subject of finding "fingers in the cookie jar."

Schaeffer implored them once more, "Isn't there anything you can do to speed this up? My family expects me in Marsh Harbour on Friday for our last long weekend of the summer, and I'd like to get out of here in the morning before the afternoon thunderstorms start to kick up. My partners are not going to want me to leave before this matter is settled."

The FINRA team leader, feeling no sympathy for trampling on a flashy yuppie's lifestyle, said, "Go ahead and go. We will file the report, and you can deal with any matters that come up when you return. You'll be back first part of the week, right?"

"I guess so," Schaeffer acquiesced. Turning to Gonzalez he added, "You can come back while they're here, right?"

Jorge nodded affirmatively. "I may have the manager on the audit stick by for the tedious stuff, but I'll come back to review the draft of the report and let you know anything you need to know before it's filed."

Schaeffer seemed to relax a little. The six of them continued until nearly six o'clock and planned to rendezvous first thing in the morning.

Anita said she would stay late and have a printout of all of the monthly manual journal entries ready for them in the morning. Jorge thanked her for her help and volunteered to stay if he could be of any help. She declined his offer, saying she just needed to program the request of what was wanted from the data-processing system, and then added with a dimpled smile, "But I will probably work up quite an appetite by eight o'clock, if you would consider taking me to dinner. You *did* say you'd call."

Jorge smiled back at her and said he'd make a few calls in the meantime. "Just let me know when you're ready."

Even timid Jorge couldn't help but notice Anita's interest in him. He felt a tingle of excitement that he was actually going to go out with her, and he didn't even have to risk rejection in asking her. For her part, Anita knew if a move was going to be made, she would have to make it. Whereas Jorge gave off an aura of great confidence and leadership qualities, he seemed very unsure of himself socially. She figured that he had no idea how handsome he was with his Latin American good looks.

Unfortunately for Jorge, one of his calls required him to return to his office. He expressed his regrets to Anita and promised to call her. Still not sure of himself, he knew he had to make good on his promise soon, or his failure to do so would be misinterpreted. He vowed to rectify this at the earliest opportunity.

Adam Schaeffer

CHAPTER FIVE

The world started to come unglued for Adam Schaeffer when he got back to the office from his uneventful two-hour flight from Marsh Harbour in the Bahamas. It was not uncommon for him to extend his weekend into Monday morning, knowing he would be at his desk at Pension Strategy Partners by lunchtime. His routine was so predictable that it didn't even occur to him to call the office before his departure to see if anything was going on that was out of the ordinary. He was up at seven, finishing a light breakfast with Marjorie and his daughters by eight. On schedule, Cay Mills, locally known as "the Admiral," picked Schaeffer up at the marina and drove him to the airstrip about a mile inland from the harbor. Schaeffer and Cay had developed a relationship over the last few summers, and Schaeffer volunteered a few dollars each year to help Cay with the youth softball league that was developing in the Abacos. There was talk that the Marsh Harbour boys were good enough to contend in the island championships played in Nassau each year.

After filing his Outward Declarations with Immigration and Customs and a quick preflight on the white Cessna 182, Schaeffer was in the clear blue sky by nine o'clock, heading west for the hundred-eighty-mile journey to Fort Lauderdale. He filed an instrument flight plan with Miami Center when they came within radio range, about fifty miles east of Freeport, climbed five hundred feet to the requisite IFR altitude westbound, and settled in for the captivating views of the local islands and beautiful waters of the Little Bahama Bank beneath him, the autopilot firmly in command of the small aircraft. The Cessna was not particularly speedy, making about one hundred twenty knots over the ground against a light headwind at seven thousand feet. He parked on the customs ramp at Fort Lauderdale Executive Airport just before eleven, giving him a few minutes to jump in the shower at home to clean up and throw on a suit before heading to the office, where he arrived at noon.

When he saw the meeting taking place in the firm's conference room, that's when things started to unravel. Stillson waved him into the meeting room with some enthusiasm, which Schaeffer entered with some trepidation, noting that Jorge Gonzalez from the company's auditing firm was already there. *This can't be anything good,* he told himself as he was introduced to the FINRA chief, Fergus Dennison, and the reason for his visit. Explanations took a few minutes, and Schaeffer's concern almost wiped the deep Bahaman tan off of his face as he gulped and tried to calm himself down. Slowly he began to realize that this was not anything targeted at him, for the time being anyway, and he began to relax a little.

Schaeffer's casual attitude lasted until the middle of the afternoon when the subject of the omnibus accounts came up, at which point he felt like he was going to be sick. He knew now that the time had come for him to pull the trigger on his plans to escape into a new world, the one he had been planning for the last several years.

The omnibus accounts contained the information that would lead the investigators to what he had been doing, and he knew it was only a matter of time before they figured it out. The bean counters arrived from the FINRA office shortly thereafter and began their review. Schaeffer understood they would need a few days to do their work and submit a report to Dennison, probably Monday at the earliest, he hoped. He decided he would have to put his plan into effect this week and be out of the country by the weekend.

His routine dictated that he would return to the Bahamas in his Cessna on Friday, so his departure should not arouse any suspicion. By the weekend he would be presumed dead, at least that was the plan. Schaeffer stayed the rest of the afternoon with the tech team from FINRA and left promptly at five o'clock to start making his arrangements. On the way home he stopped by RadioShack and bought three prepaid phones, one of which he would use to call Robbie Wells to confirm the date for the pickup. He had told Robbie he would give him a week's heads up; Schaeffer hoped the shortened notice wouldn't make a difference. He didn't know what he would do if Robbie was not available, except he could always put more money on the table. He didn't have time to recruit anyone else.

Schaeffer breathed a sigh of relief when Robbie answered on the third ring.

"Robbie," the boat bum said simply.

"Thank God I got you. I need to move up my date a little. Can you be ready to pick me up Friday evening?" Schaeffer asked anxiously.

"I'm already in the States, ready and waiting, and I've arranged for our ride."

"Ride. What ride?" Schaeffer's apprehension had him a little off his game. "Oh, you mean the boat. Got you."

Robbie continued, "It's a sweet ride too. . . . Do over forty knots." He seemed pleased with himself.

"Great. Now listen. I'll call you the morning of from this same cell number to confirm. If you need to reach me for any reason, call this number. Do you have it in your phone?"

"Sure do, boss." Robbie subrogated his conversation to make Schaeffer feel more in charge. Make him feel more comfortable, not suspecting anything. "I still need the exact GPS coordinates. I suggest you text them to me, so I can't screw it up writing them down."

Schaeffer agreed, and said he would as soon as they ended the call. Robbie said he would text a reply to confirm he had received the information.

"See you Friday at seven o'clock."

"I'll be there, you can count on it." Robbie ended the call.

Schaeffer checked the text draft three times with his sectional chart to verify he had input the numbers correctly. It was just north of Great Isaac Lighthouse marking the northwest corner of the Great Bahama Bank. His nautical chart indicated the depth at the location was over six thousand feet. Sunset was at seven twenty, the timing of the ditching carefully planned so that there would be no daylight left for a search. Robbie would arrive at about the same time, so there would be no incidental tracking of a boat loitering in the area prior to his planned arrival.

Schaeffer had done his best to plan everything out in advance to the smallest detail. He had a canvas "go bag" to carry his new identification and airline tickets, as well as a change of clothes, since he would be drenched in the short swim to the boat that was to pick him up. He planned to wrap the canvas carryall in a garbage bag to keep the contents dry. He spent the rest of the evening getting everything ready for his trip. He had already assembled fifty thousand dollars in cash through multiple withdrawals as a safeguard for his travels, in case something went wrong with the regular plans. He had no credit cards in his new identity because he did not want to leave any trail behind that could connect Stephen Anderson to the soon-to-be deceased Adam Schaeffer. In all his planning, he never gave a thought to his wife and children other than the role they would play in alerting authorities when they realized he was overdue.

When he had all his travel essentials assembled, Schaeffer relaxed a little and made himself a stiff scotch and soda. He sat back on his living room sofa and started crafting a plan to delay the FINRA geeks from finding out how he had used the omnibus accounts to assign trades weeks after they were made at his firm, which was how he was able to set a couple hundred million aside in foreign bank accounts over the last three years without anyone suspecting anything.

All things considered, Schaeffer got a pretty good night's sleep and headed to the office at eight in the morning. He tried to occupy the FINRA techs with small talk about his strategies to smooth out the effects of interest-rate fluctuations for the big pension funds, and the young crew seemed happy to engage him, since his conversation brought them up to his lofty level in the world of corporate finance. But ultimately they returned to going painstakingly through their required tasks. Schaeffer diverted them for a while, looking at capital requirements, which at the end of the day was what it was all about, wasn't it? FINRA really didn't care what was going on within the firm's structure as long as they had the capital to stay afloat through financial adversity, which was abundant these days.

When they finally focused on the special journal entries that cleaned up the omnibus accounts at the end of each accounting period, which was monthly in this case, nothing appeared unusual to the FINRA auditors, at least in the beginning. It wasn't until late Thursday that anyone on the team stepped back and looked at the adjustments from a more distant perspective that any alarm bells started ringing. Schaeffer first noticed that the team from FINRA started caucusing among themselves, whispering in quiet voices in the conference room. Around three o'clock they announced that they had completed their fieldwork and were returning to Boca Raton to prepare the report, which would summarize the results of their investigation.

Schaeffer left the offices of Pension Strategy Partners shortly after the investigators, heading for home to go over all of the final details of his plans. He would only have one chance to pull off his faked death, and once he had committed, there would be no turning back. His current life would no longer be available to him, because if he were discovered to be alive at some point in the future, he would be a criminal on the run for the rest of his life. His whole strategy was based on the premise that no one was going to look for a dead person, even if the accounting irregularities were discovered, which was likely.

He marveled at how easy it had been to move hundreds of millions in modest increments from the vast resources of the money managed by the firm over the last several years. In his capacity as the head of operations for the investment firm, the information technology department was under his control. Three years earlier, he had discovered quite by accident that the omnibus accounts could be used for more than holding miscellaneous postings in suspense until the correct ledger account for a transaction could be identified. They were primarily supposed to be used when a classification of an expense or revenue could not be identified until after the closing of a monthly accounting period. There were dozens of these each month, and if the accounting department didn't know where a transaction should be directed, it was placed in suspense, otherwise known as an omnibus account, until the matter could be straightened out.

Three years earlier in 2005, Schaeffer had ended a reporting period with a complicated joint investment transaction entered into by several clients. The allocation of proceeds required many layers of division. Not having time to make the adjustments before the month end, he just put the results of the transaction, which involved the sale of a derivative shared by five different pension plans, in the omnibus accounts of the investment sectors of the firm until he could straighten things out. The accounting for the pension funds would be slightly out of whack to an immaterial degree, but the accounting system as a whole would be in balance. Only he would be aware of the situation.

He forgot about the transaction while he was away for a week on vacation in the Florida Keys, and he didn't deal with it until two weeks later when the girl in charge of the IT department brought it to his attention. She was young, a recent college graduate with a gifted mind for data processing, who was hired for her potential as the computer-driven side of the operation became more formidable to the business.

After the accounting department completed the math for the allocations of the derivative proceeds, Schaeffer gave Anita Berwitz the journal entry to be posted manually to bring the subsidiary ledger back into agreement, the opposing postings closing out the previous entries to the omnibus accounts. It didn't take Schaeffer long to figure out that if three weeks could go by without anybody paying attention to transaction postings that the delay would give ample time for a trade to develop a profit or loss in the marketplace. This would apply to any random transaction and any trading account managed by the firm. He made a few test runs in modest amounts to make sure the system worked as planned, and then set about greatly expanding the scope of his new betting system. Anita Berwitz grew accustomed to his monthly journal entries, which she manually entered in the firm's records, so she didn't pay much attention as the years went by.

The rest of the planning was a little more involved. Through lawyers in Miami, Schaeffer was referred to a law firm in Zurich, which also had offices in Vaduz, the capital of Liechtenstein, the epicenter of monies secreted from around the world by people who wanted their wealth out of the public eye. Liechtenstein law provided for a form of trust that could be formed and operated at the discretion of a designee, usually a trusted attorney or law firm. Assets owned by such a trust could be moved at the direction of the designee and, as such, could be moved from generation to generation without tax consequences, since the monies handled by the trust were dispersed and collected at the designee's direction. He performed his responsibilities in accordance with the terms set out in the deed of trust and was not answerable to anybody unless laws of the Principality of Liechtenstein were violated, which he was trained not to do.

Through his new cadre of legal advisors Andre Shorey, née Adam Schaeffer, formed Euro Capital, GmbH, headquartered in Vaduz, Liechtenstein, which was owned by the Andre Shorey Trust at the direction of its designee, a prominent law firm with offices in all principal cities in Europe. The lawyer would respond to anyone presenting himself as Andre Shorey as long as he was able to produce the complex passcode that had been assigned to him. The new company opened trading accounts with Pension Strategy Partners in Fort Lauderdale, Florida.

Over the intervening years, Schaeffer made unauthorized trades, taking both sides of an investment position, and held them in suspense in the omnibus accounts for a period of time, usually not more than a couple of weeks, until the market shifted enough that one side of the trade produced a modest profit, while the other side of the trade had a corresponding loss. It was a zero-sum game, basically, so at no time was the investment firm's capital ever affected, at least that's what Schaeffer assumed.

When he felt the transaction had "matured," as it were, he included the posting of the loss to one of the many funds he oversaw and the profit to Euro Capital, GmbH. These investments were in highly leveraged short-term derivatives, to produce the most bang for the buck in a brief period of time. The amounts were unnoticeable in the hundreds of transactions flowing through the investment accounts each month. Euro Capital did quite well, obviously, slowly over a three-year period. More recently, Schaeffer had learned about the market in interest rate swaps, basically betting on the health of the residential real estate mortgage market, which had been exploding in recent years.

What better way to hedge interest futures, Schaeffer noted to himself. So, for the past year, he had been able to source an investment banker who would sell him both sides of an interest rate swap for a flat fee, which he held in the omnibus accounts until a market swing dictated the transaction be closed out. Until now that market had been relatively quiet, but recent disclosures of major investment houses having financial difficulty made the prospect of big market adjustments encouraging.

Schaeffer's next hurdle had been to arrange for a fake identity to exit the country and get to Europe undetected, after the unfortunate accident that would result in his "death." Ironically, for this, he turned to one of his clients for help. Many of the pension funds under his supervision were located in the Northeast, where historically the union bosses and ultimately management had ties to organized crime. Joey Bangoni, affectionately known as Joey "Bag of Donuts" attributable to his substantial girth and fondness for Krispy Kreme, was a Wharton graduate and financial genius who oversaw the dozen or so longshoremen's unions' pension funds that were clients of Pension Strategy Partners.

Schaeffer correctly surmised that Joey would be a good place to start to find a new identity for his "friend" who needed to leave the country. Joey didn't ask any questions but said he would think about it and get back to Schaeffer. A week later, he called and gave Schaeffer a South Florida area code number to call and identify himself as a mutual friend of Joey "B," whereupon he would be advised of the requirements to provide Adam's "friend" with what he needed. He cautioned him that it would be expensive, because forged documents just didn't cut it anymore in a world with governmental cyber capabilities. Schaeffer was told to be careful in this regard, to do it right, or risk being caught at the airport. *He wouldn't want that for his "friend," would he?*

So, Schaeffer wasn't surprised when the person on the other end of the line informed him it would be twenty-five thousand dollars, non-negotiable, for the required new identity, and that it would take a minimum of three weeks for delivery, possibly longer. The mysterious source explained that for the passports to be reliable, they had to be real, and that was the time required for an appropriate deceased person to be identified and a valid passport to be applied for. The package included a driver's license, Social Security card, and other assorted documents needed for travel outside the United States.

"Twenty-five thousand?!" Schaeffer exclaimed. "How do I know you will deliver?"

"You're the one who wants the new identity. Take it or leave it. It makes no difference to me," was the glib reply. "We both know who set this up, right?"

Schaeffer knew he had no leverage and agreed. He had to trust that Joey "Bag of Donuts" wouldn't mislead him. The amount was too inconsequential for him to make the effort.

As instructed, Schaeffer paid his local CVS Pharmacy a visit to obtain passport photos to be used in his new identification and delivered them to a Hispanic-looking man at the News Café on Ocean Drive in Miami Beach, along with a ten-thousand-dollar deposit for the transaction. In accented English, Schaeffer was instructed to wait until he was contacted for delivery instructions, which would be made on the fly, so as to conceal the identity of the provider, that no contact should be initiated by him. He should have the balance of the cash ready so that the transaction could be concluded on short notice.

The contact seemed very abrupt and authoritative, making it apparent that this was serious business and all instructions should be strictly followed. By the end of the next month, Schaeffer received a call to meet a young man wearing a Boston Red Sox T-shirt and a Miami Marlins bill cap, again at the News Café on Ocean Drive in Miami Beach, at ten o'clock on a Tuesday morning in July. He was advised that he would have two minutes to inspect the documents and hand over the cash, or there would be no deal. He met the same tatted-up Hispanic, probably in his early twenties, looked over the contents, handed him in the envelope, and hurriedly exchanged his envelope containing the cash.

By now, Schaeffer had possession of the documents for over a year, and even used them once on a trip to the Bahamas as a rehearsal to vet their effectiveness. Enduring the immigration process on his way back from Nassau was nerve-wracking, to say the least. He chose the Miami International Airport to ensure that he would not run across an immigration or customs official he might have dealt with before, figuring it would most closely duplicate the process he would encounter when he left the country for good. Stephen Anderson, his new identity, experienced no difficulty at all leaving and reentering the country, which gave Schaeffer great comfort as he planned the rest of his departure.

CHAPTER SIX

Friday morning brought a typical hot, humid day, with air mass thunderstorms forecast for the afternoon. *It's as good as any day to die,* Schaeffer thought as he started his morning, trying his best to leave his home the same as any other day. He pulled up the spread on his bed in an attempt to straighten its appearance and gathered the things that would be necessary for his excursion. He put his change of clothes in a plastic garbage bag and stuffed his new identity and first class Swiss Air ticket in a small leather case and put it on top of his change of clothes.

Next, he removed the sixty thousand dollars of cash he had accumulated and separated ten thousand in an envelope that he planned to give to Robbie, as agreed, placing it in a side pocket of the duffle he was going to use. The balance of the money was a little more problematic, as he knew he would have to declare that he was taking more than ten thousand dollars out of the country or he risked a problem going through security at the airport. Taking the money out was perfectly legal; he just had to disclose it along with a reasonable explanation, extensive travel in Europe being perfectly acceptable.

Since he planned to purchase a serviceable briefcase to put some books and magazines for his journey at the airport, he opted to place the money at the bottom of his duffle for the time being and transfer it to the briefcase before he passed through security. After a thorough review of his possessions, all he would have for the start of his new life beginning today, he closed up the duffle, zipped the side pockets, and put it under a stack of to-be-washed bedding in the laundry room. Next to it he placed two heavy-duty plastic garbage bags for securing his belongings for the short swim from his sinking plane to Robbie's boat.

With his heart rate noticeably elevated, he drove to his office, where he would spend the rest of the day trying to behave the same as any other day, talking to his associates about his plans for the weekend in the Bahamas. Some of the morning he spent with his office laptop going through documents and downloads, hoping to leave nothing behind that could give away his plan. His last use of the MacBook Air was to file his instrument flight plan from Fort Lauderdale Executive Airport to Marsh Harbour in the Bahamas, departing at 6:30 p.m. with an expected ETA of 7:55, or an hour twenty-five-minute flight, putting him on the runway in Marsh Harbour just before the thirty-minute after-sunset curfew.

He called his friend Sawyer in the Marsh Harbour customs office to alert him that he would be arriving after normal operating hours, something Sawyer didn't mind because he knew there was an extra fifty bucks in it for him. If everything went as planned, Schaeffer would be safely on his way back to Fort Lauderdale by the time anyone in the islands suspected he was overdue.

After a day of doing his best to behave as normally as possible, interesting to him in that he had to make an effort to identify how he appeared to others on a normal day, he left downtown Fort Lauderdale for home to make a quick change of clothes and pick up his travel duffle, new identity, and airline tickets. After another thorough double-check that he had all he needed, he double wrapped his duffle in the two Hefty garbage bags and placed them in the trunk of his Mercedes. He gave the home he had been living in for the past twelve years a quick going over before turning out all the lights and climbed in the driver's seat. He hadn't the slightest regret about what he was leaving behind, no thoughts of his family, or anything. Schaeffer was totally focused on the new life he was about to begin, absent the family baggage of a wife and kids to get in the way of his freedom.

When he got to the small executive airport, Banyan Air Service already had his plane pulled out on the ramp and fueled. Schaeffer punched in his security code at the gate, gaining access, and drove out on to the ramp by his Cessna 182, a perk available to aircraft owners. With no one paying any particular attention to his activities around the airplane, Schaeffer unloaded his peculiar-looking baggage and put it on the right-hand front seat. He didn't know how much time he would have after ditching, although he had researched as much as he could what he could expect to encounter in a water landing of a small single-engine airplane with fixed gear. He had learned the results were not guaranteed, as sometimes the airplane flipped over, and sometimes it didn't. Well, he would be a lot smarter in an hour or so.

Bobby, the lineman, removed the chocks from under the nose wheel as Schaeffer began the walk-around part of his preflight procedure. "You off to the Bahamas again, Mr. Schaeffer?" He was familiar with Schaeffer's summer routine. Schaeffer nodded. Bobby continued, "You know you are everybody's idol around here, commuting to the islands every weekend. See you on Monday."

"Sure thing, Bobby. Thanks for the help. I'll be back Monday morning, if you could have the car detailed and ready for me," Schaeffer added, thinking this would be a nice touch to help establish his intentions. He slipped him a five-dollar bill, knowing that Bobby would be expecting fifty more for the wash and wax when he came back after the weekend. He did pretty well for himself cleaning up the fancy cars of the regular customers while they were away on their airplanes.

With his gear stowed away on the passenger seat next to him, Schaeffer finished his walk around, checking the oil and draining the fuel tank sumps to make sure they were free of contaminant. Inside, he turned on the master switch and checked the flap operation. Satisfied that everything was in order, he settled in the left seat and put on his seat belts, and yelled, "Clear!" out the open side window, and turned the ignition key to the start position. After a few grinding revolutions, the six-cylinder engine sprang to life, settling in at a smooth six hundred rpm. The radios cackled, and the instrument panel came to life when he switched on the radio master. He let the engine warm up while he programmed his Garmin GPS with his flight plan, direct Freeport direct, knowing he would be cleared direct to Marsh Harbour as soon as he crossed the ADIZ, the boundary of territorial waters for the United States. There he would cancel his instrument flight plan, which would no longer be required legally.

Schaeffer picked up his clearance as filed from ground control, released the brakes, and began his taxi to runway eight as instructed. After a brief run up to verify that the propeller governors and magnetos were performing correctly, he called the tower and received his takeoff clearance. The little Cessna accelerated down the runway and became airborne in less than a thousand feet. Schaeffer turned toward Freeport at the instruction of Lauderdale approach control, and began his ascent to seven thousand feet, his assigned cruising altitude. He glanced at his watch, 6:30. *Right on schedule,* he noted.

About ten minutes into the flight, he crossed the Air Defense Identification Zone, when Miami Center called. "Two alpha sierra, you are cleared direct Marsh Harbour, maintain seven thousand."

Schaeffer replied, "Roger Miami Center. We'll cancel now and proceed VFR at seven thousand five hundred."

"Cancellation received, proceed VFR. Do you want flight following?"

"Negative, Miami." Schaeffer didn't want continued radar surveillance. Even though Miami Center could track him, they would soon lose interest in his flight when they had no reason to communicate with him, part of the plan. In fact, Schaeffer had given this part of his plan of action a great deal of thought. He had considered staying on the instrument flight plan and declaring an emergency when he got to the rendezvous, but this alternative was fraught with potential problems.

Although he would have the benefit that his ditching would be known on an official basis, providing some confirmation to his demise, he would risk that the Coast Guard would be faster than anticipated in its response. He figured if they were really on the ball, the Jayhawk rescue helicopters could be on the scene in twenty minutes. His Cessna might not even have sunk, and with their FLIR imaging, he would not even have the protection of the approaching darkness, since their synthetic vision capabilities would overcome that hurdle. They would also be aware of the fishing boat departing the area and might decide to investigate, either of which would disrupt his carefully laid out plan.

No, the better plan was to be one of those planes that was just "overdue," so as not to arouse concern or a search until it was way too late. He also knew that a slow descent, such as he might experience if he just had an engine failure, might alert air traffic control in the unlikely event it were noticed on their radar screens, triggering a similar response and risk.

So, the better of his options, he concluded, was to proceed to the rendezvous, confirm that his ride was there to bring him home, and descend as rapidly as possible, trying to simulate some sort of control surface failure, fire, or something of that nature. That course of action would have the least complications, even though Schaeffer knew his radar track would get a lot of scrutiny after the fact, but not in time for him to be tripped up.

"Roger that, squawk twelve hundred, and have a nice flight," the Miami controller replied.

Schaeffer changed his transponder code to 1200, the VFR code, and set the coordinates he and Robbie had agreed to for the rendez-vous in his Garmin. After another fifteen minutes, he was nearing where he was planning to ditch, and he began scanning the water in front of him for a sign of Robbie and his center console fishing boat. With the last of the sunlight at his back reflecting off the white can-opy of the boat, it would be hard to miss. Schaeffer pulled the power back to idle, and when his speed permitted, he put the flaps to the approach position. As the little Cessna slowed to about sixty knots, he began a steep bank angle to the left, simultaneously applying some right rudder to commence a tight slipping, spiraling descent, and always keeping the fishing boat in sight out his pilot's side window.

When he got to a few hundred feet, he slowed his descent and started a long downwind pattern away from the boat, so he would have a good bit of distance to negotiate his water landing to be as close to Robbie as possible.

Just above the water now, he added power to arrest his descent as he passed the fishing boat almost at eye level. He could see Robbie at the helm as he passed by the boat. Schaeffer tightened his belts up as much as he could stand and locked the shoulder harness in place. He continued downwind and extended the point where he would begin his approach about a mile from Robbie for a water landing. Momentarily he lost sight of the vessel as he headed west into the last of the setting sun on the horizon until he started his 180-degree turn for his final approach. He opened both aircraft doors to prevent them from jamming shut in the ditching.

Then he slowed to sixty knots, lowering the flaps to their fullest. Dragging the plane in at thirty-percent power, he was able to keep the Cessna flying at a little less than fifty knots. His heart rate was above a hundred beats per minute, and his hands were so sweaty he could barely maintain a solid grip on the control yoke and throttle. Heading now on a path that would put him next to the fishing boat, Schaeffer slowly let the last few feet of altitude evaporate as he carefully eased the airplane toward the water. His timing was almost perfect as he felt the wave tops just kiss the fixed landing gear, passing abeam the fishing boat.

For a moment, Schaeffer thought this was going to be easy when suddenly the landing gear found purchase on the water. The nose tipped in earnest toward the water just as the plane suddenly banked hard to the right, catching the right wing in the surface. The impact was considerable. Schaeffer was thrust violently forward, and he felt a stabbing pain as his lap belt pulled mightily against his hips, and the rotation of the fuselage to the right pressed the shoulder harness hard against his neck and left collarbone with such force that he thought it might break. The plane rotated ninety degrees to the right and upended on its nose, and the weight of the engine began pulling the aircraft under.

Then as suddenly as it happened, the violence of the controlled crash subsided, the plane immersing nose down momentarily and then righting itself as the more buoyant wings reached the water. The Cessna wallowed just a little, settling itself right side up. Without the airstream to hold them shut, the doors slowly opened as the sea poured in unimpeded. In a heartbeat, Schaeffer was waist deep in water. The effect was just what he needed at the moment, as it startled him out of his shock, and he began to react. He unfastened his belts and grabbed his garbage bag–wrapped duffle, easing out the pilot side door. The bag caught for a bit on the locking mechanism, tearing a small hole in the outer bag, but in a moment, Schaeffer was sputtering in the water, clinging to his life's possessions, floating and providing buoyancy for his short swim to the fishing boat.

In his worst nightmare, Schaeffer had worried that his plane might not sink right away, leaving evidence for the Coast Guard that he didn't perish in the ditching. He needn't have been concerned, as the nose had resumed its downward position, and the wings were no longer at the surface. Only the tail section was clearly visible above the water, and it was heading down very quickly. Soon the whole plane would be gone, headed for the depths in six thousand feet of water, no longer recoverable.

Robbie was already moving the Cape Horn into position to pick up his co-conspirator. When he was a few feet away, Robbie cut the motors and put the swim ladder in its stainless fittings at the back of the boat. Schaeffer dog-paddled his belongings to the stern and handed them up to a grinning Robbie.

"That was awesome, man!" Robbie shouted at Schaeffer, his excitement swallowed by the vastness of the twilight. "You put that thing down right next to me; that's some flying demonstration you put on," he said with a smile as he grabbed the garbage bag with one hand and hoisted it over his shoulder into the boat. "Are you okay? Did you hurt anything in the crash?"

Schaeffer's heart rate was only just starting to return to normal. He thought it peculiar that Robbie didn't help him up into the boat, but rather left him to his own devices as he backed up to the console seats by the engine controls, not taking his eyes off him. The boat was swaying gently in the ocean swells, abeam the waves, which had started the small craft rocking from side to side. Schaeffer finally got enough purchase on the top rung of the swim ladder to get his left foot solidly balanced on the bottom rung. With considerable effort, he raised his waterlogged bulk out of the water, rung by rung, until his weight, increased noticeably by the drenched clothes he was wearing, toppled him over the flat well of the transom. Exhausted from his short struggle to swim to the boat, he lay on the back of the transom in a heap while he normalized his breathing and heart rate.

"There she goes!" shouted Robbie, nodding in the direction of the floundering Cessna. Schaeffer looked over his right shoulder just in time to see the airplane nose down in the water at an abrupt angle, lifting the tailform high in the air. The narrow aft end of the fuselage disappeared remarkably quickly until the horizontal and vertical stabilizers slipped beneath the waves. One eighty-two Alpha Sierra was making its final voyage to the bottom of the sea, over a mile away beneath them. As he witnessed the loss of his airplane, Schaeffer had no emotional reaction to the event other than what a shame it was that he would never be able to use it again.

He rolled his weight onto his knees on the stubby platform at the back of the boat as he turned around to face Robbie, prepared to lift his soaking bulk over the transom. Much to his surprise, when he looked up, he found himself staring into the barrel of a stainless steel automatic pistol held firmly in Robbie's right hand. Robbie grinned over the top of the weapon and said firmly, "Why don't you take a minute and rest right there. I think we have some things to talk about before we can complete our transaction."

"What the fuck, Robbie!" Schaeffer uttered in exasperation. He began to raise his hands in a reflexive motion, stunned speechless. He felt the small waves lap against his feet, constantly refilling his boat shoes with water, the left one slipping off his foot and sinking into the depths below. The slow rocking of the boat in the beam sea caused him to lose his balance, and he lowered his arms to hold on to the stainless handrail on the side of the boat in an effort to keep upright. "What the hell are you doing?"

"No need to keep your hands up. This isn't cops and robbers," Robbie said evenly. "Just stay where you are while we discuss a few matters about our financial arrangement."

"We already have a financial arrangement! I've got ten thousand dollars cash for you to take me back to Fort Lauderdale. What are you talking about?" Although Schaeffer knew quite well what this was about: a shakedown for more money.

Robbie nodded. "Yes, that was our deal. However, on reflection, that just doesn't feel right, given your situation and the money you just gave up to Neptune. I think we need to renegotiate."

"Renegotiate! How are we going to renegotiate? I'm on my way out of the country. I don't have any more money here. What the hell are you thinking? Just let me get in the boat," Schaeffer pleaded, desperately looking around for some form of salvation. Seeing none, he tried to stand so that he could climb over the transom.

Robbie fired a shot over Schaeffer's head. "Adam, just get your ass back down on your knees. I'm trying to be reasonable here."

The effect was immediate, and Schaeffer lowered himself back down, trying as best he could to get into a position of leverage. His ears were ringing. "What the fuck!" he exclaimed again. Realizing that he was in no position to negotiate anything, he knelt as carefully as he could to ease the pain he was feeling from the hard fiberglass shelf under him. His back was killing him, and he was beginning to feel a chill from the air as the sun dipped below the horizon to his left.

Robbie leaned up against the center console seat and switched the pistol to his other hand, freeing up his right hand to lift the garbage-wrapped duffle up on to the adjacent console seat. As he began trying to tear the plastic covering, he continued his argument.

"You know as well as I do that there is a lot more at stake here than warrants paying me just ten thousand dollars. I'm willing to wager you have a lot more to deal with than the ten thousand. You wouldn't have risked what you have otherwise. You know, I could kill you right now and take whatever I find here. That would be easiest and safest for me. I'm trying to do you a favor and make a deal, which will still get you back to Fort Lauderdale, at considerably more risk to me than if I just shove you off the back of the boat or put a bullet in your head. It makes no difference to me; by tomorrow the world will think you are dead anyway. There won't even be a crime to solve—the perfect scenario for murder, don't you think?"

Schaeffer knew he had to give himself time, time for the circumstances to change in his favor, or he was screwed anyway. So he just nodded in agreement as he looked about the boat for some kind of weapon he could use to defend himself. He figured if Robbie was serious about not killing him and did decide to take him back to Florida, there would be many opportunities for him to make a move. Robbie couldn't make him stay on the stubby swim platform for the whole journey. He tried to delay, anyway. "I told you, other than a few bucks to get out of the country, all the cash I have is the ten thousand I brought for you," he lied.

"Well, let's just see about that. You stay right where you are while I take a look in your bag, and we'll see what turns up." Robbie used his index fingers to tear apart the plastic covering the duffle, while still holding the semiautomatic in his left hand, not focusing so much on where it was pointed. They both knew he had plenty of time to place a well-aimed shot from close range if Schaeffer made an aggressive move from his kneeling position behind the transom.

Robbie alternated his attention between Schaeffer and the garbage bags, finding the heavy-duty plastic harder to deal with than he would have predicted. Finally, he got his index fingers to poke two holes in the bags just below the tie wrap that sealed them at the top. He pulled aggressively to open the neck of the bags, a job made more difficult by the rocking of the boat, which forced him to lean heavily against the console seats, bracing his weight with his foot against the side of the boat.

Schaeffer watched him struggle to manage everything, the gun, the plastic, and his balance all at the same time. He noted that Robbie had his hands quite full doing all this and keeping an eye on his captive. *Maybe I will get an opportunity sooner than later,* he thought. At that moment, the little boat rocked more severely than it had been, and Schaeffer saw Robbie lose his concentration for a moment while he dealt with the added motion. Just as Robbie managed to widen the hole in the double-wrapped duffle, Schaeffer lost his balance as well and rolled on his side, almost falling off the back of the boat. Holding on to the aft grip on the starboard outboard engine cover, he tried to regain his balance as his head momentarily crossed the plane of the transom. Robbie noticed the change of position and immediately waved the pistol in his direction with a warning to stay where he was.

"The wave just caught me by surprise, is all," Schaeffer offered in explanation.

Robbie went back to the task of pulling the garbage bags around the sides of the duffle so he could unzip it and access the contents. Schaeffer resumed his uncomfortable position, but not before he glimpsed the fishing gaff wedged in its mounting clips under the gunnel on the right side of the boat, just in front of him. The shaft was one of the extendable ones that could be lengthened by loosening the two-part tube and sliding the housing forward. The shaft was made of aluminum to keep it light, but the hook was solid stainless steel, beautifully curved in a half circle to a point as sharp as one could imagine. It was within easy reach when the opportunity arose, and Schaeffer was looking for that opportunity intently.

While Schaeffer contemplated how he could use his newfound weapon most effectively, Robbie began looking into the duffle to examine its contents. In the folder wedged alongside Schaeffer's change of clothes Robbie found an eight-by-ten sheet of paper. Keeping his Smith & Wesson loosely aimed in Schaeffer's direction, he pulled it out and tried to read it in the fading light, now just a soft glow from the sunset.

"What have we here, Mr. Anderson, I see it is . . ." Robbie smiled, noting the unfamiliar name on the slip of paper. "You have a boarding pass for a Swiss Air flight to London tomorrow morning. How interesting."

Robbie folded the boarding pass in half and put it in the right front outside pocket of his cargo shorts. Wedging himself between the center console seats for stability, keeping the pistol in his left hand, Robbie set about going through the contents of the duffle in earnest. Without the need to deal with the constant rolling of the vessel, he felt more confident in what he was doing, paying less attention to Schaeffer huddled on his knees on the small platform at the back of the boat. Next to the folder that had contained the boarding pass, he felt the hard edges of the passport. He fished it out and examined it in the failing light as well.

"Aha! You're a pretty resourceful dude, Adam. This looks like the real thing with your picture on it and all. Mr. Anderson again, I see. So, that's how you're planning to disappear. I always wondered what your exit strategy was going to be. Looks like this is not a temporary thing you are planning, is it?" He put the passport in the pocket of his cargo pants along with the plane ticket.

Schaeffer nodded, suspecting the more Robbie figured out, the less chance he was going to have to get out of this alive. His heart was pounding, and his knees were screaming at him due to the pressure and abrasion from rolling on the hard surface of the aft platform as he tried to maintain his balance while the boat rocked in the gentle swells. He did not think of himself as a street fighter, particularly, but he knew he would have to make his move in the next few minutes, or he would not have the strength to pull it off.

Robbie resumed his interest in the duffle and its contents. He pulled a folded linen blazer part way out the top and fumbled around the rest of the clothing to get at the bottom of the bag. After a minute's groping, he felt the wrapped packets of currency on the bottom. "That's more like it." Robbie smiled to himself as he reached deeper to get a purchase on the money. He had dealt with enough banded currency in his travels to recognize it by feel, but his mind wanted to see just what he had discovered. He tried to scoop it up in one hand, but that proved ineffective, so for just a moment, he put the pistol on the seat beside him so he could use both hands.

Now! Schaeffer thought, knowing in the next few seconds he would either be dead or victorious. The boat rolled a little to his left, and he anticipated the roll back to his right to time his move out of his awkward position. He lifted his right knee and put his right foot on the platform and, in one springing motion, scrambled over the transom and reached with his right hand for the shaft on the gaff.

Robbie was just starting to notice that his captive was no longer in position as Schaeffer got a firm grasp on the gaff handle. Standing now just a few feet away from Robbie, who did not have freedom of movement in the narrow space between the seats and the console, he first jabbed at the bearded man to back him away from the pistol, which was still sitting precariously on the seat next to him.

Robbie jerked his right hand out of the bag in an involuntary reaction to grab his weapon. Panic was not the best choice of response, as his quick motion sent the Smith & Wesson clanging to the cockpit floor, sliding toward the bow. Robbie raced after it on his hands and knees as fast as he could. Schaeffer did not know where the pistol had ended up, but he wanted some protection from Robbie, so he moved around the right side of the console, putting it between the two of them. As he peeked around the front of the console, Robbie was just regaining his grasp on the automatic, turning to his left to see where his quarry was, thinking Schaeffer was still at the back of the boat.

Bad guess. Schaeffer wasted no time in arcing a huge swipe with the gaff beyond Robbie's head and pulling the hook on the end toward him as hard as he could. The shaft bounced off Robbie's cheekbone about a foot from the sharpened point as Robbie reversed his turn, not seeing his attacker at the rear of the boat. The point of the gaff entered the base of Robbie's skull just above the C1 vertebra and penetrated about two inches in the soft tissue just below the bone of his skullcap. He was just finishing his rotation to the right as the gaff hook made its connection, causing Robbie to back away instinctively from the source of the blow, but the penetration of the point of the gaff had an immediate effect on his central nervous system. He did his best to get off a shot at his assailant, but the weapon was in his right hand, making it difficult to aim it with any precision, because he was turning to his right.

The loud report of the discharge was deafening in the stillness of the twilight as the bullet flew wide to the right, passing through the upper center console and windscreen into the darkness. But the effect of the noise had its reaction, as a startled Schaeffer gave a second mighty yank on the gaff, pulling the hook fully into the back of Robbie's head, so far that the point of the gaff emerged through his mouth, knocking out a front tooth and pinning his head to the back of the seat rest in front of the console. Robbie managed to squeeze off one more round in his death throes. It passed through the console base and embedded in a longitudinal stringer in the hull below the cabin sole.

Schaeffer's heart was beating out of his chest as he surveyed the carnage before him. Robbie's cheek was pressed up against the clear plastic windscreen with a grotesque expression on his face, almost comedic, as in the way a child presses his face across a windowpane to gain a reaction from those watching the effect from the other side. Schaeffer pushed and twisted the gaff hook but was unable to free it from Robbie's head. Blood spurted from Robbie's mouth and neck for the fifteen or so seconds that his heart continued to beat, and then the blood flow lessened to a trickle. His right arm hung loosely at his side, and the Smith & Wesson dropped from his fingers as they lost purchase on the pistol grip, the gun clattering to the cabin sole below.

CHAPTER SEVEN

Slowly, Schaeffer collected his wits as he did what he did best: put together a plan to get out of the area. He felt no emotion for the life he had taken. If he felt anything at all, it was a minor regret that someone whom he had liked and trusted had turned on him, betraying an agreement that had been reached previously. Nervously he searched the darkening sky overhead for any indication of a search underway, unlikely as that possibility was. It was even more important for him now to make a successful departure from the area. Murder was involved, bringing into consideration a whole new set of complications. Correctly Schaeffer surmised that no one would be looking for Robbie, and his sudden departure from South Florida and the Bahamas would not be unexpected, given his scurrilous past.

Well, I can't think of a better place to hide a body, he told himself, letting go of the considerable pressure he still held on the gaff. Released of its burden, Robbie's body slid down to the floor of the cockpit in a heap, and blood began oozing from his wounds again. Schaeffer pulled him by his armpits onto the forward settee. He noticed with some disgust the odor coming from the stain in Robbie's cargo pants as his sphincter and bladder muscles gave up their grips. Schaeffer didn't want anything to do with that part of his victim. He glanced around the boat for something he could use to weigh down the body, because he knew if he just threw it overboard, it would likely float for quite a while, risking discovery.

At the front of the boat Schaeffer saw the outline of the anchor well on the deck of the bow, and he had his solution. He climbed carefully over the messy remains of his friend—oddly he still thought of Robbie as a friend, or at least an accomplice—and opened the locker. Inside he saw a galvanized steel Danforth anchor and about fifteen feet of chain attached to a sizable coil of anchor rope. He pulled out the whole lot and set it on the floor. Beginning with the anchor itself, Schaeffer carefully wrapped the chain around the body, positioning the anchor at Robbie's chest. Every time he lifted Robbie's torso to pass the chain under, more blood poured from the neck wounds, and the boat was quickly becoming a mess. As extra insurance, Schaeffer wrapped the body with the anchor rope so that it was fully secure, unlikely that any part would become separated as it made its way to the bottom of the ocean.

When he had finished securing the body, Schaeffer rolled it to the wide part of the deck near the bow. It was very dark now, and the three-quarter moon would not appear for another couple of hours, so he returned to the control side of the console and found the switches for the running lights and an overhead lamp for the forward part of the boat. With his workspace illuminated, Schaeffer set about the actual burial at sea by rolling Robbie's body along its axis to the edge of the boat. With a last glance at Robbie's contorted face, he gave his accomplice a final turn and watched him splash into the dark water. With his arms and legs bound, Robbie's body lay flat on its back for a brief moment, his sightless eyes staring vacantly toward the heavens. Finally the weight of the twenty-pound anchor and its associated chain on his chest pulled him under as his body rotated a half turn to face down and began its final descent to the bottom, over a mile away.

Schaeffer returned to his belongings and replaced them carefully in his duffle, recovering them as best he could with the remnant of the garbage bags to protect them from any occasional spray on the trip back to Fort Lauderdale. It was only then, when he felt the folder that had contained his passport and plane ticket to freedom, that he realized the new dimension he had added to his attempt to flee the country. He recounted visually that Robbie had put both items in the outside pocket of his cargo pants as he rummaged through the duffle.

"Oh shit! Shit! Shit! Shit! Fuck! What have I done?" He ran to the side of the boat and looked over for any sign of Robbie's remains, but saw none. He buried his face in his hands as he felt a well of total dread arise in his chest, now that the realization had hit him that his ticket out of the country to take him to his millions in Europe was on a one-way trip to the bottom of the sea, and there was nothing he could do about it.

Ever so slowly, he regained his senses. With no identifiable reaction of any kind in his features, Schaeffer began the process of making another plan. The twin Yamahas started at the push of the buttons, purring almost silently behind him, as Schaeffer expanded the chart plotter screen and eyeballed a heading back to Port Everglades, almost due west. As he accelerated slowly onto a plane, turning toward the glow barely visible on the horizon, his mind began working out the details of what confronted him when he got back. He felt no sadness about killing Robbie, nor was he overcome with regret that he had lost his path to Europe and his millions. It was what it was, and now he would just have to deal with it.

With the throttles at three-quarters, producing nearly four thousand rpm, Schaeffer was making good progress toward his waypoint on the chart plotter, just outside the jetty at Port Everglades. Wedged comfortably in the driver's console seat, he braced himself against the footrest to hold his position as the Cape Horn outraced the gentle following seas, only occasionally pounding into a trough as he overtook a wave crest. After a few minutes, his foot slipped off and banged against the cooler beneath the seat. He investigated his new discovery and was pleased to find a few Kaliks floating in the melting ice. *That's an unexpected good fortune,* he thought as he pulled one out and removed the cap with the opener built into the side of the cooler. *They think of everything,* he mused.

It was nearing eleven o'clock when he cleared the sea buoy and throttled back to avoid drawing attention to himself. Schaeffer felt overly exhausted from his trip, now that the adrenaline rush from his ditching and murder was wearing off, and he tried to focus on what he was going to do next. He needed to find a place to ditch the boat where it wouldn't be noticed for a few days. There was still evidence of blood on the cockpit sole, not particularly unusual for a fishing boat, but he knew he needed to get rid of as much evidence of a struggle as possible. It was his plan to leave the boat abandoned where it would undoubtedly be found and identified as the victim of Robbie's theft. He hoped the authorities would assume it had been taken for a joyride, would return to its owner, and leave it at that.

The obstacles that faced him ran through Schaeffer's mind. He needed to stay dead, his main defense against capture, since no one would be looking for a dead person. He needed a place to stay out of sight while he figured out how he was going to get out of the country, and he knew he was in no condition right now to do any rational thinking, so he focused on finding a safe place to hide out and get some needed rest.

Inside the jetty he turned north, ironically retracing the path Robbie had taken about seven hours before. He could see from the track lines on the chart plotter that the Cape Horn had begun its journey from Bahia Mar, or thereabouts, so he wanted to get past that area as unnoticeably as possible, lest the craft be recognized by its owner. Schaeffer surmised that the boat was a tender from a mega yacht, because he could see the tagline at the bow that must be attached to a towing eye in the hull on the stem near the waterline, common on these types of boats. They all had similar appearances, so Schaeffer hoped he would not be noticed if he gave the big marina a wide berth as he passed it on his way to the New River, which would take him west and back south where the water was close to I-95 and anonymity.

On his way west up the river at idle speed, Schaeffer left the helm to find what he could use to clean up some of the mess and blood. He needed to work in the dark, not risking turning on the overhead lights, to avoid being seen. He found a bucket and mop in the lockers below the sole and in the small cabin trunk and began making the boat look as presentable as he could. As he knelt by the side of the cabin trunk, he found Robbie's front tooth wedged in a seam on the floor and thought to himself how fortunate that was. He threw it overboard and looked for more evidence of foul play.

By the time Schaeffer had gotten upriver to the interstate, he had the boat cleaned up about as much as he thought practical. He switched out the mop for a rag and did his best to wipe down as much of the boat that he had touched that he could remember, hoping that evidence of fingerprints would be removed, knowing that if an investigation proceeded that far he would be screwed anyway. He left the damp rag on the seat next to him for final touches just before he abandoned the craft.

He passed under the high overpass of the expressway and turned south into the expanded boat basin that was known as Marina Bay, a onetime upscale marine and residential entertainment center, now relegated to a graveyard for cheap storage of mega yachts and smaller sport fishing boats. He circled around the western peninsula of the basin and followed the canal to the southern end, where he was surrounded by commercial docks offering boatyard services. Schaeffer tied up at the end of one of the finger piers. After he shut off the engines, the quiet of the still evening enveloped him, given away only by the occasional car passing on State Road 84 a few yards away. He gave the helm and throttles one final wipe, secured his belongings in his duffle, and stepped off the boat, searching the area for signs that he might be observed. Seeing none, he crossed the parking lot and access road to the edge of the highway and crossed to the other side where he saw the outlines of a desolate-looking Red Roof Inn, complete with bar and restaurant, an intermittent neon sign announcing a vacancy, sections of it unlit or dimly misfiring.

He debated changing some of his clothing, but decided he looked all right for the moment, opting instead to save what was fresh for tomorrow when he would have to go outside in the daylight where he would get more scrutiny. He tucked his shirt in his pants to look a little better. There was nothing he could do about his missing shoe. One was better than none, he thought.

It was after midnight by the time Schaeffer got to the entrance off the motel parking lot. The office was barely lit from the inside, indicating the operation was open for business. He pushed the buzzer on the side of the door as instructed for access after normal business hours. After a moment, a disheveled-looking older man emerged from the backlighting, appearing as though his evening had been interrupted, which it had. Schaeffer could see the flickering of a television coming from the hallway behind the service counter as the old man ambled to the front door and unlocked the deadbolt. Opening the door a crack, he asked brusquely, "What do you want?"

"What do you think? I want a room for the night."

The old man opened the door farther and scoped out the mostly empty parking lot. Turning his attention back to Schaeffer, he asked, "Where's your car?"

"I hitchhiked, just got dropped off at the exit ramp," Schaeffer replied, nodding over his shoulder in the direction of the interstate, happy that he had come up with something plausible on short notice. He hadn't planned on an inquisition, but it got worse.

The old man wasn't done giving Schaeffer a hard time. "Why are your clothes all rumpled?" Then looking down at his feet, he added, "And where is your other shoe?"

Schaeffer ignored his questions, as he didn't really have an adequate answer.

The old man continued looking at him suspiciously. "Let me see some ID."

"You've got to be kidding!"

"It's the law," the old man said matter-of-factly.

Schaeffer was starting to get a little exasperated. "What do you think this place is, the Waldorf Astoria? Just give me a room." To himself he said, *If this old fart only knew what I did to the last guy who dicked around with me.* Calming a little, he offered, "Give me a room for a week, and I'll give you a thousand dollars cash." He noted the posted rate behind the counter, sixty-nine dollars a night. That got a response, and the old man opened the door wider to let Schaeffer in. He went behind the reception counter and pulled out a room key attached to an oblong plastic tag, which identified it as belonging to room 116.

"For you, a room next to the pool. I assume you don't need a receipt," the old man said sarcastically.

Schaeffer thumbed ten hundreds from the side pocket of the duffle from the money he had originally brought for Robbie while the old man's back was turned toward him. They exchanged the barter, and the old man let him out the courtyard side door of the office to find his own way to his room, not particularly difficult at a two-story, thirty-six room dump. As he crossed the patio, Schaeffer could see a film of crud on the surface of the pool, and a pile of palm leaves crowding the strainer at the shallow end, which was making gurgling noises as it tried to skim dirty water from the pool.

One sixteen was at the end of the east-side units, the corner of the pool just visible from the door. The air was off when he entered the room. He found the light switch on the wall next to the door and lit the place up. Better than he would have guessed, until he closed the door and realized he could still hear the gurgling of the pool skimmer echoing off the courtyard walls. Schaeffer solved that annoyance by turning on the package air conditioner on the back wall to the highest fan setting, full cold. Slowly the stifling air began to circulate, and the room chilled down, much to his relief.

Schaeffer was bone tired from his all-day ordeal, unable to think clearly beyond knowing that he had some big mountains to climb. His knees were tender to the touch from the time he had spent on the transom of the rolling fishing tender, and his back ached from fighting the pitching motion of the trip across the Gulf Stream. His clothes had long since dried, although they felt a little scratchy on his skin from the salt they had accumulated. He didn't care. With the last of his energy, he locked and dead bolted the room door, closed the curtains, and turned off the light. In two big steps he flopped onto the surprisingly comfortable king bed and was instantly asleep, scratchy clothes and all.

The sun was well above the horizon when he was awakened by the loud exhaust of an eighteen-wheeler backing off its diesel exiting from I-95. His sleep had been so sound that it took him a minute to sort out where he was and the circumstances that had brought him here. After a few minutes of stretching and waking, he made his way to the bathroom to pee. He had not urinated that he could recall since the evening before when he had powered up the fishing boat to get back to land. He found his Dopp kit in the duffle and took his time to shower and clean actual and metaphorical dirt from his previous day's activities. He did not bother to shave, thinking instead that a little growth on his face would help him blend into the landscape of lost souls who frequented this crummy area of town.

After a cup of coffee, courtesy of the small automatic maker in his room, he felt much better equipped to meet the challenges of the day, which were to figure out how he was going to get out of the country to his money and avoid being identified in the meantime. As he sat on the edge of the bed, he contemplated his resources and how best to employ them to meet his objectives. First and foremost, Schaeffer knew he had to remain invisible. Nobody would be looking for a dead man, so he could not take advantage of or make any use of anything from his past. No cell phones, credit cards, nothing that could lead anyone to believe that he was not at the bottom of the ocean somewhere between Fort Lauderdale and the Bahamas. That left him with a single change of clothes, just short of sixty thousand dollars cash, which he would have to be careful using, lest that draw attention to himself.

He could not rent a car, or risk driving one, because of the possibility that he might be stopped randomly by a cop, unable to produce any identification to explain himself. He could not get help from anyone who knew him or could figure out who he was. His overriding concern was how he was going to get an identity and documents to enable him to get out of the country. He did not know how to contact his previous source, and he couldn't go back to Joey Bangoni without exposing what he had done. He did recall adding the passport provider to his contacts on his MacBook Air, but that was at his office, and the risk seemed too great to try get access to his former place of employment. That would have to be as a last resort. Perhaps he could find another provider, but the quality of the goods might not be as satisfactory.

These and many other thoughts ran through his mind as he sat on the edge of his motel bed. His stomach began to rumble, and he realized he hadn't eaten since the previous afternoon, so he slid his duffle under the bed and set out barefoot, walking east on State Road 84 in search of a diner or coffee shop. As he approached the interstate and the overpass, he saw a half dozen or so homeless derelicts stowing their encampments, relieving themselves against the cement buttresses and generally preparing themselves with their cardboard signs for another day of panhandling. Saturday was not a good day for that activity; they did better with the working people who were commuting to work, who seemed more sympathetic to their circumstances.

A half mile farther down the road, Schaeffer knew there would be more choices, but it would require that he climb the state road overpass, and there really wasn't any provision for foot traffic, particularly for someone without shoes, so he was really confined to the west side of the interstate for the time being. Out of options, he retraced his steps to the crummy excuse of a restaurant at the Red Roof Inn to curb his hunger.

Schaeffer took a seat at a booth by a window and looked over the menu, which was obviously designed to offer the selections through pictures with as little text as possible. An uninterested waitress offered him a cup of coffee in a heavy unbreakable mug, stained from years of service, and took his order from where he pointed at the menu. There were not many people in the restaurant, but there was some activity in the parking lot, particularly around the Dumpster. He was deep in thought, oblivious when his food was put before him a few minutes later. After he ate, he gave the Dumpster a visit where he found a ratty pair of tennis shoes with broken laces. The fit was not great, but suitable for getting around until he could find replacements.

Jorge Gonzalez

CHAPTER EIGHT

Jorge was more than a little troubled by the sudden appearance of the FINRA team, particularly when it was reported to him that they had pivoted their focus to the omnibus accounts of Pension Strategy Partners. He had not stayed in the offices for the whole time the investigators were there, since most of the work was detailed tracing of transactional data, more suited to his audit staff. He preferred instead to spend time on some of the more senior matters he faced regarding his upcoming formal admission to the accounting firm partnership at Arthur White & Company. When the team members returned to the Miami office after the FINRA staff left the Pension Strategy Partner offices to prepare their report, he tried to put his concern behind him.

His brothers had called him earlier in the day and teased him about his "big business" working hours, suggesting he join them in the Keys for a weekend of fishing and diving, and that seemed like a good idea to Jorge. They picked him up at his apartment in South Beach and suffered the Friday afternoon traffic down the Overseas Highway to Islamorada, where they stayed with friends who had a fishing boat. Jorge really enjoyed the time he spent with his big brothers, although they gave him a lot of grief about his lack of tan.

"You spend way too much time inside, Jorge. You need to get out more," Valeriano chided, thrusting his sun-darkened chest forward.

"Yeah, Jorge. Why you want to push around all those pencils? We could have a lot more fun selling hubcaps," Carlos chimed in, slapping Val on the back as if the two were in agreement.

Jorge's older brothers teased him at every opportunity, but they would walk through a brick wall for him if they had to. The weekend of fun and saltwater had its desired effect on Jorge. He hadn't given FINRA or the investigation a thought for over twenty-four hours. Sunday afternoon, after he cleaned up and put on some fresh shorts for the trip home, Jorge found the Post-it with Anita's cell phone number stuck to some loose bills in his front left pocket as he was shifting contents. That put a smile on his face, and he thought he would give her a call on the long drive home to see if she might like to have that cup of coffee or a light dinner even, maybe. He thought he would be back in plenty of time.

Sitting in his relegated rear seat, Jorge made himself as comfortable as he could while Carlos's powerful Mustang churned its rear wheels on the marl driveway as they pulled out onto the highway. The tuned exhaust made conversation problematic, but Jorge hoped the distraction would keep his brothers from hearing him make a call to a girl, something they would not let loose of easily. He waited until the two of them were in animated conversation about the weekend before pulling out his phone and dialing Anita's cell number.

"Hello," she answered in a matter-of-fact voice after a few rings, as though debating whether to pick up on a number she didn't recognize.

"It's Jorge."

"Oh, the cookie jar man. What's up?" Anita responded cheerfully, referring to their conversation a few weeks earlier.

Jorge felt less sure of himself now. "I hope it's all right that I called. You gave me your number, remember?"

"You bet. I thought you forgot . . ." In a softer tone now, she added, "But I'm glad you called."

More relaxed, he said, "I'm on my way back from the Keys with my brothers, and I wondered if you might like to grab a bite to eat, or something?" Jorge was already thinking this call was not a good idea; he didn't even know where she lived, could be north of Fort Lauderdale even. Her reply put him even further off balance.

"With all of you?"

Really flustered now, Jorge stuttered, "N-n-no—just me. I'll be home by four. I, I'm sorry, maybe this isn't such a good idea. I don't even know how far away you live."

Anita interrupted, "No, no, I think it's a great idea. I have no other plans, and I'd love to see you. I live in Oakridge in Dania with my parents . . ." She hit herself in the forehead with her palm, thinking it was dumb to tell him she still lived with her parents. "Why don't we meet somewhere?"

Encouraged, Jorge suggested, "Great! I live in South Beach. Do you know Houston's in Aventura? It's about halfway."

"Sure, you mean the one on the water in North Miami Beach?"

"Yeah. That's the one. I'll meet you there at seven. It shouldn't be too crowded on a Sunday, off season."

"Perfect, Jorge. It will give us a chance to talk about Adam Schaeffer."

"Adam Schaeffer? What about Adam Schaeffer? Why would we want to talk about him?" The hairs on the back of his neck raised at the mention of Schaeffer's name.

"Haven't you heard?"

"Heard what? I haven't heard anything about him. I told you, I've been in the Keys with my brothers." He regretted his tone as soon as he heard the words come out of his mouth.

"You don't have to bark at me," she shot back. "I just assumed you knew. It's been on the news. He's *missing!* He left Fort Lauderdale late Friday afternoon for the Bahamas, like he always does, but he never arrived. The news this morning said the Coast Guard is searching, but it's presumed he crashed somewhere en route. His radar track ends halfway across the Gulf Stream."

"Anita, forgive me. I'm just shocked. I was with him last Wednesday when the team from FINRA showed up, and he told me he was leaving Friday, but I had no idea anything was wrong until this very minute. I guess we will have something to talk about, assuming we're still on. I'm sorry I had an attitude for a moment."

Jorge felt her voice soften as she said, "Not a problem. It's kind of nice to know you can amp up from time to time. I'll see you at seven at Houston's." She hung up the phone with a smile on her face, speculating how the evening would go.

Valeriano turned around in the front seat of the Mustang. "Who you talkin' to, bro? Did I hear you say Ahneetaah?" He whipped his index finger against his middle finger, making a loud popping sound, the way he did when he wanted to get attention.

Carlos looked sideways from his seat, trying to read Valeriano's face. "Anita? Who's Anita?" he asked.

"Just some girl I know," Jorge said defensively.

His brothers exchanged glances and said loudly in unison, "ANITA!" dragging out the last syllable.

Carlos took his eyes off the road and turned completely around in his seat to face his youngest sibling, chiding, "You holding out on us, bro? What's the deal? Who is she? Is she one of us? What's her last name? Where does she live? Come on. Give it up, Jorge!" As his front wheels started to cross the centerline, only a honk from an oncoming car brought his attention back to the highway.

Valeriano bounced up and down in his seat, prepared for something big.

Jorge was really feeling the pressure now. He didn't know how to respond, so he played up the newness of the relationship, hoping that would get his brothers off his back. "She's just someone I know from work, and I've never even gone out with her; we're just friends and we're going to talk about, well, work, that's all. She just told me her boss is missing, possibly dead."

Carlos was watching in the rearview mirror. "You're lying, Jorge. I can see it in your eyes. There's more to the story. What more do you have to tell us? What's her name?" Carlos wasn't really concerned. He and Val were just messing with their little brother, not expecting him to drop a bomb.

"Berwitz," Jorge said quietly.

Carlos kept up with his needling, not really paying attention. "Where's she from? How long you known her?"

The questions kept coming when the lights went on for Valeriano. "Whoa. Back up there. What did you say her name was?"

Jorge was evasive, knowing what was coming. "Anita," he answered.

More serious now, Val shouted, "Fuck you, Jorge! You know what I mean. What's her last name?"

More assertive now, Jorge leaned forward in his seat and said firmly, "Berwitz! Her name is Anita Berwitz!"

Carlos took all this in, while trying to pay attention to his driving, but he couldn't contain himself at this latest turn of events, and he broke out into uncontrollable laughter, barely able to get out the words, "So, I'm guessing she isn't a Latina, then, huh?" He was laughing so hard he started to pull over on to the shoulder.

Valeriano punched him good-naturedly in the arm. "Carlos, this isn't so funny," he said, taking it far more seriously.

Carlos was still convulsed with laughter. "I can't wait to see the look on Mama's face when you bring her over for dinner. I'll just hazard a guess; she isn't Catholic, either?" Still laughing, he checked his mirrors and pulled back on to the road.

Jorge felt the need to defend himself, and Anita as well. "Will you guys get off my case? We're just friends, and we're just having dinner. I think you're getting a little ahead of yourselves."

Val suggested jokingly, "Maybe we'll just tell the family her name is Anita and leave it at that. Jorge, you know for us this is a big deal; we don't see you around women all that much, so when one turns up, our imaginations run away with us. But Carlos makes a good point; if this goes anywhere, you are going to have to be very careful how you present it to Mom and Dad, or you are going to have a real mess on your hands."

Defensive again, Jorge replied, "I see lots of women. I just don't expose them to creeps like you to run them off."

Carlos, never at a loss for a retort, smiled in the rearview mirror. "Guess you don't have to—you do that all by yourself."

With everyone's feelings hurt, even if only for the moment, the conversation stifled for the time being, Carlos returning his full attention to the highway, Valeriano to the radio in search of a good Latin beat, and Jorge contemplating the substance of the interchange among the brothers, for it was not totally without merit. They completed their journey without further controversy, dropping Jorge at his apartment on Euclid Avenue in South Beach in plenty of time for him to clean up and make his dinner date.

<hr />

Jorge parked his Beemer in the lot at Houston's at seven on the dot and made his way to the entrance where he spotted Anita in line waiting to get the attention of a hostess. The restaurant was a little more crowded than he expected, and he had to worm his way past a few patrons to reach her. She smiled up at him as she sensed him approaching. A moment of awkwardness passed between them. As he debated putting out his hand, she leaned toward him on her toes, offering her cheek, which he brushed gently with his lips while moving his hand to her waist in one motion. Embarrassed, he hoped she hadn't noticed his blunder. He could smell the lightest of fragrance wafting from her in the charcoal-scented air, something like garde-nias from his mother's garden. He liked that.

A busy hostess grabbed two oversized menus from the side of the stand when they asked for a table for two, Jorge holding up two fingers, and hustled them to a booth on the lower level overlooking the water. After some introductory chitchat, he asked Anita about the obvious issue. "So, what's this about Schaeffer missing? I didn't have a chance to look at a paper or anything."

"It's all over the local news. Apparently, he left Friday afternoon for the Bahamas, like he always does, but he never arrived in Marsh Harbour. I looked it up on Google Earth. It's in the northern Out Islands, east of Grand Bahama."

"That's all we know?"

"There was a little more on the local TV news. He flies a small single-engine plane, and he was on a flight plan originally, but he cancelled it after he crossed the Gulf Stream, which is apparently nothing out of the ordinary. His radar track shows that he was on course for his destination and lost altitude suddenly south of Grand Bahama Island until it disappeared. They suspect he had some kind of severe mechanical difficulty, but nobody knows, because nobody was paying attention to him after he cancelled his flight plan. The authorities only became aware when his family contacted them in Marsh Harbour and a search was started. It was dark by then. I think they're still searching, but it doesn't look good. What do you think?"

Jorge sat pensively for a moment, noticing how Anita's subtle eye shadow brought out her green eyes, giving her face a bright, emer-ald appearance. He became lost momentarily in her spell, until she regained his attention.

"Jorge."

Coming back to the present moment, he said, "Yes, what?"

"I asked you, what do you think?"

"Oh, I think that's really odd. I was with him just the other day, and I'm sure you saw him that morning. It's probably going to require an amendment to the financials, a subsequent event, since he was a principal of the company and the effective chief financial officer."

"What's the matter with you? Is that how you think about everything? Just how they affect your precious statements? The man is probably dead! He has a family. He was my boss . . . I worked with him almost every day for three years."

Jorge flinched at the rebuke, because it was not what was in his heart. He reached for her hand across the table and gave her a warm smile. "I'm sorry; that's not at all what I was thinking about. I was distracted by how pretty your eyes are, and I was not focused on what you were saying. Forgive me."

Anita was disarmed. She gave his hand a squeeze and reached for cover, her menu. Looking down at the selections, she said, "I'm sorry I snapped at you, my bad. Is there anything in particular here you like?"

Their server came by the table and identified himself as Mitch, confirmed by the badge on his right breast, and took their drink orders, a Corona with lime for Jorge and a Cabernet for Anita.

Jorge closed his menu. "The burgers are always good, I think. I don't eat here much."

The tension normalized for the moment, Jorge and Anita made small talk over their burgers and fries while the sun lowered, reflecting orange and pink off of the condominium windows across the Intracoastal from the restaurant. Thoughts of Schaeffer's disappearance kept nagging at Jorge as he tried to keep his concentration on the beautiful woman seated across from him; he didn't hold much stock in coincidence, and he couldn't help associating the timing of the peculiar arrival of the FINRA investigators with Schaeffer's missing airplane. He decided he would look into it further in the morning.

When he finished his meal, Jorge lost himself in Anita's beauty. He stared at her blankly until she could no longer pretend not to notice, and finally she said, "Jorge, what are you thinking?"

He snapped out of his trance and gave her question serious thought. "Like before, I guess I was just thinking about you and how pretty you are. Maybe I think about you more than is probably normal." He felt unguarded, vulnerable.

Anita blushed at the compliment, and then realized that Jorge had spoken from his heart, and her mood softened. "Aw, that's sweet, Jorge," she said, and she reached for his hand.

Jorge suddenly realized that he had made a real connection with this beautiful woman. They just sat in silence for a few moments until Mitch brought the check. Jorge settled the account, and they left the restaurant, each feeling that their relationship had reached a new dimension.

———✺———

As it turned out, Schaeffer's disappearance only served to heighten everyone's anxiety with the FINRA investigation. Upon his arrival at the Miami office Monday morning, Jorge found the entire staff glued to the business channels on the TV monitors, where excitable journalists were spreading the rumor of an impending announcement that Lehman Brothers was expected to file for protection under Chapter 11 of the federal bankruptcy laws. The failure of this huge venerable institution was attributable to highly leveraged investments in the housing markets. While the possibility had been known for some time, Wall Street had presumed that someone would take advantage of the opportunity to buy them, thus averting a financial meltdown. Attention of all regulatory agencies was redirected to institutions even remotely connected to the securities business, not the least of which was FINRA.

Jorge was summoned to the managing partner's office at ten o'clock, where he was greeted by the somber faces of his bosses, Dickenson and Adams. Dickenson spoke first, "What's going on at Pension Strategy Partners?" Walter Adams just glared at him.

Jorge gulped. "Nothing that I know of. As you know, we finished the engagement, filed with the PCAOB timely. Everything's fine as far as I—"

Dickenson interrupted, "Why is FINRA involved, then?"

"They showed up for a routine review last week just after we signed off on their financials. Their report is supposed to be out today, I believe. Why? Have you heard anything different?"

Adams jumped in, "Fergus Dennison of the Boca Raton Investigative Office has requested, as in *summoned,* you as the engagement partner, and me as the senior audit partner, to meet today at the Pension Strategy offices at two o'clock. That doesn't sound routine to me."

Jorge swallowed. "I don't know what to say. They were limiting their inquiries to the month-ending adjustments to the omnibus accounts when I left last week. It's all pretty routine stuff. You may recall I spoke to you about it at the end of the fieldwork, and we both agreed it wasn't worth pursuing."

"Well, apparently FINRA thinks it is. Pack up your working papers on that stuff and bring them to my office so we can go over them in case we have to be prepared for something. We'll take them with us, assuming we don't see anything out of the ordinary. This Lehman business has everyone on pins and needles. I don't want any surprises."

Jorge deliberated a moment before deciding to continue with the other recent development. "I'm sure you read about the missing investment banker this weekend."

Dickenson looked up suddenly. "You mean the missing airplane?"

"Yeah, that one. He is a principal in the firm and its chief financial officer."

Dickenson and Adams looked at each other, dumbfounded. Dickenson said, "Are you fucking with us?"

"No, sirs. I just found out about it last night, and Walter, I was going to talk to you about it this morning to see if we need to amend our filing to add a subsequent event."

Dickenson cradled his head in his hands in frustration. "Holy shit! This just keeps getting worse and worse." He looked up. "Walter, you and Jorge go down there and do the best you can to see what this is all about. We have already opined on these financials, so we're on the hook for the consequences. Jorge, I don't know what to say to you. It looks like you may have stepped on your dick the first time out of the starting gate."

Jorge and Walter Adams spent the rest of the morning reviewing the audit files that dealt with the omnibus accounts. They saw nothing of particular interest, other than noting that the activity had increased that year over last. All items placed in suspense were cleared within thirty days of the closing of any accounting period, and nothing was outstanding at the end of the year that wasn't also closed to a standing account within a reasonable time. Mostly they were postings where the proper account couldn't be identified within the accounting period. The transactions almost always involved hedging strategies consistent with the industry and the mission of the client's business. In the last year, many of the strategies included buying and selling credit default swaps in the housing market where interest-rate changes could have an effect on underlying values of comingled mortgage obligations. This was also consistent with Pension Strategy Partners' primary business purpose, to protect pension investment values, so that company earnings would not be impacted by adjustments to income for future pension benefit obligations.

Feeling they had things under control, Jorge and his immediate superior took the working papers in the trunk of Jorge's Beemer up to PSP's offices on Andrews Avenue in Fort Lauderdale. They were not prepared for the buzz saw they ran into when they got there. The conference room was filled with "suits" who Dennison introduced in such rapid-fire succession Jorge couldn't put names on the faces. All he got out of the introductions were members of the Federal Bureau of Investigation, Securities and Exchange Commission, and other government agencies.

In short order, Adams and Gonzalez were informed that irregularities of significance were discovered in the investigation, when coupled with the disappearance of a principal and chief financial officer, warranted a full investigation. In the meantime, Pension Strategy Partners was being ordered to cease all investment activities until the full investigation could be completed. The FBI agents were there to secure the premises and its contents and to enforce compliance. Employees were to vacate their workstations by three o'clock, excepting a few key personnel who would remain behind to help the FINRA investigators navigate the information technology and accounting systems.

Adams was perplexed. "Under what authority are you ordering the office to cease operations when you haven't even concluded an investigation?"

"That would be under this authority," Dennison replied smugly, producing a court order from his briefcase, sliding it across the table to the senior accountant.

Jorge and Adams looked at it together. Jorge said aloud, "This order is in regard to a failure to maintain adequate capital balances. It says nothing about irregularities that need to be investigated. What gives?"

Dennison continued, "Frankly, it's really all we are concerned with at the moment. Our mission is to monitor the health of investment banking firms, which I'm sure you can appreciate in view of the failure of Lehman Brothers"—he looked at his watch—"which has been official for about two hours now. Failure to meet minimum capital requirements is one of the few things upon which we can take immediate action."

More frustrated, Jorge blurted, "But capital requirements are at the top of our procedures checklists. No way could we have missed something like that."

"Well, I think you did," Dennison replied. "The firm housed several large transactions in the last several months, which took short and long positions on interest rate swaps before they were cleared to customer accounts."

Jorge jumped up. "So what?! The net result of a long and short position on the same investment is zero; it has no effect on capital."

Adams winced, sensing what was coming. Jorge looked at him with confusion on his face. "We talked about this, Walter. You agreed. Capital was not affected."

"Let's wait to hear what he has to say, Jorge. I think I know where he is going."

Dennison continued, "I think it has occurred to your boss, Mr. Gonzalez, that there is an effect on capital."

"How so?"

Dennison continued, "The sides of the straddle have to be considered separately in the calculation. The percentage requirement for a long position is three percent capital, and for a short position, five percent. As long as the investments were Pension Strategy Partner investments, they are responsible for the capital requirement. As you know, this firm has operated at the edge of the envelope with regard to capital requirements, and the last set of straddles put them over, after the two percent difference is applied. That's all we need to shut them down. Mr. Adams, your firm has opined on these statements, so I will leave it to you how you deal with the fallout; that is none of our concern. With the collapse of Lehman Brothers, I don't think you are going to find any ears sympathetic to getting around this, and I have my marching orders on how I must proceed. So, I think it's time to make the announcement, and get on with it."

The entire staff was called together for a group announcement by Dennison on the second floor in the central office area. Amid exasperated pleas for reconsideration from the principals of the firm, crying and histrionics from employees, the personnel of the investment firm were advised of the closing of the office, and people began packing up their belongings and heading for the parking lot in shock. The personal effects they were permitted to take were inspected by the government officials to ensure that nothing proprietary was leaving with them. The mood varied from disbelief to anger and bewilderment as forty employees vacated the building. Anita Berwitz and a handful of others were asked to stay behind to help with the ongoing investigation. As Dennison corralled the few he was asking to stay on, Anita looked over his shoulder and gave Jorge a pleading look. He could only respond with a shrug.

After Dennison gave Anita and two others their marching orders, he returned his attention to the auditors and signaled for Jorge and Adams to join him in the conference room.

"What the fuck is going on?" Adams demanded when they were seated. "What could you have possibly uncovered that would require such draconian action?"

Dennison ignored the two principals, who were standing outside the glass conference room door, rapping on it to get attention. Finally, he acknowledged them with a dismissive wave of his hand, telling them he would be with them shortly. Then he turned to the two accountants.

"This is serious business, and our reaction is standard operating procedure to protect investors." He opened his briefcase and spread some worksheets on the table where all three of them could see them. "These are the suspense account adjusting entries for the last year showing the amounts in suspense and the accounts the adjusting entries were posted to for the past year. On the far columns are the PSP sectors that generated the transactions, and in the last column the principal who authorized the adjustment. Notice anything?"

Adams and Jorge looked over the spreadsheets, quickly at first, and then more closely. There were pages and pages to review. After a few minutes, Dennison called their attention to the authorization column where about a half-dozen trades were highlighted with a felt-tip pen. Each transaction identified Adam Schaeffer as the person responsible for the adjustment by his initials. Looking back across each line, Jorge saw that each of the adjustments dealt with placing an interest-sensitive trade in a client account. All of the transactions appeared to be hedges of one form or another; some were either purchases or sales of credit default swaps purchased through an intermediary. Many of the transactions were substantial in value, but they were split into smaller pieces before allocating them to customer accounts.

Jorge considered what he was looking at for a moment. "I don't see anything particularly unusual here. Some of the transactions are somewhat large for the pension funds they are managing, but those are divided into smaller amounts before assigning them to customers. We looked at all that during our fieldwork."

Dennison smiled. "Now look at these." He pulled another sheath of worksheets from his briefcase and spread them before him. "These are the original purchases of the hedges that were made in the house account and placed in suspense. Also note the ones that were authorized by Adam Schaeffer."

Adams and Jorge began looking closely at the detail in front of them. Adams didn't notice anything at first, but Jorge started to purse his lips as the pattern began to emerge. He noticed that most of the hedge strategies authorized by Schaeffer were duplicated, not in an ordinary sense, but that both sides of transaction were purchased. He nudged Adams in the arm. After making eye contact, he pointed at several examples with two fingers, so Adams could make the connection. It was impossible to see unless you had all the activity in one place, but clearly, for one reason or another, Schaeffer's pension strategy plan involved buying both sides of an interest-sensitive investment product.

"Why would he do that? I don't get it," Adams asked, looking at his junior partner with a quizzical expression. "It's a zero-sum game for him. Whichever way the investment goes, the other side of it cancels it out. How can that work for his clients?"

Dennison grinned, as though he had just filled an inside straight. He loved dragging the discovery phase out and watching the synapses connect on people's faces as the realization set in. "I suggest you go back and look at the first set of spreadsheets where he posts the adjustments from suspense."

Jorge and Adams saw that all omnibus accounts were cleared between two and four weeks after the originating transaction, enough time for the investment to have moved, even if only a little bit, in market value from their original costs. About half of the Schaeffer-authorized transactions were placed in a single account, Euro Capital, GmbH, a Swiss-based client.

"Let me guess," Jorge speculated, staring at Dennison. "If I were to compare the market values of these postings to their original costs, the profitable side would end up in the account of Euro Capital, GmbH, and the loss side would end up on some other client's books."

"Bingo," Dennison said with some glee in his voice. "There's more. Your client has failed to take into account the effect on capital that the purchases and sales of credit default swaps have during the time they are on Pension Strategy Partners' books, in the omnibus accounts, before the obligations are transferred to client accounts. Since their capital requirements are barely met anyway, they fail to meet regulatory capital requisites from time to time while the investments are in suspense. Primarily based on that failure, FINRA is required to exercise ERA, Expedited Remedial Action, to force the investment firm to cease all investment activities.

"In a nutshell, that's why we have taken . . . what did you call it . . . *rather draconian action*. You fail to meet capital requirements, and you are out of business. Simple as that," Dennison concluded. Having gone through the technical explanations with the auditors, he waved at the impatient principals, who were still hovering outside the conference room door, for them to join in the meeting.

The group spent the rest of the afternoon discussing what came next. Surprisingly little attention was paid to the fraud that was uncovered, as Dennison said it was out of his jurisdiction for the most part. He said it was a matter for the FBI and the SEC, although he predicted that it wasn't going anywhere, since the perpetrator was missing, presumed dead, and the money offshore undoubtedly. At the end of the day, Adams and Jorge rode silently back to the offices of Arthur White & Company, neither able to look each other in the eye or carry on a conversation.

CHAPTER NINE

Jorge couldn't believe how fast his world could unravel in just a couple of weeks. Whoever said government bureaucracies couldn't respond swiftly was sadly mistaken when it came to ducking for cover. Under pressure from an administration in Washington, DC, the Boca Raton office of FINRA did its best to put the incident behind them, not wanting to be accused of improper supervision of an investment banking firm in its jurisdiction. From a government standpoint, if someone could be identified and held accountable, then the problem was solved. For Dennison, the culprit was a regional accounting firm that was in way over its head auditing a company that managed public funds. His position was that Arthur White & Company lacked the manpower and experience to run such a sophisticated engagement and included that conclusion in its final report.

The report ended up at the Accounting Standards Executive Committee in New York, where proceedings embarrassing to Arthur White & Company triggered a review of their status as a member firm of the SEC Division of Public Accounting Firms, a prized watermark to their reputation. In less than two weeks, Jorge went from being an upwardly mobile junior partner in his chosen profession to unemployed. The State Board of Accountancy took administrative action, suspending his license to practice public accounting, pending another investigation, who knew when that would take place, and Jorge found himself not only unemployed, but unemployable.

He still recoiled in anger when he thought of the meeting he had in the days following September 15 in Dickenson's office, when he was informed that the firm held him responsible and accountable for the audit failure of Pension Strategy Partners.

"How can you put this all on me?" he had pleaded. "Walter." He turned to face his partner. "You know I brought this to you when we finished the fieldwork. We talked about it . . . discussed delving into it further, but agreed it was not necessary."

Adams looked away, not able to make eye contact. "You weren't straight with me."

"What do you mean?"

"You didn't tell me the full extent of the activity in the omnibus accounts."

Jorge almost jumped out of his chair. "Of course not!" he shouted. "That's why I brought it to you, to ask if we should investigate further. You said no, that we were already over budget, it wasn't worth pursuing."

Adams smirked. "That's not the way I remember it."

"You're a fucking liar! How can you go to sleep at night? I'm not saying I was right, but I brought the matter to you, because one of my staffers brought it up, the unusual activity. I was relying on you for guidance."

Dickenson interrupted, "Be that as it may, an engagement for which you were responsible has caused this firm considerable embarrassment, possibly even administrative charges. We cannot avoid taking some kind of action, and unfortunately for you, it results in your removal as a partner in this firm, and that's the end of the matter. Be advised that we will be notifying the Florida Institute of Certified Public Accountants and the State Board of Accountancy, as required, of your termination."

It took the State Board ten days to formally request Jorge to mail his actual certificate back to them. It had been decoupaged to a piece of decorative mahogany, along with his other certificates and his college diploma, where he had displayed them proudly on the wall in his office. He FedEx'd the whole piece of wood to Tallahassee with a note telling them where they could display it. He cleared out his office of personal belongings and put them in the trunk of his car. He was so disgusted, he didn't even bother to unpack it when he got home. Jorge spent the next several days moping in his apartment on Euclid Avenue, trying to imagine how he was going to tell his parents about the inglorious end to his career.

After two days of drinking beer and watching television, he finally decided he needed to get off his ass and do something. He tried several times to reach Anita on her cell phone, but his calls kept going to voicemail. He was saddened that his promising new relationship was also down the drain. He assumed she blamed him for her misfortune. Jorge turned his attention to Pension Strategy Partners. The whole situation just didn't sit well with him, so he began gathering all the information he could find on Schaeffer and his missing airplane. In the middle of his search, his cell phone rang. The caller ID indicated it was his mother.

"Hi, Mama," he sighed into the phone.

His mother began a tirade in Spanish, which was unusual for her since both his parents made a big deal about speaking only English in the home ever since they had emigrated from Cuba, a sign of respect for their new country. "You such a big shot now that you don't have time for your family. We haven't heard from you for almost two weeks. Carlos says you're dating a new girl named Anita. Is she a nice Cuban girl? Why don't you come by tonight and have dinner with your brothers; they're coming. I'll make something nice—we'll have pork and potatoes. You can tell us about your girlfriend."

Jorge reverted to English. "Slow down, Mama. I'm not having a good day. A lot has happened. I'll come by tonight, and we can talk about everything."

"Jorge, what's going on?" his mother continued in Spanish. "You sound depressed."

"Not so many questions, Mama. I'll tell you all about it tonight. I'll come by at six, okay?"

"Six o'clock, then. Don't be late."

"I won't. Bye, Mama."

Jorge dreaded telling his parents that he had lost his job. He knew how proud they were of him, that he made it out of the Mariel cycle of poverty and cultural alignment that had captured his brothers, who lived between cultures, unable to leave Cuba behind, Colonial America just out of reach. Santiago and Adriana had placed their hopes on their youngest, pushing him to Americanize, apply himself in school, and graduate from college, the only one in his family to succeed at that.

Now, he had become a pariah in his new American world of suits and financial respectability. Anger welled within him as he determined to clear his good name and give the finger to those dilettante pricks on Brickell Avenue for what they had done to him, how easily they had used him as a scapegoat and thrown him under the bus to take the heat off of them. There was more going on here, and he was sure as hell going to find out what it was.

Dinner at his parents' house couldn't have gone worse, meeting Jorge's expectations. At first Carlos and Val tried to move the conversation in the direction of Anita, thinking it would be good fun to put their saintly little brother under the gun. Jorge bobbed and weaved like a prizefighter to deflect the conversation from Anita's ethnic background.

Finally, he just burst out at the dining table. "Would you guys please leave me alone about that? I have much more important news to tell you, and it's not going to be pleasant."

123

That sobered everybody up. A look of loving concern spread across Adriana's face like a passing shadow. Carlos and Val sensed a bomb coming, and Santiago just looked dumbfounded. At the very least, Jorge had everyone's attention. With eight eyes focused solely on him, Jorge knew he had to deliver.

"There has been a complication at my workplace." He paused.

"Workplace? Last I heard, bro, you owned a piece of that workplace." Carlos picked up on the nuance immediately. "Val and me, we have a workplace. You *own* a piece of a business."

"Apparently not anymore," Jorge said quietly, looking down at his napkin.

Adriana put out one hand to her son, the other to her mouth in disbelief. "What do you mean, Jorge?"

Jorge spent the next half hour explaining the best he could in lay terms how his first big client was involved in something a little off, and that he was being blamed for not discovering it. The subject matter was far too complicated for him to explain all the intricacies, but he did the best he could. They understood the important parts. He had screwed up and had been fired for it. Adriana began weeping into her napkin while her husband just sat in his chair in disbelief. Carlos and Valeriano felt anguish for their brother, who, in their guts, they knew was not to blame for his downfall but was too proud and honest not to accept some responsibility.

"So, there you have it," Jorge concluded. "Oh, there's one more thing. My former firm has notified the State Board of Accountancy that I was responsible for the audit failure, and they will ask me to surrender my CPA certificate in the next few days."

He couldn't contain himself any longer. Shoulders hunched forward, he put his face on his folded arms and sobbed uncontrollably. No one moved to comfort him; they were so astonished. Tears began to run down Adriana's cheeks as she felt the anguish in her son. She started to reach for his shoulder to comfort him but stopped when Santiago nodded tersely at her.

"Let him be," he cautioned. "Jorge needs to get this out. He feels responsible, and it's not something his mama can fix. He's a grown man, and he needs to deal with it the way a grown man does."

Carlos and Valeriano sat transfixed, alternating glances between their father and their brother. The table fell into silence while Jorge composed himself. Slowly he sat up and wiped his face with his sleeves.

"Forgive me," he said. "Papa's right. I got myself into this mess, and I guess I'm the only one who can get myself out. I don't really think I have done anything wrong, at least I can't think of anything I would have done differently, other than ignoring my boss's recommendation. This is just a peculiar situation with a rogue client in a toxic market environment, a perfect storm, and everybody's looking for a scapegoat. Unfortunately, I'm it."

Adriana needed to ask, "Jorge, surely there is something you can do. Your whole future can't be wiped out by one bad person. You have worked so hard your whole life. It can't just end like this."

"There is, Mama." His face showed some determination for the first time since his brief meltdown. "I need to expose what this man has done and show that it is not something that would ordinarily have been discovered in an annual audit, which fraud is not necessarily. It's complicated, but if I can demonstrate I performed within acceptable guidelines, I can clear myself. As for my job, I don't think I would want that job back anyway."

Valeriano jumped in, "Would it matter if you caught this guy? Then would it be okay?"

Jorge answered, "That's the funny thing. It might, except that he's presumed dead. You remember in the news about the guy who disappeared flying to the Bahamas?"

"Yeah, he was never found. The Coast Guard called off the search a couple days after he went missing."

"His name was Adam Schaeffer. He was the CFO of the company I was auditing, the one who was manipulating the books. So there's no one to find, no bad guy to take my place."

"That sucks," Carlos and Valeriano said in unison.

"Boys!" Adriana admonished with a glare.

Jorge reached for his mother's hand. "I'm so sorry I embarrassed the family, Mama. You and Papa have done everything for me, and I have let you down."

She took his hand. "We know you are sorry, and it changes nothing," she said, although Jorge knew that was not really true, which was confirmed when Santiago added, "You will make everything right, son, and everyone will know."

Trying to change the subject, Adriana smiled at her husband and sons as they were preparing to finish up. "So, Jorge, do you want to tell us about this girl Carlos mentioned, Anita?"

"There's nothing much to tell, Mama. She won't return my phone calls."

Traffic was light on I-95 as Jorge was making his way from Little Havana to South Beach, so rather than take the causeway east across Biscayne Bay, he decided to continue up to Fort Lauderdale. He didn't know why, but the mention of Anita's name put her and Pension Strategy Partners on his mind, and he just felt compelled to swing by and see what was going on, if anything. Surprisingly, as he drove north along Andrews Avenue, he could see lights on in the building, although as he approached he did not see much activity going on inside. There were a couple of cars in the parking lot; one of them was Anita's Camry.

The wrought-iron front gate was draped with hot-yellow crime scene tape, as was the entryway to the side door from the parking lot and the stairs to the second-floor parking garage entrance from outside. Jorge drove past. His heart was beating rapidly, but he wasn't sure if it was due to the police tape or the fact that he saw Anita's car on the lot. He made a U-turn before he got to Cypress Creek and circled back to the entrance. Cautiously he entered the parking lot. He could see movement in the second-floor window, Anita's office he estimated. He wanted so much to go in and see her, but he was fearful of getting in more trouble, knowing that he had been warned away, which was made more forceful by the police tape.

Since he'd had no contact with Anita, he had no idea what she was thinking. They had not spoken a word since the announcement, although he knew she had been asked to stay on to help with the investigation into company activities. He knew he couldn't just go knock on the front door. Jorge scrambled around in his glove box for a piece of paper. Finding none, he remembered he had boxes of the stuff in his trunk. In the dim trunk light, he found a piece of a cover sheet, something unimportant, and crafted a note to Anita asking her to reach out to him, that he really hoped she would call him. He placed it under her driver's side windshield wiper.

Feeling that he had taken his first positive step toward reuniting with Anita, Jorge pulled silently out of the parking lot and headed toward home. He hoped no one had observed his unauthorized visit.

Anita Berwitz

CHAPTER TEN

Rachel Anita Berwitz was born at Mount Sinai Hospital in Queens, New York, on November 7, 1980, just a few blocks from her family home in upscale Astoria. Philip, her father, had a good job as a manager of a furniture distribution business, which provided him with a regular paycheck and medical benefits, enabling the family to live a modest but comfortable lifestyle. Privately, however, he was driven by an entrepreneurial spirit that caused him to save every penny he could from family living expenses, hoping to be prepared for an opportunity should one present itself. He valued his ambitions more than his spiritual needs, the care of which he left to his wife, Lea, who saw to it that the family engaged in conservative Jewish traditions. She had preferred that her daughter be called Rachel, but for some reason, it just hadn't stuck.

Anita didn't remember much about her early childhood, outside of the preschool monitoring she received at the nearby synagogue on Crescent Street, which she attended most days from the time she was out of diapers and able to communicate. The Astoria Center of Israel was a block-long complex of buildings that comprised the temple itself, as well as a grammar school for members of its congregation and spaces for community activities and gatherings. All in all, Astoria was a close-knit community, definitely a Jewish neighborhood, where everyone looked out for and took an interest in their neighbors. As a child, the young girl with the dark curls and unusually green eyes had trouble pronouncing her mother's preferred given name, Rachel. Anita with its simple consonants and broad vowels was easier for her to deal with, the lip curling "R" and the soft "ch" being more difficult for her. Eventually Lea gave up and went with the name Anita preferred, hoping privately that she would be able to make the conversion at some later date.

Anita was never aware of the controversy as a child. She was bright and got along with others, expressing a quick wit even as a youngster. Her friends at preschool valued her participation, and she absorbed the religious teachings she was exposed to with enthusiasm, thinking of the teachings more as interesting history lessons than preparation for entry to a grown-up Jewish community. By the time she was five, she was allowed to walk the few blocks from her townhome to the Astoria Center in the company of two or more friends or neighbors, and she was well adjusted to her own little world. Toward the end of her first year of formal school, her father and mother sat her down in the living room for a family talk.

The setting itself proved a little intimidating to young Anita, as most serious family business was dealt with at the dinner table, where places were set with rigidity and formality every evening at exactly six o'clock, but this was different. Her father explained to her that the family would be moving to a new part of America called Florida, where he had managed to take advantage of circumstances with the help of his employers to buy a retail furniture outlet in Dania. He was going to be a businessman and own his own company. Most of this was lost on poor Anita, as she had always assumed her father was a businessman since he left for work every morning wearing a suit and tie, like other businessmen she had seen on television.

What she did understand clearly was that she was going to be uprooted and moved to a new home, away from her friends and spaces where she felt comfortable. Her mother understood her concern and did the usual things one would expect to calm her daughter's fears, pointing out what a beautiful place Florida was, tropical like she had seen in books. She would be able to play outside every day because the weather was always warm and sunny. This was a good thing, because she would have so many new friends to play with. Her mother reminded her how much Anita had enjoyed the beach at the Jersey Shore on the few occasions the family had made the jaunt, and now she would be able to go to the best beaches in the world almost whenever she wanted.

The following September, Anita and her family found themselves in tropical South Florida, living in a modern Bermuda-style three-bedroom home just west of the Florida Turnpike, about five miles from the Atlantic Ocean. Although the weather was nice, Anita soon realized she would not be walking to the beach as advertised. To help with her social adjustment, Anita's parents arranged for her to begin second grade at the nearby Levitt Hebrew Academy, where she made friends quickly. Soon she was an established fixture in her neighborhood, enjoying a number of friends with whom she played regularly. Her religious education continued as before, and she and her parents attended temple routinely, continuing their conservative Jewish lifestyle.

Philip Berwitz could not have made a better career move, as his furniture business flourished in a growing South Florida economy. By the time Anita was twelve, the Berwitz family business had expanded to three stores located at the south end of Broward County. After studying the Talmud for six years, Anita celebrated her bat mitzvah at the local country club, no expense spared by a father proud to introduce his daughter to the ranks of womanhood. Anita was beginning to fill out to the metaphor. She was stunningly beautiful with dark hair and contrasting green eyes, and the figure she was growing into began to take shape as well.

Anita had a sense that she was pretty, but the overall effect was enhanced by her mother's conservative urging that she not overuse makeup the way many of her friends did. Her father enforced strict rules on dating activities as she passed through puberty, insisting that his daughter's whereabouts always be known by her mother or father. Some of the constraints placed on Anita as she neared driving age caused her to display a vein of rebellion, but she did not act on it irrationally in a way harmful to herself. Instead she expressed herself with sarcasm and humor, which others sometimes found biting. Although she did not feel a deep religious connection, she continued to attend temple regularly with her parents, mainly to keep peace within the family. Her mother was the disciplinarian, allowing Philip to wear the white hat in contentious matters. In his eyes, Anita could do no wrong, and his job was to support her and make sure that she had the resources to reach whatever goals she set for herself.

After Anita became mobile with a driver's license, her boundaries extended. She worked summers in the back office of her father's furniture business, learning something of the world of commerce. She decided that was something she wanted to pursue. After high school, Anita wanted to go to college away from home, something her parents did not agree about, and so a compromise was reached that Anita could board at the University of Central Florida in Orlando. This allowed her to live away from her parents for the first time, but it was near enough that her mother and father felt the distance was manageable. Anita enjoyed the full college experience. The relatively young university had grown to nearly the largest in the state system, and its fledgling football team had just joined the ranks of division 1-A, the big leagues, which made for an exciting campus environment.

Anita began dating more seriously compared to the cautious high-school romances she had sneaked from the watchful eyes of her parents and ultimately lost her virginity to a second string jock in her freshman year. The experience left her a little disillusioned, and she became more selective in her dalliances through her graduation in 2002. Her interest in business had shifted more to the technical side while she was in college, and she took her degree in computer sciences, which gave her a skill she could market immediately upon graduation. Her father offered her a position in his furniture business with the stipulation that she return home to live while she sought out a suitable mate. Her mother was anxious to have grandchildren, but the idea was not consistent with Anita's view of her immediate future.

She did take the job and the housing proposal on a temporary basis, putting her skills to work in a serious overhaul of the business data-processing and accounting systems. Philip was more than a little disappointed when he was informed that his daughter wanted to place her abilities in the business world outside the family influence. After a year's work and a successful conversion to twenty-first century information technology systems available for her father's business on her résumé, Anita landed a job in a large IT department for an investment banking and advisory firm, Pension Strategy Partners, in Fort Lauderdale. The learning curve was steep, but Anita did well and found herself the assistant manager of the department after just two years in the job. She kept peace with her family by continuing her residence in the Oakridge home in Dania, which made her mother happy.

Her father behaved as though he was doing her a favor, helping a struggling college graduate with expenses by allowing her to live at home while she made her way in the world, until one day he saw a copy of her tax return and realized that his sweet young daughter was making nearly six figures on her own. He felt a little foolish after taking note of her success and, at the same time, burst with pride that he and Lea had done a good job preparing their daughter for the world. He still felt the need to be "helpful" to Anita from time to time, such as buying her a new Toyota Camry for her twenty-seventh birthday.

Since her college years, when Anita's selection of dating opportunities were not generally good choices for her, she had become very selective in potential suitors. As a consequence, her romantic life fell into the doldrums. This was not surprising considering she was living at home with her parents, and men who expressed an interest in her had to pass through the prism of her higher standards, as well as those of her parents, whose optics were more geared to prospective grandchildren than anything else. So it didn't go unnoticed when she slipped out late one Sunday to meet "some guy I know from work" for dinner in North Miami.

———∞———

When Anita had started her job at Pension Strategy Partners, she was a little overwhelmed at the volume of transactions that comprised an average trading day for an investment banking firm. Her supervisor, who was also an accountant by training, was very helpful in teaching Anita how to break the massive amount of transactions in so many accounts into smaller, easier to manage activities. He gave her good advice when he cautioned, "Never, ever go home at the end of the day unless you have every account posted and closed with the day's activity. If you leave anything for tomorrow, you will slowly build a canyon that you will not be able to bridge. So, stay as late as you have to, but complete each day fully."

Anita learned that the boutique investment firm had a market advantage over other larger, more established firms because it could react more quickly to perceived market trends without having to go through burdensome bureaucratic policy committees, but that flexibility meant that she had to manipulate a system with a lot of special requests by the principals. By 2005, Anita had mastered the job of keeping the company's software up and running and was promoted to assistant manager of the IT department. It was only natural that at the end of her first year, when her mentor and boss took another position, she was selected to take his place as the IT boss in the corner office.

Anita didn't have much cause to interact with the principals of the firm. When she did, it was attributable to a need for a special adjustment to the financial records or the result of some kind of snafu in the reporting system, so not generally a happy situation. Just before the year end, Adam Schaeffer asked to meet with her about a special project he was working on, and they arranged to meet on a Wednesday after the markets closed, when the IT needs were relatively routine. She met with him in his office on the first floor, where she was impressed by the obvious attempt to create a Wall Street–style environment. The ceiling edges were all dressed in maple crown molding that matched the woodwork from the chair rails to the floor. The walls were covered in rich grasscloth wallpaper, and the furniture was all of the highest-quality woods and fabrics.

Schaeffer's office was on the northwest corner where his bay windows offered views of the well-planted courtyard and fountains, the north-facing window yielding a sight line to the bigger office buildings on the west side of Andrews Avenue. Anita was ushered in and directed to a seat across from Schaeffer's expansive desk. Wondering what this was all about, she waited while he positioned himself across from her.

The concern must have shown on her face, as Schaeffer opened the conversation with, "There is no need to worry, Anita. I want you to work with me on a special project I am developing."

Anita relaxed, her shoulders shifting lower, as she realized this was not one of the uncomfortable meetings. "That sounds interesting, Mr. Schaeffer. What kind of project is it?"

"As you know, my official role here is to oversee some of the pension strategies we use to remove volatility from the vast array of pension funds we manage. In addition to that, with my background in accounting, the duties of financial requirements of the firm have also fallen under my direction. Since we don't have an official designated chief financial officer position, those duties have been assigned to me. In addition to that, I have a reputation for being quite innovative in the hedging strategies we employ, so I am always looking for new ways for our firm to enhance our abilities."

"I see," she said, although she really didn't, so she sat and waited for more information.

"Good. So, when I come up with a new strategy for us to employ, I often try it out on an experimental basis with select clients in our general population, with their full concurrence of course. If the strategy proves to be reliable and effective, we make it available to our other client account managers, and it becomes part of our firm's policy standards for general use."

Anita thought this all made sense, and she nodded slowly to acknowledge her understanding. After a moment's reflection, she said, "How does this involve me?"

"Well, Anita, you are a very important part of the process. As you know we have very strict protocols directing how accounting adjustments can get into our system. I know you are very familiar with that because you were very helpful to us in developing them with your predecessor."

She knew what he was talking about. Some of the internal controls were weak when she first came to work for Pension Strategy Partners, and that was one of the first tasks she was assigned. Again she nodded her understanding of what he had said.

Schaeffer continued, "So, when I test out a new strategy, sometimes the journal entries have to be customized to fit the intricacies associated with it, and they may fall outside the parameters of the protocols you have set up to safeguard the assets under our control. When that happens, we have to make a pathway for exceptions to the protocol, so that we can record the transaction properly, so it is reflected in our accounts correctly."

Again Anita nodded, although it took a while for her to become completely comfortable with what Schaeffer was asking of her. He explained that he had developed a new investment technique that had two sides to a transaction, wherein each side alone might have economic consequences, but combined the two together had no economic effect whatsoever.

"You're describing what I was taught is a 'zero-sum game.' Is that right?"

"Exactly. Say, you are as smart as you are beautiful."

Anita was taken aback by the reference to her looks, flattering as it was, but somehow she didn't sense any ulterior motive in his comment. Schaeffer was emotionless and seemingly unaware that it could have been taken as inappropriate. In fact, she would come to learn that the more time she spent with this man, the more she sensed that he was devoid of any human feelings, at least where business was concerned. Everything was business, zeros and ones, just like a computer. After she made that adjustment to working with Schaeffer, everything else fell into place.

"So, how can I help you with your new strategy?" she inquired.

"Well, in simple terms, we will make the hedge, which is similar to a straddle if you are familiar with the term, on the firm's account, and then see how the investment plays out. When we know which way the market is positioning the transaction, we will have a basis for placing it in a client's account, so we will already know the outcome of the strategy. For this part of the transaction, we will need to make an adjusting journal entry to place the sides of the investment where they will be the most beneficial to our client."

"And that would be outside of our protocol," Anita observed.

Schaeffer smiled at her. "Yes."

"So, you want me to make special adjusting journal entries in our system while you test your strategy. Is that right?"

"That's exactly right. The investments I am considering will take two to three weeks to *mature,* as I call it, remember that they cancel each other out, and then we will post them to our clients' accounts as is appropriate."

"Mr. Schaeffer, I'm not sure that that will be entirely out of our protocol, as we occasionally do that now in some circumstances, and our rules can deal with it as long as the transaction is cleared before the end of an accounting period. Generally, that happens in a few days," Anita volunteered.

"That's precisely why we need to work together. Since these hedges take a little longer to *mature,* often the closing entries will occur after the end of the month, so they will not always, or even often, originate and close out in the same accounting period, hence the need for your involvement."

"I see. Well, can you draft a summary of what you are proposing for my records, so I can safely say I am operating at your direction, which is within protocol? Just to make everything proper?"

Schaeffer flinched at the request, ever so slightly, fearing that Anita may have considered a defensive move necessary. "I will get something prepared for you first thing in the morning," he replied.

He needn't have worried. As the new department head, Anita was only trying to follow the procedures she had set up for the organization when she arrived by reminding her boss of the protection protocols she had found lacking in the company's internal controls. She did not take notice of Schaeffer's reaction because she was already writing a note to herself about the request. It occurred to him that he would be long gone if an issue came to light, anyway.

She looked up from her notes. "When will we begin, do you think?"

"We can begin anytime, but I think it will be best if we wait until after the start of our fiscal year, say next month in July."

"Okay, that sounds good to me. Just let me know the amounts and accounts where you want the securities or hedges to go, and at what values they should be transferred."

Schaeffer smiled at her. "That's easy, they will always be carried at the original investment costs; otherwise, we will not have a basis for determining whether the strategy is successful or not."

That made sense to her. "Is that all?" Anita started to rise from her chair.

"Yes, for now. Thank you, Anita. One more thing." Schaeffer held his index finger in the air, as if he had forgotten something. "If anyone should ask you about this new strategy, feel free to explain that we are just working on a new technique, like we always do. You can refer deeper inquiry to me for a fuller explanation."

Anita went back to her office to review some new software proposals before going home. She felt like she had a more important role on the management team, being part of one of the principal's special projects. In July, Schaeffer began some of his investment straddles, and as he predicted, the market movement generally took a few weeks for results to be noticeable, at which point he asked Anita to make the journal entries to place the orders in the accounts he specified, which were more often than not one of the larger union pension funds or an offshore trading account based somewhere in Europe.

Schaeffer continued to test his new strategies for almost two years. Whenever Anita asked him when the testing phase would be drawing to a close, he was not very specific in his replies. Then, as solidly as things had come together, they fell apart on September 15, 2008, with the failure of Lehman Brothers, and the trickle down of pressure on the capital of smaller (and sometimes quite large) investment firms.

The previous week had been a blur for Anita, as the world had crashed all around her. For the last couple of months, things had been looking up. Her job was seemingly going quite well. As her responsibilities gained in importance, she felt better about herself, gaining confidence in all she was doing. After multiple attempts to get the attention of the sharp young accountant who managed the audit of Pension Strategy Partners, Jorge Gonzalez had finally shown an interest in her.

She knew he was quite timid, but he had worked up enough nerve to ask her out on a date, well, sort of a date. She had fortunately avoided the messy complication of introducing a nice Catholic Cuban immigrant to her conservative Jewish parents—this was a bridge she hoped she would have to cross at some later date—by arranging to meet him in North Miami, about midway between where they each lived. That the handsome, olive-skinned Latino was awkward around her only served to heighten her interest. He most certainly wasn't hitting on her aggressively, and she found his shyness appealing. Her efforts to alert him that his interest in her would not be rejected were not always noticed, but she had obviously made some progress.

Their dinner date in North Miami began with a misunderstanding and some friction as they discussed the remarkable sudden disappearance of her boss over the weekend. His clumsiness began when he tried to shake her hand as a greeting when they met at the restaurant. She wasn't going to let him get away with that, and she moved inside his outstretched arm and offered her cheek, which he dutifully kissed without enthusiasm. Anita worried that maybe she had misinterpreted his signals of interest and finally just chalked it off to inexperience and shyness. There was no doubt in her mind that she would be making all the strategic moves where he was concerned.

Then, after they were seated, Jorge seemed distracted when she brought up her boss who had gone missing. Jorge only seemed to view the situation from his perspective as an auditor and how it would affect the financials he had just put out. This offended her to a degree, and she told him so. Adam Schaeffer may not have been the warmest of individuals she had worked with, but Anita had developed a close working relationship with him since she had been involved in his new investment strategy.

For her, Schaeffer represented what was good about the American system. She knew that he came from a modest family, worked his way through college with the help of a scholarship, and paid his dues on Wall Street where he learned the finer points of his trade. He enjoyed the outdoors, captaining a good-sized motor yacht and flying back and forth to it in his own little airplane in the summer. He seemed to have a nice family, although he never talked about them unless it was something related to a story about himself.

And now Anita was about to be unemployed. In a period of less than two weeks, the firm she worked for had been shut down by a government agency. Everyone had been dismissed except for a few employees on the accounting staff and herself, each of whom had been promised salary continuation while FINRA took control of the firm assets and conducted its investigation into irregularities they had encountered. Information technology was integral to this process, as their only access to the financial records was through the customized computer systems. It would take months to bring in somebody new and start from scratch.

A condition of her continued employment was that she was not allowed to talk to anyone who had a previous connection to Pension Strategy Partners, particularly employees or former employees of Arthur White & Company, the auditors. Anita was responsible for keeping the software running so that the investment firm's accountants could close out the ledgers of each investment client, and the assets held for them could be transferred to another investment banking firm of its choice. This was a time-consuming process that would take several weeks.

While all this was going on, Anita helped the FINRA investigators try to figure out the effect, if any, that the new investment strategies used by the firm might have had on the clients. They seemed particularly interested in Schaeffer's latest project, although this didn't seem like a pressing issue for them. Mostly they focused on analysis of the firm's failure to meet daily capital requirements, justifying their decision to close the business down.

Anita was crushed to learn from the investigators that Jorge and his accounting firm were possibly in big trouble and that Jorge would most likely lose his job over this mess. She wanted desperately to call him and see how he was doing, but Mr. Dennison had been very clear: If she had any contact with anyone from that firm, she would be in severe legal trouble. She had many missed calls from Jorge's cell phone, most of which had gone to voicemail. Jorge was pleading with her to call him back, and it broke her heart that she couldn't.

CHAPTER ELEVEN

It was now Thursday evening, about ten days after the big event, and the first cold front of the season had crossed the Florida Straits earlier in the week. The evenings were cooler, and it was getting dark noticeably earlier each day. Anita was clearing the last of the requests off her desk when she took a minute to sit back and look out of her glass office and take in the surreal appearance of the unoccupied desks and cubicles on her floor. All personal effects had been removed by the employees the day they had been asked to pack up and get out. Papers and files were open on their desks exactly as they had been left. The room looked as it would in the middle of any business day—just no humans were present. The computer servers in the glass, specially air-conditioned core still blinked randomly as they had before, and the place was eerily quiet, except for the occasional horn or semi-truck exhaust letup coming from I-95, a few hundred yards to the east.

Anita looked around the floor and verified that the building was vacant. She was usually the last one to leave, and this evening she had been asked to run a complete recap of the year's general ledger, which took hours. On her way out she stopped by the security system pad to set the alarm code and verify the previous twenty-four-hour entries to the building, each identified by an assigned employee number.

Whoa, what's this? she wondered. The screen before her displayed the access codes used for entries into the building since the previous midnight. Whereas she generally recognized the entries on the logs, times and known authorized personnel, the first entry was entered at 2:38 in the morning, and the ID was not one she was familiar with. The code shown was 003, and she suspected that such a low number would have to be one of the firm's principals. She ran back to her office to look up the name associated with 003 and confirmed that it belonged to Adam Schaeffer.

This was significant, and Anita resolved to look into the aberration first thing in the morning. After resetting the security system, she exited the second-floor outside stairwell and headed to her Camry in the parking lot. As she approached her car, she could see a folded piece of notepaper tucked under the driver's side wiper. In the dim light of the parking lot lamps, she could make out a hastily scrawled message from Jorge: *Anita, please reach out to me. I have figured out a lot of stuff from the working papers that were still in my trunk, and I need to talk to you. It's really important.* He finished with his initials, JG.

Anita felt a flush of excitement as adrenaline coursed through her body, thinking of the confluence of events in the last few minutes. Instinctively she looked about the parking area to make sure she was not being observed. Her mind was racing with unanswered questions. *Why was Schaeffer's code used to gain access to the building?* The search for his missing airplane had been called off a week ago, and he was presumed dead. What had Jorge learned since the mess was uncovered? Her heart beat faster at the thought of getting in touch with him again. Still fearing the potential wrath of the authorities, Anita drove to the shopping center on Cypress Creek, her entrance to the interstate, and from the obscurity of the parking lot, she searched Jorge's cell number on her phone and called him.

"Anita, thank God you called. I was afraid you wouldn't," he said breathlessly. "I have so much to tell you, but first how are you?"

"I'm fine, Jorge. I have a lot to tell you, too. I just got your message. I know it's late, but can we meet? I don't want to leave a history on my cell that we talked for more than a moment. It's too involved to cover in a phone call, anyway."

"I'm thinking the same thing. Do you want me to come up there?" Jorge had only been home a few minutes from his clandestine visit to Pension Strategy Partners' offices.

"I've already left the office. Obviously, I got your note. How about we meet at Houston's again? It's halfway," she said.

"Good idea; I could use a drink. It's been a rough day, and I had dinner with my family, told them everything that has happened to me. I don't think I'm the shining star in my parents' eyes I was two weeks ago." Jorge sighed.

"We can talk about it in a few minutes. I'll see you at Houston's. Wait for me at the bar if you get there first."

"Ditto. Anita . . ." Jorge paused, and offered up cautiously, "I'm really glad to hear your voice. I've missed you." He was nervous because he had no way to know what her reaction to this scandal would be, whether she blamed him or not. Her words were reassuring to him.

Anita ended the call and headed south on I-95. Twenty minutes later she walked past the receptionist and looked for Jorge at the raised bar platform on the upper level overlooking the waterway. The evening was cool, and a mild humid breeze carried a scent of the Intracoastal and flowering plantings across the open restaurant. Not seeing Jorge at first, she ordered a glass of Cabernet and turned her attention to the front door in anticipation of his arrival. She found her heart was racing at the thought of seeing him again.

Within a few minutes she spotted him at the front scanning the bar for her. She was shocked somewhat to see him in a pair of khakis and a colorful T-shirt adorned with a marine graphic, wearing loafers and no socks, not the image of the conservative businessman she had come to know. She liked the relaxed look with his dark hair combed back, and he was freshly shaven.

He spotted her at the bar. Ignoring the hostess, he wormed his way among the patrons to where she was seated. "Sorry I'm late. I thought I better clean up a bit before seeing you."

Anita couldn't resist the opening, and turned her face, so that Jorge's intended peck on her cheek landed squarely on her moistened lips. *That ought to send him a message,* she thought. "If this is how you look after 'cleaning up' I can only imagine what you looked like when we spoke on the phone."

"Shorts and flip-flops." He smiled. "And I hadn't shaved for a couple days."

"Your mom must have liked that. What was it that you had to tell them?" she asked.

The bartender took his drink order. He specified a Corona with lime and turned his attention back to Anita and her deep green eyes. He licked his lips, still moist after the smooch she had laid on him and tried to refocus his thoughts on a summary of the last ten days.

"It's a long story. A lot has happened to me since the offices were closed a week ago Monday. I'll tell you in a nutshell." Jorge proceeded to explain that his firm decided they needed a scapegoat for what was being characterized as an audit failure, and that he had lost his job as a result. In addition, he explained that he was undoubtedly going to lose his license to practice public accounting, that he would probably have to surrender his CPA certificate after a brief investigation.

Anita could see the depression in his face and how his shoulders drooped as he got into the details of how he had been kicked to the curb. She listened sympathetically and reached out to hold his hand as a gesture of comfort. He held on firmly.

Jorge concluded with an explanation that he couldn't get past the coincidences of Schaeffer's peculiar trades over the last eighteen months and his disappearance. "I have the working papers in the trunk of my car still, the ones that deal with the straddles he was using as investment strategies for his pension clients. I looked at them more closely the other day, and they make no sense to me at all as a plan to reduce volatility in investment accounts, and I suspect there is some other purpose. I know I can figure it out, if I give it more time."

Anita listened patiently, aching inside for the pain Jorge was feeling. When she sensed he was nearing the end of his story, she interrupted. "You have to hear what I learned tonight. First, forgive me for not returning your calls. These investigators have made me so nervous, telling me that I could go to jail if I had unauthorized contact with you, or anyone else for that matter. I was just scared until tonight."

Jorge looked up with interest, still gripping her hand, he asked, "So, what happened tonight?"

Anita let her hand free of Jorge's grasp; she needed both arms to express her excitement. With enthusiasm and animated gestures, she related what she had noticed on the security log earlier that evening. When she was done, Jorge sat expressionless across from her, and slowly a smile spread across his face as the possible significance of this new development registered. In his excitement, he slid off his high barstool and clasped Anita in a huge bear hug. Anita went rigid for a second and then felt that she was a great comfort to Jorge and embraced him in return. "So, what do you think?" she asked as she pulled back for a moment.

"I told you I smelled a rat, and this is the smoking gun. Does anyone else know about this?"

"No. I was the last one to leave the office, and you're the first person I've talked to. I suppose I should report it to somebody from FINRA in the morning, though."

Jorge looked concerned. "Do you think you really have to . . . tell somebody else, I mean? Have they given you specific instructions to report the logged entry of everyone? Is that one of your assignments?" He looked at her, pleading.

"I guess not." Anita thought about this for a moment. "I have not been given much specific direction at all, now that you mention it. I have only been told that everything I learn since closing the firm is confidential, and I am not to discuss it with anyone outside the authorized investigators. Other than that, I have just been generally asked to assist the people from FINRA to operate the IT system and bring up specific data they request. Come to think of it, the primary specific instruction I was given was that I am not supposed to talk to you, but I guess that ship has already sailed." She smiled and reached out for his hand again.

Jorge was comforted by her physical connection, and he placed his other hand over hers. "Can we keep this just between the two of us? At least, until we figure out who, if not Schaeffer, was in the building early this morning? If there is a possibility that Schaeffer is not dead, that could change everything for me, but I want to be in control of the information."

"Sure. This is beginning to sound like an adventure. What should we do with this new information?" She gave his hand a squeeze. "It's like we're in *Casablanca*."

Jorge looked at his watch. "It's only ten thirty. Would you mind if we went back up to the building and looked around Schaeffer's office to see if we can figure out why he might have been back, if it was him? This changes the whole nature of what has happened. Just think, if Schaeffer is still alive, then he must have faked his death, and this whole mess is something of his own creation. There must be a whole lot more going on that we haven't found yet. He must know that it will all come out at some point, so he knew he was taking a big risk to come back to his workplace. His only salvation will ultimately be that everyone thinks he is dead, and the government doesn't look to prosecute dead people."

Anita smiled at him again. "I'm game for that. We've hardly touched our drinks, though."

Jorge started to slide off the high stool. "I'm not thirsty anymore." He picked up his glass and took a gulp of his beer and nodded at the door. Anita took a slug of her wine and joined him. They left Houston's hand in hand. In the parking lot, each looked in opposite directions for their cars, when Jorge gave Anita's hand a tug and said, "Come on, I'll drive." He pulled her in the direction of his Beemer.

As Anita lowered herself into the plush beige, leather seat, she rubbed her hand over the hand-crafted dash and remarked, "Nice!"

"It's one of the perks of a good job and lack of a family to support. Unfortunately, I don't have the job anymore, unless we can get this mess cleared up."

He pulled out of the shopping center parking lot on to the highway and zipped up I-95 in light evening traffic to Fort Lauderdale and the offices of Pension Strategy Partners. As Jorge turned in the adjacent parking lot, his headlights illuminated the gates to the front courtyard and the yellow police tape across the entry way. A sign posted on the driveway entrance cautioned NO ENTRY except for authorized persons, giving momentary pause to the intruding couple. Anita suggested they park behind the garage where the car would be less likely to be noticed.

She led Jorge up the outside steps to the employee entry door at the second floor. There was no traffic along Andrews Avenue, and the couple did not think it would be likely that their entry would be observed unless someone was watching the building, in which case they were already in trouble. She entered her personal code on the keypad, and the magnetic release made an audible click as the electronic purchase on the door was freed. Anita and Jorge stepped inside and heard the magnetic lock secure the door behind them. In the glow of the night lighting, Anita found the light switch for the half of the second floor where her office was.

"Won't the light attract attention?" Jorge asked.

"Not likely. It is not unusual for me to work late if I am asked to present a lot of printed data for FINRA. I think we'll be fine."

They moved to the elevator and took it to the first floor. In the dim glow of the night lighting, the offices looked regal, as the reduced light served to soften and richen the glossy wood surfaces of the bosses' workspace. They worked their way to Schaeffer's corner office, which looked out on to the courtyard in front of the building.

When Anita turned on the wall switch, Jorge was surprised to see an office that looked like it had been worked in that day and left by someone who expected to return in the morning. Everything was tidied up, in and out boxes were empty, and only a few active-looking files stacked on the credenza behind the desk revealed signs of activity. A lone Apple MacBook Air sat on the credenza behind Schaeffer's desk.

"Where should we start?" Anita asked, a little overwhelmed at the prospect of finding anything relevant.

"We start at one corner and look at everything. Look for something that might be out of place or has a gap as though something was removed." He moved around the desk. "Let's start here," he suggested.

"Wait a minute. Let's think this through," Anita cautioned. "If Schaeffer went through all the trouble to make everyone think he was dead, and he put a lot of planning in to it, why would he have come back here and risked screwing everything up?"

"You're right, Anita. He wouldn't have come back here for something he had forgotten. Removing it might give him away. He must have come back here for something he needed to know, information or something. What kind of information would he need and where would he keep it?"

They both turned and looked at the laptop at the same time. Jorge asked, "You're the IT expert. Can you tell if he accessed his laptop? If you can, and he did, then we know that what he came for is in it." He smiled at his cleverness.

Anita agreed. "Yes, if we can get access to it, meaning he does not have it password protected, I can look at the operating system logs, and they will tell us when it was last opened and which application was used. Keep your fingers crossed. If he uses a password, it is unlikely I can get to look inside."

She lifted the lid, and the Mac chimed its trademark tune as it started booting up. After a few seconds the screen lit up, icons across the bottom, and wallpaper of a nice-looking family yacht filling the screen. There was no prompt for a password.

"This is good luck for us," Anita said, spinning the desk chair around so she could sit at the computer. With Jorge looking over her shoulder, she accessed the systems icon, and selected a key to the operating system. The screen filled with computer dribble, and within seconds, Jorge was left in a cloud of nontraditional computer characters, which were unfamiliar to him. He saw references to entry logs, and after a few more keystrokes, Anita announced, "Eureka!"

"What did you find?" he asked excitedly.

"You are right. The computer was accessed at two forty-six this morning. The software activated was the address book, part of the mail system. He looked up a contact in his register."

"Can we tell which one?" Jorge asked.

"I think so. The easiest way is to just open up his contact list. Unless he did something else with it, it should open up to the contact he searched for. If that doesn't work, I can go back into the operating system and maybe figure something out. That will take a while though."

"Let's hope it's as simple as you first suggested."

Anita opened up the contacts icon. "There it is."

Jorge leaned over her shoulder to get a closer look. He couldn't help noticing the faint scent of her hair and makeup, and the moment took on a feeling of intimacy for him. The account identified itself only as "Passport Contact" and a phone number with a Miami area code. He thought about that for a moment.

Anita thought out loud, "There's no name, email address, or other information about the contact. . . . What do you think?" She looked up over her shoulder and put her hand over Jorge's, who had placed it there to support himself as he leaned over, also feeling a moment of intimacy passing between them.

"I'm just spit-balling here, but I would think our Mr. Schaeffer had planned out an elaborate ruse to convince the world he is dead and prearranged to leave the country, for which he would need a new identity. I'm sure he would have made all the arrangements in advance, thorough as he is, and this is probably a contact he used to get a new passport. Since I assume he set everything up in advance, I can only guess something went awry, and he needs a new set of identity documents. I have no idea why, but just maybe we can track him down from this number."

Anita took in a deep breath, startled. "This has all the makings of a thriller movie. I can't believe what we're on to. So, you think we should call this number?"

Jorge thought about it a minute. "Not just yet. I've spent some time looking over the work papers that were left in my trunk. I want to go back over them and see if we can figure out what he was up to. I suspect his new strategy for reducing the volatility in customers' investment accounts was really about moving money around to his benefit. It's probably somewhere offshore, and he's trying to get to it."

"Do you want to get them and we can look at them here?"

"They're back at my apartment, and I think we have pressed our luck as far as I'm comfortable for now. I'm going to go home and give them a thorough review, and then we can decide what to do."

Anita was thrilled with the excitement of their discovery and, at the same time, disappointed the evening was coming to an end. She asked hopefully, "Can't I be of some help? After all, I know a lot about the strategy he was using since I posted all the adjustments for him. We could do it together, two heads better than one and all." She was still looking up at Jorge over her shoulder, and he was close to her, his hand still under hers.

Jorge's back was killing him from leaning over, but he did not want to interrupt the intimacy they were sharing. The strain on his back, coupled with the adrenaline coursing through his system, pushed him past the barrier of his natural shyness. His sense of humor kicked in, "You mean we should put our heads together?"

"Something like that." Anita tugged on his wrist, and Jorge leaned over farther until their cheeks touched, and then he angled his lips toward hers until they met tenderly. Anita turned in her seat, placing her right hand behind his neck and they kissed for a few seconds, her lips finally parting to encourage his passion. They broke after a moment, and Jorge observed, "Well, you're right, two heads are definitely better than one. We should put them together more often."

"So, does that mean I can come with you . . . to help with the work papers, I mean?" she asked cautiously.

"You want to come to South Beach tonight?" he seemed surprised.

"Yes, well if you want me to help. We can't go to my place; I don't think my parents would appreciate a midnight visit."

"Okay. We can stop in North Miami and get your car on the way."

"Or . . ." she said, "we could pick it up in the morning. It might be easier than an extra trip in the middle of the night."

Jorge took a minute for the significance of her suggestion to work through his brain as he hurriedly tried to recall what kind of condition he had left his apartment. "Okay, great. Let's get out of here."

The couple copied down the information they needed from the laptop and logged out. Satisfied that everything was as they had found it, they took the elevator up and left the building after resetting the security system. It was just after midnight when they got to Jorge's apartment on Euclid Avenue. He parked and moved quickly to the front porch door, so that he would have a few seconds to clean up any mess he had left. He needn't have worried. A creature of habit, his apartment was as neat as his mother would have left it. He flipped on the light switch, showed the living room layout to Anita, and pointed out the bathroom facilities, should she require them. She didn't.

"Make yourself at home," Jorge instructed. He turned on the overhead dining table light, illuminating the stack of working papers, all neatly Acco-Pressed in their legal-size files. From the small kitchen, he offered Anita something to drink, suggesting a Cabernet he had open in the fridge.

"That would be nice," she said with a nod.

Anita took a seat at the table and started looking through the files, which contained mostly columnar worksheets filled with numbers and notes to the file. Each file had a table of contents on the left side, so she perused those, looking for something familiar where she might be helpful. Frustrated, she looked at Jorge as he sat down next to her and said, "I'm not sure how much help I'm going to be. This doesn't make much sense to me. I'm just looking for something familiar from the journal entries Mr. Schaeffer had me making."

"It doesn't have to. The file you're looking at pertains to the straddles he was making, where we tied out the positions that were taken and reconciled them to the house or client account balances. They all did. Where you can help me is with any information you may recall about the clients involved. For example . . ." Jorge started flipping through a few of the expanding folders and selected one. He started looking down the list of options purchased in a folder designated "Schaeffer Clients." Looking down a list he pointed at several on the page. "These are the trades he made." Then flipping ahead a few pages, he added, "These are the postings you made to book assets purchased in the accounts of clients. Do you notice anything about the clients?"

Anita looked at the names of the clients and raised her eyebrows. "Yes! Most of the clients are pension funds of our clients in the Northeast, which were handled by Mr. Schaeffer. But the straddles were split apart when they were transferred from the house account to the clients. It looks like the investments in the pension funds were spread evenly among our biggest clients, but about half seem to be to one customer, the one in Europe."

Jorge agreed. "That's the one Dennison pointed out to us. Euro Capital, GmbH is one of the clients Schaeffer is in charge of, right?"

Anita nodded in the affirmative and went on to explain further, "You probably already know this, but the three principals who started the firm brought in most of the business. The word is that they assign the clients to senior investment advisors within the firm. When the senior advisors build up an independent book of business to the extent that they may be at risk for leaving and taking their customers with them, they are made associate partners and get a piece of the action, a percentage. All the hotshots are given a lot of leeway in how they manage their investment accounts and client relations, but the three founding principals can always intervene."

Jorge looked at Anita. "Intervene? In what sense?"

"You know, like pushing some particular product where we get bigger commissions onto everyone's clients. I'm told that's quite common."

Jorge thought for a minute, sitting back in his chair. "Okay, so maybe we should take a look at some of the other partners' client investments, particularly the ones that required adjustments subsequent to the initial trading dates and see if we notice something."

Anita looked through all the files they had at their disposal for the next couple of hours. They learned quite a bit after tracing the investment strategy Schaeffer said he was testing. It was not until they looked at all the investment accounts of all the investment partners that a clear pattern started to emerge. It had not been noticed in the audit fieldwork because each of the responsible partner's accounts were analyzed separately, but when everything was looked at as a whole, what Schaeffer was really doing became apparent. He was placing opposing investments simultaneously in the house account, and after a short period, when the market values of the positions taken began to fluctuate, the assets were moved by Anita's journal entries to customer accounts. Not surprising was that all of the profitable sides of the straddles found their way to the mysterious account in Switzerland, Euro Capital, GmbH.

The open straddles alone on the day the firm was shut down were millions of dollars. Jorge could only imagine how much had been accumulated offshore over the last twenty-four months or so. He rubbed his eyes, which were now burning and red with strain, and closed the last file they had been working on. He stacked the files neatly in the center of the table.

"So, I think we have a pretty clear idea what your boss was up to, Anita."

She smiled an understanding and took a last sip of the wine she had been nursing. Jorge continued, "Your quiet Mr. Schaeffer has been siphoning funds out of the firm's clients' accounts and moving them to Switzerland to an account that he undoubtedly controls. His plan was to fake his death . . . nobody tries to find a dead embezzler . . . and get out of the United States to start a new life."

"That all makes sense. But what do you make of his coming back to the office, leaving evidence that he is still alive. Wouldn't that risk everything for him?"

"We can only guess, but I suspect that something went awry in his plans, and for some reason, he has to start the new identity process over again. It must be something really serious, or he wouldn't have taken such a big risk, as you say."

"I really don't know what to say. I kind of liked him, sort of admired his lifestyle, you know. He was successful, had a nice family, lived idyllic summers on his boat in the Bahamas, commuting back and forth. I thought he had it all. His wife, Marjorie, is really nice, and he had two daughters. I just don't get it. Why would he abandon them? He always seemed nice to me. Marjorie came by the office on Monday to see if there were any personal effects she could get from his office, but the investigators won't let her take anything until they are done with their investigation. She burst out crying because she couldn't even take the family pictures. What kind of schmuck does that?"

"Maybe he's a psychopath, devoid of normal feelings, who knows," Jorge volunteered.

"Maybe. You just don't know about people, sometimes."

Finally, at a little past three o'clock in the morning, Anita announced that she was beat. "Where do we go from here?"

Jorge paused. "For starters, I suppose I should take you back to your car, so you can get home. As for me, I need to quantify what we have learned tonight and decide what we can do to track Schaeffer down."

Anita sighed. "It's too late and I'm too tired to drive home now. I'm going to call in sick tomorrow. Can't I just stay here? I'll sleep on the sofa if you don't have a spare bedroom."

A sudden surge of adrenaline brought Jorge to a heightened state of alertness. With a smirk on his face he suggested, "You don't have to sleep on the sofa. Let's put our heads together again and see if we can't figure something else out."

Anita gave a hearty laugh and leaned across the table to reach Jorge. Their lips met in a long, lingering kiss. "You mean like that?" she asked. They kissed again and again. "Do you have an extra toothbrush?"

"Probably not, but I'll look."

"Then I'll just have to use yours."

They sat leaning across the table, faces buried in each other's necks, until Anita slowly began to stand. Jorge followed suit, while she fumbled under the table for her sandals, which she had kicked off during their work. "I'm going to text my mom that I'm staying with a friend, so she won't worry when she gets up and sees I'm not home."

"Good idea. You want to use the bathroom first? That way you get a dry toothbrush," he kidded.

"You're so thoughtful."

After they freshened up, Jorge led Anita by the hand to the bedroom, where his king-sized bed was neatly made.

"You're a real neatnik, aren't you?" she remarked. She could sense that he was nervous as she sat on the end of the bed holding his hands in hers. "You know, we don't have to make a big deal about this right now; we have plenty of time later. If you want, we can just get some sleep. I'm exhausted anyway."

Anita felt the tension drain from Jorge's body as he sat next to her and rolled her on her back. He kissed her tenderly yet passionately. "I'm okay with that; I'm beat, too." He kicked off his shoes and stripped off his trousers and T-shirt, while Anita shed her skirt and blouse as though it was the most natural thing in the world.

She marveled at Jorge's abs, running her finger up his torso to his chin, and kissed him again.

Jorge had never seen a woman so beautiful. Anita's light skin shone flawless in the dim light filtering through the window. He was aroused by the sight of her ample breasts and tiny waist above her panties, which couldn't have had enough material to serve as a decent eye patch. Together they slid up the bed and pulled the light bedspread and sheet over themselves, and nestled spoon-style on their left sides, Jorge behind her.

Jorge remembered a piece of movie history and, as he wrapped his arms around her, said, "Pardon me if I get an erection, and please forgive me if I don't."

Anita laughed out loud, reaching behind her and pulling Jorge closer to her. "You're funny. You are a funny, funny man!"

In moments they were both sound asleep. Hours later, with the sun shining in the bedroom window and muffled sounds coming from the street, they made love, slowly and confidently, with great trust in one another.

CHAPTER TWELVE

When they awoke in the morning, wrapped in tangled sheets, they smiled and talked quietly about themselves, getting to know each other better. Anita recognized that she and Jorge had taken a significant step in their relationship, and as they became more comfortable with each other, each imagined a future together, at least a short-term one, and the complications that came with it, given their divergent backgrounds. Jorge tried to explain what it was like to grow up in a strange country as an immigrant. Anita listened to his story and compared it to her conservative Jewish upbringing. They joked about how their parents were going to have difficulty accepting their children's choices.

"Why don't we just keep this our little secret for a while?" Anita suggested.

Jorge thought about that idea. "I'm not sure we can get away with that for very long," he concluded.

"How so?"

"First, my family is very close, and my brothers already know your name. The longer I refrain from talking about you, the bigger the problem will be when I do introduce you to my mom and dad. Second, you have been out all night, and that won't go unnoticed by your parents I suspect, especially if it occurs more often, which I certainly hope it does."

Anita smiled at him and stroked his cheek, the motion of her arm exposing her left breast, and Jorge felt his male urges kicking in. Anita noticed his reaction and moved closer, and they embraced again, passions stirring.

"What else?" she asked, their faces now close.

"For starters, it's my mom's birthday next month, and I'll have to invite you to meet my family. It's a big deal for us, and you have to be a part of it if we are dating."

She kissed him again and asked, "Is that what we're doing? Dating?"

"Well, it's been a hell of a second date. I would like to think it's going to continue, so eventually I suppose, we will have to bring our families in on it, don't you think?"

The reality of family quelled their excitement for the moment, and they realized they were hungry when Jorge's stomach began to rumble.

"Maybe we should get something to eat," Anita suggested. "We've got plenty of time for this later." She smiled at him.

Jorge agreed and the two of them dressed quickly, taking turns in the small bathroom to refresh themselves, and walked the few blocks to Ocean Drive where they ordered omelets at the News Café, a popular people-watching spot across from the sands of South Beach. Anita called her office and told them she would not be in today, texted her mother that she would be home in the evening, and worked out a plan for what she and Jorge would do next.

Jorge volunteered that completing his analysis of the work papers was not a priority and suggested that the clock was ticking to locate Schaeffer before he left the country. They agreed that they should pursue the contact phone number as soon as they got back to the apartment and see if that lead would produce something useful.

Back at the dining table, Jorge looked nervously at his cell phone where he had already punched in the numbers they had taken from

Schaeffer's laptop's directory. Glancing at Anita for approval, he hit CALL, and the system started ringing after a short delay. Jorge activated the speaker so they could both listen.

After a few rings a man answered in Spanish, *"Hola."*

Jorge was a little taken aback, but he replied in his native tongue, explaining that he had been given this number by Mr. Adam Schaeffer as a contact where he could be reached, a story that he and Anita had agreed upon in advance. Jorge asked the person on the other end if he would be able to put him in touch with Mr. Schaeffer, that he had valuable information Schaeffer would need in his travels. There was a long hesitation, and then the voice informed Jorge that he didn't know a Mr. Schaeffer, asking him what the call was in reference to. Jorge explained again that he had information regarding Mr. Schaeffer's travel plans that would be important to him and that he needed to reach him. Again, he was told he didn't know anyone named Schaeffer. Jorge was insistent, asking if anyone else in the office would be familiar with Schaeffer, going out on a limb that the person he had called was not acting alone, but part of an organization.

The voice repeated in Spanish, speaking firmly, "I told you, we don't know any Mr. Schaeffer, but I'll ask around, and if something turns up, I'll call you back. Is this your number showing on my phone?"

"Si," Jorge replied.

"What is your name, so I know who I'm talking to?" the voice asked.

Jorge was nonplussed, and before he could think of an alternative, he blurted out his real name, Jorge Gonzalez. The phone went dead. Jorge and Anita just looked at one another, unsure how to feel about the call.

Adam Schaeffer

CHAPTER THIRTEEN

Time passed painfully slowly for Adam Schaeffer. Since his check-in at Red Roof Inn a few nights earlier following his Atlantic adventure, he had been concerned about the number of transients moving about the rundown motel. His main concern was to avoid being recognized or getting into a situation where he would have to produce some kind of identification, since he hadn't any. He spent his days lounging around the foul-smelling pool and walking the short distance to the fast-food diner when he was hungry. The waitresses there were already treating him like a regular, and the people he did come across seemed to accept him as one of the unfortunate homeless that frequented the area. For the first few days he did his best to avoid going outside at all, fearing that he might be recognized from the TV coverage that was prominent after his mysterious disappearance.

His missing aircraft was old news now and not receiving coverage. Schaeffer was increasingly concerned about the old man who held down the fort in the motel office, because he seemed to regard Schaeffer strangely. Schaeffer knew he had nothing better to do than watch the cable television in the office all night, and he feared he might have been recognized. *Best to relocate,* he decided.

First things first, he took the downtown bus east on State Road 84 to a business area, and armed with a pocket full of bills, he searched out a mini-mart where he could purchase a prepaid cell phone that would not be traceable to him. He was also able to pick up a pair of flip-flops, so he wouldn't have to run around barefoot, having decided not to wear the tennis shoes he had found near the Dumpster. They had given him blisters. At the first opportunity, after he had figured out a source of transportation, he would augment his wardrobe with a visit to Kmart. For the time being, he would have to make do with what he swam in the other night and his change of clothes.

Armed with the ability to communicate, he checked out rentals in a more suitable area for hiding out, east of I-95, and called a few he identified in the *Sun-Sentinel* until he found an owner who would take cash for a month-to-month located just east of State Road 84, near the Lauderdale Marine Center. There were lots of transient motor yacht crews in the area, so another stranger wouldn't attract too much attention, he figured.

Most of Schaeffer's thought process since the crash was occupied with the obvious: How was he going to get out of the country before his identity could be discovered? Every day he spent in the States exposed him to the risk that someone would recognize him, or worse, that he might be detained by some random authority and need to produce identification. He could try to steal somebody's wallet, but that posed its own set of complications, and even if he was successful, who knew what kind of history that person might be trying to conceal. Regardless, he still needed a reliable passport as a first priority, and he only knew of one source where he could get that.

While he was still at the Red Roof Inn he stayed up nights weighing the pros and cons of calling the passport pimp he had used last year for a replacement set of ID for the ones he had lost. The price was steep, but he knew he had the cash. His first day after he returned from the muddled attempt to rendezvous with Robbie Wells, he knew he had to dispose of all of his personal effects that could give him away. He burned everything in his wallet that was flammable in the kitchen trashcan behind the motel. He also removed the chips from his defunct iPhone and twisted them to bits. What he couldn't burn, he wrapped in a towel, covered it with the ashes, and dumped it down the sewer drain in the parking lot behind the motel, replacing the heavy metal grate after he satisfied himself that everything had made its way to the bottom of the culvert.

Following dinners at the diner, evenings found him at the bar adjacent to the Red Roof Inn, where he struck up conversations with other derelicts who had made their ways there. His objective was to identify someone with a car he could pay to help him get around. Several of the drunks volunteered to let him use their cars, but Schaeffer couldn't risk that because of the possibility of getting stopped by the police for some inadvertent traffic violation.

Finally, he struck up a conversation with an affable fellow who seemed to have no connection to anybody or anything. Roemer, or *Rabbit,* as he called himself, was intent on finishing his existence trying to convert his government disability checks into vodka, which he liberally applied to his system. He was full of stories of a previous life as a lawyer from the Midwest, who was accustomed to a financially secure upbringing that included prep schools and Ivy League scholarships, until his mind succumbed to drugs and alcohol. This was compounded by PTSD, a carryover from his time in Vietnam, which left him unable to make decisions for himself. An irascible sort, his family could not put up with his quirkiness and eventually let him lead the life he seemed to prefer, independent but irretrievably lost.

To Schaeffer he seemed like the perfect chauffeur. He was not stupid, just severely distracted and incoherent. Schaeffer actually found him refreshing to talk to, given his imaginative background, and his inability to remember much from one conversation to the next. Roemer seemed thrilled to have an ally to pal around with, particularly since Schaeffer seemed to take an interest in his ramblings, and he was happy to provide transportation for his new friend, as long as he wasn't required to drive when he was severely incapaci-tated, such as late in the evenings. During the day, Roemer seemed to pace himself with a modicum of control.

The next morning, they began their business relationship with a few simple trips to Kmart and a grocery store, so that Schaeffer could finally swap out better garb for his foul-smelling travel clothes. Reestablished with some living essentials, toothbrush, soap, and kitchen essentials stuffed in a ditty bag, Schaeffer convinced Rabbit to drop him about a block from his new digs off of Fifteenth Ave-nue. Schaeffer did not want anyone to know where he was staying, just in case something went wrong for his transportation source. Roemer only knew Schaeffer as Andre, the name he had given him, the same name he used on the rental apartment application, Andre Shorey, taken from his alias in Europe when he set up his invest-ment accounts.

"Hey, Andre!" Roemer shouted out the passenger-side window of his Malibu. "Are you sure you want me to just let you off here?"

"Yeah, I'm sure," Schaeffer said flippantly.

"Then how will I know when you need a ride?"

Schaeffer perked up. *Maybe this guy has more going on than I originally thought,* he said to himself. "Good point." He hopped back in the car and threw his duffle in the backseat. "Make a U-turn at the light here at Fifteenth, and head east to the Seven-Eleven just past Fourth Avenue."

Roemer didn't question the instructions and pulled into the parking lot at the convenience store as instructed. Schaeffer took this as a good sign. Inside he bought Rabbit a prepaid cell phone simi-lar to the one he had purchased there the day before. Roemer was delighted to have a cell phone. "I've never had one of these before. This is a first."

Schaeffer gave him the ground rules. "First, you are to use this phone only to talk to me. Got it?"

"Yeah."

"Second, you cannot tell anyone where you got it. When I'm finished with my business here in a few days, you can keep it and do anything you want with the time left on it. Okay? Do we have a deal?"

Roemer was overjoyed. It was a flip phone, just like the ones he had seen on TV, and he had always wanted one, even though he didn't have anyone to call, nor to the best of his knowledge was anyone trying to call him. This was turning into a good day for him. First, he meets a nice guy in a bar who agrees to pay him a hundred dollars a day to drive him around, and then the guy buys him a cell phone.

Schaeffer continued, "Now drive me back to where we were and let me off at the bus stop shelter. I will call you on the cell when I need to go somewhere."

At the bus stop Schaeffer got out, grabbed his bag out of the back, and leaned in the passenger window with a final instruction. "When I need you, unless I tell you otherwise, plan to pick me up right here at the bus shelter. You got that?"

"Yeah, I'll pick you up right here when you call."

"Okay, and remember, you keep our little arrangement just between ourselves." Schaeffer shook his index finger at Roemer for added emphasis.

Rabbit nodded his assent and pulled out onto State Road 84, after his new buddy turned his back and started walking away. Rabbit considered following him, just out of curiosity, but decided against it. The man had made himself very clear—he didn't want anyone to know where he was staying. Rabbit was loyal, if nothing else. He headed back to the lounge at the Red Roof Inn, thinking that if he flashed his new one-hundred-dollar bill around, he might just get lucky.

Schaeffer walked the three blocks to his new apartment, thinking he would see how things worked out with his new accomplice. As he gained confidence in Roemer, he might consider doorstep service. For now he was cautious. His prime consideration was finding an alternative source for a passport or risk going back to his office to get the contact information for the pimp he had used before. He knew his most precious asset was everybody's belief that he was dead. Nobody looks for a dead man, and that was his best protection.

On the other hand, just making contact with a new source, and he had no idea what or who that would be, could expose him just as easily as an inadvertent slipup by revisiting his office and his laptop containing the only record he had to find the mysterious supplier of the passport he had lost in the struggle with Robbie. The thought of the bloody murder reminded him of the vacant stare in Robbie's eyes as his weighted corpse descended slowly into the depths of the Gulf Stream just over a week ago. Still, he felt no emotion about the life he had taken.

At his new digs, Schaeffer took a few minutes to set up shop, putting his new purchases in the dresser furnished in his apartment, toiletries in the bathroom, and orange juice and coffee in the kitchen. He opened one bottle from the six-pack of Corona for himself and put the rest in the barely cool refrigerator. Next he flipped on the ancient cathode ray tube television to see if there was anything going on in the news he should have an interest in. The picture was a little blurry, but good enough for his needs. He was tired from the trials of the last few days, and before long, he nodded off to sleep. Schaeffer awoke in the early evening; the sun had already set, and he felt refreshed.

He jumped in the shower to rinse off, but found he was giving himself a good scrubbing, as though to cleanse himself of what he had done recently. He considered shaving, as the stubble on his chin and neck was beginning to bother him, particularly when he was working up a sweat in the humidity, but he decided instead that the anonymity was worth the inconvenience. Feeling confident, he put on a fresh pair of khakis from the small wardrobe he purchased that afternoon, donned a polo shirt, and slipped on his new tennis shoes. His confidence grew, and with it the decision to pursue a new passport from his original source felt like the better way to go, all things considered. He looked at his Rolex Mariner and saw that it was only eight o'clock. Schaeffer felt like a good meal, so he dialed the burner phone he had purchased for Rabbit Roemer earlier in the day and waited for him to pick up.

"Hel-Hello?" Roemer answered with some hesitation. He had never received a cell phone call before, and the process left him feeling confused.

"Rabbit, can you meet me at the bus stop in fifteen minutes? I need a ride to dinner, and you're welcome to join me if you want. My treat!"

Nothing could have pleased Roemer more. The bar at the Red Roof Inn was quiet on a week night, and he had had no stimulation since he had dropped off his mysterious benefactor earlier in the day. "I'll be right there."

He slipped off the high stool and headed for his car in the parking lot. Twenty minutes later, the pair was traveling east on State Road 84. Schaeffer was thinking Italian and considered Runway 84 just down the road, until it occurred to him that he could likely run into someone who knew him there, and opted instead for Lester's Diner, a little further east. No one he knew was likely to eat there. They took a booth in the rear where Schaeffer could put his back to the rest of the diners and still keep a lookout for trouble in the mirror behind Roemer's head.

They each ordered a burger and fries. About halfway through the meal, Schaeffer asked Roemer for a favor.

"Anything," the man replied, wiping his mouth with his shirtsleeve.

"After we eat I want you to drive me by someplace. I just want to check it out. Then we can go back to your haunt and have a beer; then you take me back to the bus stop. Okay?"

"Whatever you say, boss. You keep paying the bills, and what we do is your call."

They smiled at each other, acknowledging the mutual understanding. Schaeffer's new friend did not seem familiar with Fort Lauderdale, so he had to give detailed instructions on how to get where he wanted. It wasn't difficult. From the restaurant, they went east to Andrews Avenue and turned left to go north.

"Just stay on Andrews until I tell you to slow down."

"Okay, boss."

Surprisingly, Roemer seemed okay to drive, showing no sign of impairment from his afternoon at the bar. Schaeffer was comfortable enough to slide down in his seat to avoid detection, lest they pass someone who could identify him, something that was more problematic the closer they got to his old office. After they passed Commercial Boulevard, his senses went on high alert. He kept a close eye on the buildings on his right.

"Go really slow," Schaeffer said as the coral stone building of Pension Strategy Partners came into view. He could see that the second-floor lights were on, and as they passed the hedge at the edge of the parking lot, two cars occupied spaces next to the building. Roemer had slowed almost to a crawl. "Not this slow!" Schaeffer hissed.

Roemer picked it up a little bit. As they passed the front of the building, the police barrier tape was evident as was the NO ENTRY sign at the parking-lot entrance, even in the dim lighting from the streetlights. This raised a new level of concern in his mind. The barrier tape, also evident on the outside stairwell up the side entrance, indicated an ongoing investigation, and Schaeffer realized for the first time that the authorities were probably on to his shenanigans. *They might not be looking for a dead person, but they're still looking to unravel what was going on,* he thought to himself.

"Rabbit, go to the end at Cypress Creek and make a U-turn, and drive by here again on your way back." Schaeffer slid as low in his seat as he could and still observe everything going on around the building. He could not see anyone inside. He knew now that he would have to wait until there was no sign of activity before it would be safe to return and get the contact information he needed.

After their little recon, Roemer and Schaeffer went back to the lounge at the Red Roof Inn and had a couple beers. Schaeffer probed his driver's interest in the visit, but all he could get out of him was a grin and thankfulness for the free meal and compensation. Roemer just seemed to accept at face value anything that was put in front of him. Schaeffer was comfortable that he could rely on his simple-minded new friend, and that unlike Robbie Wells, he was not looking for an angle or leverage to take advantage.

It occurred to Schaeffer that he wasn't going to be leaving the country any time soon. He figured it would be a week before it would be safe to sneak into his office, and then from past experience, he knew that the passport source would take weeks to produce anything reliable. Since he didn't have any connection to the outside world, he thought it best if he prepare to educate himself as best he could, and settle in for a while, hiding out as one of South Florida's lost souls.

With increasing trust, Schaeffer empowered Rabbit with some additional chores. He gave him a couple thousand in one-hundred-dollar bills and asked him to go to the Apple store in the Galleria mall on Sunrise just north of downtown. While he waited in the car, Roemer was instructed to buy an Apple computer with standard software. He became very nervous when Rabbit didn't return for over two hours. About ready to leave the anonymity of the parking garage, he was relieved to see him making his way down the line of parked cars with a huge shopping bag bearing the Apple logo.

"What took you so long?" a frustrated Schaeffer inquired.

"That store is so big, and they have so much to choose from. It

175

took forever for me to decide what you wanted. First I had to get someone to help me, and they told me I had to make an appointment. When I told them I wanted to buy a computer, they agreed to help, but they weren't too friendly. Damn! Then they had all these options and questions I didn't know the answers to."

"But you got it?"

"Yeah, I got it after I told them what you said I should. You know . . . that I didn't know anything about computers; it was for my grandson who knew all about them." He put the bag in the backseat and slipped behind the wheel.

"Where's my change?" Schaeffer held out his hand. Roemer rummaged around in his pocket and produced a twenty-dollar bill and some coins. "That's all?" he asked, shocked.

"That's all I got. The receipt's in the bag; check for yourself. I didn't know this stuff was so complicated. By the time you add the junk they said my grandson would have wanted, and the warranties and other stuff, it used up almost the whole two thousand. It's what you wanted, right?" He looked at his "boss" like a puppy dog.

Schaeffer just moaned, knowing that it was probably what he should have suspected. His new friend wasn't the sharpest knife in the drawer. "You did fine, Rabbit. Now let's go home. Drop me at the bus stop, and you can go back to the lounge. I'll call you if I need you again tonight."

———

Schaeffer spent the next week surfing the net. Fortunately, his building had Wi-Fi; his landlord in the efficiency apartment on the ground floor made it available for an additional ten bucks a month. He seriously doubted that the owner of the building saw much of the extras he was being charged, particularly since he paid all cash, and the manager looked a little slimy for his taste.

A search of current market activity and events clued him in on the sudden closure of Pension Strategy Partners' investment banking operations. He was a little relieved to learn that the action was taken for the firm's failure to maintain required capital balances, although he was at a loss to understand why this should be an issue. Perhaps he had not been found out, but surely it was only a matter of time.

Schaeffer used his prepaid cell phone to call "Andre Shorey's" attorney and investment advisor in Liechtenstein to see if any inquiries had been made regarding his accounts through Euro Capital, GmbH. Again he was relieved to find out that none had been. His lawyer asked if there was any difficulty at Mr. Shorey's end, as he had been expected earlier in the week. Schaeffer, as Shorey, explained that he had been delayed, but that he fully expected to be in Switzerland by the end of the month. The lawyer went on to suggest that Mr. Shorey might want to consider closing out the credit default swap sales he had transferred to his account since there was a growing concern about the condition of the mortgage market in the United States, and the values of CDOs—collateralized debt obligations— were starting to fall. Schaeffer advised that he would watch the market and advise of any action to be taken when he got to Europe.

Further investigation of the mortgage markets confirmed what he was seeing on his TV. All the markets were in disarray. The Dow had continued its decline from earlier in the year, and now, just as Schaeffer had put his plan to leave the country in place, the Fed had taken over Fannie Mae and Freddie Mac, Lehman Brothers had been allowed to go bankrupt, and the insurance underpinnings of the mortgage markets, such as AIG, were at the abyss economically.

For the most part Schaeffer was unaffected by these market collapses. When he transferred his side of the straddles he had purchased to the Euro Capital account, the investments only remained there through the end of the month, when they were swept automatically to the primary investment account managed by his lawyer and investment team in Zurich. Then the investments were liquidated and reinvested in more conventional short-term securities. His only exposure was for the limited investments that had been made since the beginning of the month. The irony was not lost on him that his straddles in the CDOs he had made in recent months might now be working to the advantage of the pension funds where he had placed the purchases of interest rate swaps.

The following Wednesday, Schaeffer decided he could not wait any longer. He called Rabbit in the morning and requested a late-night ride. "Can you keep it together until midnight?" he asked, worrying about his driver's consumption of alcohol. "Why don't you go to a movie or something? I need you to be in good working order. We can get a late-night snack and some coffee at Lester's, and then I want to go back to that place on Andrews Avenue to look around."

Roemer said he was okay with that, and they made arrangements to meet at the bus stop on State Road 84 at midnight.

When Roemer showed up, he did not look like he had been to the movies, as Schaeffer had recommended, but he wasn't completely wasted either. To be on the safe side, Schaeffer insisted they make a pro-longed stop at Lester's Diner to get some food and coffee in his friend. They took their time talking about Rabbit's imaginative past, which now included two years at Princeton, a stretch in the army, and completion of college at Northwestern in the mid-1980s. When Schaeffer listened to these stories, he just rolled his eyes, although he had to concede that Rabbit was not stupid, just not quite right in the head.

A little after two in the morning, Schaeffer felt it was safe to head to his old office. He thought surely that everyone would be gone by this hour, and he was right; the building was dark except for a pale glow from the interior night-lights. He instructed Roemer to park in the garage around back where his car would be concealed in the shadows and told him to wait with the lights off and not open any doors until he got back. He said he would not be long. The plan was relatively straightforward. Schaeffer planned to enter through the second-floor employee entrance. He assumed his former passcode would still deactivate the security system, actually counting on it, since he had no other method of entry short of breaking in, and that's the last thing he would want to do.

He took the outside staircase, assuming the front gate would be locked, and punched in his access code on the magnetic door panel. He was relieved when he heard the audible click of its release, and he tugged the heavy door open and entered the dimly lit back hallway. He didn't want to attract attention by turning on the office lights, so he followed the glow of the emergency lighting for the exits to the grand staircase. On the executive level, he was comfortable enough with his surroundings to find his way to his office and his laptop, which was on his credenza, where he had left it. The internal lighting was bright when he opened the lid, and there was almost a full charge on the battery.

Quickly he opened up the address book and typed in "passport." The card opened to an account named "Passport Contact," and he copied the number in his burner phone for later reference. He considered deleting the account but decided that it would look more suspicious than leaving it there, giving it too much significance. *If someone investigates that far, I'll be long gone,* he assured himself. He closed the laptop and retraced his steps, resetting the security system, and left the building by the same second-floor entrance he had just entered, hearing the magnetic click as the door swung fully shut. A heavy tug on the door handle confirmed the building was again fully locked and secure.

Roemer and Schaeffer rode back to the bus stop in silence. When they got there Schaeffer directed Rabbit to his apartment around the corner, feeling confident that his new friend was proving pretty reliable. "I was wondering where you were actually living," Roemer mused out loud.

Schaeffer acknowledged him with a friendly slap on the back. "Just between us, right buddy?" Schaeffer confirmed the new confidence he was giving. "You can pick me up here from now on, okay?"

Rabbit felt elated. This was the first relationship of importance he had enjoyed since he bailed on his family years ago. He felt needed and his efforts welcomed and appreciated by this strange guy who seemed to have cash money whenever he needed any. A sense of loyalty developed within him for the man who did not treat him like a wacko. He hoped he would have more opportunities to express that loyalty as time ran on.

<hr/>

Schaeffer waited until mid-morning to call his passport contact. The connection rang and rang, finally going to voicemail with a simple instruction, "You know the routine," followed by a beep. The first time he got this, he hung up, fearing a message could leave a trail back to him. *Better to keep trying until I get someone,* he thought. On his third try, Schaeffer finally got through. The voice had the same Spanish accent he recalled from his call over a year ago. He didn't want to identify himself, so Schaeffer played it the same way he had the first time, explaining he was referred by Joey B, reminding the mysterious voice on the other end that he had used his service once before. He thought it might be corroborative to mention the name the passport was issued in, so he mentioned the passport was issued to a Stephen Anderson. He explained further that he needed a replacement.

"Don't mention any names!" admonished the Latino on the other end. "If you used us before, then you know the drill. Do you need a replacement or a completely new identity?"

"It's not for me; it's for the same friend I called you about last time."

"I'm sure it is; it's always for someone else," came the sarcastic reply. "Do you know if your friend used the other passport, or if it can be connected to any kind of difficulty?"

"Why do you ask?"

The other man's tone sounded impatient. "Why do I ask? Because I need to know. That's why I ask! It's my business to know! Does he need a whole new identity or just a replacement?"

Schaeffer thought about this for a moment. He didn't really need a different identity, and he knew the one he lost in the scuffle in the Gulf Stream worked because he had made a test run with it to the Bahamas and back. "A replacement will be fine, if that's easier, but he will also need the driver's license and Social Security number."

"Good. That makes it easier. You need to get passport photos to me; we can set that up now. Deliver them to the same contact at the News Café at two o'clock Friday. You remember the guy? Bring the ten thousand deposit, and I'll call you at this number when it's ready. The balance will only be five thousand. Replacements are easier than getting originals," the voice added as an afterthought.

Schaeffer didn't want to press it, but he needed to know. "How long will it be this time?"

"It'll take what it takes." Then softening somewhat, the man added, "Not as long as last time, since this person already exists in the Federal database. Figure two weeks, maybe less."

"That's good to hear," Schaeffer responded.

"You'll get a call from me when everything is set. It probably won't come from this number, so be on the lookout; I don't leave voicemail, and I won't call more than twice." The line went dead.

Schaeffer relaxed for the first time in almost two weeks. His shoulders slumped as the tension went out of his body, and he lay back on his bed where he had been sitting. This was doubly good news. He had a path out of the country, and he would not have to wait too long for his passport. Every day he stayed in South Florida risked his being spotted in some random way, which would undo all of his carefully made plans.

Joey Bangoni

CHAPTER FOURTEEN

The view of Lower Manhattan across the Hudson from the Jersey shore was spectacular from the twenty-seventh floor of the New England Commerce Bank, next door to the U.S. Treasury building. One World Trade Center's construction cranes pierced the blue sky defiantly, as if to show the island city that its heart could not be broken by terrorists or anyone else. Joey Bangoni never got tired of his view and wondered why anyone would want an office on the other side with only the stepsister city on the west side of the Hudson to look at, unless of course Wall Street played a role.

Such was not the case with Joey, who had come from the tough streets of Jersey. He was a big guy as a kid, leading him to think of himself as athletic scholarship material and a candidate for a Big Ten football program some thirty-five years ago. Those dreams ended when he tore his ACL during his junior year of high school. The doctors told him the damage was not repairable and that he would never play football again. Fortunately, Joey posted reasonable grades, good enough to get him into Rutgers where he graduated with a bachelor's degree in finance in 1979, just before the economy went haywire after the federal government came up with the brilliant idea that savings and loan institutions should be allowed to go into the real estate development business.

During his college years in New Brunswick, Joey took advantage of his size to make some extra walking-around money acting as an enforcer, providing muscle to Newark-based mobsters who needed assistance collecting debts on local business investments. He was a hard worker and loyal to his employers. This did not go unnoticed by the leadership of the local underground, so when Joey found himself unemployable with his new finance degree, they took him in. Joey was rewarded for his talents, both physical and scholastic, and before long he found himself moving upward in the organization to what most would recognize as management. With an acquired background in construction and accounting, he found his niche in the labor union side of the business where he became a superstar.

Whereas the sedentary life was not conducive to fitness, Joey swapped his reliance on muscle to brains. Huge may have been his success, but it also found his waistline. As he moved higher on the management ladder, he became affectionately known as Joey "Bag of Donuts," instead of his given Bangoni, although not often to his face. In spite of his efforts to stay in shape, his gut hung visibly over his belt, which was cinched tightly at his hips.

Mr. Bangoni was now the chief financial officer of the American League of Labor Unions—ALLU—a spin-off from the breakup of the AFL-CIO in the 1950s. An association-like organization made up of member unions, mostly from the Northeast, ALLU represented them in Congress and provided advisory services and management expertise, especially to those unions that were too small to afford the overhead of top-heavy management structures.

The member unions tended to be hard-lined blue-collar labor, such as dockworkers and longshoremen unions from New York, as well as construction-related unions from New Jersey. The employees comprising these member unions totaled nearly 100,000, so the total amount of pension funds of the whole group under management was staggering. As the chief financial officer, Joey's time was split evenly with state and federal compliance matters and worker pension fund activity. Although each of the union pension funds was segregated, most of the member unions opted for ALLU to oversee the investment advisory services, so that economies of scale could be negotiated with the larger investment banks who had custody of the funds.

Part of Joey's job was to fine-tune the investment advice and negotiate the fees on behalf of the group. It was in this capacity that Joey had engaged the services of a boutique advisory firm in Fort Lauderdale, Pension Strategy Partners. He had been impressed with a young former Goldman Sachs partner named Adam Schaeffer, whom he had met at a fixed-income investment symposium in Miami. Schaeffer had gone out on his own with two other investment bankers to specialize in reducing the volatility of pension funds primarily invested in bonds. Schaeffer explained that his firm could cushion the peaks and valleys in the bond market by investing in certain hedges and futures. If the pension fund would subordinate to the investment strategy, the process did not even require a huge separate investment by the fund, which eliminated a mountain of paperwork and authorization by the regular custodians.

Although Pension Strategy Partners had clients from all over the United States, the ALLU members as a group were far and away the investment banking firm's biggest client. Over the last decade, Joey's union pensions had fared well in the arrangement. They hadn't made or lost money of any significance, but that was the idea anyway. The hedges provided relief for dips in the market values of the primary investment bonds, caused by increasing interest rates, in exchange for losses when decreasing interest rates caused the bonds to value at a premium. As advertised, the overall portfolios stayed relatively flat as the market went through its inevitable cycles, which was the objective.

On Thursday, Joey parked his Escalade in the third level of the Commerce Bank parking garage and took the elevator to the twenty-seventh floor. ALLU's offices used the whole floor plate, so the lift opened directly into the reception area.

Sheila, the young ebony-skinned receptionist, smiled at him as he walked to the left of her console to the executive office doors. "Good morning, Mr. Bangoni," she said in a singsong voice.

"Good morning, Sheila. Are you set for an exciting weekend?" Joey replied, not really interested but engaging when he needed to be. He felt he got good mileage from the small things, and this girl may very well have gone to his same high school. He valued that she had enough interest in herself to apply for and take a job in the corporate world. Sheila in turn appreciated that senior management took notice of her at all.

Joey walked the executive corridor to his corner office at the end of the hallway. His secretary, Karen, handed him the day's *Wall Street Journal,* Thursday, September 25, 2008. He surveyed the highlights, noting the lead article to the effect that Congress had reached agreement to bail out the financial system from the lingering effects of the subprime mortgage crisis. *Not surprising,* he thought. The rest of the world news paled in importance, including attempts to prevent some senator named Obama and John McCain from Arizona from getting on the ballot in Texas and China's third successful launch of manned spacecraft.

The rest of his morning was taken up with union conference calls during which he did his best to reassure the leadership that barring a total meltdown of the financial system, the assets of the member pension funds were all conservatively invested in high-quality, fixed-income securities. Moreover, he added that most funds took advantage of hedges against sudden volatility in the bond markets as an added precaution. It was an easy sell, since the uncertainty of the markets was driving money to fixed-income quality, forcing upward pressure on those investments. Much of the rest of the day was taken up with individual calls to the financial officers of the pension funds who wanted to hear the "inside story," thinking there was more to tell than what was on the conference calls.

In the late afternoon, as the fall sun neared the horizon, the brilliance of the reflection from the glass towers of Wall Street became a distraction to Joey's work, and he pushed the button by his knee under his desk to close the modesty blinds on his east wall. He didn't notice the outside line flashing on his phone until the speaker piped up with Karen's voice informing him that he had a call on line one. Before Karen could explain, Joey interrupted, "Who from?!"

"He didn't say, sir. He just told me he was your travel agent in Miami, and that you'd know what it was regarding. Do you want me to inquire further?"

"No, no, I'll take it," Joey stuttered, suddenly on high alert. He took a moment to reflect on the possibilities prompting this call before pushing the flashing button on his phone. His travel agent in Miami was a euphemism for a source of alternative identities, a need that arose from time to time in his past when he was using his muscle on the streets. The Cuban refugee, known only as Camilo to Joey, had set up shop in a travel agency on Calle Ocho in the heart of Little Havana in Miami, a good cover for his clandestine services. When Joey and his enforcers occasionally made a misstep, one of his team would need a reliable source of new identity, particularly if he needed to leave the country.

Camilo had found a way to create identities that would pass considerable scrutiny by forging them from records of real people who had died young and therefore had birth certificates from which to build a credible history. The selection was given careful consideration, the persons selected having died before they could establish traceable histories of their own, such as driving licenses or employment records. The process was time consuming but infallible. Joey thought back to the last time he had any involvement with Camilo. The dots connected quickly for him, when he realized that he had referred Adam Schaeffer to him almost two years ago, remembering that Schaeffer said he needed an identity for a "friend." Joey knew what that meant, but it wasn't of concern to him at the time, but he did monitor the investment hedges of Pension Strategy Partners for a while thereafter.

Now Joey remembered that Schaeffer had died in a plane crash in the Bahamas or somewhere just a week or so ago. It was not unexpected, given Schaeffer's request, but he revisited the recent investment strategies anyway. The purchase of credit default swaps by Pension Strategy Partners had been an initial concern, but with the mortgage market in collapse, those investments were proving to have been a good idea of late. He pushed the flashing button and put the phone to his ear.

"*Hola,* Camilo. How are you doing? We haven't spoken in some time. What can I do for you?"

"Mr. Bangoni, I am sorry to trouble you, but there have been two occurrences recently that may be of interest to you. I thought I should call and make you aware."

"Thank you for thinking of me. What are they?"

Camilo had Joey's full attention now, and he continued, "You may recall you referred someone to me about a year and a half ago who was in need of our product."

"Yes, I remember."

"And, if you follow our local news, you may be aware that a person whose image is the same as the person for whom we prepared documents has been reported missing, lost in a plane crash, I believe," Camilo explained.

"Yes, I am familiar, and somehow not terribly surprised," Joey added to show he was well informed.

Camilo continued, "Well, I had a very interesting call earlier today from the same individual, at least I think it's the same individual, asking me to prepare replacements for what I gave him before. I'm quite confident it's the same person, but I will be able to confirm it when I see his head shots after he sends them to me. He says he lost the originals."

Joey thought for a moment. "Let me get this straight. So, you think the guy I sent you last year is the same as the guy who supposedly disappeared in his plane, and now he's back looking for a replacement ID?"

"It fits. My guy who met him to collect payment and get photos says it's the same guy we all saw on TV a coupla' weeks ago. His name was Adam Schaeffer. That ring a bell?"

Bangoni was cautious. "I don't want to be connected to his mess, but yes, I do know the man. He was a business associate."

"I understand your concern. There is more you should know."

"What's that?"

"Yesterday I had another call, somebody I don't know, inquiring if I knew the whereabouts of Adam Schaeffer. Said he needed to get in touch with him with important information about his travel plans."

"So, what did you tell him?"

"Whaddaya think? I told him I never heard of the guy. He kept pressing, so I said if I heard anything I would call him back. He gave me his name, Jorge Gonzalez, and then I hung up. Another tidbit, the guy was Cuban. Talked to me in my own language. You want me to do anything?"

Joey was stunned. "Camilo, there are a lot of moving parts here; I need to think about it . . . do a little research, and then maybe I will need to take some action. We have some common interest in this situation. Mr. Schaeffer may be a liability to both of us. I don't want to talk about it anymore. Let me do some thinking, and I'll call you from a different number. Did you tell your client that you would help him out?"

"Of course," Camilo answered. "That's what I get paid for. But I don't want anything coming back on me. If I have a problem here, I need to know about it."

Not completely sure of himself, Joey answered with confidence anyway, "I think we're in the driver's seat. He still needs you, so we have access to him. If there isn't a problem, then you can fix him up, and he'll be on his merry way. If not, we can deal with it. I'll call you in a few days. You know the drill, right?"

"Yeah, sure," Camilo answered, not feeling so confident. "How much time do we have?"

"Unspecified. I told him I'd get back to him. He needs to get me some stuff. We can pick whatever time we want."

"Good. I need a few days to work up a plan and see if there is anything here for me. I'll let you know what I figure out."

Both ended the call without acknowledgment. Joey leaned back in his chair and rotated it so he could look down the Hudson.

Several things occurred to him at the outset. Schaeffer wasn't very good at this disappearance stuff. He had already exposed himself to his passport pimp, so he had left a trail for someone to follow. Also, it would appear that he had already put his plan into effect by faking his own death, but something must have gone wrong for him to need replacement identification. Joey mulled over the possible cause of what Schaeffer was up to, and he could only come to one conclusion. It was money! More importantly, whose money?

Joey had a restless night and got to his office early the next morning. After checking his email, he turned to his desk and rang Karen on the intercom. "Get me Chuck Ford in investments and tell him I need to see him in my office as soon as he can get here."

"Yes, Mr. Bangoni."

Moments later a tall, thin middle-aged man rapped on the door frame of the office. Joey looked up from his *Wall Street Journal* and motioned Ford to the chair in front of his desk. Ford looked across at his boss, his eyes darting around the room and his shoulders tensely hunched. An office summons from "Bag of Donuts" was not something people in the accounting department looked forward to.

Joey sensed his tension, and smiled. "Relax, Chuck. I just want you to look into something for me."

Ford's shoulders relaxed noticeably as the tension drained from him. "Sure, anything, Mr. Bangoni."

"Ten years, Chuck. We've been working together a decade. Would you please call me Joey?"

"Yes, Mr. Bangoni." He sat further back in his chair, but still cautious in his manner.

Joey smiled, thinking Ford was expressing a sense of humor, which he wasn't. "Chuck, you look after the alternative investment strategies our pensions are involved in, don't you?"

"Yes, sir."

"Then you'll be familiar with a small investment firm we use in Fort Lauderdale, right?"

"Yes . . . Joey," Ford said cautiously. "That would be Pension Strategy Partners. They advise us and purchase straddles and hedges for our members' accounts. Some of them are way out there. Why do you ask? Is there a problem?"

"None that I'm aware of. That's why I asked to see you."

"I see."

"Chuck, what I would like you to do for me is review their investment activities for, say, the last two years, and give me an informal report on how they're doing. Nothing official. I just want to get a feel for their performance, you know what I mean?"

"Yes, sir. You know, their purpose isn't really to perform, as it would be for an investment advisor? Their investments are designed to smooth out overall market values for the pension fund portfolios. So, sometimes their results are positive, and sometimes negative, depending on what interest rates are doing." Ford looked proud of himself for having pointed out this distinction.

Joey looked at him as if he were nuts. "Of course I know that, you idiot!"

Ford's shoulders hunched up again.

"But as interest rates rise and fall, the hedges should in turn do the same, so overall, after a period of time, the market values of the hedges should be somewhere near even, don't you think? I want you to see if that's the case."

"Got it," Ford replied sharply. "I'll get right on it . . . have something for you by Monday morning."

"Good. And remember, don't make a big deal out of this. It's not a formal investigation. I just want to get a feel for what's going on." Joey thought he already overplayed his hand, and he did his best to calm it down. If something came up at a later date, he didn't want anyone connecting his previous interest in Pension Strategy Partners and some future event, whatever that might be. He returned his attention to the *Journal,* and when he looked up Ford was gone, fast as a superhero.

Joey was unable to concentrate for the rest of the day. He suspected at some gut level that he was going to hear something interesting on Monday from Mr. Ford. The hedging strategies involved many millions of investment, given the total value of the member pension funds under his direction. There was certainly a lot of room for funny business, especially considering that these investments didn't really have a profit motive. Performance would be hard to track, frankly even often overlooked.

Joey took the afternoon off and tried to put the matter out of his mind while he focused on a round of golf at Liberty National just south of his office. Even the views of the Statue of Liberty and Lower Manhattan could not keep his mind from returning to the issue with Adam Schaeffer and the possibilities of what the man was doing. The little prick was certainly involved in some kind of scam for him to want to abandon what appeared to be a successful life and disappear. The bigger questions were who was he scamming and did this present an opportunity? He would just have to wait until Monday to find out.

———〰———

Chuck Ford was waiting in the reception area when Joey got to the office after an uneventful weekend. A mild temperature afforded Joey two more opportunities to play golf, and he took advantage of them, both with the usual suspects at the club. Not a high-stakes gambler, he kept his losses to around twenty bucks, his pride more damaged than his pocketbook. After he got settled and glanced at his email to see if there was anything important that needed immediate attention, he nodded at Chuck Ford to join him in his office. Ford sat across from Joey's desk with a stack of printouts and worksheets crammed into an expanding file. Joey couldn't help but notice that Ford was beaming.

"So, what did you find out, Chuck? You look like you ate a canary." Ford looked up cautiously as he began to pull the contents out of the folder. "Never mind the detail. Just tell me generally what you found out."

Ford stopped and looked Joey in the eyes. "I almost don't know where to begin, Mr. Bangoni."

"Joey," he reminded him.

"Yes, sir, Joey." Ford still found that difficult, but he did his best. "In a nutshell, I went back to 2005. For the first half of that year, the investment hedges appeared to do what they were supposed to do, that is, countered the market effect of changing interest rates. Then about midyear, the investment strategies correlation to interest rates began changing. Whereas, as you suggested on Friday, the historical ratio of profits and losses was nearly even, they began to shift, slowly at first, and then to nearly one hundred percent losses, regardless of what interest rates were doing. The trend became more noticeable as time moved on."

"That's very interesting, Chuck. Can you give me an estimate of the total losses since, say, the third quarter of 2006?"

"I knew you'd ask me that." Ford began shuffling the papers nervously, trying to find the summary sheet.

"Relax, Chuck. I just want an estimate."

"As you know, we oversee nearly forty union pensions with tens of billions in securities. It would take me considerably more time to review them all, but based on what I have seen, I would guess the losses are north of two hundred million."

Joey's eyes bulged to the size of saucers. "Two hundred million!"

"That's my best guess, Mr. Bangoni." Formality had returned. "Possibly more. There is something notable, though."

"What's that?" Joey asked, not believing anything could shock him further.

"Just recently the credit default swaps that Pension Strategy Partners has been purchasing for us are taking off. With the collapse of the mortgage markets, I believe we could sell our positions back to the investment bankers who sold them to us for quite a profit, nowhere near, of course, what our total losses have been, but something. You know we've been advised by regulators that Pension Strategy Partners has been shut down, so we are in the process of moving all of our member accounts to other brokerage firms. I can look into liquidating those positions, if you like."

Joey thought about this for a moment. "Just keep everything as it is for the time being. Find out if the houses that sold us the swaps are financially sound and able to pay us out if the mortgage market continues its spiral. You know, the government is going to have to bail out AIG if this continues. That should give us some comfort."

"Okay, we'll just proceed as we have been. The mechanics of moving all of these accounts is difficult enough as it is, and our alternative investment bankers are scrutinizing everything we are moving. The individual pension trustees have to sign off on all of this, so it is truly a nightmare logistically. Do you want me to continue my analysis?"

Joey looked concerned. "Yes, continue, but don't make it a priority. Just put me in the ballpark with an estimate; better yet, just let me know if the number changes significantly from two hundred million."

Chuck Ford stuffed his papers back into the folder and made his retreat. As he was going out the door, Bangoni called after him. "Just keep this between us for the time being. I don't want to get anyone's panties all in a bunch right now while there's so much other financial panic going around. Just focus on what you have to do to get these accounts resituated." Joey spun around in his chair and stared at the wall behind his credenza, marshaling his thoughts. *So that's what the little bugger has been up to.*

The picture was clearing up for Bangoni. Schaeffer had been running a scam with his biggest customers, probably straddling investment opportunities, and somehow giving his clients the short end of the stick while taking the profitable side of the straddles for himself. It didn't make any difference how he cooked the books at his end. For sure that money was well hidden offshore by now, which explained why he wanted to get out of the country under an assumed name. Actually, it was kind of brilliant. He faked his own death, so no one would come looking for him. *Who looks for a dead person?*

Something had obviously gone wrong that he needed to replace his new identification. What, exactly, didn't matter. What was important was that he was still in the country, and if he could be found before he left, there was a golden opportunity to recover the money, and since the perpetrator was presumably deceased, no one was accountable. This was perfect! The hard part had already been done. All Joey had to do was get control of the situation, cash in, and maybe tie up a few loose ends. At least one other person was on to Schaeffer, this guy Gonzalez. That was a loose end.

Things were falling into place for Bangoni. He opened the lower drawer on the right side of his desk and pulled out an old flip-style cell phone. He looked up a number from his handwritten Day-Timer and called. As expected, he listened to a recorded message, another phone number in the 305 area code. He dialed it from the burner phone and heard Camilo's voice answer.

Joey identified himself and asked, "Are we okay on this phone?"

Camilo responded, "I am if you are. What's up?"

"Regarding our conversation last week."

Camilo interrupted, "You mean about the missing pilot?"

"Yeah, that one," Joey said sarcastically. What other conversation had they had in the last fifteen months?

"Just want to make sure we are on the same page. What do you want me to do?" Camilo said defensively.

"So, I think I have an opportunity here, but I need to get physical control of this guy Schaeffer, if that's in fact the same guy."

"I can confirm it. I have his passport photos right in front of me. It's the same guy, all right. Only now he looks like shit, unshaven."

Joey continued, "First a question. How do you ordinarily make your deliveries?"

"I use a courier and set up a meet at some public place. Why do you ask?"

"I need you to set up a meet somewhere where I can interrogate Mr. Schaeffer, someplace quiet where we won't be disturbed, if you get my drift. Could we use your travel office?"

"You mean here, at Viajes Mundiales, in Little Havana?"

"Yes, that would be perfect. You have parking in back, as I recall, and a storage room at the rear, right? That would be perfect for what I have in mind."

"Joey, you're asking a lot. You know I never transact my side business at my travel agency. It's the only legitimate operation I have, and I sense that you want to use it for a messy purpose, am I right?"

"Camilo, I fully understand that this might put you in a difficult position. We will take every precaution to ensure that everything goes smoothly. Your place would be perfect. I may need shielded access to your parking, and a place where people won't be asking too many questions. The location must not be intimidating, or the people I need to draw in may become suspicious."

"I don't know, Joey. This could get messy, and as I told you, it's my only legitimate outlet. I need it to stay that way, because it's how I present myself to the community where I live. And besides, the travel business is fun."

"Camilo, this is really important to me. We've been friends a long time. I can make it very worth your while. I mean *very* worth your while," Joey offered.

"Very? What do you mean *very?* How many commas are we talking about?"

Bangoni knew he had him now. It wasn't a question of how, but how much. "I don't have a good enough feel for how much is at stake until I interview Mr. Schaeffer. But if it's what I suspect, there will be enough for a comma, and maybe halfway to a second comma. It all depends."

"You mean half a million dollars? If that's what we're talkin' about, I'm in."

"There's no guarantee, Camilo. I could walk away with nothing. I want you to trust me that I'll do my best to make it very worth your while. You've never known me to be cheap."

"You promise to keep me out of it?"

"All I need for you to do is set up the meet. Tell Schaeffer to meet you at Viajes Mundiales on October eleventh at ten o'clock in the morning; that's a Saturday. You don't even have to be there, other than to let us in, and we'll take it from there. After you have that scheduled with him, call the other guy, I think you said his name is Gonzalez, and tell him that Schaeffer is planning to meet you at your office at ten o'clock to see if we can get him there too. I suspect that if he has figured out what we have figured out, he will make it for sure. That way we can tie up all the loose ends at once. Can you do that?"

"I think we have a deal. I'll make the calls and confirm with you when everything is in place. I'm trusting you with the payoff, Joey. Don't let me down."

Bangoni felt comfortable he had a deal. "I would never do that, *amigo*. If this works out, there will be more than enough money for all of us."

"Joey, one more thing. Do I still get this guy his replacement passport?"

"I don't think he'll be needing it. Wait a minute. It's conceivable we may need to get him out of the country. Yeah, go ahead."

"What I figured."

With the meeting arrangements in place, Bangoni referred to his Day-Timer and selected a local number he had not used in many years. He called on the same burner phone. The answer was a simple, "Yeah?"

"Mario, is that you?" Bangoni asked.

"Who's askin'?" Mario responded with a bored attitude.

"It's Joey B. Remember me?"

Mario's mood lightened considerably. "Bag of Donuts? My God! How are ya, Joey? I haven't talked to you in at least fifteen years. I heard you made it to the big leagues. Why you callin' me?"

"Mario, it's good to hear your voice again. You know, I'm the CFO of the ALLU now. Life's been good to me since you and I ran around beating up people for a living. Listen, something's come up, and I need some help with a job . . . some muscle. Do you think you can still handle throwing your weight around?"

"God, Joey. I don't do much of that anymore, but I still have contacts. What, or who, do you need done?"

"I need someone I can trust, Mario. I'd prefer it be you, but if you want to bring someone else along, that could be okay, provided you can vouch for him. The job is in Florida in about two weeks. I need to sweat some information from a businessman, and maybe make him disappear after I get it. There will be one other person that needs to be dealt with, too."

"You mean wet work. I can still do that, and I have a younger colleague I can bring along to help with the heavy lifting. I know him; he's good. I trained him. What's the job pay?"

"Scale, Mario. It pays scale, although I don't even know what that is anymore. You'll have to tell me."

Mario had a fast answer. "Five a day plus expenses. More if wet work is involved."

"Five hundred a day apiece. That's reasonable." Joey knew that wasn't right, but he said it anyway.

"That's five thousand," Mario interjected with emphasis.

"Wow. I've been out of the game too long. Maybe I should have stayed in it if you can command those rates."

Mario laughed.

"I think you're doin' okay. Give me some details."

Bangoni filled Mario in on the details and made arrangements for them to fly to Miami on different flights and rendezvous at a hotel the night before in Miami Beach. They planned to visit the travel agency on Friday to scope out the territory and make whatever additional arrangements would be required. He suggested they make advance preparations to be armed, although he hoped firearms would not be necessary.

Mario started talking about old times, but Bangoni backed him off. He said they would have plenty of time to revisit the past when they assembled for the job.

201

Jorge Gonzalez

CHAPTER FIFTEEN

Jorge and Anita stared at each other in disbelief. Although she could not follow the specifics of the conversation Jorge just had with the mysterious contact because it was in Spanish, she understood that the dialogue lasted long enough for it to have some significance, and there must have been some connection to the person on the other end because she heard Jorge leave his name.

"What a dumb ass I am!" Jorge finally spoke.

"What did he say, Jorge? You talked over a minute. Why do you think you're a dumb ass?"

Jorge looked at her blankly, and finally said, "He said he didn't know Schaeffer, but I got the feeling he was lying, because he asked me if he could reach me at this number." He held up his cell phone. "And he asked me for my name, and like a dummy, I gave it to him."

"So what?" Anita answered. "The important thing is we made a connection and maybe we'll hear something back."

"But what if he tells Schaeffer I'm looking for him? He'll bolt, and we'll never make contact."

Anita tried to calm him down. "You don't know that. Maybe Schaeffer will want to find out what you know. It might work the other way around. We'll just have to wait and see."

"Maybe."

Anita and Jorge spent the rest of Friday, the last one in September, lounging around his apartment on Euclid Avenue. Infatuated in the early throes of love, the two had a hard time keeping their hands off one another while they sat at Jorge's table poring over the work papers. Anita was helpful in identifying the trades and adjusting entries made the months following them. She even remembered some of the conversations she had with Schaeffer when he explained the various strategies. In particular, she relayed the conversation she had with him about the shift in the type of product he used in his straddles. Although it made no sense to her, Anita explained to Jorge that Schaeffer had decided to accelerate the effectiveness of the leverage of interest rates by switching from conventional interest rate swaps to credit default swaps, which he purchased and sold through a broker who dealt with the bigger investment banks, like Goldman Sachs and J.P. Morgan.

"Why on earth would he do that?" Jorge asked her.

"Well, the way he explained it to me, the mortgage market was booming with the explosion of home and apartment sales putting upward pressure on mortgage interest rates, which had been initiated at below market prices. He told me that rates at renewal of the adjustable ones would skyrocket, having an exaggerated effect on mortgage portfolio values."

Jorge considered that for a moment, then agreed. The acceleration factor would be greater than a value based solely on a cap rate change in the market.

He proved his theory with a quick check on the internet, but something was nagging at the back of his mind. He had already figured out how Schaeffer was making his profit, after Anita explained how he placed house account investments in the customers' accounts as much as thirty days after the original investment was made. With her help he identified the account common to all the straddles, which was Euro Capital, GmbH. He surmised it was owned and controlled by Schaeffer, further explaining why he wanted to disappear. He summarized his conclusion out loud to Anita.

"Okay, so let's review what we know for sure. Your boss was trading both sides of a hedge, waiting to see which way it went, and putting the profitable side in his offshore account, and sticking the side with the loss in one of the firm's pension accounts. We didn't notice it because not all the pensions were Schaeffer's clients, so we didn't see them all together on one book. It took Dennison to see that, because he was looking for something different. He was looking for the effect on capital for the trades taken as a whole, whereas we were just looking in the trading accounts separately, so we didn't see the big picture."

It didn't take a genius to figure he was trying to get out of the country, and that probably had something to do with the mysterious phone number they had called earlier in the morning. *If it were me, I'd be long gone by now. Why risk hanging around?* Jorge thought. "So, our best guess is that while he was trying to get out of the country, something went wrong for him. It doesn't matter exactly what, but it certainly involves his identity and passport. That's why he had to come back to the office. He would never have set all this up, just to expose himself by coming to the office. He hit a snag."

"Makes sense to me. But what could it be?"

"As I said. It's not really important what, just that it happened. I don't think he flew back in his plane. There were too many people looking for him, and where would he hide it?"

"The ocean would be a good place." Anita smiled, proud of herself.

"Right on. And if he ditched it somewhere out there, he would need a way to get back. That's a lot of ocean out there. He probably had to have some help, and a lot of stuff could go wrong. We know he obviously lost something he needed to get out of the country. I doubt he would try to leave from the Bahamas. There would be a record."

Anita agreed, nodding slowly. "I agree, it really doesn't make a difference to us. We just need to know that he's still here and figure out a way to find him. Our only connection is the phone number. We know he went to a lot of trouble and risk to get it, so the contact is valuable. We'll just have to wait. You said the guy you talked to denied knowing him but became more accommodating at the end? Maybe we can find someone who can track the phone if he doesn't call back."

"Doubtful. If Schaeffer is involved in anything shady, which we know he is, that phone won't be registered to anyone." Jorge bit his bottom lip in contemplation. "Something else is bothering me. We know Schaeffer was shortchanging his clients by placing the losing end of the straddles in their accounts, taking the profitable sides of the transactions in his Euro Capital account."

"Right, soooo . . ."

"Then explain to me the rationale behind the purchase and sale of credit default swaps. Schaeffer placed the purchases of them in the pension fund accounts and put the sales in his offshore account." He noticed that Anita looked perplexed and explained further, "The result was consistent with what he had been doing, that is, the pension clients lost money for a couple of months, but now, with the mortgage markets collapsing, the pension funds are making a fortune while the offshore account is losing a fortune, assuming they are still liable for paying off the swaps. Do you think this market mess has caught him unaware, the failures of Lehman Brothers and of his own firm biting him in the ass?"

"He never mentioned any of those concerns to me, ever," Anita said thoughtfully.

Jorge threw his hands up in the air. "Then he really fucked himself! What timing. If the markets hadn't begun a collapse, he might have gotten away with this indefinitely. The losses are insignificant to the pensions, maybe not even noticed, since their effectiveness isn't measured in a traditional sense of profit and loss. It's an interest rate strategy. Unless someone is looking for it specifically, it might never come to light in a boardroom."

Jorge and Anita spent a chunk of the day discussing possible scenarios, but ultimately, they realized that they were likely at a dead end if they didn't hear back from Schaeffer's phone contact. As the sun reached the horizon, the pair stepped out for a quick bite at the Ocean Café in one of South Beach's art deco hotels across from the water. The subject of Jorge's mother came up.

"Do you really want me to attend your mother's birthday celebration?" Anita asked cautiously, knowing the decision would put a lot of pressure on him. Jorge looked up from his menu. She studied his reaction and added, "You know your brothers are going to give you a hard time about me. I like your plan to consider facing this head-on. They would have to be more respectful if I'm there. I'm assuming, of course, that our relationship has progressed beyond just hooking up." She gave Jorge an intense look, suggesting that was the real purpose of the conversation. At the very least, his answer would be a litmus test regarding his true feelings.

For once, the subtlety did not go over Jorge's head. He reached his hands across the table and took a firm grip on her hands. "Your support while my life is crumbling means everything to me." He pleaded with his eyes. "Regardless of what we decide, you know I was attracted to you from the very first. We both know I'm a little shy and frankly considered you way outta my league."

"You bonehead! I've been flirting with you for three years. How can you not have noticed? I practically had to put my number on autodial on your phone. Frankly, if Schaeffer hadn't tried to off himself, we still might not be together."

Jorge smiled inwardly, remembering how awkward he always felt in Anita's presence, never able to work up the courage to ask her out. He always got lost in her beautiful green eyes, her long dark hair, and her outrageously hot figure. Of course he had feared her rejection if he made a move, not to mention the possible consequences of an unwanted workplace advance. For sure he was on an emotional rollercoaster right now. On the one hand, his professional life was in the toilet, something he had been focused on his entire life. His identity, sense of value, and importance to his family were bound to his professional success.

On the other hand, deep in the emotional throes of a burgeoning love, augmented by pheromones raging in his system, Jorge bubbled from within at the joy and excitement Anita brought into his life. As bad as things were going for him professionally, he felt he could slay a dragon with her by his side. The mere fact that she would willingly choose him gave Jorge all the confidence he needed to face the challenges before him. With this newfound strength, he made his decision.

"Anita, you're right. I have to face this sometime soon, and it might as well be now. But you have to prepare yourself for my family's reaction. My brothers will tease you, inappropriately I suspect. My parents will be cordial, but their disappointment will be palpable. It won't be because they are anti-Semitic, just that they didn't contemplate a marriage in the family outside their religion. I don't want your feelings to get hurt."

Anita smiled at Jorge, noting the irony. "Jorge, when the tables are reversed, I suspect you won't get off so lucky. My parents will *not* be cordial after they learn that I am seeing a Catholic boy. My dad and mom will not be able to get their heads around the fact that I may make a commitment outside of their religion. I am already well beyond the age when I should have been bringing grandchildren into the family. So be ready. When it comes to family acceptance, you may well be getting the short end of the stick."

Jorge solemnly nodded his understanding, and then his face brightened. "You know, we could find some amusement in this. We don't have to just sit back and take a lot of abuse. Let's figure a way to have some fun with this."

"What do you mean?"

Jorge thought for a moment. "Well, my brothers don't really care about any of this. It only has value to them to give me a hard time. My parents, while disappointment is an issue, will really be fine with everything in the long run. Your parents, on the other hand, will be genuinely upset, you say."

"Right." Anita nodded her head slowly in agreement, still not knowing where Jorge was going with this.

"What if we made it sound a lot worse than it is, so that by comparison our relationship doesn't seem as offensive?"

"Go on."

"Maybe we should tell them that our relationship is serious, and that if it continues, you are considering converting."

Anita threw her head back in laughter. "Yeah. That's a great idea. I could even tell them I'm going to take some classes, or whatever it is you do, in preparation for my confirmation. That would really set them straight," she added sarcastically.

They had a good mutual laugh for a moment, and then reality set in.

"I guess that's not such a good idea," Jorge said somberly.

"Let's get serious. This is not a joke. It's not funny to plan to make my parents more upset. We need to give this some serious thought. They are my parents, after all." Tension rose in her voice. "Maybe we're getting a little ahead of ourselves here. We have only been seeing each other a couple of days, intimately anyway. Let's not try to plan out a whole future that might not be in the cards."

Jorge tried to lighten the mood a little. "You're right. Will you visit me when I'm in prison?"

"Now you're being childish."

Time for a reset, Jorge decided silently. "First things first. Will you come with me to my mother's birthday party a week from this coming Wednesday? It's in the evening. I would love to introduce you to my family. We'll take it from there. What are you going to tell your parents about where you have been the last couple of days?"

"I'll tell them I've been with you and see what their reaction is. I think I should go home tonight. Maybe we can get together over the weekend. You okay with that?"

Jorge felt the tension leave his body. "Of course. Let's order."

They finished dinner around eight-thirty and retrieved Jorge's Beemer from the valet. Anita realized that her car was still at the restaurant in Aventura, and that Jorge would have to drive her up there to pick it up. She did not relish the reception she would get when she got home around ten that night. They kissed passionately in the parking lot when they retrieved Anita's Camry, and Jorge suggested returning to his apartment for another night.

Anita would have liked nothing better. "I would love to, but it would just add complications to what I'm going to tell my parents. It's best I go home tonight. You can dream about me."

The corners of Jorge's mouth curled upward. "Won't be the same . . . Anita?"

"Yes."

"I can't tell you how much your support means to me."

"Just the support?" Anita lifted an eyebrow, and Jorge melted as he took in her beauty, backlit by the parking lot lamps.

"Everything. Just everything! I could jump over the moon."

Anita moistened her lips and gave him a final peck as she slid behind the wheel of her car. Jorge felt empty as he watched her drive off. He slowly climbed in his BMW and headed toward I-95. He didn't know how he was going to make it through the night, and he had only been with her twenty-four hours.

Jorge spent the majority of his time on Saturday reviewing his working papers, hoping he might be able to determine the magnitude of the theft. He was comfortable that he knew how, and now he wanted to figure out how much. Mostly he was trying to fill his time doing anything constructive, but his mind kept returning to thoughts of Anita. Conservative by nature, he was not used to experiencing emotions so overpowering and out of control. When he thought about his dinner conversation with her, he realized the topic of their families was very advanced considering their intimacy was only a couple days old. He felt comfortable that he could trust her, as she could him, and that was added reassurance they had a relationship that could be built upon.

His bubbly anticipation at the possibility of seeing her that evening was burst when she called to say it would be best for her to stay home Saturday evening. She explained that she planned dinner with her parents and had decided to begin exploring the subject that she had met someone. Anita promised to give him a full report in the morning, then added, "You may want to call your family and give them a heads-up if you're *really* thinking of including me at your mom's birthday celebration."

Jorge froze at the prospect of facing his family. The cold reality that he had to face the music about his new romance stiffened his backside like a bucket of ice water. Tentatively, he picked up his cell phone and called his mom to ask if he could stop by, explaining that he had something he wanted to tell her. He needed to alleviate her concerns by saying it was good news but had nothing to do with work. Adriana said she would be happy to see her pride and joy that evening. She suggested that maybe he could get his brothers to join them for dinner, too.

Actually, Jorge thought that would be a good idea. His brothers might soften his parents' reactions when they started to needle him about his new girlfriend, which they most certainly would do, causing his parents to come to his rescue. He got ahold of Valeriano on the first ring and made his request of his brothers. When he explained the reason for the dinner, Val was only too happy to volunteer his and Carlos's participation. Jorge could hear his brother shout over the noisy shop sounds in the background to Carlos in Spanish, "Hey, Carlo! Our baby brother is going to tell Mama and Papa all about *ah-nee-taah* tonight at dinner. We should go, yes?"

Overhearing his older brother, Jorge pleaded in their native tongue, "Come on, Val. I'm looking for a little support here. Please don't you guys give me a hard time in front of Mom and Dad. Don't make this worse, please."

"Oh, you can count on us, little brother. I don't think we will have to give you a hard time," Valeriano laughed. "You're going to do that all by yourself. Just think, Mama's pride and joy dating a nice Jewish girl from Miami. The family will be so proud," Val teased sarcastically.

That night at dinner Jorge was under so much stress that he didn't even notice that the evening was going rather smoothly. Every time his mother reminded him that he had mentioned he had something to say, he managed to pivot the conversation in another direction. Adriana had gone to a lot of trouble to make a nice chicken casserole with fresh vegetables and plantains, but after fifteen minutes of Jorge's diversionary flattery, she had had enough.

Santiago, ever the quiet one, sat amused as he watched his youngest son keep avoiding the subject he had brought the family together for, and he couldn't help noticing how his older boys kept rolling their eyes at each other, revealing they shared a secret of some sort. He sat smiling at the performance, waiting for the imminent outburst. He was rewarded when Adriana finally slammed her palm on the freshly ironed linen tablecloth and directed her attention at Jorge.

"Enough of this nonsense, Jorge! You said you had some news for us. I think you should tell us. What is it?"

The silence hung in the air like a fart. Valeriano and Carlos glanced at each other, getting ready to enjoy the moment.

Jorge squirmed in his seat. "Mama, I have met someone."

Adrianna beamed and said gently, "Jorge, why didn't you just say so? You've met someone, how nice. Tell us about her. Is she from Miami? This must be serious for you to bring it up so specially."

Carlos and Valeriano exchanged nervous glances, and Santiago picked up on it immediately. He leaned forward in his seat from the other end of the table from Adriana, sensing something important was coming. There was a pause, as Adriana looked at each of her family in turn. "What is her name? Have you known her long?" she asked quietly.

The tension in the room was palpable.

Carlos blurted out, "Tell her, brother, and don't mumble the way you told us that day in the car."

Jorge thought of Anita's beautiful green eyes, and he was emboldened, ready to rip off the Band-Aid. "Mama, her name is Anita Berwitz," he said clearly. "I have known her for a few years from work; she works for one of my clients."

"Former clients," Carlos corrected, rubbing salt in the wound. Santiago admonished him with a look, shaking his head slowly.

Jorge continued, "Right, *former* clients. But we have been together only a short while."

The color drained from Adriana's face. "Jorge, don't tell me you're serious about this girl. She's Jewish, isn't she? There would be no place for her in our family."

"Mama, it's early in our relationship. But I can tell you now that my feelings for her are very strong, as are hers for me. If things continue, there will be a place for her in my family, and I am part of your family. I want your blessing to bring her to your birthday party, so you can meet her. You will like her very much."

Adriana was absolutely shocked. Her hands began to shake ever so slightly, but noticeably to Santiago. She reached for the only words she could muster, trying to put off the reality. "It is not possible. My birthday is for family! Your new girlfriend is not part of my family. I forbid it."

Santiago realized that his wife was close to setting immovable boundaries, and he needed to avoid that at all costs. "Quiet, everyone! Let's drop this discussion before we say things that cannot be unsaid. Carlos, Valeriano, stop your smirking. This is not something to joke about. I know you get great satisfaction out of ribbing your brother, but this is not an appropriate time for that." He looked across the table at his panic-stricken wife and tried to reassure her. "Adriana"—he lost himself in her eyes—"this is not the end of the world. Jorge has told you this relationship is new. None of us knows where it will go. In the meantime, I know we have raised a well-adjusted son who is capable of making good decisions. I'm sure that anyone he brings into his family will find a place in our family, because that is the way it is."

For the first time, Adriana let her fear emerge. "I'm not so sure we have done the best job of raising our son. Look at the choices he has made lately. He has lost his job, and maybe more. Now he wants to bring someone to our family who does not believe in Jesus, our savior. I am not in favor of her coming to my birthday party and exposing our shame to others." She folded her arms across her breast and sat defiantly, ramrod straight in her chair.

Jorge was crushed, and he looked at his father for help. Santiago looked at his son with a loving smile and suggested, "Maybe your mother's birthday isn't the right time for this, Jorge. Have you thought of that?"

"Papa," Jorge said with some conviction, "I have already told her, and I will not disrespect her by telling her that 'now isn't a good time.' Have you thought for a minute that maybe this is as difficult for Anita and her parents as it is for Mama?"

Adriana snorted and turned her face to the side, as if not wanting to hear such blasphemy.

Valeriano made an observation. "Jorge, probably it's not a good idea to suggest that her parents would be as upset that she is dating a Catholic boy, but we get your point."

Both of the brothers knew that the opportunity for needling Jorge had passed them by, and Carlos added his two cents. "Mama, things have changed in the world. Val and I see it every day. The Cuban community is spreading itself out. Let's not be so set in our ways. We should at least meet this girl. Val and I just want to see what kind of girl our brother can come up with."

Adriana glanced at them and noted that they were older than Jorge and, to date, hadn't set much of an example, both still unmarried. They ran around all hours of the day and night partying, doing business with Lord knows whom. Val and Carlos retreated back into silence. The meal ended in subdued quiet.

When Jorge left, his father gave him some words of encouragement. "Son, I'll talk to your mother. We'll work something out. You plan on bringing your girl to the birthday party. I hope she's pretty tough."

After Jorge left, the brothers, Santiago, and Adriana spoke for a short while. Adriana was still insistent that she was not open to Anita coming on her special day.

Santiago gave Carlos a two-fingered pop on the top of his head. "You two knew about this. Why didn't you give us a warning? You just sat there gloating."

"Sorry, Papa."

"Do you know this girl? Have you met her?"

Carlos answered, "No to both, Papa. We've just heard him talking to her on the phone, and we teased him about it. We didn't know it was anything serious, but I'll tell you, he lights up when he talks about her."

"Well, he's under enough pressure now, anyway. So help me make this go as smoothly as possible. The gathering may help diffuse the situation. All of the attention won't be on the poor girl."

Valeriano was concerned. "You heard Mama. She said she wouldn't even speak to her if she came. She's painted herself into a corner, and you know how stubborn she can be."

"Yes, but your mama is also a gracious lady. She won't let that happen," Santiago said without conviction.

—⁓—

Jorge called Anita on his BlackBerry when he got home. They compared notes and found they had each come up with similar results. They agreed to meet in the morning and go to the beach. Jorge suggested they meet Sunday midday if they wanted to get the good rays, as the sun was moving further south this late in the year. Anita drove down in her Camry and parked in a space she found on the street. They threw some beach towels and lotion in a canvas bag and walked the few blocks to the ocean. Once lathered and positioned on the sand, surrounded by unlimited circus-like acts common to South Beach, they began discussing their respective conversations with their parents.

Jorge told her about the cool reception he got from his mom. Anita listened patiently but did not appear to get upset. When he finished, she said, "Maybe your dad is right. Maybe we should look for a better time."

Jorge shook his head. "I don't think so. You are more important to me than that, and I won't allow my family to disrespect me, let alone you. I think we should go, unless my father calls me with something outrageous. We just need to give it some time. When Mom meets you, she'll melt, just like I did."

Anita brushed his brow with her fingers, giving him a juicy kiss on the lips.

"What about your parents?" he asked.

"My parents focused more on me than you. My mother actually called me a *shiksa*. My father was hurt, as though I had betrayed him."

"What's a *shiksa?*" Jorge asked innocently.

"It's a Jewish girl who affiliates outside her religion or just a non-Jewish girl or woman in general. Whatever, it's about the worst thing a Jewish mother can say to her daughter. You would be a *shkutz,* the male version. They were very dramatic with a lot of arm waving and shouting. I'll probably have to endure some more. It's an ethnic thing, and part of the healing process for them."

"Looks to me like we're in the same place. My brothers said my mom was more upset that your parents might be upset by the arrangement than she was."

"Mine would be, too, if they knew. I don't think I'll mention that to them. I'll just tell them your family invited me over for a birthday celebration. Maybe they'll be jealous."

They both laughed.

Anita spent the rest of the afternoon at the beach with Jorge, alternating brief dips in the warm ocean. Jorge marveled at Anita's flawless skin, which glowed from the color she was getting from the sun. She was only a shade lighter than Jorge's natural olive color. After the sun neared the horizon, they got a quick bite to eat and walked back to the apartment on Euclid Avenue, where they made love before Anita grabbed her things and headed north toward Hollywood, lamenting over Jorge's pleas to spend the night.

Jorge spent the next two days in a funk. Without anything to do but worry about his future, his mind continued down dark possibilities that might be in store for him. He managed a dinner with Anita on Tuesday night, but she hadn't much time for him during her busy workdays. His brothers volunteered some part-time bookkeeping jobs at their boss's service stations. The work was awkward for Jorge, because he didn't know how to record some of the peculiar transactions involving purchases of aftermarket parts. The sales were easy to record, but when he questioned Val or Carlos about the cost or source of some of the inventory, he was rewarded with a casual, "Don't worry yourself about it."

Jorge tried to explain that the sales records left a trail, and if they didn't record a sale, they were liable for tax evasion. Conversely, if they didn't identify a cost of the product, they were overpaying their taxes. He gave the matter some considerable thought and devised a way to account for the mysterious inventory without disclosing where it came from. Word of his creative abilities spread in the Little Havana community overnight, and he received requests from other businessmen to massage their bookkeeping. It wasn't very remunerative, but it did occupy his time, and that was helpful.

The rest of the week flew by as Jorge continued his efforts to bring creative accounting to Little Havana. In just a matter of days, he had developed quite a reputation for his abilities to think outside the box when it came to reporting some of the underground business activity rampant in the community. He worked up an hourly rate for his services, which supplied him with a reasonable cash flow that week to supplement his dwindling reserves, and would help him keep up with his living expenses, such as rent, as long as he was willing to offer his unique services. A couple of restaurants that were relying on his abilities provided delicious meals on Wednesday and Thursday, for which he was thankful.

On Thursday evening, Jorge designed a conservative but dignified letterhead to give his growing bookkeeping and advisory business a little branding. At the top it identified him as: JORGE GONZALEZ, CPA, and listed his apartment address as his office location. To add a little official prestige, he added in the left margin that he was a member of the Florida and American Institutes of Certified

Public Accountants. He knew that this did not complete all of the requirements to form a new business and that he was probably lacking numerous local operating licenses, but the stationery's purpose was only to serve as a platform to brand himself and send out professional-looking bills for his work. The logo was printed at the top of all of his correspondence and memoranda.

On Friday, when Carlos got his first official statement and accompanying letter, he teased Jorge about his pompous effort to promote himself. "Val and I make a lot more than you do, little brother, and we don't have no stinkin' fancy stationery."

Jorge looked up from the tight office space at the back of the service station, where he did his bookkeeping, and smirked at his brother.

Val came in from the shop wearing his greasy overalls. Overhearing Carlos's remark, he came to Jorge's defense. "Yeah, that's right, Carlos, but on the other hand, we don't want most of our customers to know where we work, either." He took the statement from Carlos's dirty hand and gave it the once-over. "Not bad, Jorge. You look almost like a real business, like that fancy place you used to work for."

Jorge sat back in the old-style colonial desk chair, which slid around on the wood floor unbidden, resulting in peculiar postures for its occupant. He dug his heels in to crawl his way back behind the desk and a sitting position. Carlos and Valeriano both laughed at his struggle, when an idea suddenly jumped into his eldest brother's head.

"Say, Jorge. Mama's birthday isn't until Wednesday. Why don't you bring your new girlfriend down here tonight to meet your brothers, and maybe have dinner down the street at Café Versailles? Your treat."

Jorge was taken aback. "You're kidding. What makes you think I would subject her to you two without the protection of the rest of the family?"

Valeriano obviously thought it was a good idea. He nodded his head in excitement. "Seriously, brother. It would make things better. You would get two of us out of the way, and she would have two more allies on Wednesday when she gets to meet Mama and the whole family."

Jorge thought about it. The idea made sense if Anita was available and if he could keep his brothers in line. "You guys aren't going to give me a hard time, are you?"

Carlos and Val laughed together.

Val volunteered, "We'll be on our best behavior, we promise."

The elder Gonzalezes were overcome with curiosity to see what kind of woman their little brother could have romanced, especially one he would want to bring home to his family. Lord knew, neither of them dated women who were Mama-worthy. Jorge always teased them that the local girls his siblings associated with all wore their underwear on the outside.

Jorge got out his BlackBerry and dialed Anita's cell.

She answered on the third ring. "Hi, babe. I was hoping you would call. Are we going to make plans for tonight? I haven't seen you since Tuesday."

"I miss you, too," Jorge said and then told her what he had in mind.

Anita agreed to meet them at Café Versailles at eight o'clock. He told her how to find it and the best way to get to Little Havana, assuring her the area was safe for her to travel alone.

"What's the dress?" she asked.

"Very casual. There's parking in front, but if it's full you can park at the gas station across the street, just east of the restaurant. The sign says, U Pumpit and Parts, it's where Carlos and Val work. We'll be inside the restaurant holding a table. It gets really busy around that time."

"Okay, great. I'll go home and change and get a toothbrush. See you at eight."

Jorge couldn't resist. "You're being a little presumptuous, aren't you?"

Anita's reply was quick, "Okay, I'll leave it at home, guess I won't be needing it."

Jorge realized his flippant reply wasn't the smartest, and he apologized, "Forgive me. You'd better bring it."

"You're sure your brothers are cool with this, right?"

"Are you kidding? They're about to wet themselves."

"Funny. Eight, then. Bye."

Valeriano and Carlos high-fived each other.

Jorge asked, "The restaurant isn't too touristy, is it?"

Val grinned at Jorge. "No, it's perfect. Has a lot of class and it's historic. We may even see some original revolutionaries."

At six o'clock the night crew arrived and got some direction from Val and Carlos as to the cars that were being serviced. Jorge made a quick run home to clean up while his brothers made their ways to Hialeah to do the same. They agreed to meet at the restaurant at seven-thirty. All three brothers parked at the service station, hoping it would free more space so Anita would have a place to park, although they knew things would be tight at eight o'clock on a Friday night. They walked the block and a half in mild temperatures with a little humidity in the air. They got one of the last tables alongside the great framed windows facing the street. Inside was a little noisy with the crowd. Hard surfaces covered most of the restaurant, intensifying the tableware clatter. The back wall of the restaurant was covered with ornate etched glass populated by statuettes around the perimeter. The ceiling featured acoustic panels framed by fancy millwork, giving the space a classy look, just as Valeriano had described.

They sat at a square table with their backs to the other diners, facing the windows where they would have a good view of the arrivals. A waiter took their orders for Coronas with limes, and they inspected their surroundings, eavesdropping on the conversations around them, while keeping an eye on the parking lot to make sure they didn't miss Anita's arrival. There weren't any parking spaces open that they could see from where they sat. The beers arrived, and Jorge looked at his watch, ten 'til eight. The brothers talked briefly about their mother's birthday, speculating as to how it was going to go.

Val said, "I talked to Dad last night, and he told me nothing much had changed. He was starting to get a little worried, but he told me he couldn't really talk to Mom about it . . . said she'd have to work it out for herself. He felt confident she would."

At eight they ordered another round, as Jorge's brothers watched him rubbernecking around the parking lot and the front door. Carlos and Valeriano enjoyed ogling the more attractive patrons of the restaurant, just short of being obvious enough to get busted. Jorge was focusing his attention outside at the arrivals.

"Whooooieee! Val, check out that girl." Carlos pointed with the long neck of his beer bottle out the window to the cars in the lot.

Just walking up the sidewalk and turning in the lot was a very attractive brunette. She was in a hurry, carrying a medium-sized bag over her shoulder on a strap. The sun was below the horizon, so her figure was highlighted by the parking lot lamps located in the corners of the lot. Her shapely brown legs moved powerfully and purposefully toward the front door. She was wearing sandals and a light-green, mid-waist halter top of some fine, sheer material that highlighted her slim waist and ample breasts. Her dark hair flipped back and forth with her effort, hanging nearly to her shoulders.

"Check out the ta-tas on that one," Carlos added for emphasis.

Jorge looked up just in time to see Anita pull on the glass front door, and he switched his view to the inside as he watched her come through. He jumped up from the table, admonishing his brothers, "You assholes. That's Anita!"

Carlos and Valeriano looked across the dining room dumbfounded, their mouths hung limply open. Utterly speechless, they watched the beautiful young woman make eye contact with their little brother, smile broadly exposing her dimples, and nod an acknowledgment of recognition as she made her way to the table. They watched in awe as Jorge returned her smile and stepped forward to embrace her, adding a peck on her lips when she neared.

Jorge turned to his brothers and smiled proudly, gesturing to the two of them with a wave of his hand. Carlos and Valeriano were too stunned to make it to their feet.

Jorge introduced Anita to them. He pointed to each as he said their names. Anita extended her hand and shook each in turn. Valeriano was the first to recover. Grinning from ear to ear, he slowly made it to his feet. He noted Anita's firm grip on his hand, which she released after a perfunctory pump, switching to Carlos, who had yet to regain his composure. Ever the lady's man, he finally stood and came around the table to give Anita a hug, enjoying the moment of physical contact. He stepped back, holding Anita at arm's length, taking in the whole package.

"We are so excited to meet you finally, Anita," Carlos said.

Valeriano, ever the comedian, added, "Indeed. We are so pleased to see that you are not one of Jorge's imaginary friends. Surely he could not make up someone as beautiful as you." He turned to Jorge. "And as for you, little brother, you are way out of your league!"

Anita and the brothers laughed at Jorge's expense. They took their seats at the table. Holding Anita's chair with an exaggerated flourish, Carlos tried to take command of the scene. There was no doubt who was really in charge. Before Carlos and Valeriano could begin an interrogation, Anita began pumping them with questions of their memories of Cuba and what it was like growing up in a new country.

Carlos summarized the family's ride across the Straits of Florida during the Mariel Boatlift and the adjustment to growing up in Alabama and learning a new language. "It was harder for us because we were a little older than Jorge. It seemed he learned to speak English in about a week. He fit in with his friends at school in no time."

Val took over. "Carlos and I were a little older, as he said, but we also had each other. We were a curiosity for the rednecks in Gadsden, but we did okay. Our parents never felt comfortable until we moved to Miami, where they had some relatives, and most people they knew spoke their language. That seems like a long time ago now."

Jorge felt a little excluded, so he jumped in. "You'll see for yourself at dinner Wednesday night."

His brothers looked at one another with some apprehension. Anita picked up on that from their expressions.

"Relax. I know about the stand your mother has taken," she said.

Carlos and Val slumped in their chairs.

"How do you think your mom is going to handle my being there?" she asked.

The brothers all shrugged. "We have no idea," Val said. "It's not like her to paint herself into a corner like this. Our father thinks she will work things out. She's the spiritual leader in our family, and she's really sweet. That's why we thought it would be a good idea to meet you first, to kind of take the edge off."

"I appreciate that. I can see that you three are really close, even though Jorge tells me that you pick on him all the time," she joked, smiling.

"We do," Carlos admitted. "It's because he gets all the attention. He was always Mama's perfect little boy, and Val and I were the troublemakers. He went to college and works in a fancy office, while we steal hubcaps for a living." Carlos punched Jorge affectionately on the upper arm. "Well, I guess he used to work in a fancy office. Now he's unemployed and helping Cubans cheat on their taxes."

Jorge blanched at the reference. "I'm helping you and your business neighbors stay honest about your bookkeeping for a change," he insisted. "If it weren't for me, you could all be going to jail."

Carlos gave him a dirty look. "We've been doing fine for a long time without your help, little brother. The aftermarket car parts business has been good to us, and we're proud of it."

"What's the aftermarket parts business?" Anita asked, turning to Jorge.

"It's more like the after-hours parts business, hon. You know those cars you see with the spinning hubcaps or the ones at night that are lighted underneath in purple? They supply that stuff," Jorge said with sarcasm. "And—"

"Okay, Mr. BMW," Carlos cut him off, "just remember, we don't set the fashion, we just supply it."

The waiter brought a pitcher of margaritas, breaking the growing tension. Anita could see the abrasive relationship the Gonzalez brothers shared, but she could also see the deep love and respect they had for one another. She lamented the poor person who would try to come between them, but she took comfort in the fact that they seemed to treat her as one of the team. The conversation turned to Adriana, as they discussed her possible reactions to Anita's attendance at the birthday celebration. All they could come up with was a wait-and-see attitude and hope for the best.

As they finished their meal, which consisted mostly of sharing a variety of Cuban dishes for Anita's sake, Val reached across the table to take her hand, looking directly into her eyes. "Anita, just for the record, Carlos and I think you are terrific. I have no earthly idea how Jorge managed to attract the affection of someone as beautiful as you, but we're so happy for him that he did. Don't worry about our mama. Things will work out somehow. She adores him, even in his somewhat embarrassed state right now. If it's in the cards, we will all welcome you into the family, if you'll have us." He released her hand.

The table fell silent for a moment. Anita started to well up with tears as she began to understand that Jorge's family had a lot more depth than showed on the outside. Carlos was a little abrasive, a stereotype of the macho Latino, and Valeriano was a milder version of the same. They both still spoke English with the slightest hint of an accent, which only made them more intriguing, but they were considerate and sensitive to the core, and they shared Jorge's intelligence and sense of commitment to each other. They finished their meal with a small cup of Cuban coffee, a formality Jorge explained. Anita didn't think she would ever get used to it.

Valeriano suggested they share contact information. "So we can find our little brother when he doesn't answer his cell phone," he explained.

They texted the information to one another before they got up from the table. They stood together and, amid hugs, two-cheek kisses, and reverie, bid their farewells until Wednesday. Carlos's hug lasted an inappropriate extra moment, prompting Jorge to admonish him. "Carlos, get your hands off my woman!"

Anita reacted immediately, raising an eyebrow. "So, is that what I am now, *your woman?* Is that how it is?"

"It most certainly is, my dear," Jorge smiled. "You're family now."

Val piped up, "Like I said when we sat down, little brother, you are way out of your league, and you have your hands full."

The four of them laughed as they made their way out of the restaurant. Anita and the Gonzalez brothers walked abreast up the street to retrieve their cars.

Carlos said farewell at Anita's car. "Drive carefully. There are a lot of *locas* out on a Friday night, and you've had a few margaritas."

Anita looked over her shoulder as she bent to get in her car. "Fortunately, I don't have far to go." She gave him a knowing smile.

Standing alongside Valeriano between their two cars, Carlos whispered to his brother, "That's one lucky son of a bitch, our brother."

Val nodded his concurrence, and they exchanged a wink.

Jorge was disappointed that he and Anita couldn't drive to his apartment together. He didn't want to be apart from her for even a second, but there wasn't a good way to deal with the cars.

"What's the best way to get to your place, Jorge?" Anita asked him.

"Just follow me. We'll go north at the first light to the Dolphin Expressway and get on the MacArthur over Biscayne Bay and it dumps you out on Alton, right near my apartment."

Anita had a rough idea what he meant, and she knew she would recognize where she was when she got across the bay. Thirty minutes later, they pulled up to the apartment. There was only one space, so Jorge gave it to her and he parked a few doors down. They met at the front door and waited while Jorge fumbled for his keys, finally unlocking it and stepping into the small foyer. Jorge still had his keys in his hand when Anita wrapped her arms around him and planted a wet, erotic kiss on his lips. They kissed for a moment, and Anita relaxed her grip on his shoulders and put her head in the crook of his neck. He loved the fragrance about her and drank it in, holding her closely.

Anita lifted her head to his ear. "I love your brothers. They made me feel so welcome, particularly Val. He's really bright, isn't he?"

"He's more like me, if that's what you mean . . . not as rough around the edges."

"Yeah, like that. I really like Carlos, too, though. Don't get me wrong."

"I know what you mean. Carlos is the oldest, and when we were young in difficult circumstances, the responsibility for our well-being fell to him, when Dad wasn't around. It was pretty traumatic for us, particularly when we packed up and left Cuba. Imagine riding on a dirty, open train and then crossing what seemed to us like an ocean to get to America. I was only about seven, so it was all an adventure for me, and somewhat for Val. But Carlos was old enough to know what was going on, how uncertain everything was. I'll never forget the young couple who sailed us across the Straits to Key West. The guy was as big as a mountain with long blond hair. And his girl, I don't think they were married, was really pretty, too. He seemed to me to be a Scandinavian god, like Thor, or something. I can still remember his name. It was Durk."

Anita felt her heart ache in her chest, imagining what it must have been like for a seven-year-old to set sail at night across an ocean. She stood on her toes and kissed him passionately.

"Make love to me, Jorge," she whispered hungrily in his ear.

Jorge was happy to oblige. They fumbled their way to the bedroom, kicking shoes off, unbuckling belts, and shedding halter tops along the way.

In the morning, they made love again, slowly and tenderly. Jorge marveled at Anita's beauty as he glimpsed pieces of her emerging from the sheets. How could he be so fortunate? His personal problems melted away in her embrace, but eventually they had to surface from the euphoria and face the day.

Anita slinked into the bathroom first and suddenly reappeared, passing through the bedroom to the living room, littered with the evening's garments. She picked up her handbag and reached inside as she walked back through the bedroom to the bathroom. In the doorway, she turned and faced Jorge who lay on the bed, head up on one elbow, intrigued.

Anita reached in her handbag and pulled out a toothbrush and wriggled it in front of her for him to see. "See? I didn't forget. Now we don't have to share."

Jorge laughed at her playfulness.

"Would it be presumptuous of me if I left it here?"

"I would be very disappointed if you didn't," he replied.

They spent the day together until late Saturday afternoon, when Anita felt a further delay in seeing her parents would be counterproductive.

"Maybe we should plan for me to meet them?" Jorge suggested tentatively.

"I think we better get your parents out of the way, first. Then we'll tackle my parents."

Jorge was relieved that he only had one set of disgruntled parents to deal with this week. Anita had only just driven out of sight, and he missed her already. They spoke by phone on Sunday and planned dinner for Tuesday night to go over any last-minute ideas that anyone might come up with before Wednesday. Anita asked Jorge what he planned to do the rest of the week, and he explained the pseudo accounting business he had set up.

"It's just to occupy my time until my situation resolves itself," he said.

"So, that's what your brothers were referring to at dinner Friday night. You are back in the accounting game again, working in Little Havana. Cool! Have you heard anything from the Florida Board of Accountancy?"

"Not yet, but I'm expecting a slap on the wrist of some sort. They said my case was under consideration, and that I shouldn't hold myself out as a CPA until the matter was resolved."

"You won't get in trouble with what you're doing now?" Anita asked.

"No, as long as I don't hold myself out as a CPA or render my opinion on financial statements, I should be okay," he answered.

He immediately regretted putting CPA on his letterhead, but he didn't mention it to Anita.

CHAPTER SIXTEEN

The noise and interruption by employees looking for paperwork in the cramped space set aside for office work at U Pumpit proved too much of a distraction for Jorge, so he decided he would relocate his bookkeeping supervision services to his new clients' places of business.

"What, you don't like us anymore?" Carlos asked when Jorge informed him he was taking his fledgling accounting firm on the road. "Our gas station doesn't meet your professional standards, like that fancy glass office building on Biscayne Bay?"

Jorge took a moment to explain why it would be better for him to use client-provided space. "Besides, it's better for me. I bill by the hour, so they see me put the time in, and their records are there if I need additional information."

Val overheard the exchange from the shop and shouted, "Makes sense to me! You're kinda in the way here, anyway. No offense."

"None taken."

In fact, the brothers were all distractions to each other as the tension built over the approaching family gathering. There was still no word on how their mother was going to deal with the position she had taken about Jorge's Jewish girlfriend. The uncertainty weighed heavily on Jorge, and it was noticeable to others.

Jorge plodded through that Monday paying visits to his new

clients where he assisted their bookkeepers with the systems and charts of accounts he had recommended. Many did not fully understand the subtleties of the changes he suggested, but they took comfort knowing a properly certified public accountant was overseeing their financial records. He actually enjoyed working from the business establishments he served, because he felt more involved in the companies' activities.

Spending a few hours in different locations with different people gave him a refreshing beginning at each visit. He also enjoyed the opportunity to reacquaint himself with his heritage as he became more aware of the smells wafting from the local eateries and the sound of the language he had learned as a child. Invariably though, the Cuban connection in his activity guided his thoughts back to his family situation. It reinforced his sense of loyalty to his family, particularly his mother, which conflicted with his deepening affection for Anita.

Jorge took this conflict home with him at night, where without a dose of his new love, his dreams of the future he imagined with her seemed to be ever further from his grasp. He could not focus on television, so he turned to his audit work papers as a diversion from his fears. Finally, he went to bed where he slept fitfully, sensing an ominous cloud drifting overhead. Just marking time now, he poured effort into his new business on Tuesday, dreading the approaching confrontation with his mother, which was contrasted with the excitement he felt knowing that he would be having dinner with Anita at the end of the day. Jorge took comfort anticipating her steady reassurance he had come to rely on.

He was winding up a meeting with the owner of a local art store that featured watercolor scenes of 1950s Cuba painted by expatriates. As the working day neared its end, he felt a wave of nostalgia at the oversized views of the agricultural countryside that had been painted from memory by refugees who had actually seen them firsthand. They reminded him of the fields where his father used to work and where he used to play with his brothers and the other migrants who serviced the farms south of Havana. Many of the paintings were of the old city, but Jorge had never been in the city center, having passed it by on the train ride from Camagüey. He didn't remember much of that trip other than the smelly coal-soaked air, and that he had to pee off the back of the open freight car holding on to his father's hand while he relieved himself.

The irony of the memories was not lost on him driving home, considering that he and Anita were meeting for dinner at Houston's, which had become their default restaurant because it was midway between where they lived. His front door stuck on the small pile of magazines and letters the mailman had dropped through his mail slot when he tried to open it. He released the pressure on the stuck door and reached around to grab the mail. As he lifted it, Jorge noticed right off that the top letter was from the Florida State Board of Accountancy, Department of Compliance.

Jorge's heart rate increased twenty beats per minute in the blink of an eye, and his hand started shaking. This was the letter he had been dreading for the last three weeks. He shouldered the door open as he tore at the envelope with both hands, kicking it shut with his foot behind him, the rest of the mail tucked securely under his armpit. In three purposeful strides, he reached the small dining table and deposited the rest of the mail and magazines on top. His hands were trembling as he fiddled with the folded tip of the letter. Finally, he got it spread in his fingers, verifying the letterhead. He skipped the salutation and went right for the meat.

The Department of Compliance of the State Board of Accountancy has completed its review of the complaint filed against you by the Florida Institute of Certified Public Accountants. Our review has taken into consideration all of the relevant circumstances of your failure to follow

Board-adopted audit standards in connection with the financial statements of Pension Strategy Partners opined by your employer, Arthur White & Company. At the recommendation of the Board, your license to practice public accounting in the State of Florida is suspended herewith.

This suspension is indefinite until such time as you have filed a formal request for readmission to practice before this Board and is subject to completion of remedial audit training as outlined in the attached document. You are required upon receipt of this letter to return the original of your Certificate, No. 9095 which was issued on May 6, 1996 to the offices above.

What an appropriate ending for a shitty month, Jorge thought.

This guy Schaeffer was the gift that kept on giving. While there was some room for argument about his not meeting audit standards, he was not alone in the failure and, in fact, had completed his work on the engagement under the full supervision of the senior audit partner. *I'll bet he didn't get one of these letters.*

Jorge sat round-shouldered on the dining chair as the consequences of this letter began to scroll through his mind. So much for his new accounting business, for starters, not to mention that he would never be able to work for a respectable public accounting firm in the future. His only hope was to somehow find the schmuck who caused this mess and bring the matter into the light. He felt every dash of encouragement he had been entertaining drain from his body and a deep depression overcame him. At that moment his BlackBerry began its jingle.

"Ho, ho, Jorge," a cheerful voice greeted him. "Are we still on for six thirty at Houston's?"

Jorge looked at his watch; it was already five forty-five. "I didn't realize it was so late," Jorge answered nervously. "Let me jump into a pair of shorts and a T-shirt. I'm sick of wearing this suit that doesn't impress anybody. I may be a couple of minutes late, traffic you know."

"Not a problem. Jorge? Are you okay? Your voice sounds a little shaky."

"Yeah, I'm okay. I just got a little bad news, that's all," he answered.

"Oh no! It's not about your mother, is it?" Anita sounded concerned.

"No. I've heard nothing on that front. I'll tell you about it when I see you. 'Bout an hour, then?"

"Yes. See you then. Love you." Anita ended the call.

Jorge was halfway out the door when it dawned on him how Anita ended the conversation. *Love you,* she had said, casually, almost as if it were automatic. That was a first. Two simple words and his day was turned completely around. He wanted desperately to call her back and tell her he loved her, too, but he knew it was too important a message to be frivolous. He wanted to look Anita in her emerald eyes when he said the words. He couldn't wait.

Jorge and Anita ended up competing for the same parking space near the walkway to the restaurant, coming from opposite entrances of the lot. Jorge magnanimously yielded the space to her with a dramatic arm gesture through the windshield, and he continued searching for the second-best available spot. Anita waited for him at the edge of the walkway where they embraced and kissed for a moment, then continued hand in hand to the front door near the water. They were early enough to be seated right away at a table with a water view where they could admire the small boats on Maule Bay and watch the sunset reflect off the condominiums a half mile east on the ocean.

The orange glow augmented Anita's refreshed tan from the time she spent poolside at her parents' home on Sunday. She studied Jorge's expressionless face and decided to jump right in. "So, what's the bad news?" she asked.

With just a little drama, Jorge pulled the folded letter from out of his pocket for her to read. Anita took the letter and read it slowly. She looked up at Jorge and put her hand across the table to take his hand and offer comfort. "Is this as serious as it reads?"

Jorge considered this for a moment. "It is," he said finally. "My career as a certified public accountant is finished for all practical purposes."

"But it says you can reapply," she interrupted.

He just looked at her and smiled, the way a parent might respond to a naive child's question. He recognized the hurt look on Anita's face, and he set about correcting his pandering. "You're right. But the issue is that for the rest of my life, whenever I have a box that asks, 'Has your license ever been suspended or revoked?' I will have to check it. No respectable accounting firm will ever give me serious consideration. In my business, it's like having a felony on your record."

"Oh," she sighed. "Will you have to stop the accounting work you're doing in the meantime?"

"No. I'm not really doing anything that requires me to be a CPA, but I'll have to take it off the letterhead, just put 'accounting services' or 'consultant' or something." Jorge looked across the table at Anita, his mouth downturned and his eyes sad.

Anita sat back in her chair and studied him, realizing that this new development was not what was troubling him. "What's really wrong, Jorge?" she said softly, again leaning toward him, trying to show her concern.

At that moment the waiter interrupted to take their beverage orders. Neither had given a thought as to why they were at the table, and his arrival startled them, diverting their attention to the menus. While they considered their options, the waiter left to get the drinks, white wine for Anita and a Corona for Jorge.

Finally, Anita looked up to face Jorge and asked again, "You were going to tell me what's really bothering you."

Jorge shifted uncomfortably in his seat. "It's all of it. Just everything! My life is a mess, and every day I am reminded of just how bad everything is."

Anita, sensing his pain, felt a tightening in her chest. She tried to conceal the hurt she was feeling at his general statement that his life was a mess. Jorge continued his explanation, totally unaware of the effect his words were having on her. "In just three short weeks I've lost my job, forfeited my professional credentials, and alienated members of my family. I am adrift, and I cannot imagine what kind of future I have to look forward to, now that I've wasted years of education and training."

Anita stiffened with fear that she was going to suffer the fallout. Worry rose within her that her relationship with Jorge was not included in those three weeks. She wondered if the inadvertent "Love you" she blurted out at the end of their call an hour ago had put him off. It had just slipped out, seeming perfectly natural at the time, although they had never actually used the "L" word in conversation before. On the one hand, she felt sad for the pain Jorge was experiencing, but on the other, she was scared that maybe she had misinterpreted his feelings for her. Her heart ached, and a tear began to form in the corner of her eye. As she took this all in, her mind raced, imagining an ending to a story that hadn't even been written yet.

"Is that all that's happened to you in the last three weeks that's important to you?" Her voice quivered just a bit as she said the words carefully.

Jorge woke up from his pity party in an instant. "Oh my God, no!" he gasped, suddenly realizing how wrapped up he had been in himself. He felt the need to console her and stood, taking her hand in his, and moved alongside her chair. Squatting next to her, he reached for her face and cradled it in his shaking hands. He kissed her fully on the mouth and tasted the salt of the tear, which was now running down her face. Jorge felt more pain than he had caused. He backed from her face a few inches, so that he could look her directly in the eyes. "You mean everything to me. Do you understand me?"

He concentrated on her reaction to see if he was getting his message through.

"Anita, from the first moment we met, I knew you were the one. I just couldn't imagine you would have an interest in a nerd like me. Please forgive me. I was only thinking about myself." He hesitated a few seconds for effect and kissed her again. "Anita, I'm very much in love with you. I could not have survived these last two weeks without you." Then he folded her in his arms, tasting lots of salt now, but they were tears of joy.

Anita hugged him back even harder, smashing their cheeks together. "Really?" she mumbled in his ear, still uncertain. "The way you sounded I thought you were getting ready to dump me."

Jorge just hugged her more tightly. "Never gonna happen," he said.

By now the patrons at the tables around them were beginning to take notice of the two lovebirds having an intimate public display of affection. Jorge felt self-conscious, so he moved quietly back to his side of the table and took his seat. At first the restaurant was silent, and then he heard a single clap, then two, then more. In a moment, the entire upper level of Houston's where they were seated was giving applause.

"What happened?" Jorge heard from a lady at the table behind him.

"I think he just proposed," replied the man with her, loud enough for both to hear.

Jorge's olive skin reddened, and he couldn't wipe the grin off of his face. Anita giggled uncontrollably. They just sat and took in the moment until the waiter reappeared with a tray containing an ice bucket, two champagne glasses, and a bottle of Brut.

Jorge was confused. "That's not what we ordered."

"Compliments of the management." The waiter smiled as he began his performance opening the bottle. "We got the impression you were celebrating something special, and we wanted to participate." He filled their glasses and asked if they were ready to order.

"Why don't you give us a few more minutes to enjoy this?" Anita said, taking control, and held up her glass. "Thank you so much for thinking for us."

Jorge held up his glass in the direction of the departing waiter and turned to clink with Anita's glass. He said, "Let's not say anything. We don't want to spoil it for them."

Anita chuckled. "Tell them what? You should know that in the conservative Jewish tradition, you did just propose to me, ya know. Don't think you can wriggle out of it. I'm soiled goods if you don't keep your promise, and my father would have you rubbed out."

They had a good laugh, and Jorge was perfectly comfortable with the jest. Since he had heard nothing from the family about his mother, he and Anita didn't have much to talk about on that front. Jorge felt he could manage anything with Anita by his side, and she knew he would place her first if they ran into difficulty. After dinner, they left an oversized tip for the waiter and said their goodbyes in the parking lot without all the drama they had expressed inside. They agreed Anita would meet Jorge at his apartment the following evening at five thirty, and drive to his parents' house together.

CHAPTER SEVENTEEN

In the morning, Jorge decided to put in a few hours in Little Havana to occupy his mind. He knew he couldn't get through the day unless he had something to do. Things were humming at U Pumpit when he got there, and his brothers shot some lighthearted verbal abuse his way about the coming family dinner, although Jorge knew that they were as concerned as he was about how the evening would unfold. He was already tensed up in anticipation to the point that his back ached.

The three brothers were committed to a wait-and-see attitude, even though this didn't seem like much of a strategy to Jorge. Val had suggested several times that Adriana's birthday party might not be the best time to introduce Anita to the family. He reminded Jorge that this was more than just immediate family. About six cousins and aunts and uncles would be there as well. Jorge was not open to a change of plans at this late date.

"It's a matter of principle to me," Jorge replied. "In the long run, if Anita becomes a permanent part of my life, she would never forgive me. It's best I deal with it now than for the next several decades."

His brothers were understanding of his feelings and volunteered to try to stay close to her, so she would not feel isolated, even though they were not convinced the relationship would endure. Jorge did not have a history of long-term relationships in their experience.

Valeriano winked at his brother and suggested to Jorge, "You're sure it's not just because you're getting laid, Jorge?"

Val was rewarded with a whirling screwdriver hurled in his direction. "You know, I was thinking, how are you going to deal with the language situation? Most everyone will be speaking Spanish, and she doesn't."

Jorge thought about that. "It's a good point. I guess we'll have to stay close by and translate for her. You guys could help with that. I hope she won't think everybody's talking about her."

"Get real, brother. You know that's all everybody will be talking about."

Jorge just sighed. He hadn't given a thought to all the logistics, he was so preoccupied with the personalities. So nervous that he was actually feeling a little sick to his stomach, Jorge left the gas station at three thirty to give himself time to go home and clean up. Anita had agreed to meet him at his apartment at five thirty to shorten all the required traveling. That would give them time to fortify each other and discuss any last-minute strategies they might come up with. She had already told her parents she would likely not be home Wednesday night, using late-night travel after drinking wine as an excuse. Neither of her parents was confused by what this meant.

Jorge showered and straightened up his apartment, clearing the stacks of work papers from his dinette table and shoving dirty clothes in his closet. The dress was casual, so he opted for khakis and a polo shirt. He slipped his feet into a pair of well-worn topsiders, no socks. He heard Anita's car pull in front of the building as he approved his appearance in the full-length mirror on the back of the bathroom door. He felt he looked a little preppy for the family's standards, but *I'm not really dressing for them,* he reminded himself.

Anita felt comfortable enough to give the front door one rap before letting herself in. "Jorge, I'm here," she announced.

Jorge stepped out of his bedroom and saw Anita standing in the doorway, highlighted by the late-afternoon sun coming in from the kitchen windows. He was just stunned by her appearance. Still glowing from two days in the sun, she was still dressed in her work clothes, a navy pantsuit over a puffy white blouse, which augmented her figure.

"You're not wearing that to the dinner, are you?" he asked.

She held up a small travel bag for him to see. "Of course not, dummy. I assumed you wouldn't mind if I changed here." She stepped toward him, and they exchanged perfunctory kisses, just short of ones that would lead to passion.

Jorge could detect the sweet odor of the shampoo she had used to wash her hair that morning as Anita walked past him to the bedroom and deposited her bag on his hastily made bed. She turned and smiled at him. "Just give me fifteen minutes. I want to jump in the shower before I change."

Jorge busied himself with a few emails on his Mac while he waited for Anita to reappear. He heard the shower stop and thought about paying her a visit in the bedroom. Glancing at his watch, he decided he didn't have enough time for the consequences. He could hear her humming an Alicia Keys' tune among the quiet noises of her dressing. On schedule, after fifteen minutes, Anita opened the bedroom door and posed, model style, for Jorge to pass judgment. She was perfect, draped in a salmon-colored sundress and sandals. Backlit by the light from the west-facing window, she looked like something out of a *Vogue* casual photo shoot. Jorge could not conceal a small gasp as he devoured her beauty: glowing skin, dark hair falling lightly to her shoulders. Her shapely legs were visible through the backlighting.

"Is this casual enough?" she asked from her modeling pose, turned half sideways, one leg bent at the knee, one arm against the doorframe for support.

"You're perfect," was all Jorge could manage.

"I'm not too casual, am I?" Anita asked, suddenly concerned at Jorge's lack of reaction. Then she realized that he was just overcome, and she went to him to give him a kiss. He looked so adorable taken off guard as he was that she wanted to gobble him up. They embraced for a moment, Anita above him, Jorge still seated in his chair.

The intimacy of the moment helped relieve some tension, and Jorge did not want to spoil it by trying to stand. He could smell the faint essence of her perfume, very subtle, yet intoxicating. Finally, standing from his awkward position, he kissed her deeply and passionately. The strain of their impending ordeal melted away as he imagined that no one in his family could possibly be unfavorably impressed by this woman.

"Is it time? Are we ready to go?" Anita asked, concerned that their passion might lead to another delay if they didn't begin the journey. Jorge released his hold of her and looked at his watch.

"It's six. With rush-hour traffic we'll get there around six thirty. That's perfect."

Anita turned toward the bedroom, Jorge still managing a firm grip on her hand as she tugged to get free.

"I'm just going to get my purse and the card I got for your mom," she said, thinking Jorge had other plans. "I hope that's all right?" He laughed and let go of her hand. She returned with a small leather handbag with a strap over her shoulder and a card in her hand. "Did you get your mother something?"

"Do you mean a present? We don't do presents, family tradition, we never had any money. It saved a lot of embarrassment," Jorge explained. "What does your card say?"

"It's a simple birthday card. I added a note that I hoped we could become good friends."

"Good luck with that," Jorge said sarcastically. Anita just frowned.

The traffic on the causeway delayed them a few minutes, and as they made their way west on Flagler, Jorge's right leg began to shake, making it difficult for him to maintain a steady speed. Anita noticed his tension and put her hand on his thigh.

"I'm nervous, too," she said, trying to calm him. "How much farther?"

"We're almost there, just ahead on Thirty-sixth Terrace."

Jorge felt somewhat inadequate for the circumstances. *He should be comforting Anita,* he thought. He had no idea what to expect, how he should enter his parents' home, what he should say, where he could begin, and he told Anita so. He reached for her hand for support, and she gave it a squeeze.

Anita beamed her most confident smile. "Let's just go in and act as though there is no backstory. Just take me inside and introduce me, as you would anyone else you might bring. Don't worry about me. I'll be fine." She didn't really feel that way, but at the very least it gave them a plan to execute.

Jorge turned left off of Flagler onto Thirty-sixth Terrace. The house, a typical one-story cinder-block Florida home painted a tropical green with white trim, was set back on the small lot, making room for a double-wide cement driveway in front. There were some cars parked along the street, indicating they were not the first to arrive. Jorge pulled in the available space behind Carlos's Mustang in front and turned the motor off. He and Anita sat in their seats holding hands for a moment, steeling up the courage to go inside.

A moment had passed when they heard the screen door slam at the front of the house. Jorge's mother was descending the front cement steps, and she made her way slowly toward the passenger side of the BMW. Anita beheld a handsome, mature woman approaching her side of the car. Adriana was wearing a simple skirt and blouse. She wore no makeup, other than a light coloring of lipstick, and her curly hair was a medium brown with just a speckling of gray, yet the worry lines on her face could not hide the engaging warmth emanating from within her. Adriana moved confidently, with purpose, to the passenger door and opened it. Anita was frozen in anticipation of what might come next. Jorge's right leg began shaking again as he took all of this in. Adriana smiled at Anita from her heightened vantage, extending her hand toward her.

"You must be Anita," she said in a soft voice, accented from her Cuban heritage. Adriana bent over, as though she intended to get in the car. "Dear, would you mind scooting over just a little bit, so I can sit next to you?"

Anita was stunned speechless, and she reacted immediately by sliding her butt to the left until her left cheek was planted firmly on the center console. Adriana stooped and sat on the vacated half seat Anita had made available to her. Jorge had no idea what to expect. His heart was pounding over a hundred beats per minute, but he was powerless to react, isolated across the console from the two women.

Jorge looked out the windshield at the front door, which was still open, shaded only by the screen door, behind which he could see faces of his brothers and others who were obviously jockeying for position to observe. Undoubtedly they were also unaware of what was about to transpire.

I guess we'll all find out in a minute, Jorge thought. He watched as his mother took Anita's hand in both of hers in a loving, comforting gesture. The stillness in the car was palpable, disturbed only by the noise of the rush-hour traffic moving along Flagler, a few doors away. Adriana looked directly into Anita's eyes.

"When I knew Jorge was going to bring someone special to my birthday party, I thought to myself that this might be awkward for her, coming from outside our community, not knowing anyone or what to expect." Adriana spoke from her heart, although Jorge could tell his mother was a little nervous herself. "There are so many family here, and most of them are speaking Spanish, that I decided I should stay close by you to make all the introductions, so that you will feel comfortable in our home. So take your time to compose yourself, and we'll go in together and I'll introduce you around."

Anita's heart stopped for a few beats while she absorbed what was going on. This was not at all what she had expected, and Jorge's mom was not at all what she had imagined.

Adriana leaned back and looked across to Jorge and said, "You can look after yourself. We'll see you inside."

Jorge had finally figured it out, that his mother had painted herself into a corner and found a gracious way out. His emotions got the better of him, and a tear rolled down his cheek as he mouthed to his mother, while Anita was still turned away from him, *Te quiero, Mama.* He opened his car door, and Anita and Adriana wriggled across the passenger seat and started for the front door of the house. Jorge could see the faces scurry away from the screen door to keep their eavesdropping and peeping from being observed.

Unable to restrain themselves, most of the family gathered around the front of the living room near the front door. Santiago stood at the front to start the reception. He had no idea what his beloved Adriana had in mind, but he always felt confident that she would find a gracious way to resolve the difficult position she had put herself in. His faith in her was rewarded as he watched her march toward the steps hand in hand with a beautiful young woman. He could see them speaking quietly to one another.

Valeriano pushed his way to the front and held the screen door open so they could enter. As Anita, on the left, passed him, they touched briefly and kissed each other on the cheek. If Adriana noticed the familiarity between the two, she gave no notice. Santiago, on the other hand, glared at his middle son and then directed his gaze to Carlos, raising his eyebrows. Carlos gave him a shrug in return, but it was clear to Santiago that his sons had been holding out on him. The last time they spoke he had been told they had not met Jorge's new young lady, but clearly they had. He felt a pang of jealousy as he returned his gaze to Anita, who was now standing directly in front of him with her hand extended.

He was vaguely aware that Adriana was speaking to him in English, something she rarely did, and he realized he was being introduced to her. He felt an awkwardness as he extended his hand to shake hers, and then suddenly overcome by the unexpected turn of events, he reached his arms around her to give a light hug. "Anita, it's so nice to meet you finally," he said.

"Thank you for including me," Anita responded, still somewhat stunned, but feeling she should say more. "It smells delicious in here," she added, noting the aroma of the roast coming from the kitchen and the many spices she was unfamiliar with. She blushed at her stupidity. *I might as well have said 'I carried a watermelon,'* she chided herself, reminded of the awkward scene from *Dirty Dancing* when Jennifer Grey's character tries to impress Patrick Swayze's Johnny.

Everyone in the room began jockeying for position to meet the new arrival amid hushed conversations in Spanish, and with the primary introduction out of the way, Adriana made a statement to the group.

In accented English she announced, "I am pleased to present Anita, Jorge's new girlfriend . . ." She turned and whispered to Anita, "It's all right to say that, isn't it?" Anita nodded in the affirmative. ". . . to our family. You will all have a chance to meet her individually. Since it's *my* birthday, I have a request of you. That is that for the rest of the evening we will all speak English so that our guest will feel a part of this celebration."

Everyone in the room nodded their concurrence, and the room came alive with conversation. Jorge stood behind everyone, still at the front entrance, feeling about as useful as a doorknob. The circumstances of Adriana's previous position regarding Jorge's new girlfriend were known by everyone in the family, so this outcome was a pleasant surprise to all. Valeriano could see his father heading his way, so he moved closer to Carlos for support.

Santiago approached and gave his two sons simultaneous finger snaps on the top of their heads, which he could barely reach, in the manner he had when they were children. In Spanish he said, "Why did you keep it a secret from me?" He tried to show anger, but it just wasn't in him. He was so relieved that Adriana had worked her magic.

"We're sorry, Papa," Carlos answered quietly. "We just met her Friday night, briefly at dinner with Jorge. We thought it would help."

Santiago embraced his sons. "All is well," he said.

The evening went smoothly, although Adriana was not the center of attention. Anita felt welcomed into the family, and she quickly learned of the close bond they shared as expatriates. Dinner was a cultural experience for her. Santiago had cooked the roast pork in the oven, and his brother and Adriana's sister had brought side dishes of *arroz congri* and *yucca con mojo*. The flavors and spices were all new to her, although the garlic was a little excessive for her taste. All in all, she loved the meal. Anita was surprised when a platter of flan with six candles, one for each decade, replaced a traditional birthday cake.

"No meal is complete without flan," Jorge explained.

Anita was intrigued; she had never had it before. The pan looked like an oversized crème brûlée, with a caramel topping, but it was not as sweet. After she tasted it, she thought she preferred it that way. The evening ended with the usual well-wishing. Anita remained behind with Jorge and his brothers, but the conversation seemed to reach an awkward pause. Jorge nodded to Anita as the hour drew late and suggested they make their way home. Anita picked up her handbag and moved to Adriana to say goodbye. As she started to wish Jorge's mother a final happy birthday, she suddenly remembered the card she had purchased that afternoon. She fumbled around in her bag and produced it.

"Oh, my goodness, I almost forgot your card, Mrs. Gonzalez."

"Please call me Adriana," Jorge's mother said with a smile. She took the card and read it, her lips moving slowly as she took in the handwritten message. "Thank you, Anita. I think your wish has already happened. We look forward to seeing you again in our home, when perhaps we can spend more time learning about you. I'm sure Jorge has already told you a lot about us."

Jorge was overjoyed at how well the evening had gone. He gave his mama a prolonged hug and whispered in her ear in their native tongue, "You are very special, Mama. Thank you, thank you."

She replied, "It's a changing world, Jorge, sometimes things take a while to sort out. I think your lady is charming."

On the way back to South Beach, Jorge and Anita were absolutely giddy with excitement. Anita told Jorge she thought what his mother had done was the most amazing thing she had ever experienced from a parent, that she knew it must have been difficult for her, given that she had made her earlier feelings known so publicly.

"You're so right!" he responded. "My dad told Carlos that he knew she would work it out some way. Boy, was he right."

They rode in silence the rest of the way, admiring the brightly lit Miami skyline and the still waters of Biscayne Bay as they crossed the MacArthur Causeway. When they turned off of Fifth Street onto Euclid, the flashes of a fireworks display were visible to the southeast, and the soft sounds of a musical celebration carried through the open car windows.

"Must be something big going on down by the beach," Jorge murmured. "You want to go down there and check it out?"

"Not tonight. I'm tired and I've had a long stressful day. I just want to get into bed. I told the goons at the office that I wouldn't be in until after noon tomorrow."

Jorge didn't need additional encouragement; he'd seen plenty of fireworks before and it probably wasn't going to be easy to find parking if there was something big happening on Ocean Drive. He stepped on the gas, imagining what was awaiting him in the bedroom.

"By the way," Anita continued, "they told me that the investigation was just about completed, so I may be out of a job by the end of the month, too."

"That's just more time we can spend together." He smiled at her. Nothing could bring him down off the high he was feeling. He began to realize how much of his emotional energy had been absorbed by worry over his family situation the last ten days or so.

CHAPTER EIGHTEEN

The young lovers awoke to a dreary, drizzly morning. A cold front had moved through during the night, and the wind was howling out of the southwest, chilling the master bedroom in Jorge's apartment. Anita came out of the bathroom wrapped in a towel, shivering. The floor in the room was old-style terrazzo, and it was cold. Jorge propped his head up on an elbow and admired her golden skin, particularly where her tan line showed just above the white towel tucked in around her ample breasts.

"Jesus, it's cold in here. Everybody thinks it's cold up north in the winter, but it's nothing compared to a cold humid day in Florida . . . and these floors! Why don't you have carpeting?" she whined, climbing in bed next to him.

"That's your 'Good morning, Jorge'?" he teased. "First of all, Jesus is my guy. You have to get your own guy. And a word of caution, don't use his name that way around my mother."

Anita fired right back. "Give me a break. Half of you Cubans are named Jesus. How would she know which one I'm talking about?"

Jorge sat up in the bed and laughed. "So, that's how it's going to be. My mama warned me as we were leaving that there would be challenges."

Anita pulled Jorge on top of her playfully and gave him a kiss. He could smell the fresh scent of soap on her neck from her shower, and he took her full kiss as an invitation.

Later in the morning, Jorge pulled on some shorts and a sweatshirt. Anita borrowed one of his long-sleeve tees that fell to her knees, and they relocated to the small living room. Jorge turned on CNN, and they ignored the drone of the news in the background while they decided what to do. Anita said she was hungry. Jorge was, too.

"It's too messy to go out," he said. "I know what we'll do. I'm going to make you the best French toast you have ever had."

"Oh, really! I'll have you know I make pretty good French toast myself," she challenged.

"Okay. I'll make you a bet. I'll make my French toast, and if you don't agree that it's the best you've ever had, I'll forgo sex with you for a month."

Anita frowned. "That sounds like a lose-lose to me. Or maybe it's a bribe. I can't tell which." She was intrigued, and she watched as Jorge began rumbling around in the kitchen. First he put half of a package of bacon in a huge iron skillet and put it on a burner. Then he found a baguette of French bread in the metal-lined bread drawer and began cutting it in inch-and-a-half slices.

Anita looked aghast. "How long has that been in there? It must be stale. I'm not sure I'm liking where this is going."

"Just watch and learn. It won't make any difference."

Anita could hear the bread crunching as he sawed at it with a serrated kitchen knife. Then he put half a dozen eggs in a large mixing bowl and began stirring it with some milk and any spice he could find in the cabinets, not measuring anything. In went nutmeg, salt, pepper, vanilla extract, cinnamon, and brown sugar, lots of brown sugar. He stirred it vigorously and sampled it to his satisfaction with his fingertip. The bacon began to separate as it sizzled. He put the strips on folded paper towels when they were done. There was about a half inch of bacon grease in the skillet when it was emptied.

"What are you going to do with that?" Anita asked impatiently.

"Shush! You can't question an artist about his work." Then he added a stick of butter to the spattering pan, and he took it off the stove to cool. One at a time he soaked the bread slices deeply in the batter he had made, and flattened each piece with a spatula, so that when it expanded, it absorbed the seasoned eggs. He repeated the process and when he had four slices laden with dripping batter, he placed them in the oil-filled skillet and watched them sizzle.

"Just four, two apiece?" Anita asked. "That's all we get? I'm hungry."

"Don't get your panties in a bunch. You'll see."

"I'm not wearing any," Anita replied coquettishly.

She was always quick with a retort, Jorge had learned. He didn't figure he was going to be winning many verbal sparring contests with her. She seemed to have an instant answer for everything. "Set the table," he commanded.

"Aye, aye, sir!" Anita saluted and got silverware out of the drawers and put placemats on the small dining table. She found maple syrup in the refrigerator door. "All set," she said.

As they cooked, the slices of French toast puffed up to more than three times their original size. He tested the side, which was basically deep frying, and when it was a deep golden brown he flipped it over to do the other side, sealing in the slowly cooking batter. Jorge used the bottom of his sweatshirt as protection from the hot iron handle and carried his creation to the table. He plopped the heavy slices on their plates, and they settled in the butter and bacon grease that oozed from them. Jorge poured two cups from the coffee maker and sat down to observe Anita's reaction to his labor.

Anita poured syrup on her French toast and cut a piece with her fork. "Hot!" she exclaimed as she put it in her mouth tentatively, savoring its texture and taste.

Jorge sat anticipating her reaction, which was immediate.

"Oh, my God!" she exclaimed, mumbling with her mouth full. "I apologize for doubting you. This is the best thing I have ever tasted."

"Really?"

Quickly she cut a bigger piece and began stuffing her mouth. Again she said, "Oh, my God. This is magnificent. The outside is so crisp, and the inside is like custard. It's amazing." She bowed her head in reverence. "You are the French toast king. You are so going to get laid this month," she added with her mouth full, but still finding room for a bite of bacon.

Jorge enjoyed watching her stuff herself in a very unladylike fashion, confirming that her reaction was genuine. They finished the meal in silence.

Finally, Anita sat back in her chair. "I'm stuffed!"

"Me, too."

"Do you have enough batter to make another one?"

"There aren't enough statins in all of this hemisphere to keep our cholesterol under control if we have another one. But, no, I don't think there is enough," he added.

"Point taken," Anita conceded.

They turned their attention to the television, which was filled with talking heads droning on about the deepening financial crisis. It appeared that the economy would continue to deteriorate before it would get better. The newscaster said it was going to be a long haul before the country could work its way out of the mess it was in. Congress was debating a bailout of some sort, and this was becoming a driving force in the upcoming elections to determine who was going to lead the country for the next four years. The United States was considering the possibility of its first African-American president.

Jorge and Anita were mesmerized by the controversies that were developing before their very eyes when Jorge's BlackBerry jingled.

He took it off the charger cord and answered. "Hello?"

Anita heard him switch immediately to Spanish as he motioned her over to him, gesturing wildly with his index finger at the phone. "It's the Schaeffer contact!" he mouthed excitedly.

"You contacted me a couple of weeks ago about Adam Schaeffer," the voice continued in Spanish.

"Yes, yes. Have you been in touch with him?" Jorge acknowledged. "Do you know where I can find him?" He remembered the sound of the voice.

"No. I don't know where he is right now. But I know where he is going to be on Saturday."

"Where's that?"

"He will be going to a travel agency in Little Havana to make some travel arrangements. Do you know the area?" the mysterious voice asked.

"Yes, I'm familiar with it," Jorge answered.

"Look for him at Viajes Mundiales at ten o'clock in the morning on Saturday, October eleventh. It's on Calle Ocho, just west of Twenty-seventh Avenue, but before the cemetery on the north side of the street. You got it?"

Jorge repeated the message to make sure he had it right. The caller confirmed his read back. "Just one more thing," the caller announced.

"What's that?"

"Don't ever call this number again. Got it?"

Jorge said, "Yes," and the line went dead.

He sat down in his chair, dumbfounded and staring into space.

Anita waited a moment, and then became impatient. "So what's the deal, Jorge?"

Jorge gathered his senses and looked at her. "That was the guy from Schaeffer's contact list that we called two weeks ago."

"Duh! What did he say?"

Jorge told her the substance of the conversation.

She nodded, trying to prompt him along. "Soooo, this is a good thing, right? Why aren't you more excited?"

Jorge was contemplative. "Sure it's a good thing. It's what we've been hoping for. But now we have to figure out what to do about it."

Anita grew more exasperated. "What's to think about? We know where he's going to be and when. Let's go get him."

"I think it's more complicated than that. Let's talk about it for a minute. We have to keep in mind what our objective is. It's not only to bring him to justice. I want my record to be cleared so I can have my future back," Jorge explained.

"Doesn't catching him do that?" Anita asked.

"Only partially. We don't want the authorities to focus on what he may have done wrong faking his death. We have to tie him to the securities fraud. If we can establish that, the audit standards I have been accused of failing to meet are beyond the scope of the audit, and they will have to give me my certificate back."

Anita nodded. "Exactly, so we have to catch him, like I said."

Jorge shook his head. "There's that, of course, but I think we need to think about this some more." He went on to explain what was troubling him. He found it odd that the mysterious contact, after denying he ever heard of Adam Schaeffer, would make a gratuitous call to tell him otherwise when there wasn't anything in it for him.

"I see what you mean. It's almost as if someone wants you to know how to find Schaeffer. Is that it?"

"That's what I'm thinking. We may have put up a red flag when we called that number. For some reason, someone wants us there, and I'm trying to figure out who that could be, and I can only think of two possibilities."

Jorge was in full-concentration mode now. He was the plodding, methodical auditor Anita had known when she met him, working through all the possibilities and consequences. It was a part of him she admired and respected even though it contrasted with the playful lover she was attracted to now. "What are they?" she asked.

"Either it's Schaeffer himself who sees me as a threat and wants to tie up loose ends—"

Anita put her hand to her mouth, momentarily cutting off his words, suddenly realizing there might be an element of danger to this adventure.

He continued, "Or someone else who has figured out what has been happening and wants to take advantage of the situation."

"And wants to tie up loose ends," Anita finished the sentence for him. She thought about that for a moment. Then she asked, "But why would you be a loose end to someone like that? Wouldn't they just want the same thing we do, to find Adam and turn him over to the authorities?"

"Maybe, but we have to keep in mind that we are dealing with the theft of tens of millions of dollars, possibly hundreds of millions; we don't know how long he has been doing this. That's a lot of money and a lot of temptation, and there might not be anyone even looking for it or aware that a huge fraud has taken place."

"I see."

"Since Pension Strategy Partners was closed down, has anyone from FINRA or the other agencies asked you anything about a fraud? Or suggested in any way that one might have occurred?"

Anita thought for a minute. "Jorge, your right! The only thing they have been investigating is the firm's failure to meet capital requirements and by how much. That's why they were shut down."

"That's what I thought."

"And they don't particularly impress me as being the sharpest bunch of guys, based on the questions they ask me and the documents they want me to reproduce. That head guy, Dennison, only comes by when it works around his tee times. I think he spends most of his time on the golf course."

Anita and Jorge spent more than an hour looking at the problem from every conceivable angle to determine the best course of action. Anita leaned heavily on just going to the police or the FBI. Jorge felt he needed to learn more about what Schaeffer was up to, where he had been the last three weeks, and why he hadn't already left the country.

"Surely he hasn't stayed here in Florida just so he could trap me into exposing myself. That wouldn't make any sense. He planned his departure well in advance, and had we not made that call, he would have no idea I could be a 'loose end.' No, I think it's unlikely that he set this up."

Anita suggested, "How about the FBI then?"

"Again, I don't think we have enough to excite them."

"But you have all those working papers. Can't you show that to them?"

"First of all, I and my firm created them. It's our work. Second, it would take hours in front of one of their forensic accountants just to explain what we had, and I don't think they would be interested. They will pay attention when we produce Schaeffer."

"So, what then? You just plan to walk into the travel agency on Saturday and waltz out with Adam Schaeffer?"

"Something like that." Jorge smiled for the first time since receiving the phone call.

For the rest of the morning and well into the afternoon, the young couple worked out a plan for Anita to surveil the agency while Jorge went in to assess what was going on and who was involved. She would alert the police and 911 after she got a text from Jorge that he had the information he needed, or if he sensed that anything was amiss or he was in any sort of danger. In the meantime, Anita would use the last few days of work before the offices were shuttered to see what she could find out regarding the intentions of the government agencies who were wrapping up their investigations into Pension Strategy Partners.

Joey Bangoni

CHAPTER NINETEEN

Joey checked into the InterContinental Hotel in downtown Miami on Friday afternoon, October 10, the day before he was set up to intervene in Adam Schaeffer's travel plans. At the reception counter in the main lobby, he was given a written message to be delivered upon his arrival. It read simply: *We're in 717 and 718. Call when you get in.*

Joey managed his own luggage, a small bag on wheels, to the elevators across the lobby from reception and rode one to the ninth floor, where he found his spacious room with a view of downtown and the Miami River. He set his case on the bed and called one of the room numbers he had been given. Mario picked up on the first ring.

"Hello."

"Hi, Mario. It's Joey. When did you get in?"

"Angelo and I got here yesterday. We had to pick up some special equipment, if you know what I mean. Ya wanna meet up?"

Joey knew he was referring to weapons, something they could not risk bringing on an airplane. "Yeah, that's a good idea. We have some things to talk about before tomorrow. It's too early for me to get a drink. Why don't you come up to my room? I got a nice view. Nine twenty-one."

"Be right up. Okay to bring Angelo?"

"Sure. I gotta meet him sometime, right?"

A few minutes later, Joey opened his door to greet his old enforcement partner from the early eighties. Mario gave him a huge bear hug, clapping him heartily on his back. They were about the same age and height, but Mario had not taken the best of care of himself. His huge gut belied his love of pasta, whereas Joey, although himself overweight, had made an effort to stay somewhat in shape. In spite of his efforts, his girth had thickened since his football years, but not to the same degree as his old friend's.

Over his shoulder Joey could see a young man in his early thirties, clearly wiry and fit, but nearly a head shorter than the two older gentlemen. He had intelligent eyes that moved about, taking in his surroundings while his head stayed motionless. Joey invited them both into his oversized room and motioned them to take seats near the window where a small sofa and armchairs were clustered around a marble coffee table.

Mario looked around the room, noticing the fifty-inch Samsung on the far wall across from the king-sized bed. "Nice digs," he said. "You always had a little class. I knew you were going somewhere when we were young."

Joey took the small sofa, while Mario and Angelo took the armchairs. Angelo looked like a little boy sitting in the company of the huge men. Mario introduced him, "Joey, this is my friend Angelo Amorico. Don't let his size fool you. You would want him on your side if things got ugly, and he is not intimidating, so he works effectively with people in our business."

Joey thought this was a little peculiar for a business where intimidation is part of the deal, and he said so.

"It's not always about muscle. Nowadays we try to negotiate where we can and back it up with the heavy stuff. Twenty-first century image, ya know. So, tell us what you have in mind."

Joey spent the next twenty minutes going over his plan, which included containing two individuals in a secure location in Little

Havana, so that they could be interrogated. He gave a little background on the nature of the information he was looking for, including that a white-collar crime was involved and that he was looking for access to the money that had been stolen. Joey did not divulge any information about the magnitude of the crime, just that his mark had his fingers in the unions' tills.

"Who's the other dude?" Mario asked.

"He's collateral damage, I suspect. I don't know much about him, other than that he has stuck his nose in my business and may know something. I've arranged for him to arrive at our location at about the same time as our target, a guy named Adam Schaeffer. When I get what I need from Schaeffer, he is of no further use to us and probably needs to disappear. I want to find out what the other guy knows, his name is Gonzalez. If he can identify us after we deal with Schaeffer, then he has to go, too. We'll decide on that after this goes down."

Mario and Angelo nodded their understanding. Joey suggested they take three cars so they would have maximum flexibility.

"Mario, let's jump in my rental and drive over there so we can assess the setup. On the way back, we can swing by the airport and pick up another car if we decide we need it. You guys have a car already, right?"

Mario nodded in the affirmative.

A half hour later, with directions provided by the relatively new GPS system, Google Maps, the trio pulled into the side parking lot on Calle Ocho in Little Havana. As they exited the car, Angelo noticed the sign on the side of the white building: ESTACIONAMIENTO ADICIONAL ATRAS DEL EDIFICIO. He stepped around the side of the building to survey the parking at the rear and the access to the back door of the travel offices.

"How does it look?" Mario asked.

"Should work fine. There's lots of room, and a cement-block wall shields the back of the lot from wandering eyes. The back door is right in the middle of the building. We should be able to transfer *stuff* from the building to the trunk of a car without any problem," Angelo said matter-of-factly, as though he was talking about loading boxes of stationery. "Also, there's no other way into the back lot."

Joey observed the duo's thoroughness and approved, nodding to Mario. "The kid's sharp."

Mario gave him a thumbs-up as the three men walked around to the front entrance. Angelo grabbed the door handle and stepped back, holding the heavy glass door open for his bosses. A jingling bell announced their arrival when they stepped into a large office space occupied by metal working desks, each with a flat computer screen whose alternating screen savers depicted magnificent vistas of well-known world scenes, from historic Rome to romantic Caribbean getaways. The walls were covered with similar vacation destination posters. No one was in evidence until a roundish older man stepped in the room from a back office. It was almost five o'clock.

"Mr. Bangoni," he greeted Joey. "Long time no see."

"Hi, Camilo. Good to see you again." Joey smiled and thrust out his hand. He started to introduce Mario and Angelo when Camilo interrupted him, glancing back and forth between the bigger man and the smaller one.

"No names, please. I don't wanna know anybody. I let everyone go early today . . . told them to get a head start on the weekend. I want to have as little to do with this business as possible."

"Got it," Joey said.

Joey explained that he needed to use the whole office for a meeting at ten o'clock the next morning and that he would be finished by midafternoon latest if everything went smoothly.

"I'll make this easy for you," Camilo began. "No one will be here after this afternoon until we open Monday morning at nine. Just make sure you're gone by then. Clean up after yourselves, and we'll have no problem." Camilo was not naive, and he could imagine what was probably going down. "I just don't want to draw any attention to this place or me."

"Again, got it," Joey reassured his friend. "We'll leave the place just as we found it. Can we look in back so we know what we have to work with?"

Camilo showed the trio the way to the storage room in back, down a short hallway past a couple of private offices, one of which appeared to be Camilo's. The space was the full width of the office space, with boxes stacked along one wall and unused office equipment and a portable table with paper-cutting tools occupying the rest of the room. Some filing cabinets took up another corner. There were some metal folding chairs stacked next to them and around the table, which also contained some photographic equipment. Small high windows provided ample light from the outside across the back wall, too high for anyone to look through.

"This is perfect," Joey said to no one in particular.

Mario and Angelo nodded their agreement. Camilo handed Joey a key, which Joey put in his pocket.

"That's for the back door. I'd prefer no one see you come through the front door. Might attract attention. You can unlock the front from the inside to let your visitors in. Just remember to lock it before you leave."

"Any alarm system?" Mario asked.

"No. Not much here worth protecting," Camilo answered.

Camilo and Joey talked for another fifteen minutes about this and that while Mario and Angelo surveyed the rest of the premises. When they finished, they returned to their boss's conversation and stood patiently, signaling that they were ready for departure.

Joey said his goodbyes, reassuring Camilo once more that he would leave everything as he had found it. The trio left by the back door and returned to the InterContinental Hotel to rehearse their strategy for the following day.

Adam Schaeffer

CHAPTER TWENTY

Adam Schaeffer rubbed his strained eyes, red from watching the disassembly of the financial markets in real time on CNBC, one of the few channels of value that came with his apartment package. He did not want to expose himself unnecessarily by opening an upgraded account with Comcast, so he made do with what was available on basic cable. In the evenings, he occupied his time watching countless reruns of sitcoms going back decades on obscure channels he had never heard of.

The drop in the Dow had everyone in a panic, and the rapidly increasing rate of default in the mortgage markets combined to show Schaeffer just how wrong he could get things. Whereas interest rates were rolling over on adjustable mortgages, which should have made the CDOs more valuable, the opposite was happening. The increase in rollover rates was causing massive defaults in mortgages that had been placed by unqualified borrowers. His need to get to Europe grew every day, or he would have to make an investment adjustment by phone to unload the credit default swaps he had sold. He was losing the better part of a million dollars each week by putting it off.

Early in October, Schaeffer got the call he had been waiting for. The mysterious accented voice had told him to pick up his replacement passport and driver's license in Little Havana at some travel agency called Viajes Mundiales on Saturday, October 11. He looked up the website on his computer and studied the map of the area to familiarize himself. Next, he called Roemer to nail down the date for transportation to Miami, and they chatted about additional needs Schaeffer might have for transportation, which were few.

Rabbit had been Schaeffer's whole social world since he got back to Fort Lauderdale, and he enjoyed having someone to speak with from time to time. They had an occasional meal together, and sometimes a drink, although Schaeffer tried to avoid alcohol as much as possible so he could keep his wits about him. He needn't make a misstep, causing his ongoing existence to be found out, after he had gone through so much trouble to stay in the shadows. They made plans to see a movie that evening.

Schaeffer had not shaved since his arrival, and he was taking on the appearance of one of the unfortunate homeless slobs he had seen camping out under the State Road 84 overpass at the expressway. His usual dress was wrinkled khakis and a T-shirt, shod only in what were now well-worn tennis shoes. He fit right in with the crowd he observed in the vicinity of the bus stop near his apartment. A floppy straw hat completed his disguise. No one he came in contact with would ever guess that the slob they saw usually had thousands of dollars in his pockets.

The occasional movie Schaeffer and Rabbit took in at the local multiplex helped occupy time in a safe place. That night they planned to see *Iron Man,* a moronic thriller based on action heroes Schaeffer remembered seeing as a kid in comic books. Rabbit was looking forward to it. Schaeffer took comfort in the quiet darkness of movie theaters where he knew it was unlikely he would be recognized. Knowing that Roemer was not out drinking in public where he could inadvertently say something he shouldn't was an added blessing. Roemer continued to be an adequate companion. He accepted that his new friend diverted any discussion about his circumstances, although it was not hard to figure out that Schaeffer was on the lam.

He, on the other hand, was perfectly willing to discuss details of his peculiar past, which Schaeffer found intriguing.

Roemer had come from a seemingly privileged background that included New England prep schools and two years at an Ivy League college, followed by three tours in Vietnam where his life apparently disassembled. As near as Schaeffer could put together, Roemer got addicted to the adrenaline of combat, booze, drugs, and hookers, possibly exacerbated over the years by Agent Orange sprayed on the fields where he did battle. It all came to an end when he was severely wounded and returned to his family in 1973, just as American involvement in the war was drawing to a close.

He tried to pretend he was the same, but in fact he was very damaged. He finished college and law school, got a job, married a Midwestern girl, and started a family in an attempt to live what he thought was a normal life in Ohio. After years of depression, the anger and self-loathing got the better of him, as did the alcoholic crutch he used to lessen the pain he felt inside. The coup de grâce came in the form of rock cocaine, which appeared on the scene in the early nineties. Unmanageable at this point, his family threw him out, and his life turned to the streets. A couple of arrests put him in rehab clinics, which were effective in turning him away from the hard drugs like crack, which he could no longer afford, but they never dealt with his underlying issues. He had become a lost soul of the street where he had learned to make his way effectively and where he felt most comfortable.

Adam Schaeffer, who as a general rule didn't feel much emotion for anything, found the time he spent with his new friend pleasurable. He figured he had another week to kill, and Rabbit offered an interesting diversion. A couple of days before he was scheduled to pick up his replacement documents, Schaeffer had dinner with Roemer and shared his plans to leave the country. Roemer was saddened that he was going to lose a companion he had spent so much time with and from whom he had benefited financially, and he expressed his feelings to Schaeffer.

"I'm really sorry, buddy," Schaeffer replied. "You have to have known that I have been waiting for things to come together for me, so I could get on my way. This isn't my life. You must know that."

"Yeah, I figured as much. You obviously have a lot of money. That's not normal for someone on the streets. You have to be careful that someone doesn't try to separate you from it." In fact, it had truly never occurred to Rabbit to do exactly that. He sincerely considered Schaeffer a friend.

"You have been solid with me, and I will do the best I can to take care of you before I leave," Schaeffer said in what he thought would be a comforting manner, although feelings of that type were foreign to him. He just needed to keep Roemer in line just a few days more. "I have a couple more things I need to do that you can help me with, if that's all right with you."

"Anything."

"Tomorrow I need you to take me to the Miami airport so I can get some airline tickets. Then tomorrow night we'll have a farewell dinner, and Saturday we go to Miami again where I have some business to take care of, and then you can take me to the airport for the last time."

"I can do all that."

"Good . . . and all I ask in return is that you keep your mouth shut about me. You never met me; you never saw me. Get me out of your memory, no matter what happens."

"You got yourself a deal." Roemer stuck out his hand, and Schaeffer took it, keeping his eyes locked on Rabbit's eyes for emphasis.

The next day, they followed the plan. At Miami International Airport, a dubious Swiss Air ticket agent accepted roughly five thousand dollars cash for a first-class ticket to Zurich on the 7:15 nonstop the next evening.

"May I see your passport, Mr. Anderson?" the agent asked.

Schaeffer was flustered, not expecting this. He felt around his pants pockets as though looking for it and then remembering. "I don't have it with me right now."

"That's not a problem. I was just going to include the information on your reservation to save time when you check in tomorrow. Just be sure to bring it with you, or you will not be able to board." She smiled.

Schaeffer returned to where he left Rabbit in the short-term parking lot. As they drove off, Schaeffer gave his friend some new instructions. "I want to stop at a Kmart or something and pick up a blazer and trench coat. I can't travel to Europe looking like this."

Rabbit found his statement about his destination odd but said nothing. He just filed the information away for future use. Schaeffer told him that when they left for Miami in the morning he would take everything he needed with him, so they wouldn't need to return to Fort Lauderdale after his business in Miami in the morning. The two concluded the day with a couple of errands and a farewell dinner at Runway 84, a popular Italian restaurant down the road from the bus stop.

Jorge Gonzalez

CHAPTER TWENTY-ONE

J orge and Anita sat on the front patio of the Habana Café, almost directly across the street from Viajes Mundiales on Eighth Street in Little Havana. They had an unobstructed view of the travel offices where they could see the comings and goings of anyone entering the building.

"What's your plan, exactly?" Anita asked him.

"I'm thinking we'll just watch from here. When we see Schaeffer enter the travel office, I will follow him in and confront him."

"And you think he'll just roll over and allow you to turn him in to the authorities?" she questioned.

"I'll think of something. After I go in and sort things out, I'll come out and give you the high sign and you call 911 and tell them a crime is in progress. Give them the address. I'll figure out a way to keep him there until the cavalry arrives. You have the thick packet I gave you?"

Jorge was referring to the package of the summaries and conclusions from his work papers detailing what Schaeffer had been up to in the theft of millions. It contained all the evidence he needed to absolve him of a violation of audit standards, what he would need to clear his name. They were copies of the originals he had made at Kinko's, which were still in his apartment.

"It's in the backseat of your car." Anita was a little unsure of how this plan was going to work out, but she trusted Jorge's judgment, hoping everything would fall into place. "Do you want me to get them?"

"Not right now. Just have it available when we turn Schaeffer over to the authorities." He handed Anita the keys to his Beemer, which was parked on the street. "Just in case," he said.

"In case of what?" Anita frowned, showing some alarm.

"So you can get the evidence out of the back, for one thing."

"Oh, yeah," she realized. "What's the other?"

Frustrated that he showed weakness, Jorge said, "I don't know. Just in case something comes up, and you need the car." Anita did not find this comforting.

The waiter came by and asked in Spanish if they wanted another cup of coffee. Jorge apologized for tying up the table and asked if it was a problem if they stayed for a few more minutes. The waiter glanced around the mostly empty café and said they should stay as long as they liked, cautioning that things would start to get busy around lunchtime. Anita raised an eyebrow, not understanding the rapid-fire Spanish.

"You're good to stay here after I go in to keep an eye on things and make your call," he explained.

The waiter refilled their coffees, so they would have something in front of them, and retreated into the kitchen to give them some privacy.

"If I drink this I will have to pee, and I might miss something," Anita remarked.

"Me, too. Let's just sit and watch."

They didn't have to wait long. About two minutes after ten, a somewhat wrinkled and dirty blue Chevy Malibu worked its way slowly west on Eighth Street, halting in front of the travel agency. Jorge and Anita could see two men in the front seat pointing at the sign painted on the front window. The passenger got out and motioned for the driver to proceed, giving him a few abbreviated instructions. Had the scene not been somewhat comical, Jorge might not have paid any attention to the disheveled passenger who emerged. He looked pretty sloppy in his unpressed khakis and T-shirt. He wore a floppy straw hat to shield his face from the sun, and he sported an unkempt beard. Suddenly Jorge realized it was Schaeffer.

Pointing he said, "Anita! Look. There he is."

Anita squinted to get a better look through the glare of the early morning. She immediately recognized her old boss and quickly reached out to lower Jorge's arm. "Put your arm down, Jorge. You don't want to call attention to yourself. You might scare him off. You're right. I can hardly believe it's him. He must have been living in a culvert somewhere."

Jorge nodded. "He doesn't look like he's been enjoying his ill-gotten gains. I'm guessing he's been trapped here since he faked his death."

They watched as Schaeffer looked both ways nervously and crossed the sidewalk to the entrance of Viajes Mundiales, slipping quietly through the front door. Jorge gave him a few minutes to get started with his business, whatever that might be. He stood and gave Anita a kiss on the cheek.

"Well, I guess it's now or never," he said nervously.

She reached out to grab his hand as he turned to leave the table, tugging gently. "Be careful, Jorge." Then she added, "I love you." She held her grip a moment longer for emphasis, fearing what was to come.

"You remember what to do, right?" Jorge said, a tremor in his voice. "I'll come out when I'm ready and give you a thumb's up. Then you call the police."

"Got it."

Jorge crossed the busy street. Dodging traffic, he was rewarded with a brief horn. He jumped up on the curb and took eight steps to the front door of the travel agency. He could not see any activity inside mainly because of the darkly tinted window, which set off the colorful scripted business logo VIAJES MUNDIALES painted in yellow and blue across the front windows. As he opened the door, he heard a chime, one of those springy bells merchants used to put on their front doors to alert them when customers came in.

The lights were not on inside, and it took a minute for Jorge's eyes to adjust to the dim light coming in from the outside. He heard noises of some physical effort and voices coming from the back of the offices. This got his full attention, and adrenaline started pumping through his system. He was considering his options, which included a retreat out the way he had come in, when a large, casually dressed man, entered the room from a back hallway. He seemed at ease, not threatening, and then he spoke in smooth English, not accented as Jorge would have expected.

"Welcome, Mr. Gonzalez. We've been expecting you. Please come in." He extended his hand in greeting. "I'm Joey Bangoni, and I've come a long way to meet you and to learn more about your interest in our mutual friend, Adam Schaeffer." He had an easygoing manner highlighted by his broad smile.

Jorge did not feel threatened by him, other than the circumstances. He took his hand nervously and shook it, but when he tried to release his grip, the man did not let go.

"Why don't you come in back where we can visit for a bit?" Bangoni said, still smiling.

Now Jorge started feeling very uncomfortable. "I'm not sure about that, Mr. Bangoni." Jorge started to withdraw, and Bangoni still would not ease his grip. Jorge began to panic and tried to release his hand. As he tried to pull his hand free, Joey bore down, the thick muscles of his forearm bulging, encasing Jorge's hand in a viselike grip. Unable to free himself and sensing an attempt to struggle with the big man would be fruitless, Jorge allowed the larger man to guide him toward the rear hallway, directing him with his other hand positioned in the small of his back. When Jorge stopped his feeble resistance, he noticed Bangoni's physical pressure relax as well. He seemed to have a sense of just how much corporeal dominance he needed to get submission from his subject. Slowly, but awkwardly, as Joey still had a hold of Jorge's hand and a prodding piston fist in his back, they made their way down the hallway to the storeroom at the rear of the offices.

As Jorge passed first through the doorframe, the scene before him sent chills down his spine. The room was not large, and the walls were lined with filing cabinets and unused office junk. In the middle of the room was a portable conference table, the kind with folding legs, with metal folding chairs staged around it. Seated at the center of the table with his back to Jorge was Adam Schaeffer, his hands restrained behind him by a plastic tie wrap, the kind electricians use to bundle wires together. He didn't look the worse for the wear to Jorge at the moment, but then Jorge realized he had only arrived minutes before Schaeffer had. The restraints left no doubt what was to come.

As they entered the room, Schaeffer turned his head to the side nervously in an attempt to see who had entered, but the restraints prevented him from craning his head enough, so he waited for someone to say something. Bangoni motioned for Jorge to take the chair next to Schaeffer. Jorge sat down, putting his hands behind him in anticipation that he was going to get the same treatment as Schaeffer.

"Don't worry, Mr. Gonzalez. We're not going to tie you up . . . for now," Bangoni said quietly.

Jorge noted the two men standing off to the side just observing the goings-on. One was huge, clearly out of shape with his gut hanging over the top of his belt, and the other was a fit-looking younger lad, about his own age he guessed. The big guy, who looked like a mafia thug, was clipping his fingernails absentmindedly, as though he had no real interest in the proceedings, while the younger one was very alert, his eyes darting about the room.

"You!" said a startled Schaeffer when he was finally able to see his table mate. "What are you doing here?"

Jorge could see Schaeffer's confused mind connecting the dots as he tried to make some sense of his situation. Schaeffer didn't look the same in his rumpled khakis and T-shirt, face unshaven.

"As I thought, you two know each other," Bangoni said as he moved to the opposite side of the table and tried to rest his bottom on the edge, facing his captives. Feeling the metal legs starting to wobble, he thought better of his choice of seats and relocated to the chair opposite.

Jorge's stomach felt like it was sinking as the intimidation of his surroundings overcame him. In an effort to appear unconnected to Schaeffer and his recent activities, he asked no one in particular, "What's this all about?" Looking at Schaeffer and responding to his earlier question, he exclaimed, "What am *I* doing here? What are *you* doing here? You're supposed to be dead!"

Schaeffer just lowered his head in submission. "Well, shit happens," he said.

Bangoni interrupted the exchange by tapping his fingernail on the Formica tabletop. "Let's dispense with the charades, if you please, gentlemen. You both know goddamn well why you're here. You invited yourselves here," he said with emphasis, all manner of pleasantness gone from his voice. "What I want to know is why." He turned to face Schaeffer directly. "Adam, you have come to disappoint me. I have been a valued associate for years . . . given you all sorts of business, helped you out with personal matters, and how do you reward me? You steal from me and my pension funds. I find this very upsetting." Then turning his attention to Jorge, he said, "As for you, Mr. Gonzales, I have absolutely no idea who the fuck you are, but somehow I think you are in this up to your neck. Isn't it funny how large sums of money bring people together? So, here we are. Who wants to start?" Bangoni looked from one of his "guests" to the other. "Let's start with you, Adam. We'll do the easy stuff first. Who is this guy?" he asked nodding at Jorge.

Schaeffer wasted no time trying to cooperate. "He's an accountant. His firm does the audits for Pension Strategy Partners," he said nervously.

"That right, Mr. Gonzalez?"

Jorge's heart was beating fast. He was scared, but he couldn't think of anything he could say that would get him out of this mess. His only hope was that they would find him of no interest and let him go. He stuck with the truth. "Yes, that's right. I used to be the engagement partner for Arthur White & Company, who audits Schaeffer's firm annually. We had just completed the audit when Schaeffer disappeared."

"I see." Bangoni made a pyramid of his fingers, elbows on the table, as he considered the information. "So, that's the connection. Have you two been working together? Is that it?"

Suddenly an idea hit Jorge in the head like a bolt of lightning. Things fell into place for him in a hurry, and he felt a sense of urgency to take control of his part of the conversation. From what Bangoni had just told them about his disappointment in Schaeffer having stolen his money, Jorge figured that he was here to get his money back. That made Jorge somewhat irrelevant and therefore vulnerable. Jorge couldn't help Bangoni get his money back, only Schaeffer could, and Jorge suspected that his life was very dependent on Bangoni believing he was relevant.

Schaeffer started to answer Bangoni's question. "He's just a dumb accountant. He doesn't know anything. In fact, his firm gave us a clean opinion on the audit they just—"

Jorge panicked. He moved his leg around the side of the chair leg and kicked Schaeffer as hard as he could in the ankle, but not so hard that the others would notice. Schaeffer stopped midsentence and glared at Jorge, who looked him squarely in the eyes.

"Come on, Adam. Let's not put this off. You and I are in a difficult situation here, and I don't see any point in dragging this out. I appreciate the gesture to leave me out of it, but he's going to find out anyway." Jorge turned to look at Bangoni. "Yes, we were in it together. How do you think we slipped past the scrutiny of the SEC, our auditors, and regulatory agencies?"

Schaeffer started to object, but Jorge ground his heel into the toe of Schaeffer's shoe.

Bangoni considered what he had just heard, but he wanted some verification. "So, tell me. How did you do it?"

"It took years, almost three," Jorge answered. "Adam figured out how to work the financial records, and he handled things internally. My job was to make sure that nothing suspicious came up in the audit process. We spread the target clients across various spectrums of the firm, so the hedges and straddles we used wouldn't be noticeable to the accounting staff that reported to me. I deliberately constructed the audit plan and scope of the engagement to steer my people away from sensitive areas. I was also helpful keeping government regulatory agencies at bay."

Schaeffer just looked on with his mouth agape, unclear whether or not he should go along with Jorge's story. He couldn't see a reason not to, since the dummy was trying to take partial credit for a massive fraud. He was surprised that Jorge seemed to know as much as he did. He was curious to find out how much of a trail he had left behind.

Bangoni looked at the both of them. "So, where's the money now?"

"Offshore, Switzerland," Jorge answered before Schaeffer could say anything, trying to make his relevance to the situation more believable.

"Wonderful. We're finally getting some clarity here," Bangoni said with a satisfied smile. "So, here's the sixty-four-thousand-dollar question," he began, making reference to the 1950s game show, "How do *we* get it?"

Schaeffer decided he could add to the story Jorge was spinning. "That was my part. I needed to disappear, à la the plane crash, to go get the money. Gonzalez was to stay behind and clean up any messes that might arise after I left. As it stands, it's the perfect crime. No one knows that any money is missing. Only the pension funds were affected, and among the billions they have under management, our investment strategies only represent a fraction of a percent of reduced return, so it shouldn't stand out."

Jorge nodded in agreement, feeling better that Schaeffer didn't give him away.

"I noticed," Bangoni observed. "And if I noticed, I'm sure others will too, eventually."

Schaeffer was helpful again. "You only noticed because you found out I wasn't killed or lost at sea, probably because I went back to your source to get some new identification to leave the country."

Bangoni nodded his head to confirm what Schaeffer had just said. "But you haven't answered my question. How do we get the money?"

Jorge jumped in again. "That's where it gets complicated."

Bangoni frowned. "It's not really complicated, kid. Just tell me how to get my money back."

"It takes both of us. We used a lawyer in Switzerland to set up a structure that requires both of us. Adam set up the banking arrangements, but I have the passwords to access them. The lawyer formed the investment company that holds the assets."

Bangoni made an observation. "So, you two don't trust each other?"

"Would you?" Jorge asked rhetorically.

"How much money are we talking about?" Bangoni pressed. "Don't fuck with me. I've got a pretty good idea."

Jorge looked at Schaeffer, who said, "Over two hundred million. It varies, because some of the investments are still in their original trade form. Most of it has been converted to U.S. Treasuries."

Just then they heard the jingle of the mechanical bells on the front door. There was a slight pressure change in the room as the wind blew in the open door. Bangoni stared at Angelo and Mario, an alarmed look on his face.

"Did you guys leave the front door unlocked?"

"You were the last one to use it, boss. You wanted the Cuban guy to get in, remember?"

"Shit! You're right. Get out there and get rid of whoever it is."

Angelo and Mario moved quickly to the hallway. As they moved to the front of the office, Bangoni could hear a woman's voice call out, *"Hola, hola, Camilo?"* followed by a burst of rapid-fire Spanish.

Joey thought for a minute and made a decision. He jumped up from his seat across from his prisoners and started for the front office. Halfway, he turned and slapped his palm across the top of Jorge's head. Having Jorge's attention, he pointed his sausage-sized finger right at Jorge's forehead and warned, "Don't you even think of cutting Schaeffer loose, or I'll personally cut your nuts off! I'm not done with either of you yet."

Having made his point, he went to the front to defuse the situation before his heavy-handed crew could make matters worse. When he got to the front office, he confronted an intense older lady wearing an actual bonnet while she streamed unintelligible Spanish at Mario, who was gesticulating wildly that she should turn around and leave. They were not having much luck getting the woman to understand. Bangoni stepped in between them and did his best to intervene. Thinking Italian and Spanish had the same origins, he tried that first.

"Chiuso, chiuso," he repeated, Italian for closed. It didn't seem to have any effect. The woman ranted on. He tried another tactic. *"No es aperto. No es aperto."* This seemed to have the desired effect, *aperto* being Italian for open.

"Aha," the woman said. *"Abierto. Si, entiendo."* She turned and made her way to the front door.

"Make sure you lock it this time," Bangoni instructed.

Angelo put his eyes as close to the glass as he could to make sure the lady was walking away from the building. Satisfied, he returned to join Mario and headed back to the interrogation room.

While all three were out of the room, Schaeffer faced Jorge with a pleading look on his face. "Quick, cut me loose. We have to get out of here. What are you doing anyway?"

Jorge looked around the room for something sharp that he could use to free Schaeffer from his bonds. He tugged at them to see if he could force the tie wrap to snap, but it was designed to hold wire bundles for decades and wouldn't yield.

"It's no use, Schaeffer. The goons have guns tucked in their waistbands. We wouldn't get far," Jorge whispered. "They're on their way back already. I heard the lady shut up. She was looking for the owner, Camilo. Bangoni got her to leave. Listen to me. I have a two-inch thick dossier on you and everything you have been up to. If you ever manage to leave this building alive, which is doubtful, your ass is grass. Anita Berwitz has everything, and if she doesn't hear from me, it's going right to the FBI, so you have no future if you don't cooperate with me."

"So, what's your plan?" Schaeffer asked.

"Just follow my lead. We have to convince this thug that it will take both of us to get to the money, or he'll kill me when he figures I can't help him, and you as soon as you tell him what he needs to know."

"So, what do I tell him?"

"Just let me answer the question when he asks how we get access to the accounts in Switzerland and go along with it. If you do that and we get out of this alive, I may cut you some slack. You're not the only one whose life has gone in the toilet since you *died*."

"Sit back down in that chair, kid, or I'll put some restraints on you, too," Bangoni cautioned as he entered the room from the hallway, seeing that Jorge was up out of his chair.

"I was just stretching my back. It's sore from sitting." Jorge made an effort to lean backward at the waist with his hands on his hips, as if to alleviate the strain from a sore back.

"I'm sure you were," Bangoni said sarcastically. "Quit screwing with me. I'm running out of patience." His words guided Jorge back into the chair. "Let's go over this one more time. How do you guys get control of the money?"

Schaeffer looked at Jorge to take the lead, as instructed. "It's in an investment account of a Swiss company, Euro Capital, GmbH, who is authorized to move the money around at the request of its agent and attorney in Liechtenstein."

"What's his name?" Bangoni asked.

"Not important. What you need to know is that he will only take instructions to transfer the money from Adam and me, together. We cannot act independently of one another."

"But you told me only Schaeffer was leaving the country. You were going to stay behind and clean up any messes that might surface. You said something about passwords."

"That's right," Jorge thought fast. "Only one of us has to be there in person. The other can concur with his instructions by verifying his identification."

"You mean the passwords?"

Jorge realized he had painted himself into a corner. Passwords wouldn't get the job done, if Bangoni was going to have to keep him alive. "It's not really a password. It's like a test."

Bangoni was getting visibly frustrated. "What is this, fourth grade? What do you mean a test?"

Jorge swallowed and spoke patiently. "It's like when you make a wire transfer. You know, when the bank wants to verify who you are."

"What do you mean?"

"They have a bunch of basic questions only you could know the answers to. Like what was the name of your first pet, or what kind of car do you drive, how many stories does your house have—"

"Okay, okay, okay!" Bangoni interrupted impatiently. "I get it. I do it all the time. So, what you're telling me is that all the money is overseas. You can only transfer the money in cooperation with one another, and that one of you has to be there in person for that to happen. Is that right?"

"That's correct," Schaeffer said, while Jorge nodded his agreement.

The frustration on Bangoni's face distorted his features. He put his elbows on the table and folded one hand over his fist. His brow furrowed while he gave the matter intense focus. This was not what he had anticipated. He had assumed he would just come to Florida, pick up Schaeffer, and rough him up until he gave him the information he needed to get the money, and then make him disappear. As soon as he learned what the Cuban knew, he would most likely dispose of him, too.

Now it looked like a trip to Europe would be involved, and that would require transporting an unwilling detainee to a foreign country and forcing him to perform in front of a third party. First, he had to be convinced that he wasn't being handed a line of bullshit. If what he had been told checked out, Joey figured he could cut Schaeffer in on the deal. Schaeffer ought to go along with that, if his only alternative was to get turned over to the authorities or killed. As for the Cuban, he could be held physically and made to perform to save his life.

Bangoni returned his attention to the gentlemen across the table from him. "So, here's how this is going to go down. I need some information to verify what you have told me. If it checks out, Adam, you and I are going to Switzerland." Turning to Jorge he said, "And you, kid, are going to be a guest of my friends here, so that you can handle your part of the authorization. After we have successfully moved the money to accounts I can control, you can go home." He returned his stare to Schaeffer. "Adam, I don't have as much leverage over you, and I need you to cooperate with me, so I am willing to consider cutting you in for a small piece of the deal to help me pull this off. Your alternative is to die right here and now. Is that clear enough for you?"

Frightened by how this was unfolding, Jorge answered for him, "I don't get it. Why don't you just turn us in to the police? There's a trail where everything is, and in time, your pensions will get all their money back."

Bangoni threw his head back and roared with laughter. "You are really naive, kid. You have committed the perfect crime. It seems to me that the victims don't even know they have been robbed. What makes you think I want to get the money back for them?" When his shoulders stopped shaking from laughter, Bangoni got serious again. "So, if you want to see tomorrow, tell me something to give your story credibility, like something I can check out."

"Like what, specifically?" Jorge asked nervously. He couldn't think of anything he could offer up that would confirm the story he had concocted.

"For starters, who is the attorney acting as your agent in Zurich?" Jorge's heart, already racing, started pounding. He had no idea what Schaeffer had done or what arrangements he had made. He certainly didn't know a name of a lawyer that could be checked out. He turned and looked at Schaeffer and saw that his eyes were bright with concern.

Schaeffer was also at a loss for how to answer, so he did the only thing he could under the circumstances. He told the truth. "The lawyer is a guy named Reinhardt Proksch. You can check him out, but he won't talk to you about my accounts without going through the protocol," he added.

Bangoni took out a pen and grabbed a piece of paper off the end of the table. "How do you spell that?"

Schaeffer repeated the name slowly and spelled it for Bangoni.

After a moment, Bangoni motioned Mario to the table from the corner where he and Angelo had been observing. As Mario approached, Bangoni gave him instructions. "Restrain the kid. For safety, tie wrap him to the chair, as well. Same for Schaeffer."

Jorge held his hands together in front of him in the hope that they wouldn't tie his wrists behind his back. Schaeffer looked awfully uncomfortable to him restrained the way he was, and he wanted to avoid the discomfort if he could, not to mention the advantage to having his arms in front of him. Mario pulled a tie wrap from the sheath of them on the filing cabinet, looped the band over the wrists as they were offered, and cinched the bitter end through the eyelet. Then he made another loop from a second and cinched it to the perforation in the seat frame at the front of the chair, positioning Jorge's hands between his legs at his lap. He then secured Schaeffer's hands to his chair frame as well.

Bangoni motioned for both Angelo and Mario to join him at the end of the table. He menacingly cautioned his two detainees, "Don't even think about trying to get up from these chairs. If I hear any commotion coming from this room, the pleasantries are over. My colleagues and I are going to work out some logistics in the front office while you wait here. When we come back, we'll be ready to go get some money." For effect, Mario pulled the nine-millimeter Glock out of his waistband and waved it across their faces. Angelo was already moving through the hallway to the front.

Frustrated, Schaeffer said with sarcasm, "Where would we go hogtied to the furniture?"

Bangoni, ignoring him, called ahead to Angelo, "Boot up one of those computers in there so we can check out this lawyer and look at some airline schedules."

"I'm on it," he replied.

Again, Bangoni repeated his threat, this time reinforcing what he said with the point of his meaty index finger on the chests of Schaeffer and Gonzalez. He got his point across. When they left the room, Jorge asked Schaeffer what they were going to find when they googled the lawyer.

"He's my real lawyer. They'll find something. They can't call him. It's Saturday afternoon there."

"Let's hope so," Jorge replied.

Joey Bangoni

CHAPTER TWENTY-TWO

"You don't look happy, boss," Mario said after they found seats around the desks in the front room.

Joey considered this for a moment. "I'm not really unhappy, considering we found two needles in haystacks this morning. What are the odds that we could bring both of these characters together at a time and place of our choosing? It's just that it is going to be more difficult than I had envisioned. I thought we would only have to deal with one of them, get what we needed, dispose of them, and get our money. Go home rich! Now we're going to have to work for it."

"So, what's the plan?" Mario asked.

Angelo sat quietly at a computer station on one of the desks, waiting for the computer in front of him to boot up.

"First, see what you can find out about this guy," Bangoni said, handing the piece of paper with Proksch's name on it to Mario, who passed it along to Angelo, who then began typing. "If the lawyer is legit, then Schaeffer obviously must know him, so the rest of the story is probably accurate. I think he's too scared to lie at this point. He knows he's fucked no matter what he does, but he may have a way out if he cooperates." Looking at Mario, he continued, "Do you have a place where you and Angelo can put the kid on ice for a few days, until Schaeffer and I can get to Switzerland?"

"Sure, boss. I know just the place. We got friends in Miami all over."

Angelo let out a soft whistle that got everybody's attention.

"What you got, Angelo?"

Angelo smiled at what he had to report. "I just googled his name, and a ton of stuff came up about him. He has several websites in all languages, German, Russian, and others. He advertises his specialty in helping people manage their money offshore in countries where it will be safe and private."

"Good job." Bangoni smiled.

"No, wait. There's more! There is a link to an article from the *New York Times,* wait a minute . . ." Angelo clicked on it and studied the screen as the news article came up. His lips moved slowly as he read through the first few paragraphs. "Here it is. It seems that this guy Proksch is rather famous. This article says he is being investigated for money laundering. His clients are pretty big guys, like the president of the Ukraine. Apparently, no one has been able to nail him yet."

"Good. Keep researching." Turning again to Mario, he said, "So, here's what I'm thinking. You and Angelo take the Cuban and put him on ice for a few days. It will be Monday at least before I can get Schaeffer to Europe. I will call you with updates so you can have Gonzalez ready to perform on command. After we get what we need from him to make transfers, get rid of him. We won't need him anymore, and he knows too much."

"Got it," Mario said.

"And, Angelo, check the flights out of Miami to Zurich this evening. I'm going to need two tickets, first class."

"What names do you want them under?" Angelo asked.

"I'll go as myself, no other choice. I'll have to check with Schaeffer to see what his new name is. Then you can make the reservations."

"No problem. There's a seven fifteen from Miami direct on Swiss

Air," Angelo informed him, seemingly pleased with himself that he was able to stay one step ahead of his new boss. He hoped it wouldn't go unnoticed.

Bangoni got up from the desk-side chair. "Mario, let's go check on our friends in the other room."

Mario and Bangoni went down the hallway to the back where his "guests" were bound to their chairs. Mario stood at his post in the corner while Joey pulled the third folding chair around the table backward and sat resting his arms on the seat back. He looked them squarely in the eyes.

"So, this is how this is going to go down," he said in a measured tone. "Adam, you and I are going to make a quick trip overseas. By the way, I need the name you were planning on traveling under and your new passport."

Schaeffer squirmed uneasily in his chair. "The name is Stephen Anderson, but I don't have the passport. That's what I came here to get, remember? I already have a reservation on tonight's Swiss Air flight from Miami."

"Aw fuck!" Bangoni got out his cell and called Camilo's most recent burner number. Everyone listened to Bangoni's side of the conversation. "Did you get the new identification for our guy. Yeah, yeah . . . I know I told you that, but now I need it. Good, good. Your middle desk drawer. I'll look. Thank you."

The significance of the conversation was lost on everyone in the room except Jorge, who understood very well that if the phony passport pimp, who was obviously the proprietor of the travel agency, hadn't had the ID made, it was because Bangoni did not plan on Schaeffer ever seeing the light of day. This did not look good for him as well, and the need to free himself from this situation was now of paramount importance.

"Mario, keep an eye on 'em while I go look for Schaeffer's new passport."

Mario moved toward the center of the room, as if his presence there would be a factor keeping Schaeffer and Gonzalez at bay. Bangoni returned a moment later with a fresh passport in his hands. Examining it carefully, he said out loud, "This guy does really good work. I can't see anything to indicate it's not real."

"It's because it is real," Schaeffer chimed in. "That's why it's so expensive."

Bangoni returned to his chair and continued his discourse. "When we get to Zurich and your lawyer, Proksch's office, you and your Cuban friend are going to do your dance to transfer these assets to a company under my control. If that goes smoothly, Adam, I'll leave you with enough money to get by."

"What about me?" Jorge asked hesitantly.

"You? First, you are going to be the guest of my friend Mario here, and if you do your part correctly, well, you get to walk away. I will know where to find you if you do anything stupid, so don't even think about it. *Capisce?*" The last word, spoken in Italian, was meant to impress upon Jorge the nature of whom he was dealing with. Bangoni got up from his chair to see about getting on Schaeffer's flight. He looked down at Schaeffer and asked, "Where's your ticket?"

"It's in my car," he answered, not being specific, knowing that his ability to get out of the country was walking down the hallway in Bangoni's left hand. He held out little hope that he could manage his way from the room and get Rabbit to whisk him away to safety. Mario started to follow his boss out of the room, but Bangoni motioned him to stay. While his back was turned for a moment, Jorge could see the Glock tucked in the waistband of his britches. He had a sinking feeling.

Anita Berwitz

CHAPTER TWENTY-THREE

A nita's nerves were getting the better of her as she waited patiently for Jorge to reappear at the front door to give her the signal to call 911. Embarrassed that she had taken over the outside premium table for over an hour, she made her situation worse by ordering another cup of coffee, requiring her first to drain the previous one. She knew she would have to pee soon, and she didn't know how she was going to accommodate keeping an eye on the storefront of the travel agency and do that at the same time. For now, she just watched and worried.

She looked at her watch. Almost twenty minutes had gone by since Jorge had crossed the street and disappeared behind the front door of the travel agency. Anita began drumming her fingernails on the tabletop in nervous frustration. Down the street she saw the strangest looking woman wearing a bonnet adorned with fake flowers approach the travel agency. She wore a mid-calf cotton dress, and she paused as she neared the agency door. She reminded Anita of granny on *The Beverly Hillbillies* reruns she had seen. After some consideration, the old lady wrestled the door open and went inside. After several minutes, she reemerged waving her arms, obviously not happy with her visit.

Anita's concern amped up a bit after witnessing the strange behavior, and she left a twenty on the table, gathered her purse, and crossed the busy street to see for herself. She didn't want to interfere with whatever plans Jorge had developed; he had been quite clear about that, but this delay wasn't in the plan, as far as she knew. Anita looked as best she could through the heavily tinted front windows but could see no activity inside. There were no noises that would give away what might be happening, so she went around the building to the back. There was only one door in back, and the windows were too high for her to look through, so she returned to her table at the café to continue her vigil. After another twenty minutes, panic began to take hold.

Anita searched the directory of her phone and found the number Valeriano had given her the night they had dinner. She selected it and listen to it ring. After four rings it went to voicemail. Naturally the greeting was in Spanish. Really in a state now, Anita pushed redial.

Valeriano answered on the second ring with a string of rapid-fire syllables. Finally, he shifted to English. "Ah, it's you Anita. I just now looked at the front of my phone, and I see your name. *¿Que pasa?*"

Anita was frantic with fear. "Val!" she shouted, her voice trembling. "I think Jorge is in trouble!" She started to spill her circumstances incoherently over the phone.

Val interrupted her. "Whoa, pretty lady. Slow down. All I got is that Jorge is in trouble. Back up and tell me again what he's doing."

Anita took a deep breath and tried her best to calm herself. She explained that she and Jorge had found the person who had caused all the trouble with Jorge's audit and that Jorge had gone to a meeting where he could confront the man. She further explained that Jorge was to signal her when it was time for her to call the police but hadn't come out of the building. She ended by saying that she thought the man they were after could be dangerous.

Valeriano became immensely concerned for his little brother. He listened to Anita's story and whistled over the shop noise for Carlos to come over. All he had to say was that Jorge needed help, that he was right here in Little Havana. "He's just a few blocks away, man!" Val exclaimed. He told Anita to stay on the phone after she gave him the address.

"I know the Havana Café," he said. "Carlos and I will be there in five minutes. Carlos, bring your 'Stang round the front. I'm going to get some bats out of our softball gear bag. Hurry."

Valeriano ran to the back of his Ford pickup and reached in the bed for his softball satchel. He and Carlos played in a regular league after work at the park down the street. It was a favorite pastime of the Cuban community and quite competitive. He withdrew one aluminum and one Louisville Slugger wooden bat from the canvas bag and hopped in the passenger side of the Mustang, which Carlos had slowed only slightly as he passed his brother at the front of the station on to Calle Ocho. They sped east and double-parked in front of the café. Horns blared as they got out of the car and rushed to where Anita was sitting at an outside table. Val ignored them. Carlos gave his signature finger-popping wrist snap at one car whose driver shouted an obscenity out the passenger-side window.

"Show me where you last saw him," Valeriano told her.

"He went in the front door across the street." She pointed to the spot.

"You mean Viajes Mundiales?" Val asked.

"Yeah, right there!" She shook her finger for emphasis.

Carlos looked stupefied. "You've got to be kidding. Everybody knows that guy. He's where you go to get identification. Half of this community would be out of here if he didn't take care of their needs. That's no travel agency. I don't think the owner's ever been out of Miami."

Anita, calmed a little now that Jorge's brothers were here, said, "That makes sense. We think the guy we're after is trying to get out of the country. He faked his own death, so now nobody is looking for him. Except we are. And maybe someone else is. I don't know how many people are in there."

Carlos looked at his brother. "What do you think, Val? Should we just bust in the front door and see what's going on or what?"

Valeriano, ever the thoughtful one, said, "I don't think we should do anything stupid. Something is obviously going on. If it were just the two of them, one of them would have come out by now, whether it's good news or bad news. Let's go around back and see what we can learn. If nothing, we'll bust in."

"I was just in back," Anita said. "There is only one door, and the windows are up high, just to let light in. You can't see anything inside."

Val smiled at her and said, "You went over there by yourself and checked it out?"

Anita nodded.

"Damn, girl! You're beautiful *and* you got balls."

Anita wasn't sure the mixed metaphor was a compliment, but she took it as one from Val's smile.

"Carlos, move your car to block the entrance to the side parking lot, and we'll go around back together. That way, no one is going to get away in a hurry. It will tense them up, whoever is inside. Anita, you stay here, and if you hear us shouting, call the local police."

"I don't know the number," she said matter-of-factly.

Heading to his car, Carlos said, "Just call 911. It's faster 'cause they will reach out to the closest assistance. Say there's been a shooting. That brings them fast."

Carlos moved his Mustang, much to the relief of the cars that were stacking up behind him. Traffic returned to normal as Val crossed the street on foot. The two brothers moved behind the building and stood with their bats at the ready on either side of the rear door, listening for clues from inside. Anita couldn't stand the stress of not knowing what was going on, so she crossed the street to the side parking lot and worked her way to the edge of the building, where she could peer around the corner to the rear parking lot. She could see Valeriano and Carlos positioned on either side of the door, their bats raised to a striking position, and their heads craned to the door, listening.

Suddenly the door opened, and an athletic-looking man, about Jorge's age, stepped into the sunlight with a set of car keys in his hand. As he passed between Carlos and Valeriano, he turned to his left. Anita noticed a startled look on his face, and she could clearly see an automatic pistol in his waistband at the back of his pants. He retreated backward, trying to distance himself from his adversaries while keeping his eye on them, as he reached behind him for the pistol.

Anita was amazed at the blinding speed with which he drew the gun and chambered a round. Carlos made a threatening move toward him with his bat at the ready, and the young man drew a bead on him, preparing to fire. Valeriano took the opportunity of the split second the gunman refocused his attention to swing for the left-field fences, connecting squarely with the exposed side of Angelo's head. Simultaneously the weapon discharged, the shot flying wildly in the air as Angelo's head snapped to the side at an unimaginable angle. The weapon discharged again, harmlessly into the ground this time, as Angelo slumped to the pavement in a disjointed heap. As he lay there, his right leg extended and twitched spasmodically, his eyes staring vacantly into space.

Anita didn't need another prompt. Fumbling in her purse, she pulled out her cell phone and called 911. It seemed forever, but it was only three rings before she heard a calm woman's voice, "911, what is the nature of your emergency?"

"There's a shooting in Little Havana!" she shrieked into her phone.

"Calm down, ma'am," the voice responded in even tones. "Can you give me an address? Are you in any danger now?"

Anita took a deep breath, knowing that she had to be calm to be effective. "I am on Calle Ocho in Little Havana . . . southwest Miami, at a travel agency called Viajes Mundiales, across the street from the Habana Café. I don't know the address, but it's near Seventeenth Avenue, maybe a little west of there. Please send help. There has been a shooting, and more have guns. We need help in a hurry."

The dispatcher was telling Anita help was on the way, that she should stay on the line, when Anita burst out, "Oh my God! No. No. No. My friends. They're going in. They're going in the building where the gunmen are."

The dispatcher updated Miami dispatch that there might be multiple shooters involved, as well as multiple victims.

Anita stood frozen with fear as she watched Carlos rush to the back door, pull it open, and run in, crouched and swinging his aluminum bat viciously from side to side. Valeriano moved to a more cautious position outside the doorframe and peered inside to see what he was up against. Then he spied Angelo's discarded pistol at his feet and he picked it up tentatively, holding it in one hand and the bat in the other.

Jorge Gonzalez

CHAPTER TWENTY-FOUR

Jorge looked on helplessly as he watched his brother Carlos flail his baseball bat ineffectively in the back of the room. Carlos was trying to set a perimeter of safety around himself. After being told of Bangoni's plans, Jorge knew he was a dead man if he ever got in his captors' car, and he had refused to participate. Bangoni had told him he had no choice and sent Angelo out the back to bring the car closer to the back door where they would have a better chance of putting an uncooperative passenger in the car without being observed.

At first Mario backed away from the potentially crippling blows when Carlos came through the door. Everyone had been taken off guard when they heard two gunshots immediately after Angelo left. Mario had moved to the nearly closed door to get a better look, and he saw Angelo down, probably dead, he guessed after seeing the blood pooling from the side of his head across the cement pavement. Now, with an enraged Carlos crouching before him with a wild baseball bat in his hands, Mario drew his nine-millimeter from the back of his pants and pointed it at Carlos's head.

Bangoni backed away from the table where Jorge and Schaeffer sat, careful not to be caught in the fray. He had lost his taste for extreme violence over the years and preferred to sub such work out. He saw Carlos make eye contact with the kid, and he made the connection that they knew each other. Jorge confirmed this when he shouted, "Carlos!" followed by a stream of Spanish.

Mario made a threatening gesture with this pistol intended to stop the bat-wielding intruder's rant, but when he saw Carlos had the "red mist" look in his eyes, he chambered a round in his Glock and took aim at Carlos's midsection.

Jorge felt helpless, but he knew he had to do something. He stood from his chair trying to take some action. As he rose, the tie wrap connecting him to the bale on the bottom of the seat came tight, and the seat did what it was designed to do, fold up for storage. Jorge's hands came to rest naturally on the chair frame, and he picked up the folded chair, feeling empowered that he now had some sort of weapon himself. He feared that Mario was about to kill his brother, so while Mario was focused on his target, Jorge raised the chair high over his head and brought it down as forcefully as he could on Mario's forearm. The Glock discharged as the chair frame impacted Mario's arm, and the bullet whizzed between Carlos's legs, narrowly missing his manhood before ricocheting off the polished cement floor and embedding in the wall opposite. The sound was deafening in the enclosed space.

Mario's arm bent at an awkward angle, both the radius and ulna cleanly broken, one protruding from the skin in a compound fracture. Carlos rendered him unconscious with a bunt to the top of his head. Mario's Glock skittered across the floor and ended at Bangoni's feet. He picked it up and pointed it at Carlos, who in his mind was still behaving irrationally, looking for more targets to swing at.

"Put the bat down!" he said sternly.

Carlos continued to close the distance between himself and sudden death. Seeing that his warning was unheeded, Bangoni switched his strategy. Turning, he aimed the pistol at Jorge's head and commanded again, "Put the bat down."

His assessment was rewarded. Carlos shrugged apologetically at

Jorge and reached forward to put the bat on the floor. At that point Valeriano revealed himself in the doorway, his Louisville Slugger at his side and the nine-millimeter aimed in Bangoni's direction.

Joey had but a second to make a decision, and he was not really ready to face the rest of his life in a cell. He kept his bead on Jorge but directed his attention to the newcomer in the room. "Nobody else has to get hurt here. I don't want to hurt anybody. I just want to get out of here and take that other guy with me," he said calmly, nodding his head at Schaeffer. "He is of no interest to you, so why don't we just call this an impasse, and you let us walk out of here, and we'll forget this ever happened."

Valeriano looked quickly at Jorge to gauge his reaction and saw him move his head ever so slightly sideways.

"No deal, Val," he said in Spanish. "I need this guy to clear my name. He's the one who stole all the money and bankrupted my client." Then to Bangoni in English, "No deal. You put down the gun, and you can go. Otherwise my brother will put a bullet in your head."

Jorge was shaking from the knees down, but Bangoni could not see that below the edge of the table. Mario was beginning to stir from his folded-over position on the floor, which proved a momentary distraction.

Joey Bag of Donuts considered his options and came to the conclusion that his best bet was to try to get out of here. If he killed the Gonzalez kid, he would surely be killed himself. If he tried to shoot the new arrival, he would most likely suffer the same result or be batted unconscious by the madman, who was still moving closer, bat at hand. "Can I take Mario?" he asked, looking at his friend who was just regaining consciousness.

"Okay, put down the gun, first. Then grab your friend and get out of here," Jorge said.

Bangoni did as he was told, slowly placing the pistol on the table, eyes darting back and forth between Valeriano and Carlos. As he let go of the pistol, he closed them for a split second, awaiting the inevitable, but no shot rang out. Relieved beyond belief, he stepped around the bat-wielding Cuban and stooped to help his old friend to his feet. Mario needed a moment more to orient himself before he could safely straighten his legs beneath him.

Wobbly but firmly in the grip of Bangoni, the humbled pair made their way down the hallway toward the front entrance of the travel agency. Bangoni could hear the sound of police sirens as he neared the glass door, and as he and Mario made their way into the bright sunshine, he was confronted by a determined, young brunette who was waving her arms at the approaching squad cars in an attempt to direct them to the crime scene.

Anita was shocked at the sight of two big men leaning on each other, one balding with a huge lumpy bruise on the crown of his head; the other trying to help him along. The first police unit screeched to a halt diagonally to the curb, blocking egress to the fugitives. Seeing that things appeared to be under control, at this end anyway, Anita ran inside the building to find her beloved Jorge, fearing the worst after having heard more gunshots since calling 911. She called out, "Jorge! Jorge!"

"In the back. Everything is okay. You can come back!" Jorge shouted happily.

Anita entered the back room to see Carlos and Jorge hugging it out. Jorge appeared to have a metal folding chair hanging from his wrists, which suddenly sprang open, making the reunion difficult. Valeriano opened a pocket knife and cut the tie wraps from Jorge, freeing him of the chair, and clasped him in a fierce embrace. As the brothers group hugged, uniformed police entered from the back door and the hallway, assessing the carnage as they entered the room. Valeriano wisely placed the nine-millimeter on the table where everyone could see it so that the police would know he was not a threat.

Finally, after poking and prodding her way into the hugfest, Anita wrapped her arms around Jorge, squeezing with all her might, forcing her ample breasts into his chest. Then he kissed her with passion, while Schaeffer, looking up in confusion, could only observe from his seat. The police, having no knowledge of the cast of characters, placed everyone in the center of the room while they identified that Anita was the one who called 911. With her help, they took statements from everyone and separated the good guys from the bad guys. They gave Anita and the Gonzalez brothers permission to leave with the promise that they would not leave the area and be available to come in for further questioning when needed. They called the coroner to deal with the body in the back parking lot and marched Bangoni, Mario, and a confused Adam Schaeffer out the front door to the waiting squad cars for rides to the downtown precinct.

Rabbit Roemer

CHAPTER TWENTY-FIVE

Rabbit Roemer sat in his Chevy Malibu a block and a half down from where he had let Schaeffer off for his meeting on Southwest Eighth Street. The day was sunny and warm, but not hot. The remnants of a cool front had taken the moisture out of the air, so the humidity was at tolerable levels, and Rabbit felt comfortable sitting in his car with the windows open, enjoying the six-pack of Coors Light he had purchased at a convenience store near where he had parked. His car was facing east on the south side of the street, so he had a good view of the activity around the travel agency. Schaeffer would be easy to spot when he came out, and he had told Roemer that he would be no more than a half hour at most.

Rabbit paid no attention to the time, as he was enjoying himself, but when he cracked the tab on his third beer, he thought to consult his watch. This seemed to be taking longer than he had expected. He watched with amusement when an old lady entered the agency and emerged a few minutes later, seemingly upset about something or other. He couldn't help but notice the very attractive dark-haired girl cross the street and look in the windows before walking around the building through the parking lot and out of sight.

He glanced at the seat next to him and realized he had set the sweating bag containing the beer on Schaeffer's new blazer, the one they had picked up for his trip to Switzerland later today. He moved it aside so as not to get it wet. The navy-colored coat was atop Schaeffer's leather travel bag, and out of curiosity, Rabbit rummaged through it, not intending to take anything, just curious and trying to kill some time. He found the usual stuff in the top and middle sections, but when he unzipped the bottom section, he hit pay dirt. Inside were four banded bundles of cash, each indicating ten thousand dollars. There were some loose hundreds in there, too.

It would normally never occur to Rabbit to take advantage of a situation like this, Schaeffer having been so generous with him these last few weeks, but when he heard the sirens and saw the approaching police cars close in on the travel agency, his priorities began to shift. He watched as the pretty girl waved the officers to the curb. Two big guys emerged from the front door of the building, one seemed to be helping the other, who seemed to be hurt. His feelings of panic began to rise as the moments went by and the two big guys were escorted to the squad cars. Then the final straw put Rabbit over the edge. His buddy, "Andre," was led to the second police car. He watched as the officer placed him in the backseat, offering a protective hand over the top of the man's head to avoid banging into the squad car doorframe as he got in.

Rabbit had had enough. His PTSD kicked into high gear, and he motored swiftly, not so fast he would draw attention, down the street. He passed the police cars and gave his bewildered friend a broad smile as he patted the travel bag on the seat next to him.

Key West ought to be really nice this time of year, Rabbit remarked to himself as he entered the right lane in anticipation of taking the southbound entrance to I-95 and the Overseas Highway to the Florida Keys.

EPILOGUE

In the first quarter of 2009, as the markets continued their slide, the financial world was just beginning to come to grips with the magnitude and ripple effect of the real estate crisis that first reared its ugly head with the failure of Lehman Brothers. The tentacles of the grossly inflated residential markets affected every sector of the economy. A new president, our nation's first African-American, would have to deal with the mess, which included bailouts of the banking, automotive, and insurance industries. This was of little interest to the loving couple that was busy preparing for a wedding with complications.

Jorge and Anita planned to be married in June, right after Jorge received his official induction to the Federal Bureau of Investigation following fifteen weeks of training at Quantico, Virginia. Oddly enough, during its investigation of the securities fraud, the FBI was very impressed with the analytical work Jorge had done in determining that Adam Schaeffer was indeed alive and chronicling his methods to divert over two hundred million dollars to offshore accounts.

With his name cleared of wrongdoing, the Florida Board of Accountancy offered to reinstate his certificate to practice public accounting, provided he agree to complete ninety hours of continuing professional education. Jorge found this particularly offensive, especially when the Bureau had offered him a coveted position with their agency, inclusive of pay-level recognition for his years of experience, so he would not have to start at the bottom.

The icy relationship between Jorge's and Anita's families commenced its inevitable thaw as parents from different worlds succumbed to their children's choices. Jorge and Anita found humor in an ongoing argument whether her parents were more upset about her marrying a Catholic or the fact that his parents were upset that he was marrying a Jew. Adriana continued to be a voice of grace and reason where this matter was concerned. She saw clearly how perfect the match was for each of them. Anita was committed to learning Spanish courtesy of Rosetta Stone, although she had a lot of help from Jorge and his family, who did their best to teach her "proper" use of the language.

Needless to say, Jorge took a lot of teasing from Carlos and Valeriano because of his new employment arrangement. "You gonna be coming after us, Jorge? Are we going to have to shut down our hubcap outsourcing business?"

Jorge reassured them their side business could operate safely below the FBI's radar. "Although, you know, it's always good to have someone on the inside," Jorge teased back. "I'll let you know if the Feds are getting close and give you a heads-up."

The bond shared by the Gonzalez brothers was evident to everyone, confirmed when their friends and family learned that Carlos and Valeriano faced armed goons with nothing more than baseball bats to defend themselves.

As for the goons, Joey Bag of Donuts got off with barely a slap on the wrist. His defense counsel presented a case of a financial executive looking after the interests of his clients. Since nothing could be proved that he had intended to commit a crime, the worst he faced was association with known mobsters, one of whom had died in the conflict. Mario received a light sentence for possession and discharge of a firearm within city limits. His bare scalp still bore evidence of the whack he had received on the head, a noticeable calcium lump. His right arm itched when it rained, but the bones set nicely on his forearm. The cast he wore for a few weeks served to help ward off unwanted attention while he was in the prison yard. His commanding bulk protected him after that.

Valeriano was exonerated of any criminal behavior. Angelo's unfortunate death at the hands of Val's baseball bat was adjudicated justifiable homicide, attributable to the fact that Angelo had discharged a firearm in the physical exchange. Valeriano, in spite of the encouragement of his family, said he would always feel terrible about what he had done, but over time, he was learning to forgive himself.

Carlos enjoyed the attention he got as a hero in a crisis, although he never understood how he could have been so enraged as to attack a man while a nine-millimeter pistol was aimed at his head.

Adam Schaeffer took the hardest fall of the bunch. In addition to millions in civil judgments against him, he was sentenced to fifteen years in federal prison for a variety of felonies. He was fortunate that his connection to Robbie Wells had never come up in the subsequent investigations. Due to the magnitude of his theft, no one paid any attention to how he managed to find his way back to the United States after ditching his plane somewhere in the Gulf Stream.

Robbie Wells had just gone mysteriously missing. When David Nemeth, the rock star, got out of jail for his offenses, he reunited with his band, Ascension, and continued touring successfully. Their next three albums went platinum before he announced his retirement, reclaimed his beautiful schooner, *Mayan,* and set off for the Caribbean.

While Schaeffer was in prison, his wife, Marjorie, filed for divorce. Schaeffer tried to block it, having no one else on the planet who cared a shit about him. His lawyers argued in court that he had given his wife the best years of his life. Her lawyers responded that she did not disagree, and the termination of the marriage was settled before the end of the following year. She kept the motor yacht and soon met someone to share it with. Karen and Mary liked their new stepfather.

Arthur White & Company, Jorge's former accounting firm, struggled unsuccessfully to overcome the bad publicity from the Pension Strategy Partners failure. Ultimately, the partners sold out to a national financial services firm. CBIZ offered them cash for book value and stock for the balance of partner equity. CBIZ's stock fell from twelve dollars a share to about two dollars shortly thereafter.

Rabbit Roemer, bless his soul, decided to make his relocation to Key West permanent. He continued his unambitious lifestyle, enjoying the sunsets from Mallory Square in the old town. He rented rooms as they became available from local homeowners trying to make a few extra bucks, and he found plenty of company in the sea of lost souls who called the island community home.

AFTERWORD

This is my third book of fiction. Its creation is my reward in and of itself; however, with this attempt, I plan to submit my work to traditional publishers, an effort I have avoided in the past, in the hope that it will reach a wider audience. If you purchased this copy at an actual bookstore, then you know I have been successful in my efforts. If you received it via an internet site such as Amazon, then most likely I have not been successful. Either way, I am honored that you took the time to get this far, and if you liked it, I encourage you to give my previous novels a try.

If you have read my work, you may be aware that I sometimes use the names of people known to me as I develop characters for a story line. I have continued this practice in *Career,* if for no other reason than it helps me to keep the continuity of characters as I write. As before, I have decided that if I were to change the names to ones unknown to me, they would belong to somebody in the reading public, so I figure, what's the difference? Besides, it is fun. If you are known to me and your name appears in this book, rest assured that the connection ends with the name. The character bears no association to you, so please do not be offended by how he or she is portrayed. If you are known to me and your name does not appear, also please do not be offended. I just ran out of story, but I'm sure there will be other opportunities for your namesake to find its way into my fiction.

So many of you have been helpful to me in pulling this work together. Thank you to all of my friends who have sampled my writing as a litmus test to my progress; particularly I want to thank Roy Connors, a friend since high school, and Karen Krumholtz, who have suffered through the worst of the first drafts. Also, thank you, Doris Kearns Goodwin, for giving me the encouragement to start writing so late in life.

Friends helped me with cultural aspects of the book that I was not familiar with, such as the background of a conservative Jewish family from Queens. Thank you, Phillip Rich. Also, thank you to Haydee Viera and Yoharner Echemendia for insight into the Cuban community, and Dennis Ferguson—whose altered name you may recall from the text—who helped me with the inner workings of market regulatory agencies. Thank you also to Mike Swisher, who helped me think through the plot continuity. The French toast recipe is my own invention. I highly recommend it.

I particularly want to thank someone who is often forgotten in the lives of writers. A huge thank-you is due Mrs. Pemberton, who did her best to teach me grammar in the late 1950s. I know that no one would be more surprised than she that I could complete over ninety thousand words of prose, not only once, but three times. Apparently, I was paying more attention than she thought while she was diagraming and parsing sentences on the blackboard, at least based on the grades she gave me. Thank you to my family, who listens to my drivel as I run plotlines by them from time to time.

Finally I want to thank you, my loyal readers, for your encouragement and support. As long as I have that, you will continue to see my work.

Please do me a favor . . . If you could take a minute to leave a review for *Career* on Amazon, I would be most grateful. Many readers may not be aware of how essential reviews are to the success of a self-published author. When you post a review, it makes a huge difference to help new readers find my books.
Thank you,
Dick

THE BOY AND THE DOLPHIN

Following the unfortunate death of his parents, young Toby Matthias finds himself living a carefree life on Piper Cay, an Out Island in the Bahamas, at his grandparents' inn. Isolated from children his own age, Toby develops a deep and lasting friendship with an unlikely companion: a bottlenose dolphin.

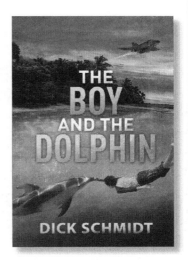

A heartwarming tale, *The Boy and the Dolphin* follows the tropical adventures of Toby and Phinney as they make sense of life in the mid-1950s. When Toby is sent to complete his education in the States and Phinney immerses herself more deeply in her dolphin culture, the best friends experience ever-increasing separations. But even while Toby serves his country in the skies over Vietnam, the boy and the dolphin share an unbreakable, decade-long bond.

MEMORY ROAD

After serving his country with distinction as a senior officer with the
Central Intelligence Agency, Stewart
Masterson is rewarded with deten-
tion in an assisted living facility by a
government agency concerned with
his advancing Alzheimer's disease.
Longing for his late wife of forty-
seven years, Masterson makes his
getaway from the facility and finds
himself on the road with limited
resources, trying to negotiate his way
from Florida to his daughter in Mary-
land, the only place where he feels
he can find happiness and relevance.

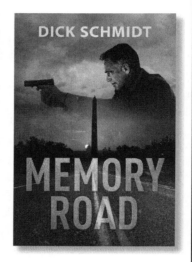

With three U.S. government agencies and the intelligence arms of
unfriendly countries in hot pursuit, Masterson relies on a lifetime
of training instincts to avoid recapture, proving he has a lot more
on the ball than his pursuers had expected. His northward travels
up U.S. Route 1 lead him from one adventure to another until the
inevitable conclusion when his fate will be decided by who finds him
first and how he responds.

This charming, suspenseful, and sometimes ironically humorous
story gives us a glimpse into a world that is far more relevant to the
brave individuals facing personal limitations than we could possibly
imagine.

ABOUT THE AUTHOR

Dick Schmidt is a lifelong resident of Florida with a background in banking, real estate development, and aviation. His time is filled with philanthropic endeavors, which he spearheads with his wife, Barbara, an international bestselling author. He has two grown children and resides in Boca Raton, Florida.

He is the author of two novels, *The Boy and the Dolphin* and *Memory Road*.

Made in the USA
Columbia, SC
06 June 2020